THERE
SHE
LIES

THERE SHE LIES

A NOVEL

MICHELLE YOUNG

Rock Forest Publishing

Cover Design by Michelle Young
Cover Photograph © Pixabay.com
Author Photograph © Youngs Photography

ISBN-13: 978-1-7750983-3-1

There She Lies / Michelle Young. – 1st ed.
Rock Forest Publishing

ALSO BY MICHELLE YOUNG

Salt & Light
Without Fear
Your Move

For Mom & Dad

"And terrors don't prey on innocent victims
Trust me, darlin', trust me darlin'"
– BAD LIAR, IMAGINE DRAGONS

It wasn't supposed to happen. The sun was up, the road was clear; the pavement was dry. Optimal conditions, the weatherman had predicted.

The wheels advanced quickly, the tires silent on the smooth pavement. Endless road stretched on for miles. The morning sun kissed the back of her neck where her curly blond hair was swept up by the slight breeze. The weather was crisp that early in the day. The heat hadn't hit them yet. There was no one but them out that morning. They had the road to themselves. It wasn't difficult to imagine they were the only two people in the world.

They'd spent weeks planning for this day, taking every precaution necessary. No one could have anticipated what was going to happen just before nine o'clock that morning.

"You ready to go?" her husband had asked her earlier that morning. She hadn't known that someone else had been listening when she'd answered, "Yes."

MICHELLE YOUNG

PART
ONE

1

QUINN
MARCH 2014

Babies. The only time any of us are ever truly innocent and blameless is when we are newborns. A blank canvas. Unfortunately for some, their blood has already been contaminated long before they start growing skin to contain it. Even before they are born, they are doomed. Life is cruel. It takes from us and it discards us—ashes to ashes.

We can only hope to live well enough while we are here, to make our loved ones proud, to leave something behind—a legacy. A child. But what if that child has already been damaged? What if their genes—the raw materials that created them—are faulty? A blackness seeping in at the last moment of conception. A curse over their life. What if they turn out to be just like you—a liar?

———

Quinn is sleepy from the long drive, her head heavy and bobbing slightly, causing a dull ache in her neck. She'd taken off her puffy coat at the last rest stop to prevent a headache, but it seems it didn't help much.

"Would you take a look at this!" her husband exclaims. "It's so beautiful!"

Quinn leans against the cool window, the frost making translucent designs on the glass as she clings to the hope that she will be able to rest a little while longer before they arrive. She had been able to nod off for a little while after lunch once they had gotten back on the highway and Cole finally fell asleep. *Sleep when the baby sleeps*. That's what everyone keeps telling her. It had taken Quinn longer than usual to settle him.

You would think Cole's top-of-the-line car seat had grown thorns overnight, the way he would scream bloody murder whenever Quinn tried to strap him into it. She was growing tired of the constant struggle each time they got him into the car.

Her forehead is cold from resting it against the window. She lifts her head slightly and slowly opens her eyes to the harsh winter glare reflecting off of the snow. While her husband is admiring the snow-covered trees, Quinn can only think about the potentially slippery and dangerous driving conditions. She's been mostly quiet during the drive, absentmindedly biting her nails.

The roads are covered in grey slush, making the old Volkswagen Golf twist and turn as it does its best to stay on course. Quinn swallows away the anxiety building inside her. Her stomach is doing its best to keep down the toasted Western sandwich she ate for lunch a couple of hours ago. She stretches her legs as best as she can in the narrow seat. The usual six-hour drive had stretched into nine due to the bad weather.

There isn't much out here but a straight stretch of road, long and narrow, surrounded by large endless rock faces and an army of evergreen trees to block any view. This morning's flurries have left a beautiful white dusting on the green trees, dressing them up for winter. With the sun slowly making its way west, Quinn can see thousands of fluffy white specks floating around their car without any idea of their destination. The large flakes are falling so slowly, almost hypnotically—it might put her to sleep once more.

If she wasn't so terrified of moving farther from her beloved hometown, Quinn might feel as though she were living in a snow globe fairy tale. She can imagine how the lazy frozen crystals might taste on her tongue as she closes her eyes and drifts off again.

Back home, Quinn had been planning to get Cole's stroller out within the next week or two so they could go for walks into town—just to get out of the house for a few hours. But looking out her window an hour later as they inch further and further north, Quinn can see that winter is still very present here in North Bay, Ontario. She stirs in her seat as the cold seems to envelop her body, making her shiver suddenly. An old memory begins to appear in her mind. The flash of an image had followed her here. Strips of red mixed with a loud crashing sound. She shakes her head, willing it away.

This is a new beginning, although, she's unsure of what waits for them at the end of the long journey. They still have a thirty-minute drive west before arriving at their new house in a town called Sturgeon Falls.

With William at the wheel, Quinn knows she's in safe hands, but she still has to reason with herself. She doesn't like being at the mercy of someone else. As much as she trusts her husband, she would still rather be in the driver's seat and be the one in control.

Quinn prefers being the one to choose the speed of every curve, to be the one lifting her foot off the gas, to be the one to make swerving decisions when necessary. She finds it difficult not knowing William's next moves, his speed, never knowing which of his sharp turns could wake Cole at any moment. She knows William is a better driver than she is but being a passenger has never sat well with her. The motion sickness is so close she can taste it.

To distract herself, she busies her mind thinking about what the new town will be like. Will she make friends there? She wonders if there will be a place to walk and push the stroller.

Quinn looks over at William's strong hands, one placed on the steering wheel, the other resting firmly on the stick shift. Her gaze moves to his sculpted jawline, appreciating the shadow of stubble. His lips are pressed closed as though hiding a secret while his eyes are intent on the road ahead, trying to predict the weather in this unknown territory.

His forearms show just a hint of the thick vein that used to be so prominent when they first met. His hairline is slowly making its way further up his forehead with each passing year. If anything, Quinn finds him even more attractive now with a few stray grey hairs poking through his dark brown hair—it's more distinguished. They're not the young kids they once were and that's quite alright with her.

William has been quiet for most of the ride, content with his thoughts and busy watching the road for icy patches. Quinn can see dark circles forming under his hazel eyes and imagines she must have a matching pair herself. Cole hasn't been the best sleeper so far.

She takes a peek behind her seat, looking at her son's reflection in the little mirror attached to the backseat, a slow smile plays on her lips. Cole is finally sleeping soundly in his rear-facing car seat. She watches for a moment to see the rise and fall of his tiny chest, a bubble forming between his little lips, the small wheezing sound of deep sleep emerging. She smiles and relaxes slightly at the sight of her son's peaceful face before facing the front.

The moving van can be spotted in the rearview mirror, the giant, white, block-like vehicle following slowly behind them to their new home. March isn't the best time to be making a big move, but what choice do they have?

It hadn't been in Quinn's plans to move in the middle of winter—or even this year for that matter. With Cole only two months old, she feels sad about leaving his first home behind. Tears brimming, Quinn wipes them quickly away, the discussion over long ago, and the decision to move well underway. There was no sense dwelling on it any longer. Their entire lives were packed into heavy brown boxes, piled atop each other, secured by thick yellow ropes and blue blankets in the moving van behind them.

———

William had first talked about becoming a helicopter pilot when they'd met seven years ago. At the time, Quinn had thought it was only a childhood dream, not something he would pursue. Yet, here they were, in Northern Ontario, about to settle down for the next several years of their lives so that William could get his commercial pilot's license, their old life far behind them, their friends and their home back in Kingston.

William had applied to Helicopters Canada's flight school two years before, and never heard back. Quinn had almost forgotten he had applied because William had thrown himself into his job as a forklift driver, quickly earning a promotion and a raise. She had gotten used to their lifestyle and their financial stability. That's when they had begun talking about starting a family. William had been a little more eager than Quinn, who had felt content with just the two of them.

They'd only been married three years when Quinn got pregnant with Cole. She had been so nervous during her pregnancy, frightened to harm the baby if she moved too quickly, coughed too loudly, or ate the wrong things.

Her girlfriends had all gotten pregnant much younger, their kids already in kindergarten by the time Cole was born. Their advice had seemed dated and irrelevant to Quinn. Most of them seemed to have warped memories of their pregnancies, elaborating and embellishing facts as they shared stories and advice.

She had felt very alone and miserable during her pregnancy. She'd put on a significant amount of weight and experienced terrible nauseating spells for most of the pregnancy, which was why she'd been so looking forward to finally burning off some of the weight by going for walks with Cole in the stroller. Quinn is disappointed that the weather up north doesn't seem to want to cooperate with her plans.

She's read online about their new neighbourhood, about the unforgiving environment and how its lavish landscapes demanded respect. Looking out to the vastness of the forest, the majestic rocks on either side of the car, Quinn feels as though the trees and rocks might close in on her at any given moment. Shivering, she turns the heat up in the car, earning a smirk from William.

The cold on the other side of the glass sends goose bumps along her forearms and she hugs herself. She swallows hard, trying to breathe through the fear of feeling trapped. A blanket of white as far the eye can see. Hunched in on herself, grinding her teeth, a disturbing thought occurs to her that maybe the North isn't happy about her arrival either.

2

QUINN

As William steers the car onto Highway 17, towards Sudbury, population 160,000, Cole senses the slight movement on the smoothly paved highway and stirs slightly in his sleep.

Quinn holds her breath, waiting for the summoning cry that will make her breasts ooze with milk. *Breast is best*, she'd been told time and time again by other mothers. Yet, Quinn can't shake the resentment she feels that her body has turned into a 24-hour snack vending machine.

She doesn't feel as though her own body belongs to her anymore. She has to be ready for Cole's every need, no matter how sore or how tired she is. She longs for some sleep and sometimes wishes William could grow breasts to help with some of the nightly feedings. She can feel her chest tightening at the thought of another restless night.

Her family doctor back home had talked to her about post-partum depression symptoms shortly after Cole was born. She hadn't been showering regularly, often felt resentful towards her family, and had been avoiding her friends. Quinn has struggled with depression her entire life and what she's been experiencing these last few months is similar, but on a deeper level. Her doctor had ordered her a higher dose of Pristiq—her regular anti-depressant was not quite cutting it.

She constantly struggles with the guilt dividing her between wanting her own space and body back, while also longing to be the most attentive and loving mother possible for Cole. After only two months, she knows she can't do it all on her own. She drives herself crazy, thinking about milestones, feedings and the best sleep training schedules. Quinn had busied herself in those first weeks, while Cole napped more than he was awake, by making dozens of colourful spreadsheets listing weekly baby activities and mom-groups to join back in Kingston—all that work and research useless now. She didn't feel up to the challenge of doing the research again in this new town.

She glances out William's window and spots the snow-covered Lake Nipissing stretching far, seemingly touching the horizon. William had been looking forward to spotting it after looking at a map.

"Almost there," William says now as he glances at the GPS Navigator on his phone for directions to the new house.

Quinn moves in her seat, inching her body forward, anxious to get her first glance at the house they will be living in for the next five years or so. She's never seen the house in person, only pictures online.

When they'd first learned of William's acceptance into the flight school, they'd agreed that renting would be best for the first while, until William could secure a permanent job. William's new teacher, who lives in the town of Sturgeon Falls, had recommended his rental property. Even though it was a decent distance from the school, William and Quinn could rent it for cheap.

The rental listing had been slim for pictures, leaving Quinn's imagination to fill in the gaps. She'd spent countless hours poring over the few available pictures, trying to dissect the house layout, determining how the rooms flowed into each other, how close in proximity Cole's room would be to theirs, where the laundry was situated, and if there was enough storage for all their things.

The voice on the phone's GPS announces a left turn up ahead, 300 meters. Quinn feels her throat tighten at the prospect of waking Cole, and all the work still ahead. It had taken her a month to pack up their belongings. She'd been able to do most of it while Cole napped, but she had progressed slowly. Her reluctance to move had made the task at hand seem impossible.

Somehow, she had managed to do it all with minimal help from William. He had worked full time until two days ago. They had worked hard together to take apart the master bed and the spare bedroom furniture, leaving Cole's room untouched until the last minute.

Quinn had been careful to wrap the fragile items in bath towels and newspaper. Every time she'd plucked an item off a shelf and wrapped it tight, she'd felt a swelling in her chest telling her this wasn't right. She hadn't wanted to move. She was doing it strictly for William.

She consoles herself by remembering that there is always the option to return to Kingston later on, once William completes his training. This thought, and the unlikely possibility that Sturgeon Falls might grow on her as William hopes, is all that she can cling to.

She's wary of finding herself isolated in this new town, away from the city centre and above it all, with the grand forest behind the house. Since learning about the house, William has been giddy at the idea of living on such a large piece of land during their time here. For weeks before the big move, he kept talking about all the wonderful things they could do while living in the woods. Promises of cozy wood fires in the evening, hot tea on the gas stove, knitted sweaters, and starry skies with no boundaries had made her heart leap.

Quinn has a soft spot for nature, but only on the weekends. She wants convenience during the week, everything nearby. While on the weekends she enjoys her woodsy hikes and feeding birds from the palm of her hand, she can't imagine why she would want to do that every day, despite William's eagerness.

The tires glide, breaking loose momentarily on a patch of black ice, lightly covered by snow, as they take a left turn on Dutrisac Road. Quinn sucks in a breath and grips the door tightly, waiting for the car to stop sliding. After a few agonizing moments, William gets control again and they keep moving forward, their tires gripping the snow.

"Yikes, that was scary," William exclaims.

The GPS chimes as they turn onto Quesnel Road, their new street. "Your destination will be on the left."

"Jake said it would be the last one on the left." His eyes are growing bigger with excitement as they near the house.

All the tension and exhaustion seem to evaporate before her eyes. He turns to her with a large grin, making her automatically calm down. Seeing William this happy helps her relax a little. *Everything will be fine*, she thinks.

"Oh! Wow, babe, there it is! Did I tell you, or what?" William boasts, obviously proud of himself for choosing a decent looking house.

"It looks nice, honey," she admits, despite her lack of enthusiasm.

William carefully backs the car in the long driveway and turns off the engine. Immediately, Cole wakes up screaming, grumpy and hungry as Quinn lets out a sigh.

Here we go, she thinks.

Reaching behind the seat to stroke Cole's cheek as William exits the vehicle to greet the moving crew, she takes a good long look at the house through the rear window of the car.

The majestic height of the house and all the white siding makes it look very similar to the snowy rock faces they'd just driven past for the last few hours. Quinn can't help but quiver at the resemblance and the dreaded memory of claustrophobia she'd felt during the drive. Somehow, she'd found herself living in the middle of the woods with endless amounts of white siding holding her captive.

3

QUINN

When Quinn steps out of the car, she almost hits her head on the door panel as her feet slide, losing grip on a patch of black ice. She quickly grasps onto the car door handle to pull herself back up to reach Cole, all cozy and snug in the backseat—oblivious to her struggle.

We need to buy sidewalk salt, she thinks as she begins to create a mental list of things to get on their first run into town.

Without her coat, Quinn feels the sharp wind cutting straight through her, chilling her right to her core. There is a damp humidity in the air, making her grit her teeth. She has to shut her eyes tight to hold the tears in, unsure if it's because of the cold or the move. She feels frozen in place as the evening's darkness begins to descend around her. Quickly, she snaps herself out of it and grabs her coat, hat, and mittens before unbuckling Cole's seat from the backseat. She places the heavy handle over her forearm and carefully makes her way up the treacherous driveway to the house.

Her first thought as they enter the house is how big it is. Do they truly need this much space? Any worries she'd had about where all their belongings would go quickly evaporates. Even from only seeing the entryway, she can already tell they will have many spare rooms with nothing to put in them for a while.

The Millers pile inside.

As Quinn shakes off her coat and hangs it on an abandoned coat hanger she finds in the nearby closet, she takes note of the unfamiliar smells and sounds of the new house. William must have just turned on the furnace. There is a moaning sound coming through the ducts. Jake had warned them that the house had been sitting empty for most of the winter, but he was glad to have someone living in it, even just to keep the pipes from freezing and ruining the entire house.

The rent is very reasonable, but the distance to the helicopter school isn't ideal. William will have to commute over an hour each day to get to and from school, leaving Quinn and Cole alone for about nine hours a day.

Quinn tries not to focus on this devastating prospect since William's previous job had been walking distance from their old home. She finds it hard to swallow all the sacrifices he's been asking of her lately, but she desperately wants to help William make his dream come true. After all, how many people get an opportunity to fulfill their dreams? She wants him to be happy, and she decides that she will try and make the best of it.

William reappears, returning from the basement, letting Quinn know they now have running water. Quinn gently lifts Cole from his seat and rubs a thumb across his chubby cheek. She leans her own cheek on Cole's fuzzy head and feels him wriggling beneath her.

After such a long drive, Quinn urgently has to use the bathroom, but William is busy directing the moving crew. She's anxious to explore the rest of the house, but Cole keeps searching for her breast. She can feel him growing warmer as he begins to get worked up. She will need to feed him.

She finds an empty corner of the living room near a bay window and lowers herself down carefully to the old hardwood floors while holding her son. She balances Cole with one hand as she lifts her nursing shirt slightly for him to access her nipple. After some searching, Cole finds what he's looking for and the fussing stops. Quinn takes a deep breath and looks around. Peace returns as she watches the large snowflakes descend and slowly create a layer over their car.

We made it, she thinks to herself.

She hadn't been sure they actually would. The weather had gotten progressively worse with every hour. There is more snow here than she's ever seen in Kingston.

She isn't sure if they brought their snow shovel with them from home, and if they had, where on earth had she packed it? She adds this thought to her ongoing mental to-do list.

———

William and the moving crew work relentlessly for several hours until both vehicles are emptied. After feeding Cole, Quinn quietly rises off the cold floor, the heat still making its way through the large house, while bouncing Cole over one shoulder until he finally releases a burp and falls asleep—milk-drunk, as William likes to say.

Quinn carefully walks across the threshold to find the main floor powder room. With one hand, she unbuttons and unzips her jeans and relieves herself, all while keeping Cole asleep on her shoulder.

Before becoming a mother, she would never have dreamt of attempting such a manoeuver. Without a place to safely lay Cole yet in this house, and with William still occupied, she has no other choice.

A few moments later, she's finished her business and washes her hands, one at a time. She uses her socked foot to flush the noisy toilet, while making a quick escape out of the small room so as not to wake Cole. Surprisingly, Cole can sleep through most anything when he wants to. Getting him to sleep, however, now there was a challenge. If it wasn't for Quinn's reliable milk supply, they'd be in serious trouble. The only indication that Cole even heard the loud noise is a simple smile across his lips.

The bay window is now a black, glossy canvas reflecting her shape, the perfect picture of a mother holding her baby. An image to make most women tear up with joy. A new home to nest, a newborn baby to love and care for. Strangely, Quinn doesn't feel very much joy, only exhaustion. With the storm brewing outside, Quinn can hardly see anything of her new neighbourhood, but with all the lights turned on in their house, she wonders who might be able to see them. From the inside, she imagines they must look like a perfectly compact snow globe, with a shining light illuminating the characters in it.

Another hour later, Quinn and William thank the moving crew and watch the large moving truck's brake lights disappear into the pitch-black outside.

"Our new home," William says as he places a gentle hand on her shoulder while lovingly rubbing Cole's head.

Quinn can't help but think that it's still just a house to her. A box with four walls, albeit, four very tall walls, but still simply a house. To her, it's not yet a home, even if her precious loved ones are all living there with her. She is discouraged and overwhelmed at the sight of all the boxes littering the floor. Instead of feeling grateful for the safety of a house in this strange new place, she worries about the time and effort it will take to turn this rental house into a place she will one day call *home*.

4

QUINN

Thankful she had the foresight to ask William to set-up the mattress on the floor in their new room when they unloaded the moving truck, Quinn easily finds the pillowcase in which she'd stuffed all the bedsheets and swiftly begins making the bed. The simple, mundane routine helps her feel calmer and more in control.

Her eyes are heavy and she craves sleep. Once finished making the bed, she walks down the hall over to Cole's new room. William is rocking the baby in the new white and grey glider, reading a book. Watching them from the door frame, she finds it difficult to believe they've just moved in earlier that day.

She feels a soft flutter in her belly when she spots the perfect white crib, all made-up and a new navy flannel sheet wrapped over the mattress. With a soft grey coat of paint, this room will come together nicely. William must have put all this together while she was in the kitchen earlier gathering bread and peanut butter to make sandwiches for dinner.

Cole should sleep for a few hours before he needs to feed again, and Quinn looks forward to sleeping on a soft mattress, without motion sickness and a stiff neck.

As William stands to place Cole in his crib for the night, Quinn makes her way back to their new master bedroom, walking softly on the pads of her feet.

The room comes with an ensuite bathroom, definitely a plus for Quinn. There's a large soaking tub, a spacious two-person shower, a toilet, and a two-sink vanity. Real luxury in the middle of nowhere. Quinn wonders why this place hadn't been rented.

As she searches in her toiletry bag for toothpaste, she feels William's arms wrap around her small waist from behind her. He slowly kisses the back of her neck, moving away some stray hairs with his warm hand to access it better.

His breath is hot and makes her whole body tingle. She closes her eyes and allows herself to be transported by his touch, losing control as his hands begin to explore under her shirt and panties. Enjoying the sensation and the dizziness, it takes her a moment to snap out of it. She reluctantly moves William's hands back to her waist and unhurriedly turns around to face him. She kisses him passionately and puts a palm on his chest, to the little dip between his pecs that she adores, and gently pushes him away.

"You know we can't," she moans regretfully.

"I know, but you look so damn sexy," he says in a disappointed tone, as though the rejection is physically painful.

"The doctor said another week should do it," she assures him, feeling the tug of remorse from turning down his advances.

Her body wants him just as much as his wants her. Normally six weeks is the recommended waiting period before having sex after giving birth, but Quinn's doctor had advised an extra three weeks—to let everything heal.

Still, she sees it as a good sign that her body is responding this way to the intimate touch that had only weeks ago caused her to cringe. The new dosage of her medication must be working.

It's been forever since they've made love and she misses the feeling of having all of him inside her. With hungry eyes, she watches him remove his shirt and runs a finger down his bare chest and across his muscular biceps. William respects the doctor's orders to wait and doesn't argue. He steps aside and removes his pants, his erection not the least bit let down by her dismissal, and turns and strides into the shower. Quinn licks her chapped lips, desire written across her eyes as she watches William's tight buttocks flex under the hot jets of the water. Her skin flushes and she sighs—it will have to wait.

———

After checking on Cole, Quinn crawls into bed, the sheets still chilly from being in the moving truck all day. Without curtains to block the bedroom window, the room feels even colder. Her thin tank top and shorts no longer seem like a wise choice for bedtime until William's warm body glides in beside her—her furnace.

Quinn allows the heaviness of her eyelids and the warmth surrounding her to whisk her away, enveloping her in a cozy cocoon. But this is the moment her mind decides to spring to alertness. The soft click of the furnace and the clank in the pipes resound through the house in unfamiliar noises, making it difficult to rest.

Her to-do list seems to stretch before her eyes; impossible deadlines to meet, insurmountable tasks to complete, endless boxes to unpack, a grocery store to find, new neighbours to meet, laundry to do, and more. Her heart rate picks up as she twirls these tasks in her mind over and over until she's falling. Her body jerks and she gasps. She's awake, blinking rapidly. It was just a dream.

The snow is still falling outside, large flakes of it dancing by the glass of their bedroom window. The hazy glow of the moon shines through the room and Quinn spots boxes piled in every corner. She grunts as she grabs the sheet to pull it over her head in denial of the work still left to be done. Tomorrow, she will have her work cut out for her.

5

QUINN

The night proves to be a long one. Cole wakes up several times. His long nap on the drive and the strange new sounds of the house have made him restless.

Quinn has a hard time calming him down; Cole seems too agitated to take her breast to feed. She's wandered the dark halls of the new house, bouncing and rocking the baby, all while holding him tight on her chest to keep him warm and comfortable. Everything that Cole manages to eat, he spits up minutes later. Quinn finally falls asleep sitting upright in the glider, holding Cole over her shoulder to keep her son from having reflux.

A few hours later, Cole stirs and starts crying again. Exhaustion grips at Quinn but duty calls.

She's not sure how other mothers survive this, or why some chose to do this again. Sure, she loves Cole, but the endless waking up and feeding schedule is starting to get to her. She starts to shake. Her entire body craves sleep and lacks nutrition. She often skips meals because if Cole has finally fallen asleep on her, she doesn't dare move. She's not sure how she will handle it if he wakes up again, never mind if she'll be able to keep up the bouncing and patting on his back to try to get him to settle down. She focuses on her breath, trying to calm her heart and empty her mind of anxious thoughts.

After a while, she finds her mind wandering through the past few weeks when she'd been constantly forgetting conversations she'd had and losing things everywhere she went. She'd stopped caring about her appearance and barely took the time to shower anymore. Her last one must have been a week ago, but she didn't care. She's sure she will get spit-up on her again the moment she puts on a clean shirt, so what's the point of changing into new clothes?

Quinn also hadn't had any energy to take Cole anywhere. She'd been busying her days half-heartedly playing with him, passing the time looking out the window, or watching TV. She lived for nap time when she'd have a few moments to herself. She knew she was slipping deeper into the dark abyss, but she'd been too tired to pull herself out.

She hadn't seen her friends in quite some time, and she isn't sure when she'll get the chance to see them again. Not until the summer, that's for sure. She isn't about to make the long drive in this weather all by herself.

She doesn't feel like seeing anyone right now either. She wants to be alone. She wants to get away from her life, even if only for an hour. Quinn spends much of her time soothing Cole while daydreaming of leaving everything behind. She gets lost in her thoughts for hours before shaking her head and releasing them to the wind.

I'm a horrible mother. She shuts her eyes, embarrassed by her inability to be the mom she wants to be. She doesn't feel like herself lately.

She's been getting anxious more regularly and retreating from others. William had mentioned this to her one day when they went grocery shopping in Kingston before the move. He'd been concerned, but she'd just waved it off as nerves about the move. She'd been so nervous about getting a parking spot near the cart return that day, worried about placing the car seat in the cart that she had gone to do her groceries the minute the store opened its doors to make sure she'd be the first one there. At the time it had seemed completely rational to her, but William had explained that she couldn't live in fear or control everything.

It seemed that lately, Quinn could only think of the worst-case scenarios. If Cole wasn't awake, her mind would be active, keeping her up with all the possible terrible events that could come upon them. She would stay up for hours, lying in bed, facing the blue glow of the baby monitor, driving herself mad by watching every single breath Cole took and released.

———

When she's sure that Cole is in a deep sleep, Quinn slowly rises from the soft chair, which proves to be quite the feat. She lowers her baby boy into his crib so he can rest on his back and places her hand on his chest to check his breathing. She's worried about him getting cold in the room. Babies Cole's age aren't allowed any blankets in the crib until they become more mobile. She finds a hat in his box of clothes and debates the possibility of waking him up versus letting him get a little chilly. In the dark she places the hat carefully over his head, feeling the thin hairs on his scalp as she brushes them into place under the knitted hat.

Quinn tiptoes out of the room, shutting the door behind her as she's done several times that night and walks downstairs to the kitchen for a glass of water.

She hasn't had much time to unpack their belongings yet, but she had thought ahead and packed one box of essentials that she asked the movers to place in the kitchen for easy access. The box holds two mugs, a lighter, a candle, paper towels, a roll of toilet paper, hand sanitizer, hand soap, tape, scissors, a Swiss army knife, some cutlery, paper plates, newspaper, a pack of matches, a few plastic grocery bags, sandwich bags with a reusable clasp, and salt and pepper shakers.

She tests the water with her hand, getting it as cold as it will get before first rinsing out a mug and then filling it half-way. As she stands by the sink, looking out of the kitchen window above it, she notices a light on in the house next door, the only other house on this part of the street.

She can see someone moving around in the dark, a shadow swiftly pacing left and right, passing in front of the small window next-door. She watches for a while, trying to make sense of what she's seeing, doing her best to make out any features of who she's spotted, before giving up and drinking her water in one big gulp. She drags her tired body up the stairs, unaccustomed to climbing them after living in a bungalow for many years.

Upstairs the halls are dark and Cole's room seems far away in the pitch black. She feels her way back to her room, palms out, reaching ahead of her to feel the doorframe. She can hear William's soft snores and sinks into the mattress to cuddle up next to him and warm up. Her feet are freezing, and she wants nothing more than to sleep a deep sleep like William always seems to.

6

QUINN

The morning is a blur between rushing to get Cole from his crib and feeding him. Quinn feels groggy and yawns as William tries to find the coffee maker amongst the sea of unopened boxes. They resolve that it might be best to drive into town for their coffee and a few items from the store to make breakfast this morning. This will give them energy for the unpacking, and also a chance to see the town for the first time in the light of day.

The snow has piled up quite a bit throughout the night, leaving a few centimeters of snow on the long driveway. They bundle up, lock the house up and tread through the fluffy snow to the car as more snow falls from the sky. William takes the brush out from the backseat and begins the extensive job of dusting all of the powder off, making sure to get every bit off the roof as Quinn settles Cole into his seat. The Weather Network is calling for more snow later this afternoon, but the Millers should be back at the house and well into unpacking by then.

Grateful to make it out of the driveway successfully, Quinn taps at her phone, trying to find directions to the closest grocery store. As they pass the neighbour's house, Quinn notices a woman dressed warmly, sporting a hat and mittens, shoveling her driveway. She looks like she's about to keel over from the hard work.

"William, stop the car," she begs. "That poor woman looks like she's struggling to shovel all that snow!"

"You're right, babe. That was a big snowfall," he adds as he rolls down Quinn's window and stretches over her to speak to the neighbour.

"Hi there!" he yells out, his voice resonating in an echo, the street silent, insulated by the snow. The woman waves back, her face red with exhaustion. "We just moved into the house next door." He points with his thumb to their house. "If you'd like, I'd be happy to help you get the snow off your driveway later," he offers, before adding that it wouldn't be before the afternoon when he can reach the snowblower in the garage, currently stacked behind other boxes.

With a frail voice, the woman yells back, "Thanks!" coughing mid-way. William waves through the open window and settles back in his seat to shut the window as the woman waddles back into the warmth of her home.

"Thanks, babe," Quinn says as she leans over to kiss his cheek, her knight in shining armor.

They make the drive to No Frills, which is surprisingly only a five-minute drive away. They hesitantly walk the aisles, familiarizing themselves with the new store, but seem to find most of what they need in the first trip through.

Less than an hour later, they're on their way back with a few groceries and hot Tim Horton's coffees in hand. Cole, exhausted from their outing, is peacefully asleep in the backseat of the car as they make their way back carefully to their new street. The snow plows have been by during their outing, making the road slightly better to maneuver. In the light of day, Quinn takes a sharp breath upon seeing the house. It looks even more like a fortress in the daytime. White on white. A big wall, a large fence, blocking her in.

In front of the house there is a dead tree with its branch reaching out to the sky, resembling a dying man on his last breath, a futile attempt to touch heaven while his roots remain deeply buried in the ground. She shivers at the thought of what wildlife exists just beyond the trees. She imagines which creatures could harm them if they ventured out into the woods for a leisurely walk. She doesn't ever want to step into the vastness of the woods that surround their house. Everywhere she looks, she feels encircled—trapped.

She dreads walking through the doors, the work ahead and the responsibility of it all. She looks forward to being all unpacked, making this cold house resemble a little bit more of a home— somewhere safe and comfortable. She longs for that warmth she had worked hard to get at their old house, and to be amongst her things, the familiarity of it all. Homes have personalities, colours, smells, and comforting sounds.

The isolation of this house makes her uneasy. She doesn't know anyone here. She knows she will meet people, but when? And will she like them? Will she fit in with the mom groups here? It's a new start, but that takes effort. It takes a lot to build new relationships. But Quinn isn't sure she has it in her to put on a smile, get all dolled-up, and present her best self to strangers.

She doesn't feel like faking it anymore. She's tired. She's doing her best to survive these early days. She's just trying to get through them. She takes a deep breath, steadying herself. Four seconds out, four seconds in.

She's used to the tightness in her chest by now. Unfortunately, it's a regular occurrence these days.

Quinn takes in her surroundings, doing her best to focus on finding five things she can see, four things she can touch, three things she can hear, two things she can smell, and one she can taste. It helps slow down the spiraling thoughts and brings her back to the present.

A breath out, a breath in, and she opens her eyes again.

The wave of panic is under control for the time being. Like the low tide, she knows it will come back to swallow her again. Drag her to the deep end, and drown her in her own body.

7

QUINN

A few hours later, they are no longer tripping over boxes and each other. Cole is happily playing on a soft blue blanket on the floor in the middle of the living room. The couch and coffee table have been moved into position and most of the kitchen items have been unpacked and put away in the cupboards.

Quinn is starting to feel lighter, more in control. *At least we can cook now*, she thinks. The thought of cooking always soothes her. Even if the stress reduces her appetite, there's nothing quite like the regular rhythm of chopping vegetables to put her mind at rest.

Next, she shifts her attention to the bookshelf William assembled earlier. He's been working through the boxes in the garage, bringing some in periodically to place in their designated rooms for Quinn to sort through later on.

She hears William walking up the steps in the garage and opening the steel door. He stomps in, his winter boots loud on the cheap black rug they picked up at the grocery store this morning. He whistles and brushes a white dusting of snow from his hat and mittens, tucking them under his armpit as he rubs his hands together.

"Getting colder out there!" He shivers, his nose red. "I finally found that snowblower. I'll go get the neighbour's driveway cleared up now and come back to help you with the rest of the boxes after," he adds.

"Alright, babe, no problem. We're good here." Quinn smiles reassuringly as she slowly approaches her husband, feeling her chest tightening with every word.

William doesn't seem to notice as he gives her a quick kiss on the lips at the door before going back out in the cold. She can still feel the sting of his frozen nose on her cheek as she watches him walk the snowblower next door. She stands there by the window until he's out of sight. Exhaling loudly, she turns around to see the mess before her. It looks like a bomb has gone off inside the house. She stares with teary eyes at the floors that are covered in old, crumpled newspapers, dozens of boxes lying half-opened, their belongings scattered everywhere.

"How do we have so much stuff?" she whines. "This is going to take forever."

Overwhelmed, she picks Cole up from the floor and holds him in her arms as she gets started on yet another box. She hands some of the crunchy newspaper to Cole for him to squish through his fingers while keeping an eye on him to make sure he doesn't get too curious and decide to put the paper into his mouth. She tries to distract herself from the work ahead and sings a familiar lullaby, more as a way to calm herself than her son, as she absentmindedly places items on the bookshelf. One item at a time, she's rebuilding their life, here in this strange town.

Her heart isn't in it, she knows. Without William around, she doesn't force the smile to come. She just works away, busying herself by moving mechanically. Doing and not feeling. But she's running on empty.

She feels it in her bones.

She's been getting dizzier lately, her emotions have been all over the place. She's caught herself on multiple occasions crying at the most random things: spilled milk, burnt toast, even a commercial with puppies in it. She's just glad William hasn't witnessed this and that she's been able to keep it hidden from him so far.

She spends the next few hours in a trance-like state, walking and bouncing Cole until he twists his body like a furious fish in her hands. It seems that even Cole wants to escape this place. Dutifully, she settles down on the couch and lifts her shirt to feed him. While he is calm, she takes the opportunity to plan the best way to attack the overwhelming feeling taking over.

One box at a time, she thinks. *One room at a time.*

That's how she'll get there. She feels herself calming down. She breathes easy as Cole falls asleep peacefully in the crook of her arm, meaning she won't have to unpack any more things for a while.

She misses her friends. She also misses her husband. She never knew how lonely she'd feel when she became a mother—never alone, but lonely.

Looking out the window, she sees only forest staring back at her. It creeps her out, how she can't see inside its darkness, only guessing at the depths of it. She imagines bears, cougars, lynx, and coyotes watching her every move, waiting for an opportune time to strike. She shivers, suddenly exhausted.

Resting her head on the back of the couch she stares up at the ceiling. The popcorn surface is stained with yellowed circles in various spots where water has gathered over the years. She falls asleep staring at the thousands of tiny dots, like snowflakes blurring over her, surrounding her, swallowing her whole.

8

QUINN

Quinn wakes up twenty-minutes later to William's heavy steps on the landing in the garage. It takes her a moment to remember where she is and that William was coming back from the neighbour's place. Cole, fussy and unhappy to be woken up, screams in a fit and doesn't settle for the next half hour. It's almost dinnertime by the time Quinn and William call it a day.

They have managed to unpack most of the boxes, the last few remaining stashed away in their room, but Quinn isn't worried about those. They are just her things, mostly clothes and make-up, which she can't imagine needing anytime soon.

She's exhausted from being up for most of the night and from all the unpacking she did throughout the day. She barely has enough energy to cook dinner. She settles for an easy penne pasta, with chicken and rosé sauce, on which she sprinkles parmesan cheese. After all, it's just for her and William, Cole is still too little for solid food.

"That lady next door, Mrs. Westover, is so nice," William explains, between mouthfuls. "She lives there all by herself. I'm not sure how she can live in that old house alone. It looks creepy." He shivers—from the cold or the thought of the house, she doesn't know. "She can barely walk up and down her driveway. How can she take care of that old place?"

Quinn contemplates that last statement and frowns.

"Are you sure she's all alone? I was up late last night getting some water in the kitchen, and I swear I saw her light on and someone much younger-looking was pacing quickly by the window." She worries suddenly that maybe someone was in Mrs. Westover's house.

"Are you sure?" William takes a sip of water as Quinn nods. "Should I go over there and ask her? Or call the police?" he offers, visibly concerned.

"Where's her husband?" she asks, suddenly hopeful for a reasonable explanation.

"She said he died a few years ago and she hasn't had the heart to sell the place." His expression was pained. "I feel bad for her," he adds, placing his fork on his plate. He reaches out and takes one of Quinn's hand in his and squeezes it. "I hope no one was in her house. That would be terrible."

Cole, who's been sitting on Quinn's lap, happily looking between his parents, suddenly decides he needs attention also and scrunches his face in a scowl. Quinn winces, already dreading the cry that's coming.

"Oh, little dude, what's the matter?" William coos as he shoves the last bite of his dinner into his mouth and stands to rinse his plate at the sink. William puts his plate in the dishwasher and walks over to Quinn with his arms extended, ready to take Cole from her so she can finish eating her dinner. He gives her a gentle kiss on the head and strides off to the living room, bouncing and singing to Cole.

Quinn watches and tries to smile, but she's so tired.

She's trying to enjoy the break, the feeling of being by herself again, but all she can think about is that it won't last. That soon, very soon, she'll become a snack vending machine again. In a few moments, Cole will cry and her breasts will leak, oozing warm milk in response, making dark circles through her shirt for the tenth time today. She releases a heavy sigh as she stands up to put the leftovers away.

Her eyes are irritated as she rubs them with her finger. She can feel that her scalp is itchy—more dandruff must be showing. She doesn't care. Quinn is doing her best, but she's struggling. If she's honest, motherhood hasn't been at all like she imagined it would be.

She had imagined laughter, warm hugs, smiles, a simple sleeping routine, outdoor walks to the park where they could set up a blanket and read books, or sing songs. She had pictured cute outfits, her body returning to her normal weight within a few weeks, walking every day, Cole happy and easy-going. But that hadn't been the case. Quinn hadn't turned out to be the motherly type.

She knows what she needs to do, and she does it, but that's all. She doesn't feel any particularly maternal instincts kicking in yet. She hasn't felt her uterus flutter with desire for another child right away after bringing Cole home, like many of her friends. Rather, Quinn has been contemplating getting her tubes tied. Not that Cole is a bad baby, but more that Quinn is a bad mother. Or at least, not the mother she'd hoped she would be.

She watches William tickling Cole's toes and feels tears sting her dry eyes. Fatherhood has come so naturally for him. Her husband so casually slipped into his new role and has made it look effortless.

Quinn had been so surprised. She had always thought she would have no problems becoming a mother, but she worried about William. Now, it was the other way around. William had never been keen on other people's kids, but when he first saw Cole, it was love at first sight. Quinn had seen the twinkle in his eyes, and she'd known right then and there that he would do anything for his boy.

Then again, he wasn't waiting on him day and night like she was. He wasn't missing out on countless hours of sleep like she was. It never felt like William sacrificed the same way Quinn did.

———

Quinn stands by the sink, her hands plunged in the hot, soapy water as she stares out the window into the night, her reflection judging her. She dreams of a warm bath, twenty-minutes of solitude, soaking in flower-scented bubbles, candles lit, maybe a good book to read, and a glass of wine in her hand. Maybe one day, but not yet.

Quinn thinks that some sleep will be good for her. That all she needs to feel like herself again is, just a little bit of sleep. She considers going to bed at the same time as Cole tonight, to catch up on yesterday's missed sleep. Just as Quinn is fantasizing about the soft mattress and warm sheets, she hears a soft knock at the door. Her shoulders drop.

"Now who could that be?" she mutters, not bothering to hide the disdain in her voice. This is the last thing she needs today.

9

QUINN

Quinn watches from the dimly lit hallway as William opens the front door, carrying Cole in his arms. From her position, she can see a middle-aged couple standing in the doorway, wiping off a light layer of snow from their black coats.

The man is attractive and slightly taller than William. He's got thick, wavy black hair, deep brown eyes, tanned skin, and almost perfectly straight white teeth. The woman, who Quinn assumes is his wife, is just as gorgeous with her medium-length, rich, chestnut brown hair, large brown eyes, and bright pink lipstick. She's significantly shorter and probably stands just over five feet tall. They are a beautiful pair, but oddly opposite in size. Both are sporting thick black winter coats and leather boots.

Quinn looks on, mesmerized. The woman removes her coat and gold pashmina scarf to reveal a leopard print blouse and tight-fitting black pants. The man is dressed sharply in a clean, light blue dress shirt, black and blue striped tie, and black pants.

Quinn suddenly feels extremely underdressed in her three-day worn grey Old-Navy t-shirt and ripped jeans. Her dandruff seems to be all over her shoulders, her head suddenly unbearably itchy. She is particularly self-conscious of the stained circles over her nipples and does her best to cover them up by quickly crossing her arms awkwardly high. If she's lucky, they might think she's cold.

"Hi!" William exclaims, genuinely excited as he welcomes in the couple. "What are you guys doing here?" he asks as he slams his large hands into the other man's palm for an enthusiastic handshake. William seems to know these people. But this thought doesn't do much to appease Quinn, who still has no idea who they are, or what they are doing here this late in the evening when all she wants to do is go to bed.

Quinn slowly moves closer, finally reaching the entryway. Standing under a light, she suddenly feels very much like she's on display.

"Quinn! This is Jake and Lena Adkins. My helicopter course instructor and his wife!" He looks over at Quinn, a large grin on his face. "Jake is our landlord," William explains as he shifts closer to Quinn, putting his arm around her.

"Jake, Lena, this is my wife Quinn, and my son, Cole." He beams with pride as he gently lifts Cole's hand to shake theirs.

Everyone laughs and they seem to have forgotten about Quinn for the moment.

"Nice to meet you," she offers anyway, her voice so soft, she's sure no one has heard her.

Shy and embarrassed, she moves out of the way, directing them inside to the living room without uttering another word. She doesn't trust her voice to sound inviting. She knows William expects her to play the role of hostess, but she just doesn't have it in her tonight. Why did they just show up like that? Don't the Adkins know Quinn and William have a baby? That they just moved in late last night and that they're tired?

Quinn's mind is spinning at the prospect of having to spend the next few hours entertaining and socializing with these strangers. Peering around the house, all she can see is dust and smeared glass surfaces. She sighs, feeling judged although she's the only one who seems to notice and be bothered by any of it.

She's dreading having to make small talk and ensure everyone has a drink to sip or food to chew on. She has half a mind to tear open a bag of potato chips and dump them in a bowl, before storming off to have a bath, like she's been craving, leaving her guests alone with Cole and William.

Instead, she grabs some cubes of cheese and dumps a few crackers on a few serving trays and turns on the kettle for tea. While the water is heating up, she resolves to sit quietly across from them on the adjoining accent chair, busying herself by holding Cole and keeping him happy.

"How was the drive up?" Lena turns to face Quinn, her eyes the most beautiful Quinn has ever seen. They are deep brown, like delicious truffles with flecks of gold in them. She feels like Lena is looking right into her soul. She wonders what she sees. Suddenly, Quinn realizes that she cares how this stranger views her.

Lena's eyelashes seem to reach her eyebrows, they are so long. They are heavily coated in black mascara which reminds Quinn of a wasp's furry legs. Quinn has to blink several times to keep her focus on the woman's question.

"Ok." Quinn finally replies, licking her lips to make sure her mouth is closed. She's unable to think of any other word, her brain seems to have turned to paste. Her lips are cracked, she realizes. So dry, to smile would cause them to split and bleed. The young mother's mouth has been stubbornly impossible to keep shut these days. She's constantly fearing the humiliating possibility of drooling.

She realizes then that it might be good for her to get out more often and interact with other adults. She hasn't had a normal conversation with anyone other than William since Cole was born late in January. Her tongue feels thick in her mouth like it's taking up too much space. Lena is smiling politely back at her, waiting for more. Quinn can detect pity seeping through Lena's closed lips in the way they pressed harder together the longer Quinn remains silent.

The awkward pause seems to drag on forever.

Internally, Quinn is screaming at herself for being such an idiot. *Just talk normally*, she coaxes herself. *Just say something! Anything!* Yet, she can't even think of anything simple to say or ask. Lately, Quinn has had trouble remembering simple things like what she did that day or what she ate. Her mind is constantly filled with Cole's feeding and sleeping schedule, leaving no room for anything else.

She can't muster anything relevant or interesting to say. What was that thing she saw recently on the news? A hurricane in the south? Before she can even think up a full sentence, Lena gives up on Quinn's reply and shifts her gaze back to William, releasing Quinn from the anguish of having to find something to talk about, but causing her more shame that she couldn't.

The men are happily getting along, chatting while Quinn and Lena content themselves with looking at Cole, the perfect icebreaker. Quinn musters all of her strength and asks if Lena and Jake have any kids—they don't. Their conversation is pretty much monosyllabic until Quinn notices a small *Om* tattoo on Lena's forearm.

"Do you do yoga?" she asks, genuinely interested.

"Yes! I love yoga!" Lena perks up instantly, enthusiastic at having found something to talk about. "I practice it every single day. I teach yin yoga at the local studio downtown. Do you like yoga?" She smiles broadly at Quinn who shifts her weight, uneasy, transferring Cole from one knee to the other.

Quinn should have guessed the moment she laid eyes on her. Lena's body is toned and lean, her posture impeccable. She glides more than walks, and though Quinn is pretty sure Lena is older than she is, her skin is visibly tight, no worry lines on her forehead. Lena radiates next to Quinn, who feels like she's suddenly sitting under a cloud, greyed by the shadow of this bubbly, shining guest. Lena oozes confidence and peace through her pores. She's probably one of those people who is nice to everyone she meets.

Quinn always feels inadequate around people like that, constantly wondering if they've made a mistake talking to her. As though, perhaps she was in the way and they were trying to talk to someone else behind her.

But no, not here.

Lena is simply a nice person—a happy person. Quinn doesn't mind her so much in this setting. Lena isn't trying to impress anyone by being nice. This is just who she is.

"Hmm, yeah, I guess. I tried it a couple of times," she replies hesitantly. "I wasn't very good at it though. I'm not all that flexible," she adds bashfully.

"Oh, but that's exactly why you need yoga!" Lena laughs good-heartedly, patting Quinn's knee lightly. "Stick with me, girl, and we'll have you bending in half in no time!" she winks.

Quinn feels her cheeks burn. She feels ashamed that this beautiful woman has touched her greasy, dirty clothes. But a part of her is hopeful. Has she just made a friend? Could it be that easy? She likes Lena, but she isn't sure they will have much in common.

The men chat as Lena continues to gush over Cole and talk about the house, must-see stores in town and the many benefits of yoga. The visit lasts about an hour with a promise to do it again soon. After the drinks are cooled and the food trays emptied, Quinn picks up the dishes and places them in the sink to wash up later. The Adkins stand to leave as Cole starts to yawn and fuss.

Quinn hesitantly agrees to go to Lena's yoga class one evening next week. Immediately after agreeing, Quinn worries about what to wear and if Lena will still like her. She's never found it easy to make friends. But as this friendship is important to William, she's willing to give it a try.

10

QUINN

Today is William's first day at helicopter school and Quinn's first full day alone with Cole in this strange new town. She doesn't know very many people, other than Jake and Lena. She feels reluctant to wake up, dreading the long day ahead.

She should get dressed and take Cole for a walk to explore their new surroundings. She also needs to fold up some of the moving boxes and take them to the road for recycling day. As her mental to-do list continues, Quinn feels increasingly exhausted. She begrudgingly drags herself up from the bed and yawns as she gathers her unwashed hair on top of her head with a scrunchie.

Laughing to herself, Quinn remembers her therapist's words from their last session on the importance of the words she uses.

"You need to change your 'should' into 'get to'. It's about how you approach something. How you think about a situation will affect how you feel about it," she'd told Quinn.

Cognitive behavioural therapy, or CBT as her therapist had called it. It's changing automatic thoughts into rational ones with the hope to eventually produce different behaviours. If only she could think herself out of being depressed. Unfortunately, she had tried and it hadn't worked.

She's tried several tricks over the years. Staring at her reflection in a mirror, saying affirmations such as 'you are beautiful, you are smart, you are worthy.' But all this had done was make her feel odd for talking to herself. She has tried walking, meditation, and she even changed her diet and tried to be more aware of her thoughts in general.

If she's lucky, she sometimes catches herself spiraling down a dark path and knows well enough to quickly turn the other way. But other times, on days like today, she just lets herself fall deeper down the hole.

She has no definite plans. She makes light of it to William, claiming it's better this way—see how the day goes, she's reassured him on his way out the door. But Quinn has never been big on spontaneity. She prefers knowing what's coming and likes planning ahead.

Trying to get herself out of her dark frame of mind, Quinn uses her phone to get online. But after a few moments of buffering, waiting for a webpage to load, to her dismay, she notices that the cell reception is spotty.

"Of course," she hisses through clenched teeth, convinced this is a plot from the universe to pull her down again. The only good spot for reception seems to be in the living room, on the window ledge of the bay window, in the same spot where she fed Cole that first night.

Scrolling through Facebook, she tries to find a mom group nearby or even a drop-in activity offered in town. After twenty minutes of searching, she comes up empty. It's several hours too early for any of the groups to be meeting, or the wrong day, it seems.

Nothing in this town seems to be open until well past nine-thirty. Quinn groggily glances at the clock on the kitchen wall that William had placed there yesterday.

It's a little after seven in the morning.

William's course is in North Bay, about a thirty-minute drive away. The class starts at eight, and in the hopes of getting ahead of traffic, he'd left early, giving himself enough time to find the school and grab a coffee on the way. Playing the role of the supportive wife, Quinn had kissed him goodbye with a smile on her face, wishing him luck and a great day. Inside she began internally crumbling—breaking at the seams and coming undone.

Only nine hours to go, she'd told herself as she'd shut the door behind him, locking the deadbolt while he got in the car.

William will be back in time for dinner tonight, assuming the weather doesn't take a turn for the worse. Quinn can't exactly hold her breath until then, therefore she decides to put on her big girl pants and make the best of it. She has a lot of laundry to catch up on, floors to sweep, beds to make, and baseboards to wipe clean. The last occupant hadn't done a great job of cleaning the grout between the kitchen tiles either. As Quinn looks around the space, she makes a mental list of all the small and bigger jobs she can spread out over the week, and those she can stretch out over several hours—anything to make the time tick by faster.

Cole has been especially needy since the move and Quinn is finding it difficult to accomplish anything at all. The only time her son seems calm and happy is when she's holding him, but Quinn feels suffocated. He's already on her half the day to nurse, and she just gave birth to him two months ago after carrying him in her belly for almost a year. She needs space. She's ready to claim her own body again, but Cole doesn't seem to get it.

Cole is reluctantly sitting in a bouncy chair on the floor of the living room and he watches Quinn move around the floor on her hands and knees, meticulously wiping the baseboards clean of debris, making the white paint shine. *Good as new*, she smiles to herself.

She's already done half a day's work and only one hour has ticked by. She sits on the floor, brings her knees in and bends her head over them. She feels herself losing control and is on the verge of crying, but instead she chooses to focus on her breath.

She's almost calmed down when Cole decides he needs her attention and begins to wail.

"No, Cole, you can't possibly be hungry again! I just fed you an hour ago!" she whines, tears threatening. Ignoring his pleas, resolving she'll feed him in thirty minutes, she gets back to cleaning.

———

Cole just gets fussier and fussier as the day goes on. Quinn only has a sliver of the energy she had this morning. She drags herself around the house, looking from room to room, for something, anything, to keep her mind busy.

With Cole, she wanders the halls. Her muscles ache at the constant weight of her growing boy. He hasn't stopped screaming for an hour and nothing Quinn does seems to work to calm him down.

She'd tried feeding him, but he'd just spit everything out. She'd tried to rock him in the glider, but that had made his screams even worse.

Finally, she decides to lay him down on the blanket on the floor to give herself a minute to think. Her brain feels muddled, like mushy peas. Barely holding it together, she knows she can't call William on his first day, but she has no one else. She wants to cry, scream, or kick something. She feels like she's cracking and knows she needs help.

Just then, there's a knock at the door. This time, she's grateful for the interruption.

11

QUINN

Quinn carefully opens the door to a shivering Mrs. Westover. Her fur hat and matching gloves make her look very refined and elegant. It seems every time the front door opens, well-dressed people walk in. Her neighbour holds out a jar of pickles and strawberry jam for Quinn to take. Quinn, who's still wearing the same shirt as yesterday, begins to redden from embarrassment.

"Mrs. Westover! What are you doing out here in the cold? Please come in. Thank you so much for these!" She moves out of the way to open the door wide enough to let her through and has to push the door closed with her hip because of the harsh wind blowing against it.

"Thank you, dear. My pleasure!" Waving a hand at Quinn, she adds in a frail voice, "Please, call me Rose. I just came by to welcome you to the neighbourhood and say hello. I wanted to see how you were getting on with the move and everything." Her eyes are a glassy blue peering from behind her foggy glasses at Cole, laying on the floor.

"Oh, thank you so much! That's very thoughtful of you," Quinn blushes, immediately feeling ashamed by the state she's in. Her neighbour must think poorly of her.

Her voice is frail, her hair is streaked with white and her movements are slow, but her skin looks very healthy and tight. *How old is she?* Quinn wonders. Mrs. Westover takes a good look at Quinn and smiles reassuringly, patting her gently on the shoulder before making her way towards Cole.

"Hello there, little one. What's his name?" She turns back to Quinn, who answers her in a tired voice.

There's no use trying to pretend she's got it all together. Mrs. Westover probably heard Cole's cries all the way from her house and came to see if everything was under control.

"What a pretty blue blanket!" Rose remarks suddenly.

Quinn feels relief and then concern as Mrs. Westover bends awkwardly towards the screaming child. Before she can protest, Rose has her hands on Cole's legs and is moving them strangely. As Quinn approaches, she realizes that the woman is pumping Cole's legs as though he were riding a bicycle.

"He's probably got some gas," Rose explains, referring to Cole's fussiness. "So uncomfortable," she adds speaking to Cole in a soothing tone.

Quinn looks on mesmerized, unable to speak or move. Of course, gas! Why hadn't she thought of that? She senses the exhaustion wash over her now that there is someone else here. She finally allows herself to relax, just a little bit.

Cole's screams seem to wind down, the pumping of his legs keeping him happy and busy. He's even managing some happy gurgling noises as Mrs. Westover smiles and tickles his toes.

She's like the baby whisperer, Quinn muses.

She's so grateful for the woman's interruption to her day that she stops worrying about the messy state of the house. It's just nice to have someone around so that Quinn doesn't have all the burden and responsibility of taking care of Cole.

After a while, Quinn picks Cole up from the floor and covers herself with a nearby soiled nursing blanket to feed him. He seems a lot more relaxed now, which in turn, helps her calm down as well. She can feel her stomach settling down and her heart beating at a more natural rhythm. Mrs. Westover has slowly risen from the floor, her cracking knees protesting before she settles in the accent chair facing Quinn. Although they haven't spoken much, Quinn feels more comfortable with Mrs. Westover than she has with anyone other than William in a long while.

"Thank you," manages Quinn, as she holds Cole close to her chest.

"It's really no problem." Rose waves her hand in dismissal. "I've seen this before." She nods with understanding and wisdom. "You're doing great. Babies are fussy at this age. It will get easier with time," she reassures her.

"Do you have any kids?" Quinn asks.

"No, never had the pleasure." The lady's melancholic smile tells Quinn there's a story there, but she doesn't pry. Instead, Quinn asks how long she's lived here.

"I've lived on this land all my life. My father owned it before me, as his father did. It's been passed down from generation to generation. I remember when our house was the only one on the block." Her eyes shine as she remembers. "I liked it that way. Just us and the forest." A sad smile spreads across her lips as she stares out the window briefly.

"But it sure is nice having new neighbours, especially now that I'm getting older," she says kindly as she looks at Quinn.

The women talk for some time, while Cole feeds happily, switching breasts partway through. Quinn learns about Mrs. Westover's love of gardening, her intensive quilting projects and her background as a daycare provider.

"That explains how you know so much about babies!" Quinn remarks, truly fascinated. Maybe moving here was a good idea after all. To have a neighbour like Mrs. Westover is going to be very helpful.

"Do you and William want any more children?" the woman asks and Quinn feels an uneasiness rush through her.

She hates this question.

She always feels like she might somehow be disappointing people if she told the truth. Cole is only a few months old, and she's barely gotten her body back! She's not ready to give it up again. Quinn isn't even sure her mental state can handle another pregnancy and all the hormones that come with it. She feels out of sorts already, having more than one kid might just throw her over the edge.

"We've talked about it." She nods noncommittally, not answering the question either way.

The truth is that Quinn is holding onto a birth control prescription that William isn't aware of. She's trying to give herself a breather—some space to get back to herself. She doesn't feel she's been the best mother to Cole yet, and the thought of having any more children so close together makes her feel anxious.

Quinn's comment seems to satisfy Mrs. Westover enough to change the subject. With Cole done feeding, Quinn isn't sure what to do next. Rose offers to hold him and Quinn places him carefully in the woman's extended arms. She seems to have the magic touch because Cole's eyes shut almost instantly and before long, his breathing is even and deep—he's fast asleep. Rose looks over at Quinn and suggests that she go and have a shower if she wants.

"We're good here for a while. Do what you need to do," she reassures with a gentle smile.

Quinn feels the emotions bubbling to the surface at this woman's kindness. She doesn't feel the slightest bit nervous about leaving her baby with the sweet woman as she makes her way up the stairs to her master bedroom.

She needs this. She deserves the break.

Quinn decides that she will enjoy a warm shower and take her time. She doesn't know when she'll get a break like this again. She knows Cole is in good hands. Mrs. Westover is like an angel sent from heaven. Rose clearly adores children. She's made a career of it and she seemed to know a lot about them. Quinn can finally relax and enjoy a bit of "me time".

12

QUINN

Mrs. Westover left an hour after Quinn came down from her heavenly, spa-like shower. She had cranked the water to the hottest setting, hoping the pricks of the jets on her back would get her out of the funk she seemed to be in lately. There was a sheen of steam on the mirror as she stepped onto the bathroom rug.

She felt luxurious as she blow-dried her long black hair and tied it neatly in a top bun, out of reach of Cole's velcro-like grip. The flowery smells of her shampoo and hair products had taken her back to a time when all she had to worry about was William and herself. She misses the simplicity of that time.

Quinn feels so good after her shower, she resolves to take better care of herself from now on. She sighs and leans over the sink to apply a thin coat of mascara.

Maybe she should make an appointment with a doctor in town. Her hormones have been all over the place since she's given birth, but lately they have been feeling a little extreme.

———

She's so grateful to Mrs. Westover for coming over and helping her out today. Quinn hopes to get to know her better over time. It's nice to know a few friendly people in town, people that she feels comfortable reaching out to.

The weather changes rapidly in this area. This morning had been frigid and windy, but now the sun was heating the living room making it warm and toasty. Quinn chooses a spot on the floor where the hardwood seems the most sun-damaged. She sits down with Cole as he looks on and feels the various soft toys and books she's taken out of a box and laid out for him. Of all the items, he seems to be most interested in his socks. They spent so much money on toys for him, but kids are funny that way. It often seems they'd rather play with regular, everyday things.

Sipping a hot cup of tea, Quinn enjoys the warm drink and the sunshine on her face. She and Cole play for a long while and the afternoon seems to go by a lot quicker than the morning. Relieved, she notices that it's finally time to start chopping vegetables for her stir-fry.

She settles Cole in the bouncy chair on the table next to her and starts peeling and chopping carrots, followed by onions, celery, zucchini, mushrooms, and garlic. She prepares a pot of boiling water for the rice noodles and makes a sauce with soy sauce, brown sugar, grated ginger root, garlic powder, salt, pepper, and vegetable oil.

By the time William comes home and walks in the front door through to the kitchen, the house smells of sweet spice and warmth. His cheeks are flushed, his skin sensitive to the cold. He places his hat and mittens on the heating vent by the bay window for them to dry and puts his hands around Quinn's waist as she works at the stove.

"Your hands are freezing!" she squeals and jumps a foot away from him, laughing jokingly.

William's tired eyes smile at her and he slowly paces to the sink to wash his hands in warm water before he returns to place them on her cheeks as he pulls her in for a kiss.

"How was today?" he asks, a worried look on his face as he assesses hers.

"Not too bad, actually." She beams up at him as he holds her close.

"Did you shower today?" He seems surprised, referring to her fresh smell, filling Quinn with a deep shame.

She shrugs away from him slightly. He must think she's incredibly disgusting for having waited so long to take a shower. She'll have to try harder to take better care of herself from now on. She's been feeling so much better since she had that shower. As though cleaning her exterior had also renewed her insides.

She tells him about her impromptu visit with their neighbour and how lovely she was with Cole.

"That's awesome, babe!" he says, grabbing a carrot stick off the chopping board and crunching on it. "You know, Jake and Lena asked if we'd want to go over to their place for dinner one night this week. I wasn't sure how that would work, because of Cole's sleeping routine, but maybe we could ask Mrs. Westover to watch him for a few hours. What do you think?" His eyes are hopeful. Quinn recognizes that William would very much like a baby-free night, probably as much as she would.

Pondering the implications, the desire for a night with her husband strongly overtakes the slight separation anxiety she feels.

"I guess I could ask her," she finally offers. "She was really great with him and seemed truly happy to help."

William, happy with her answer, scoops her up in his arms and twirls her right there in the middle of the kitchen.

Catching herself smiling, she adds, "But it couldn't be for too long, in case he gets hungry. I'm not sure he'd take a bottle just yet." Quinn wonders if they'll be able to pull it off.

A night away. She lets herself imagine it. This date would be their first since Cole was born.

The idea of a date with her husband, even a double date, makes her almost giddy. She misses him and the life they had before becoming parents. Having a kid is great, but they are still adjusting to the new dynamics of having a child, not to mention, they haven't had time to be a couple in a while, their parenting responsibilities taking over everything else.

Quinn also realizes she's looking forward to seeing Lena again. The woman has already carved a spot inside her heart, her warmth and kindness during that first meeting had made Quinn feel welcomed and accepted, no matter how she'd been dressed.

After cleaning up dinner, Quinn puts Cole to bed feeling hopeful for the first time in a long time. Things seem to be looking up. She's going to be able to get through this difficult, draining phase.

One day at a time.

She just needs a little help once in a while. Her shoulders relax. It's a relief to be well-surrounded with nice people like Lena, Jake, and Rose. As they say, it takes a village to raise a child.

13

QUINN

A few days later, Quinn gathers her courage and walks over to the house next door. She wants to ask Mrs. Westover if she'd be willing to babysit Cole for an hour or two during their double date the following night.

Quinn comes prepared with the bribe of warm, freshly baked ginger snap cookies and a box of English breakfast black tea. Seeing how she doesn't know Mrs. Westover very well yet, she's hoping this gesture will be well received and help her neighbour with her decision to babysit.

She struggles to bundle Cole into his puffy red snowsuit that zips from his feet up to his tiny chin. She places a blue hat and warm mittens on him before picking him up from the entry-way floor.

Holding him close to her chest, she exits the house and treads through the wet, melting snow down her driveway. What a difference a few days can make. The snowfall from the other day vanished overnight, it seems. She's hoping that was the last bit of snow they'll be seeing up north this year.

The slush under her boots makes tiny mud splatters on her jeans, but she is determined to make her journey towards Mrs. Westover's despite inevitably getting her pants dirty. She hasn't left the house since they did groceries after moving in earlier this week. She checks the mailbox at the end of the lane and walks down the road to Rose's door to ask her the favour.

The porch's steps are weathered and creak beneath her feet. The paint is peeling on the wood siding revealing decades of various colours beneath. There is a small crack in the front door window panel which appears to have been there for a long while. Quinn knocks, keeping her feet moving to appease Cole, who hates it when she's immobile.

From the old porch, Quinn spies long flowing white-lace curtains in the windows on the main floor. *I bet the second floor has matching ones*, Quinn thinks.

She tilts her head slightly away from the porch's roof to chance a glance only to spot a lone window at the front of the A-frame style house. She imagines the rooms having small closets and slanted ceilings. The sound of the door latch turning brings her attention back to the present. Her arms are growing tired from holding Cole and her gifts.

"Quinn! What a lovely surprise! Hello, young man," she coos at Cole. Rose smiles at them graciously. "Come in, my dears! Let me put on the kettle for some tea." She motions them inside.

Quinn unwraps her winter clothes and unbundles an overdressed Cole, littering Mrs. Westover's tiny front hall.

The women chat over hot tea and munch happily on a few of Quinn's cookies. They stay for over an hour as Cole's curious gaze takes in the house's interesting and abstract wallpaper, distracting him long enough for Quinn to enjoy her cup of tea.

The busy vintage style floral walls make Quinn queasy, but the design seems to please Cole. Quinn does admit that the patterns and colours add some warmth to the home.

She briefly considers adding wallpaper to their rental but dismisses the idea almost immediately. A fresh coat of paint will do wonders for those bare, white walls. It will help bring life back into them. There's no need for Quinn to plaster wallpaper on the walls, especially not in a place she's renting. She will be limiting her décor style to inexpensive and temporary fixes only.

Mrs. Westover shows Quinn the quilt she is working on for the Sacré-Coeur Catholic Church she belongs to here in town. She tells Quinn how the congregation is currently meeting in a nearby high school cafeteria as the church's building has been crumbling down for years and was recently deemed unsafe. Seemingly, there were issues with the roof supports and water damage in the basement.

"Unfortunately," Rose explains, "the repairs were quite extensive—about $7 million dollars-worth. Therefore the demolition will be happening quickly." Quinn notices how much Rose seems bothered by this fact and she feels sorry for her.

"My parents got married in that church. So long ago now, but I have many good memories of that place. It's been there for over a hundred years—I hate to see it go," she says with a pained expression.

Rose stands to show Quinn a wedding photo of her parents, the church in the background. Taking the silver frame that is passed to her, the young mother sees a beautiful building with two tall bell towers and gorgeous white stone walls. Quinn can only imagine the empty void the church will leave behind in the town once it's gone.

"There are plans to rebuild a smaller church in its place, but with a modern look, it won't have the same historical representation in the town," Mrs. Westover continues, visibly upset about the loss of history that will go with the tearing down of the building she's known her entire life.

———

After a while, Quinn comes clean about the true reason for her visit, and Mrs. Westover happily agrees to watch Cole the following evening for a few hours. Quinn sighs with relief and excitement for the night to come.

Finally, she will be able to reconnect with William and talk with other adults without having to worry about bouncing a baby on her hip! She smiles fondly at her son, casually and comfortably lying in Mrs. Westover's arms.

"He's such a precious child," Rose speaks gently as she carefully strokes Cole's chubby cheek. It strikes Quinn how much love this stranger seems to have for her son. Then again, a new baby is hard to resist.

Once everything is cleaned up, Quinn gets Cole and herself bundled-up once more to make their way back to their house. The sun has been shining all morning, and she finds that she's too warm with her hat on. She'll need to dig out their spring jackets and rain boots when she gets home.

She feels lighter somehow, knowing she'll get a reprieve from the responsibilities of motherhood, even if just for a few hours. Smiling, already feeling happier, she bounces Cole, able to be more nurturing, seeing a break in sight.

On her way up the driveway, she notices tracks leading to the house. She looks ahead and sees that the footprints seem to go around the house, disappearing towards the backyard.

She frowns, gripping Cole a little bit tighter.

She searches for her cellphone, feeling her heart sink, remembering that she hadn't brought it with her when she'd left earlier. After all, she had only planned on checking the mail and popping over next door for a few minutes. She hadn't thought about it when Rose invited them in for tea. William might have tried to reach her.

Unsure of what to do, Quinn rebalances Cole in her arms and carries on towards the house. Perhaps Jake had come by to check on something to do with the house while she was at the neighbour's. She'll be able to find out once she's made it back inside.

Thankfully, she had thought to lock the house behind her before heading next door—an old habit from living in the suburbs of Kingston. She searches her coat pocket for her keys, jingling them in her hands as she tries to unlock the front door. As she pushes the door open, she catches sight of a man walking on the side of the house. She startles, keys stuck in the air, her hand frozen in place. He's coming up to her from the backyard. He seems alarmed at the sight of her, surprised to see her as much as she is to see him. The man isn't Jake. She's never seen him before.

Halfway through the entrance, Quinn does her best to look confident and authoritative, all the while never letting go of Cole, fussing and overheating in his thick winter suit.

"Can I help you?" she asks briskly, making her wariness of his presence known, yet trying her best to appear poised.

"Yes, hello, Miss...?" he tries, but Quinn stays silent, giving nothing away. "I'm here for your yearly furnace inspection. My name is Rick," he says with a cocky smile as he extends a dirty, soiled hand towards her.

Quinn only stares at it, not wanting to touch it or to let go of Cole. She remembers a scam that had been going around back home in Kingston where men pretended to be utility workers, when in fact they were thieves scouting out their next gig.

"Sorry, but no thank you," Quinn manages finally. She's slowly losing her grip on Cole as he wiggles angrily, getting hungry.

Without another word, Quinn gets inside and quickly shuts and locks the door behind her. Her hands are shaking as she watches Rick's back retreating down the driveway. Her gut tells her that she was right not to let him in. Why would the furnace guy be in the backyard? She needs to call William right away and sort this out. Maybe he had arranged for Rick to come and check out the furnace, but surely he would have told her?

Before she can find her phone, her son squirms in her arms. First, she must feed Cole. She sighs heavily, suddenly exhausted.

She tries to calm her racing heart down while feeding Cole. Once he finally gets into a steady rhythm, Quinn suddenly realizes that she's starving and forgets all about the strange encounter with Rick, the furnace guy. She balances Cole in one arm as she steadies herself to stand and makes her way to the fridge. Grabbing eggs, butter, and a few slices of bread, she doesn't waste a moment, efficiently making her meal.

The aromas blending together make her stomach rumble. She loves the comforting smells of warm butter on toast and salty eggs. Regrettably, she fights the intense cravings and cooks a smaller portion. She could have eaten three times the amount, but she needs to get started on losing this baby weight.

Flipping on her laptop, she decides to check if there's a good yoga tutorial to try at home. She's pleased to find there are many to pick from and chooses a beginner level 'mom and baby' class. She's surprised by how much her body remembers from her classes all those years ago. Maybe she won't embarrass herself too much with Lena when she finally goes to one of her classes. At least, that's what she hopes.

14

QUINN

The next evening, Quinn and William welcome Mrs. Westover just before five o'clock. Rose has come prepared with a bag full of picture board books that she picked up from the local public library. She seems very excited to be babysitting Cole tonight, putting the couple at ease right away.

Quinn feels a twinge of anguish as she kisses Cole's fuzzy head goodbye. Her son looks on, oblivious that his parents are leaving. He seems content to be held by Mrs. Westover.

"You doing ok?" William asks Quinn as they drive off into the night, the evening before them. Lena and Jake also live in Sturgeon Falls, therefore they don't have very far to drive.

"Yeah, I think so," she wavers, doubt creeping in.

This is the first time she's ever been away from her son. It feels freeing, but also terrifying. Will Cole notice she's gone? What will Mrs. Westover do if he starts fussing? Did Quinn remember to tell Rose what Cole's favourite bedtime song is? Had she pumped enough milk? Did she leave out enough clean onesies? Quinn's mind starts to fret, but she reminds herself that Mrs. Westover is a professional and that she won't be far away if they need to rush home.

Plus, just in case, Quinn has given Rose a list of things to keep in mind—Cole's diaper change routine, his favourite toys, and most importantly, both of their cellphone numbers. She knows the woman has more than enough experience watching children and so she does her best to calm her worries. *Everything will be alright*, she wills. She trusts Rose.

Still, there is a tiny, minuscule part of her that hesitates.

The deep desire for a night away is stronger than any small doubt brewing and so, she forces herself to look ahead and reach over to hold her husband's hand as they make their way to the Adkins' house for dinner. Leaving the forest behind them, she starts breathing easier the closer they get to town.

It's only for a few hours, she reasons. They will be home again soon so that Quinn can feed Cole.

———

The Adkins' home is across town, which isn't far at all. They pass the hospital, a pizza place, and some car repair shops on the way. This town seems to have many snowmobile shops and a few motels off the main drag. Quinn contents herself by looking out the window, the sky clear of clouds, bright stars shining in the darkness. Before she knows it, they've arrived.

The home is a surprisingly modest, high-ranch with a one-car garage on a one-acre lot. It has large, mature birch and maple trees surrounding it and several big, round canvas-covered bushes in the front yard. The exterior is a light coloured siding, possibly a pale blue. Someone has left the outdoor lights on for them.

They park the Golf next to another vehicle, a new-looking black Lexus. *So they do allow for some luxuries*, she thinks to herself.

She shivers as she steps out of the car. The night air sends a chill right through her and she can see pale, white clouds escape from her mouth as she breathes. They walk up the uneven, concrete block path leading to the front door and ring the bell. They are immediately greeted by the loud barking of two tiny, ankle-biting mutts and Quinn shrinks, making herself as small as possible as fear overtakes her.

She hates dogs—is terrified of them.

William senses her stiffen and instinctively shifts into protector-mode. He holds an arm over in front of her, a small barricade between her and the dogs, not doing much to save her ankles. Still, she's grateful for his presence and the sense of security he exudes.

The front door opens wide and through the closed screened door, Quinn spots Lena and Jake's smiles quickly fade as they take in the scene and quickly clue in. Without delay, they shoo the dogs away to the basement and shut a gate to keep them down there for the time being. Quinn and William enter the warm home and remove their coats, placing them carefully on nearby hooks.

Following their hosts, the Millers relax as they walk the few steps up to the main floor towards the kitchen. Lena is busily stirring something on the stove and with the help of the oven light they spot an enormous chicken roasting perfectly.

The large eat-in kitchen has a rectangular table and six honey oak chairs. The table is dressed for Christmas dinner, even though Christmas was months ago. Quinn notes the red table linen, tall candlesticks, crystal wine glasses, green napkins folded into fans, laid over some expensive-looking ceramic plates and a glass bowl with fresh salad in the center of the table. There is also a wicker basket, lined with a napkin, holding delicious looking buns next to a delicate looking glass dish containing butter. The salt and pepper shakers are the only items that look out of place as they appear to be hand-painted, resembling bad sponge and stencil work—like a child's piece of art.

Quinn's mouth is watering as Jake carefully removes the chicken from the oven and the smells of rosemary and thyme fill the space. The crispy skin is flawless, giving the chicken a golden, picture-perfect look.

Jake expertly carves the bird as he talks to them. Lena is busy mashing potatoes and mixing gravy while Quinn and William stand at the peninsula looking on at the meal with anticipation, their stomachs rumbling.

As the wine is poured, the conversation flows easily. The couples have no trouble finding things to talk about tonight, the tension of the first meeting long dissipated.

Quinn surprises herself with her unexpected surge of energy. She suddenly feels elated and fun. It isn't because of the wine, because she is still breastfeeding and isn't drinking. She is just enjoying the conversation, this place, and these new friends. It feels so good to be sitting next to William, to hear his deep laugh as he recounts the old familiar stories of their first years together.

Quinn feels an admiration for her husband that she hasn't felt in a long while. Her heart seems light as she gushes with love for this man, the love of her life, the father of her child. She reaches for his hand and interlaces her fingers with his as William shares stories.

The dogs stay in the basement for the entire duration of their visit and Quinn is grateful for it. She doesn't have the emotional capacity or interest in fighting them off. When Quinn glances at the clock above the stove, she realizes they need to be on their way and they quickly begin clearing the table.

The night has been short, yet successful. She couldn't have asked for a better first night away. She can tell William is pleased. The look he is giving her makes her beam with happiness. She feels exhilarated and suddenly craves to be close to him, the old urges resurfacing with a vengeance.

A short drive later, they are back home. They spot Mrs. Westover sitting quietly in the living room, reading a book with Cole sleeping soundly in the crook of her arm.

"Hi Rose, how did it go?" Quinn asks.

"Oh, Cole is such a wonderful boy!" she beams. "We had a lovely time." She gently stands up, careful not to disturb his sleep as she hands him over to Quinn. "I hope you both had a great evening?" she inquires, curious.

They speak for a few moments and thank Rose profusely as she gets her coat on.

"Let me walk you home," William offers gallantly. Rose seems touched by his offer but assures them she can manage the short walk on her own.

"You both enjoy your night now," she waves as the door closes behind her.

While walking Cole upstairs, Quinn is full of love for her son and husband. After putting Cole to bed, she quietly pads to her bedroom, eager to find William. She's light-headed with desire for his body, ready to give in to his touch and allow him to whisk her away with his kisses.

15

The next few weeks come and go. Time keeps moving forward, yet Quinn is struggling—stuck in the same stagnant place. Despite finding a few local playgroups and new moms to connect with, she still feels so isolated and lonely. She's finding it hard adjusting to motherhood, parenting, and this new town.

Their house is so far from everyone else's that Quinn finds it difficult to maintain relationships with the others. The moms in town that she liked and connected with are either nearing the end of their maternity leave and going back to work soon, or stay-at-home moms who love every single minute of it—diaper changes, multiple feedings and all. Being near them made Quinn feel even worse.

She'd felt guilty when she'd spoken up about her struggles and feared being judged and shunned at the groups. Even if she didn't feel good being around them, being excluded would be worse. Everyone else seemed to be enjoying themselves which made her wonder why her experience couldn't be a little more like that.

———

She's been having a hard time snuggling with Cole lately. She's been more resentful towards him and his ever-changing mood swings. One moment he is smiling sweetly at her, and the next minute he's wailing and screaming. She just can't take it anymore and hates the panic that never settles within her, eating her alive, stealing her joy.

She feels like she is losing her mind.

The mere high pitch of his cries are sure to send her over the edge, grabbing for those pills, breaking her rule on drinking alcohol. Every spare moment she has is spent trying to rest her eyes or calm her heart rate.

She just can't find a regular breath—her mind is always on high alert, the cortisol spiked. The adrenaline pumps through her as though she is fighting for her life. She knows it isn't normal, but she has no idea how to fix it, or who to talk to about it.

Any time she's opened up about her mental health concerns, people have just nodded, not knowing what to say or how to help. They'd rather pretend all is fine, put blinders on, and carry on. Little did they know how much strength it had taken for her to speak up about it. A last resort at saving herself before giving up, losing all hope, and turning off the light for good.

There were friends she didn't speak to anymore, people she'd known her whole life, her own parents. They'd all preferred to turn a blind eye, to ignore her pleas for help while slowly, not subtly, putting more distance between them.

Well, this time, without having planned on it, Quinn had been the one to put distance between them and her. She missed the familiar faces, but she'd naively imagined that moving away would help her—a fresh start. She'd been terrified of leaving her comfort zone, leaving everything she knew behind. Yet, she had willed herself to try and remain optimistic, which was proving to be a bigger challenge than she'd ever expected.

A few evenings ago, Quinn had gone to one of Lena's yoga classes on her own, but even that hadn't helped to calm her down. She'd found the class quite boring and too granola for her, with its mindfulness and balance talk. She'd tried hard to locate the energy within herself, but she feared most of her light had been extinguished by heavy darkness.

The slow pace of the movements meant to bring calmness and peace had only made her mind race even more. All she'd been able to do was to think about all the stuff she hadn't done because she'd been sitting on a mat in an odd-smelling cramped space.

"Salute the sun," Lena instructed calmly as she addressed the class. "This is your practice. Try to be here in the moment as much as you can. When you feel your mind going elsewhere, bring it back to centre." She smiled and brought her hands in a prayer before her chest. "Remember, if you get overwhelmed or you have trouble with a pose, you can always focus on your breath." She nodded her head at a few members, her eyes landing on Quinn's for a beat before she'd continued.

The studio had been in a tiny loft located above the town's only Chinese restaurant. The essential oils of lavender, eucalyptus, and peppermint mixed with the greasy smell of won ton soup and eggrolls coming up through the vents had done nothing but make her stomach turn. She decided she'd stick to seeing Lena at one of the coffee shops in town, or at each other's house from then on.

———

With spring well underway, Quinn is looking forward to getting the stroller out of the garage to take Cole out for a walk. She's dying for some fresh air and hopes the warm rays of the sun will brighten her miserable outlook and give her the burst of energy she so desperately needs. Not to mention, she's hoping the sunshine can illuminate her dull skin and make her appear healthier, at least on the outside.

As she pushes the jogging stroller down the gravel road, her rain boots make sloshing sounds as she steps over the last mounds of darkened grey snow, stubbornly holding on despite the rising temperatures.

The weather is refreshing, energizing, and she knows there will be only a few months of this before the pesky mosquitos start coming out, forcing them inside the house to avoid looking like they have chicken pox.

This will be Cole's first summer. Quinn has dreams of taking him for long walks around town on the weekends with William, indulging in hand-churned ice cream, swimming at the local public pool, and maybe even discovering a nearby park for a family picnic.

The long road stretches out before her as she pushes on. Cole seems content for the moment and Quinn is glad for it. He's been teething lately, and she's finding it hard to manage. Everything she'd learned about his feeding, sleeping, and diaper change schedule is different now.

He's fussier, cries more, and even has less of an appetite. Quinn feels bad for him and the pain his growing teeth seem to cause him, not to mention the diaper rashes he is now suffering from. Even his sleep is being disturbed and he seems to be having some nightmares, waking up more often and in a panic.

Sometimes, it takes hours for Cole to settle, only for him to wake up screaming a few hours later. Quinn's exasperated. She's tried everything. Even breastfeeding doesn't soothe him. Giving him doses of children's Tylenol seems to be the only thing able to offer him some comfort lately.

Quinn has unconsciously slipped into her old habit of not taking care of her appearance. She's been finding it harder and harder to get out of bed lately and hasn't eaten well for weeks, her appetite gone. She's lost about ten pounds, but not by exercising. She hasn't showered in a week and she's back to wearing the same clothes for days, her hair tied in a messy top knot.

Her current medication doesn't seem to be cutting it. She finds it hard to smile at Cole and feels her son's searching gaze on her. His tiny hand reaches out, but she looks away, unable to give him the attention he craves from her. Sensing this, Cole begins to cry, a last-ditch effort to get Quinn to look at him.

She remembers how emotional she'd been when she'd first seen those tiny little fingers when Cole was born. She'd counted and kissed each one to make sure they were all there. Cole's little pinky had a small dot of a freckle that she'd found adorable, and she had taken to planting a kiss on it each time he lifted his small hand up to her lips. But she just can't bring herself to do that now.

She starts to feel hot under her leather jacket and long-sleeved sweater as the guilt rises in her. She's barely holding it together.

"Stop it," she says to Cole through gritted teeth. "Please, just stop it!" she begs him in a whimper. She's doing the best she can right now. All she wants is a few minutes of peace. A few moments where she doesn't need to do anything for anyone else.

Quinn looks a little way up the road and spots a lady she's seen walking out here before, a neighbour, she assumes from over the train tracks.

"*Bonjour!*" The woman waves enthusiastically as she slows down her pace and eagerly crosses the road, determined to meet Quinn and Cole.

"Hi!" replies Quinn, forcing herself to smile.

"And who is this little guy?" she coos at Cole with a French accent. "How old is he?" she smiles.

Swallowing down her disappointment that the woman only wants to pay attention to Cole, Quinn introduces her son. She should be used to it by now, having been a mother for months already. She's surprised to realize it still stings when people barely give her the time of day.

"This is Cole. He's three months old." She tries her best to look the way she imagines a new mom should look—blissfully happy.

"He is just adorable!" the woman squeals. "I'm Sylvie, by the way. I live up the road. Did you guys just move in recently? I've seen you a couple of times driving by with your husband, but never outside." She observes Quinn's face with much attention, her eyes big as she takes in every square inch of her, like she's trying to file it away in her memory.

"Yes, we moved in last month. My husband is going to the Helicopter Canada School in North Bay to learn how to be a pilot, so we'll be staying here for a while," she explains, quickly scolding herself for giving too much information to someone she's just met.

"Oh, that's so great! A future helicopter pilot!" Sylvie claps enthusiastically. "Well, welcome to the neighbourhood! It's a nice place to raise kids. So much outdoor space and there's a lot of things to do!" Quinn does her best not to jump in and ask her exactly what she means since she's been running out of avenues to try.

"Which house did you move into?" the woman inquires, looking behind Quinn trying to guess.

"The rental at the end of the road, next to Mrs. Westover," Quinn explains and notices a shadow cross Sylvie's face before it quickly disappears.

The woman smiles, but her right eyelid is twitching slightly. Quinn is about to ask what Sylvie's look of unease was about and if there's something wrong with her house, but the woman starts talking again. Did she imagine it?

Sylvie uses her hands a lot as she speaks heartily about the town. She grew up here and went to the French Catholic high school in town, Franco-Cité, but of course Quinn has never heard of it having just moved in.

"Is there anything we should check out while we're living here?" Quinn eagerly ventures, and to her surprise, Sylvie tells her about a few nearby park trails, a local blueberry picking spot, and the locally famous chip trucks downtown.

"They have the best poutine!" she mentions. "Also, make sure you take this little guy to the Country Music Fiddle Fest in the summer! Sturgeon Falls is renowned for it! People come from all over the world to compete. It's quite something." She beams with pride. "My son, Martin, is a fiddle player. Has been since he was ten. Of course, he's all grown up now, but he still plays a few pieces at the festival."

"That's a fantastic idea! Cole loves music. I'm sure he'll enjoy seeing that!" Quinn replies, but the summer seems quite far away.

"Well, I better get on! It was so nice to meet you, Quinn! You too, Cole! I'm sure I'll be seeing more of you both around! *Au revoir!*" Sylvie waves again before crossing the street to resume her power-walk, the sun's rays bouncing off her shiny auburn hair. If you could bottle sunshine and energy, it would be named after this woman.

Quinn can't help but look on, mesmerized. The noticeable difference between herself and Sylvie are undeniable. Snapping out of it, she picks up her pace. Once she reaches the train tracks, she turns the stroller around and starts making her way back to the house.

There isn't much to look at during their walks, but Quinn had desperately needed to get out of the house. She's regretting it now. Her mind is fuzzy with lack of sleep. The heat of her jacket and the glare of the sun in her eyes is making her eyes heavy and souring her mood. Despite having her hair pulled up, stray hairs are sticking on the back of her perspiring neck.

Cole, ever so intuitive, seems to pick up on every single one of Quinn's emotions. Lately, when Quinn has a bad day, Cole seems to make every effort to be even more challenging that day. He cries louder and just plain refuses to nap. She knows this, but she doesn't have the willpower to hide her face from his gaze. Her face is like stone, expressionless as she goes through the motions.

When they get home, she rolls the stroller into the shade of the garage. Quinn mechanically lifts Cole from the stroller to realize he's soaked through his pants. She feels like crying, her feelings a mix of irritation and guilt.

"Oh no, Cole! I'm so sorry. You must have been too hot in your seat." Tears brimming, she feels like a terrible mother.

Once inside, she quickly removes her coat and shirt and walks to the laundry room in her bra to grab a clean shirt from her overflowing and unfolded clean pile on top of the dryer. Cole is fussing and understandably uncomfortable in his wet pants, but Quinn desperately needs to pee, the pressure in her bladder painfully uncomfortable.

She brings him to the powder room and lays him on the floor in front of her as she goes to the bathroom, but Cole is having none of it. She washes her hands and quickly strips him of his wet clothes to reveal that his wetness was not urine, but in fact, diarrhea.

"Oh gross!" she whines. "That's so disgusting!"

With her hands up, she hesitates in the small room, unsure of what to do. If she'd had a white flag, this is when she would've used it. She picks Cole up by the armpits, holding him at arm's length, and rushes upstairs to run him a bath.

He must have soiled himself a long while ago because his earlier diaper rash has turned bright red. She mindlessly washes him with only water to avoid irritating the tender skin, and pulls him out of the tub.

As she pats him dry, she decides to give him another dose of Tylenol. She's having a hard time remembering when she gave him one last but gives him more anyway. She's not very good at following guidelines on medications, but she uses the tiny syringe to suck up some of the pink liquid, and squirts it into Cole's mouth. He loves the taste, so he gulps it easily. Quinn's shoulders relax as she thinks of the reprieve the medicine will bring.

"There you go." Patting his back, she makes a clockwise motion to help pass his gas. "Poor little guy," she fusses as she looks at the soft spot on his skull. She's always terrified of accidentally pushing it in with her chin whenever she casually rests her head on his. To avoid this, she chooses to place her cheek on his. The moment doesn't last as Cole begins to fuss once more.

"Argh. What? What do you want?" she says impatiently just as Cole, diaper-less, pees all over her shirt. The warm liquid seeps onto her pants and she grumbles loudly, quickly losing control. "What's the point of even wearing clothes?" She feels desperate, on the verge of a breakdown.

She shuts her eyes tightly, forcing the tears to stay inside. After a few breaths, she gathers her strength and stands to clean up the mess and gets them both new clothes.

It feels like every day is the same pointless routine. Feed, change, sleep, feed, change, and sleep. She doesn't know if she should laugh or cry at the absurdity of what her life has become. She's unsure of why she's even doing this in the first place. Surely she'd be happier somewhere else, far away from here.

16

QUINN

William got home late tonight, and Quinn, too exhausted to deal with dinner had made simple eggs and toast to eat before heading up to bed early, leaving Cole in William's care. For hours, she tosses and turns, getting herself tangled in the sheets.

Her sleep is restless.

In the middle of the night, she wakes with a start. Her heart beat heavy, she checks the alarm clock on William's nightstand. One in the morning. Cole hasn't woken up to feed. It's been too long.

Something is wrong.

She sits up quickly and presses hard on the baby monitor button. Zooming in with the camera, she tries to see her son on the tiny screen. She spots him, but his body looks wrong. The position is off.

Quinn harshly rips the duvet and sheets off of herself, glancing at her husband who remains obliviously asleep. She quickly runs down the hall, stubbing her toe on the doorframe, cursing to herself that she hasn't yet gotten around to buying a nightlight for the hallway.

She rushes into Cole's room and stands over him, her heart racing. She places a hand over his chest—his heart is beating, he's breathing. *Thank God*, she thinks, feeling hot tears falling down her cheeks and exhales.

Yet, something still doesn't feel right. She can't help but feel like there's something she's forgotten. Something important. Cole stirs at her touch, his body unnaturally warm. He starts sputtering, lying on his back. Quinn watches on in alarm as her son vomits. With nowhere for it to go, Cole starts gagging.

She acts quickly and lifts him from his crib, urgently patting his back. As she does, she notices that his diaper has again soaked through his onesie pyjamas. She doesn't even need to get close up to smell to confirm it's not pee.

Holding Cole tightly to her chest, she turns on the bedroom light and steps back at the sight of the bed. Unsurprisingly, there's a diaper explosion she will need to clean up later.

She lays Cole down on a blanket on the floor and begins to remove his onesie but stops short when she notices his swollen belly.

"What?" she yelps. "Oh no, oh no! What's going on?" She worriedly looks over Cole, trying to assess if there's anything else.

His skin is free of any redness, but her son seems asleep even though the lights are on and he's lying half-naked on the floor. This would normally make him cold and extremely fussy. His breathing is ragged also, as though he needs to work hard for every breath.

As Quinn sits on her heels on the floor next to Cole, she wills herself to focus. Taking in the scene, the soiled crib sheet, the swollen belly, the lethargic nature of her son, she finally realizes her mistake. She had given him too much Infant Tylenol! Her son was overdosing.

"Oh God! Oh my God!" She leaps up and takes Cole delicately in her arms. She wraps him in a blanket and runs to the master bedroom to wake William and grab her phone.

"William, wake up!" she screams as she shoves him awake. "We need to go to the hospital! Cole is overdosing!" She's hysterical, tears and snot running down her face. "Quick, call an ambulance!"

It takes a few times to wake him up completely, but William takes in the words and the scene before him and adrenaline courses through his body. Within seconds, he's up and throwing clothes on as they rush out the door, diaper bag in tow.

"It'll be faster to just drive there. Come on, let's go!" he states in quick breaths. How easily she can let him take charge. She doesn't argue with him as she sits in the back of the car, clutching Cole to her chest, not bothering to strap him into his car seat.

They make it to the hospital in only five minutes William drops Quinn and Cole off at the emergency entrance and veers the car around to find a parking spot. Quinn holds on to Cole tightly, wrapping the blanket securely, doing her best to keep him comfortable. Her son just can't seem to keep his eyes open.

"Please, please, please!" Quinn whispers desperately to herself as she dashes through the automatic doors and into the emergency room, holding her most precious bundle close to her heart.

"Help! Please, someone, help me!" she yells, frantically looking around for someone to assist her. "My son, he's unconscious!" she wails, pleading.

Within a few seconds, two nurses arrive and expertly take Cole from her arms to whisk him into an observation room. Quinn follows, with William running in quickly behind.

Through sobs and whimpers, Quinn explains the overdose error, and the staff workers tell them to wait outside in the waiting area while they work on Cole. Quinn collapses into William's arms, which are not much more stable than her own. All the strength it took her to get to the hospital has melted away.

There's nothing more they can do now but wait.

17

QUINN

After drinking several strong, bitter coffees from a nearby vending machine, William impatiently paces back and forth in front of the waiting room doors. The couple anxiously waits for the doctor to come back to let them know how Cole is doing.

Quinn hasn't been able to relax for one second since they arrived. The guilt of her oversight is eating her alive. She's bitten her nails down to the edges, chewing until there's almost no nails left. She'd been so frustrated with Cole earlier in the day, so exhausted that she hadn't been able to take proper care of her son. This was all her fault. What was going to happen to her perfect, sweet, little boy?

Suddenly, the heavy doors of the waiting room open. Quinn and William jump to their feet, alert but also dreading any bad news. A doctor in his late forties approaches them, his white coat flowing loosely behind him like a cape. He nods as he addresses them.

"Mr. and Mrs. Miller, I'm Dr. Pharand. I'm happy to report that Cole is doing fine." At this, the couple collapses into each other. The relief brings a welcome wave of emotion. Dr. Pharand leads them to some chairs before continuing.

"Cole did suffer from an overdose of acetaminophen," he explains gravely.

"He had some respiratory and gastrointestinal issues, which led to some diarrhea, a visibly swollen belly, and caused his breathing to be wheezy as Mrs. Miller had advised us upon arrival. Cole also had excessive sweating and seemed lethargic when you brought him in." The doctor pauses to let this sink in.

"Because you brought him in right away, he was only classified as Stage 1, meaning, within 24 hours of the overdose. We performed an emergency blood test to check the level of toxicity of 150 mg and we were then able to administer an antidote through intravenous to reverse the effects of the overdose." Dr. Pharand goes on to mention possible secondary effects to watch for in the future for any damage to Cole's liver and other organs.

Quinn grips William's hand tightly.

"I feel very confident that Cole will recover quickly. We will keep him here overnight just to check that his breathing returns to normal. We also want to give him some IV fluids through intravenous to keep him hydrated after the diarrhea he experienced. I expect Cole will be cleared to go home by tomorrow." He smiles now as the couple, numb with information overload, nod their appreciation and understanding.

Silent tears fall from Quinn's eyes. It could have been so much worse. They are so lucky.

"When can we see him?" she asks through some quiet sobs, dabbing a used Kleenex to her nose and putting it back in the pocket of her sweater.

"Right away, although, prepare yourselves," he warns. "Cole has a few intravenous needles and an IV bag attached to him. You can't pick him up, but you'll be able to touch him."

Her throat dry, Quinn stands on wobbly legs, weakened by exhaustion. The adrenaline has drained from her body. She grips William's hand as they make their way through the doors to see their son. She doesn't dare look over at William for fear of what she might see on his face. Does he blame her? It wouldn't surprise her if he did—she isn't so fond of herself at the moment either.

The sight of Cole's little body lying in the middle of the small hospital cot makes her take a sharp breath. He's attached to all kinds of beeping machines and tubes, making her feel nauseous. His tiny frame seems lost in the sea of white blankets.

The sides of the cot have been lifted to prevent an accidental fall while still allowing the tubes and wires to reach him. The cot is elevated so they can walk right up to it without bending down.

"Oh, Cole. My precious little boy." Quinn rushes over to the side of the cot, careful not to step on loose wires on the floor. Cole is either asleep or drugged. She's unsure which, but his eyes are closed, his breathing is even—he looks peaceful.

She kisses his forehead, glad to find it at a more neutral temperature, and brushes a finger on his cheek as she often does.

Softly, she begins to sing, "You are my sunshine, my only sunshine...," choking on the last bit of the lullaby.

In her head, she makes hundreds and thousands of promises to do better—to be better. From now on, she will be a more loving, kind, and attentive mother. She vows to work on her patience and to take better care of her son.

The sight of her usually vibrant and energetic boy lying limply like this is almost too much for her to take. She feels sick with guilt and can feel her stomach turn on itself.

She doesn't know if William, or even if Cole, will ever forgive her for this serious oversight. She bites her lower lip nervously. She's not even sure how she will ever forgive herself.

18

QUINN

The house is dark when they get home the next day. Cole had made great progress and Dr. Pharand had let them leave with a promise to return if anything seemed off with Cole's condition.

The evidence of her mistake still looms around them. The mess is spread out. There's a foul odor coming from the baby's room upstairs that begs for attention. The responsibilities don't stop even after an accident such as this. She still hasn't washed Cole's sheets and clothes. She can feel her shoulders tightening, a heavy weight— guilt upon guilt.

The tension between Quinn and William is so thick, she can almost taste it.

Her husband blames her. Even though he won't come out and say it, she can sense it. He's supportive and understanding, but she can see something underneath his reassuring smile and in the sideways glances he gives her. He doesn't trust her anymore.

As soon as they are through the door, William takes over. Still holding Cole in his arms, he begins picking items off the floor, making piles—laundry, unpack, and garbage. Quinn begins to feel hot all over, yet frozen in place. She feels ashamed watching her husband take charge.

This is her mess, her responsibility.

William has already missed class today because of her mistake, a slip-up that almost killed her son, and now he is picking up after her, too. Cleaning up everything she'd been too lazy to deal with. Tears sting her eyes as she watches, embarrassed. What does she even contribute to their lives? She feels useless.

She wants nothing more than to tell him to stop, to put it aside for the night. She longs to feel his arms around her, for him to hold her tight so she can sob without reserve on his chest. But there will be none of that.

There's an undercurrent of bitterness seeping through now. A trust has been broken. She has but one job—to keep their son alive—and she'd almost failed. She's never felt so low in her entire life.

She watches William from her position in the entryway, her feet stuck in place, transfixed by her husband's systematic movements around the house—like a fast-forward film. She finds herself unable to move. Her feet are heavy as though they are encased in blocks of cement. Ashamed, she trudges up the stairs to her bedroom. William has things under control. He doesn't need her. No one needs her.

She doesn't even stop by Cole's room, knowing the state of it. The work that needs to be done in there overwhelms her entirely. Her mind fogs over, her skin is flushed. Her eyes glaze over like a car windshield on a humid day allowing her to see only through tiny specs of condensation.

Images of her past come up in her mind and she feels a familiar panic sending shock waves over her skin.

She draws herself a bath, willing herself to relax, pushing the guilt and shame away. Moments of failure and terror always seem to bring back memories she's long ago filed away. She thought she could handle it on her own, but it's obvious that she's been lying to herself.

The air in the bathroom is stale and dense. The steam rises quickly as the hot water fills the tub. She's glad when her foot screams in agony at the scorching surface when she dips it into the tub. Quinn's slightly relieved to feel a physical pain that resembles her emotional torment. She pushes through the pain and first plunges her legs, then her entire body into the tub.

The water rises above her swollen breasts and up her neckline, covering her in water—the tide high, swallowing her. She imagines what it would be like to sink even deeper and never surface. She imagines all her problems drifting away like the steam into the air.

She lies in the tub for what seems like a very long time, dreaming about dying. Her forehead is sweaty, and the water is now lukewarm. When she finally stands, her body is bright red and hot to the touch and her fingers are pruned. She strains her ears trying to make out the sound of her family down below but can't hear anything.

Grabbing her nightgown off the hook in the bathroom, she opens the door to the sharp, abrasive, cold air of the bedroom. The shock of the different temperatures makes her skin tingle—she's alive. She has a second chance to make this right.

She walks down the hall and peers into Cole's semi-opened door. William is rocking their son in the glider in the soft glow of a bedside lamp. The sheets have been changed and the earlier mess has been cleaned up. How he's managed to clean up all the evidence on his own while caring for their son, she will never know.

She feels such love for him in this moment, at his ability to take over and fix everything. The shame from before is slightly appeased by gratefulness. She's not sure what she would do without him.

She hadn't known what kind of father he would turn out to be when she'd first announced she was pregnant. Looking at him being in control of this mess, rocking their son to sleep while reading him a bedtime story, she wonders how she could have ever doubted he would have been anything but extraordinary.

Standing in the doorframe, her face shadowed by the darkness of the hallway, William looks up from the book mid-way through a sentence and meets her eyes as she crosses the floor quietly over to him.

She stands beside the glider chair and lays a hand on his shoulder, which he grabs maintaining his steady rocking rhythm. Cole is fast asleep, his little mouth awkwardly folded in an 8, the earlier traumatic events evaporating with each passing minute.

When William looks into Quinn's eyes, she sees only affection there. The bitterness she had spotted earlier is long gone.

"Could have been either one of us," he says later as they lie next to each other in bed. "You can't blame yourself," he reassures her. But it doesn't change how guilty she feels.

If she hadn't been so tired, if she'd been more alert, more present, then maybe this wouldn't have happened. If she'd been a good mother and read up on teething remedies, she could have prepared teething rings in the freezer for him to chew on, or bought the right toys to help her son's aching gums.

Truth is, she'd been lazy, irresponsible, and inattentive to his needs.

When Dr. Pharand had asked Quinn how much Cole weighed, she hadn't even known the answer. She was embarrassed enough as it was, but it got even worse when the doctor had proceeded to explain the importance of knowing a child's weight when administering medication dosage.

Dr. Pharand had continued, explaining how to effectively weight a child by weighing yourself first on a scale, then taking the child into your arms and weighing again, then figuring out the difference to find out the child's weight. Quinn had simply nodded along, understanding the importance, but all the while thinking about how silly it would look.

She is reacting completely wrong to situations, laughing instead of crying and becoming unhinged when she's scared. She doesn't feel like herself these days. She's losing herself in this new role. How much longer will she need to do this before she becomes good at it? Will she ever?

19

As the days begin to get longer, William's course load increases by the day. He comes home more and more exhausted. He is surviving mainly on strong coffee and take-out lunches.

Quinn hasn't seen much of him lately. Her husband gets home late, shoves food in his mouth, and goes off to another room to study his course material. He tells her it is the hardest thing he's ever had to do. He's stressed out about not getting the required 90% passing grade. Quinn has never seen him like this. Between the two of them, they look like a pair of zombies. She's worried about him burning out.

His hair is overgrown—he's long overdue for a haircut. He's got permanent dark circles under his eyes and new frown lines developing and deepening by the day. She's never seen him so serious about anything. It's clear to her how much this means to him.

She does her best to stay out of his way, to help him in any way she can. She washes and hangs his clothes as well as lays them out each evening for him to dress with ease in the morning. She prepares lunches she knows will come back uneaten as the class usually goes out at lunch for a well-deserved break.

The course load is heavy. So far, they're about halfway through the material at fifty hours. William is set to start learning to fly the helicopter soon.

He tells her how he will get to start his hours by flying the school's Guimbal Cabri G2, a helicopter worth almost $400,000. The astounding amount shocks Quinn but only seems to excite William. He's so ecstatic, his right foot is jiggling happily up and down as he explains the specifics to her. It seems like a huge responsibility, but then again, this is what they are here for.

Her husband is completely enthralled with the subjects he's learning about. Every evening when he comes home, he talks non-stop about what he's learned on various aviation regulations, the aerodynamics of flight, meteorology, airframes, engines, and systems.

"Babe, today was so much fun! The guys and I went out for lunch at this new place down the road from class and Chris, you know Chris, right? Well, he bought for everyone! How nice is that?" he beams.

Quinn dreams of a meal she hasn't cooked, served to her hot on a pretty pottery plate in a semi-lit restaurant with soft jazz music playing in the background. She listens patiently when he talks about "the guys", his new friends. She's so happy for him but at the same time, she's aware of jealously seeping in.

When is she supposed to make new friends? She's getting more bitter and angry every day.

He speeds through his day, describing every detail passionately with a childlike enthusiasm before gulping his meal and disappearing to study some more.

Whenever William comes home happy, it always seems to be on the days she's had to deal with a thousand little issues. Her stressful days are becoming the norm and William doesn't seem to be paying attention. His fulfilling days make him completely miss the fact that his wife is coming apart at the seams. He no longer notices her greasy hair, her weight loss, or the fact that she goes to bed at six every night. To say she's depressed would be an understatement. She's far beyond depressed at this point and William doesn't seem to care or pay any attention to it.

She's been in this place before—felt the sinking feeling of the weight anchoring her in one spot. The last time she felt this heaviness on her shoulders, she'd gotten through it, fighting with everything she had. Now, however, stripped away from everyone and everything she loves, she's been unable to get herself out of it. She's been treading water for too long and she's tired. So very tired.

———

It's been one of those days—her new normal, it seems. Cole got up at the crack of dawn and didn't go back to sleep. His teeth are coming in at full force, making him miserable again.

Quinn feels sluggish and exhausted from staying up with him for hours last night, while William lay sprawled over both sides of the bed, oblivious. Her back is sore from carrying and bouncing her son and she feels dizzy. Cole's eyes look up expectantly. *Entertain me*, they seem to beg. She looks on, void of emotion. *I've got nothing left for you*, her eyes respond.

They spend most days like this lately.

With William starting flight training, he's gone longer hours, trying to fit in the last part of the course and getting his flying hours in. They haven't seen much of each other lately.

Quinn has been isolating herself more and more, finding it a challenge to leave the house. She feels immense pressure from other moms and from William—from everyone really—to be more, to do more.

With William being away for most of the day, many of the responsibilities fall on her. She feels like she's burnt out, both ends of the candle burning at rapid speed towards each other. What happens when they meet? Does the flame go out or does it get bigger?

Quinn understands now how sleep deprivation can make mothers do inexplicable things to their children. She's often considered shaking Cole to get him to stop crying but thankfully, she's learned to place him in the crib to settle down and walk to another room to calm herself down before returning to get him a few minutes later.

Nonetheless, she's in full survival mode at this point, barely keeping it together. The very thought of having to dress them both, pack diapers, prepare snacks, and a change of clothes is more than she can bear.

Remembering even simple things has become the biggest hassle. She keeps losing track of her keys and her phone, never leaving them in the same spots. It just seems easier to stay home and not have to deal with locating items, dressing and undressing a crying child, and pushing the stroller through tight aisles.

There are so many places that are difficult to maneuver. So many doors without proper automatic openers, or even a ramp. She's pushed the stroller through an entire parking lot, only to find out the sidewalk didn't have an access point for the stroller. She's been forced to pick up the front of the stroller while using her behind to push the door open to get inside a store—a baby store, nonetheless! You'd think they would be more considerate!

Too often, she suspects people are watching her every move, almost like they've placed a bet on her. *Will she make it inside the store or just give up and go home?* she imagines they muse. Never once does anyone offer to help or hold the door for her. Lately, she feels like most people view her and Cole as a nuisance, a blip in their otherwise relaxing day.

She's tired of apologizing to onlookers about her fussy child. *They can mind their own business*, she thinks bitterly. But inside, it breaks her heart.

She often wonders why her child is the one who makes all the noise. Cole always seems to announce his presence wherever they go. She would love more than anything to participate in the free baby-yoga classes, or arrive on time and join a playgroup in town. It's a stretch for her to stay for the entire duration of any event.

Maybe when he's older, she consoles herself.

She'll try again in a few months. All the failed attempts are getting to her.

The constant judgement from other mothers is adding to her guilt and fear of being a terrible mother. She finds herself second-guessing every single decision she makes. William hasn't been very present in Cole's life lately and the extra tasks have been too much—the final drop in the bucket.

She can barely decide what to wear in the morning even though it's usually the same as yesterday. She keeps forgetting to take her medication and to eat. She can feel her brain cells silently dying off one by one without anyone else noticing but her.

Cole screams from his crib, ready for another feed, her breasts responding to the call. She's not looking forward to the position she'll be forced into for the next hour. She feels like a robot, forced to repeat the same task over and over again. Her skin is hot. The day seems unusually warm for the middle of May.

She is exhausted from working constantly, never allowed a break. She feels immediately guilty because she knows William is working hard on his certification. She watches him cram so much information into his mind every single night. He's under high pressure, expected to get almost perfect scores on every test, and trying to get the required flying hours.

As understanding as she is, Quinn often wishes they could trade places. At least then she'd have a normal lunch break, have the chance to drink a full coffee, hot, and talk to other adults. She doesn't feel she's asking for much more than what most people take for granted when they get to do it every day.

When Cole regurgitates the entire contents of what he's spent the last hour drinking all over Quinn, she starts to cry. She cries so much that she doesn't think she'll be able to stop. Whoever said not to cry over spilled milk had obviously never breastfed a reflux-prone, fussy, and teething baby.

And just like that, both ends of the candle meet. The flame burns out.

PART TWO

20

ROSE

She can see the lights flashing from her spot by the living room window. The red and blue glow of the ambulance parked at the neighbours' house. She hasn't seen Quinn in such a long time, she wonders if something's happened to her, or to Cole. William came home from his course only minutes ago, so something must be wrong with Quinn. She would have called for help sooner had it been Cole.

She doesn't have the best view from here. Their house is quite far up the driveway, but even from here she can sense the energy radiating from her neighbours' place—desperation. Rose moves closer to the window. The streetlight shines into her dark home. She's left the lights off on purpose in her attempt to blend into the shadows. Her white nightgown makes her appear almost ghostly.

Fitting, she thinks.

Her house is rumoured to be haunted. Being the only original building left, the oldest on the street, has granted her house this reputation. She still gets the most trick-or-treaters at Halloween. Only the bravest ones make it all the way up the front porch to ring the bell.

Mrs. Westover knows there are other reasons her house makes the town wary, but it's nothing anyone could ever prove.

She's surprised at how easily it all came back when she first saw the Millers move in. How quickly she's fallen into her old patterns. Most of her neighbours have come and gone, moved far away from this place, the memories too fresh for them to stay.

Rose has a special talent—she can spot liars from a mile away, and Quinn Miller is a liar.

She just needs a way to prove it.

Mrs. Westover has taken a slow approach at first, acting like a harmless senior to get Quinn to let her guard down. Rose has been walking tentatively, as though she's awaiting a hip-replacement surgery. She even went so far as to make her voice frail. It makes her seem like she is about twenty years older than she really is. It isn't lying so much as acting—to see if she can pull it off. But if anyone were to ask her, she would tell them the truth. She's been called many things, but there's one thing she would never be accused of. No one can ever call her a liar. Rose Westover always tells the truth.

Her neighbours are new to the area, therefore they are a blank canvas. They don't know the history of this place. They don't know they should be afraid of her.

She's been cooped up in this old house her entire life. Taking care of liars has become her business. It isn't anything she can make a living off of, of course, but it helps the planet as far as she's concerned. Rose learned from her father how to take care of people like that—undesirables. People like Maddison Thomas.

21

ROSE
1971

Maddison looks over at her, eyes narrowed—trouble brewing.

Rose knows Maddison isn't a good friend, but she likes the attention the girl gives her.

They've been friends since their toddler years, growing up one concession away from each other. But ever since Maddison's parents moved to North Bay, their friendship has suffered, dwindling to almost nothing. It seems there is an unwritten rule that Rose never knew about, that city folk and country folk don't mix.

Maddison showed her true colours one day after school when the two girls still lived near each other. They had been playing outside Maddison's house when they'd started a game of tag. It had been fun at first, but quickly became a contest of who could outrun the other.

In an attempt to escape from Rose's grasp, Maddison had jumped over the fence, bending the latch just enough so that the door hung loose. They'd been unable to close it afterwards. When Maddison's mother had questioned them about it, Maddison had shamelessly pointed a finger towards Rose and blamed her for it.

When questioned, Rose had been tempted to rebuke the claims and clear her name from the false accusation, but at the last minute she'd changed her mind when she'd seen her friend in the background, pleading with her to take the fall.

Maddison had crossed her heart and glued her hands together in prayer. A sign they often used along with the words 'cross my heart and hope to die'.

Rose had been confused and slightly annoyed at Maddison for making her admit to something she hadn't done, but she was a loyal friend and Maddison had pleaded. This was the first and last time Rose ever lied.

Over the years, the girls had grown apart. Rose grew more interested in reading books and helping her father with farm work, while Maddison started going out more, making friends easily.

Rose wasn't sure her friend even cared about her anymore, so when she caught Maddison looking at her, Rose beamed with joy.

For once, the popular girl in school was paying attention to her. She'd enjoyed every moment of it. So much that she missed when the entire class started laughing at her because she'd had a sign taped to her back that read "Kick Me". So that had been why Maddison had paid attention to her, she'd realized solemnly. Her shoulders had slumped in defeat and her eyes had found her loose shoelaces. She'd stared down at her feet until she'd been sure her cheeks no longer burned scarlet. She hadn't wanted everyone to see her crying. She hadn't wanted Maddison to win.

She'd felt like an idiot.

She'd so badly wanted Maddison to be her friend again. She hadn't learnt from her past mistakes. She'd always been so trusting, the desire for acceptance so strong, it blinded her. The next time she trusted Maddison, the consequence had been much more serious.

———

Maddison had hidden Rose's inhaler far away into the locker room. After gym class, Rose had suffered an asthma attack, but no one could locate her inhaler. Getting the medication in time was a critical remedy to her severe condition.

Even as Rose's colouring was turning white, spots of red covering her face, as she was gasping for breath, Maddison had just watched on, unmoving, doing nothing. She told no one that she'd hidden the device in one of the stalls at the back of the change room, underneath some storage boxes, hidden deep in an old fold-up desk, collecting dust—good for nothing.

Rose had no choice but to regulate her breathing on her own, terrified, with the whole class watching. She hadn't been sure she'd be able to get her heart rate down to normal, or her breathing back on track. It had taken her a while, but she'd finally done it.

When all had calmed down, Rose immediately went to her locker to find her inhaler, only to discover that someone had gone through her bag. Her puffer was nowhere to be found. As she searched, another girl, Tina, came up behind her, her knees and gym shorts covered with lint, loose hairs, and dust bunnies, and handed her the inhaler, her hand shaking nervously.

"I think this belongs to you," Tina breathed, careful to keep her voice low. "It was in the storage cubby, in an old desk, over there." She pointed discreetly. Inching closer, Tina whispered in her ear, "Maddison hid it." Tilting her head slightly to the right, she indicated the popular girl.

"Thanks for getting it for me," Rose choked back, her throat still sore from her earlier ragged breaths.

Torn and hurt, Rose had debated with herself. Unsure if she should tell a teacher what had happened or keep it to herself. In the end, she'd decided to confront Maddison directly, to deal with it on her own. After all, they used to be best friends, right?

When Rose had gathered all her strength and eventually confronted Maddison, the girl had smiled sweetly back, feigning innocence.

"Why would I ever do such a terrible thing?" Maddison asked, acting perplexed, placing a hand over her heart as though she was hurt at being accused of doing something so horrible.

Then she extended her hand towards Rose and drew out her pinky finger.

"I promise you, I didn't hide your inhaler." She smiled, a twinkle in her eyes. "Pinky-promise," she smirked, forcing her eyes wide in a plea.

Rose stared at the manicured pinky finger, longing to touch it, for an intimacy reserved for only true friends. When her hand reached for the pinky, she felt a hard knee connect with her stomach, and she doubled over.

The sound of squeaky sneakers on the hall tiles resonated as Maddison ran away with her squad, laughing obnoxiously, leaving Rose collapsed on the ground in a pile of pathetic, useless waste. Only then did Rose finally realized that Maddison had never been a true friend and probably never would be. Only then did Rose realize that Maddison was a liar. And liars needed to be punished.

―――

Rose had come home that afternoon and found her father in the backyard. He'd been sweaty and swinging an axe with all his might as he often did in the afternoons. It was his exercise, he used to claim.

When Bruce saw his daughter's tear-streaked face, he asked her what was wrong. Rose had fought through the tears, her words in her throat. Gasping breaths along with spit and snot mixing in her mouth had made it difficult to articulate properly. The cut of her friend's betrayal was deep and raw.

After some probing, Rose had spilled everything to Bruce. She'd watched his face contort first in pain for her humiliation and then in anger that someone would dare treat his daughter this way. It didn't take long before her father told her she needed to teach Maddison a lesson—that she couldn't get away with it.

"Liars are the worst kind of people," he'd told her. "The world would be better without them." He'd spit on the ground to punctuate his declaration.

It was this moment Rose had in mind when, years later, as chance would have it, she had found Maddison Thomas biking along a deserted highway near North Bay.

22

ROSE
JULY 1999

Driving back from an early medical appointment, Rose spots the bright blue tank top bobbing up and down, hovering lightly over the seat of the fancy bike.

The two cyclists are so focused on the road, lost in their own thoughts, that they don't even hear her car approaching quickly. Birds squawk up above, hovering over them, the only available prey on this empty stretch of road near North Bay. The couple pedals steadily, seemingly oblivious to the oncoming threat.

Even from a distance, Rose can make out the old familiar bounce of curly, blond hair that had once made her life a living hell. Maddison Thomas, she knows, had married a man from North Bay and has two sons. Rose has kept tabs on her over the years, waiting for the perfect moment to take revenge for the pain and humiliation her one-time friend had caused throughout her entire childhood.

Because they had grown up together, Maddison had known a lot of details about Rose's life and hadn't hesitated to use them to bully her. Only concerned with her popularity and social status, Maddison had never worried about hurting others or talking behind someone's back. She'd lied to the teachers, to her own parents, and if Rose had to guess, even to her husband.

Rose had had a pretty good idea of what she would do if she were ever to see Maddison Thomas again. She'd been hoping for just such an opportunity to make things right again.

———

She had spent the last ten years or so putting liars in their place—hunting them. It was a passion of hers, a job only she could do. She wasn't squeamish. She'd been exposed to this lifestyle from an early age.

Rose was five years old the first time she saw someone die. Accidental drowning. The boy had been eight years old, a good swimmer, they'd said. They'd claimed it had been a horrible accident, but Rose had watched her father push the boy into the water.

When she'd caught a glimpse of the boy's dead body floating in the water, she was surprised to find that she was curious rather than frightened. She'd never seen death before, not like this. She didn't know what it looked like in real life. The boy's body had perplexed her. How could humans die but look relatively the same as they did when they were alive? She found the thought very confusing, but also intriguing. She became obsessed with it. She needed to find out more.

The second time she saw someone die, she was older.

Her sister Joyce had gotten pregnant and decided to abort the pregnancy herself because no self-respecting professional would perform it after the second trimester. She'd already tried the three nearest local clinics, only to be rudely sent away.

This was a problem she'd have to fix herself.

The determination in her eyes, her emotionless face has remained with Rose to this day.

Joyce had almost died during the procedure, however she'd gotten that baby out of her and kept on with her life as though nothing had happened. Rose had been mesmerized by the swift efficiency with which her sister had achieved her task. Watching her sister be so purposeful, so business-like about the decision to dig out the baby, putting her emotions aside, had stuck with Rose. It was around then that Rose began to think about bloodlines and families.

Could people who were related to each other, who shared similar genes, be capable of performing similar acts? Was the desire to kill and torture as commonly passed down as the colour of hair or the shape of a face? Could a murderer gene be passed down through generations?

The idea that Rose could have inherited the murderer gene didn't scare her. In fact, it excited her. She rationalized it by thinking that most people were born capable of killing. Many people were already murderers even though they didn't see themselves this way.

Some just happened to be more committed to it than others.

Everyone's killed an innocent spider in passing and splattered a pestering mosquito, wiping the insect on a pant leg without regret. Many have even killed a scurrying wild animal or a dozen frogs standing idle in the middle of the road in the dark hours of the night.

What makes one murder worse than another? The intent behind the kill? The lack of remorse? The species killed? The size of the victim?

Rose had begun experimenting in secret after that.

She still remembers her first roadkill.

The headlights shining brightly on a red fox, its small frame appearing before her at the last minute on the road. His eyes wide as tennis balls looking right through her soul searching for mercy. He didn't find it—she never even slowed down. It was almost like playing chicken—who would move first?

Of course, he'd lost.

Rose didn't feel anything when her car ran over his limp body, a thud-ump-thud-ump, just like a speed bump. That was all that indicated the fox had ever been there. A bump in the road.

She knew someone else might have stopped the car and checked on the fox, made sure he was ok, or at the very least, finished it off to put it out of its misery, but she hadn't. She didn't care. He'd gotten in her way; it was his own fault he'd gotten hit and was now staining the road with his blood.

She still remembers the exhilarating feeling that had spread through her entire body immediately after. The fox had been a symbol. She was no longer someone weak who only killed bugs and plants on purpose. Rose was capable of more. Hell, she wanted more. She knew her thirst for this new passion wouldn't be satisfied with a few road kills, so she started studying.

She had generations of examples to follow. There had been many in her family who shared the same interests. Yet, some of Rose's relatives had been caught and imprisoned, but she wasn't going to get caught. She was too smart for that.

Her father, Bruce, had taught her well. He'd been able to avoid the law until the day he died. His cases were never closed. He would always say that only the guilty get caught. So as long as you didn't feel guilty about your crimes, then you'd never get caught. He had lived his entire life in peace, waving to the local police officers as though they were friends, snickering all the way home.

Bruce had also used the tactic of hiding things in plain sight. Anyone who ever suspected anything would look under beds, in the dark corners of the basement, or in the shed in the backyard. But no one ever took a second look at the tall bookshelf that camouflaged a secret room, one her dad called his playroom. Rose had lost count of how many 'friends' he'd taken there who had never left.

Bruce had nearly been caught once at a neighbourhood pool party one summer when he *accidentally* hit a boy in the head with a stainless-steel barbecue set case. Since then, he'd been more careful. He'd opted for victims of lower social status. His favourite were hitchhikers or street kids whose parents had given up on them long ago.

Bruce had been careful never to let his children see him in action. He had preferred to finish the job alone. Rose had never before actually seen any of her father's victims die, but she'd heard them.

Their house was the only one for miles in the centre of what used to be her great-grandfather's old farm. Part of the large plot of land they'd inherited with the house was surrounded by a large forest, bordered by a wet marsh. Over the years, Rose's great-grandfather had built several buildings at different ends of the property. Every building was a secret 'hobby' area. As time passed, they'd all become private cemeteries the rest of the family could use for their own extra-curricular activities.

No one else could hear a thing out there.

They lived quiet lives, for the most part. No neighbours to watch over their comings and goings. This was their safe place.

Since there were no secrets regarding their interests within the walls of their own home, evenings would be spent swapping best kill stories and sharing tricks.

Over time, they'd broadened their 'hunting' area in order to keep the authorities away from their property. They'd gone away on 'road trips' and 'vacations' where they'd picked up a few strays, as Bruce liked to call them. Basically, unlovable, unmissed, pathetic excuses for humans.

In public, they were just a normal, close-knit family who kept to themselves and was well-liked in the town.

———

Rose's instincts kick into high gear upon seeing Maddison on that bike in the middle of a secluded area. She follows close behind, and not thinking twice about it, she guns the engine and aims right for Maddison, tasting revenge on her tongue.

Upon impact, Maddison's and her husband's bodies make a loud thump, similar to the fox on the road from all those years ago. Rose can feel her heartbeat slamming hard in her chest, not from regret, but from exhilaration, her younger self thanking her for finally taking care of this vile human being. She's finally gotten her payback for all the pain Maddison had put her through.

———

When Rose comes home and parks her car in the garage, her husband, Max, notices the large indent on the bumper of her red car.

"What's this, hun? Did you hit something?" he asks her, worried, looking her over. She nods but doesn't elaborate.

Rose knows her husband has his doubts about her past.

Her father hadn't been pleased that she'd chosen to marry an out-of-towner even though Rose had argued it would be safer that way. In the end, Rose had convinced Bruce that her quiet, reserved husband wouldn't speak up even if he ever did learn the truth. And if he ever did, Rose promised she would take care of it. He was a quiet man who kept to himself and didn't ask questions. Rose had nothing to worry about.

For years, Max never questioned her when she insisted he shouldn't explore the buildings on the property, explaining they were her father's things and she didn't want to disturb them. *Too many memories*, she'd claimed. Of course, dead things can't be disturbed.

Max had never asked her what she'd done with all the stillborn babies she'd birthed at home, all five of them. Every time, she'd brushed him off explaining that they had been taken care of and that they were now at peace. She always wondered if there was a reason she wasn't able to reproduce, that maybe she was being punished.

But that evening, Max questions her about the state of the car. He insists on making a call to their insurance company to open a claim. He even offers to take her to the hospital to get her checked over.

She watches him silently as he slowly paces around the car again, inspecting every inch. She wonders what he's thinking. He's sweating and keeps glancing at her out of the corner of his eye.

He knows there's more to the story. Still, she refuses to tell him. If he would only ask her point-blank, she would be honest. Then he'd be in on it too and she could gauge how he would react. She imagines Max would be appalled at first, but then hopefully he'd come around after hearing Rose's point of view.

Rose doesn't feel guilty about what she's done. If anything, this little 'incident' has put a jump in her step. For years she'd been hoping for the chance to get back at Maddison Thomas and, as luck would have it, their paths had crossed once again.

———

That night after they'd both been in bed for some time, Rose feels her husband carefully slipping out of bed, armed with only the faint beam of a flashlight to light his path. He must have brought it up to bed with him earlier without her noticing. Rose quietly reaches over to Max's nightstand table and slides open the drawer.

She opens the safe and slowly pulls out his nine-millimetre. Armed with the loaded gun, she makes her way to the landing.

She watches Max climb down the stairs one by one on his tip toes, doing his best not to make a sound. Grabbing some discarded leather gloves on the hallway dresser, she follows him out the door. He steps into his shoes, opens the back door and heads towards the backyard, making his way through the overgrown grass in the direction of the buildings. Curiosity has finally gotten the best of him. Rose copies his movements so as to not alert him to her presence, following a few feet behind, keeping her position hidden.

Holding her breath, Rose silently prays he will change his mind—reconsider and turn around. She wills him to come back to bed and forget all about it. Instead, Rose watches her husband fiddle with the lock on one of the buildings. Somehow, he found the key in Rose's nightstand, the one she'd kept hidden under her nightgowns for years.

Following close behind, Rose nervously anticipates how he will react when he sees what's inside the building, knowing his response will determine her next move. The door creaks loudly in the silent night as Rose watches, waiting to decide her husband's fate.

Unfortunately, he doesn't respond well.

23

ROSE
MAY 2014

It's two o'clock in the afternoon the following day when Rose hears the sound of a car door at the neighbours' house. She's been enjoying some of the black tea Quinn brought over during one of her visits.

Getting up from her seat at the kitchen table, she turns down the volume on her radio on her way to the living room window. She enjoys listening to afternoon talk shows to keep her company. Growing up with a large family, she often feels dread at the empty silence stretching between the walls of her home.

Since Max's untimely death, she's been living here alone, minding her own business. Her daycare days long behind her, she had missed the purposefulness of having a job. She now spends her days observing, watching—hunting.

At the window, Rose gently pushes aside the curtain to get a better view. She's surprised to spot a wobbly-looking Quinn being assisted out of the vehicle, leaning on her husband's arm as he carefully walks her over to the house.

The couple walks slowly, with their heads down. They take their time walking up the steps leading to the front door, and Rose notices bright white gauze bandages taped to both of Quinn's forearms. Understanding courses through Rose as she watches, a tight smile forming on her lips.

Quinn had slashed her wrists then. The young mother had wanted to die. Even went as far as harming herself. Rose might not have to kill her after all. If Quinn is close enough to the edge, maybe all she needs is a little push in the right direction. Rose feels exhilarated at the idea. It's been a long time since she's had the privilege of choosing someone's fate.

Lost in thought, Rose catches William's eye looking in her direction. Caught staring, Rose gives him a sorrowful little wave, pretending to be the well-meaning neighbour, but inside she's mad at herself. She wanted to remain in the shadows, to watch but not be seen.

It's too late. He's spotted her.

William disappears inside the house for a moment and then runs back to the car as a light rain begins to fall. He tries to cover himself with his hand, a useless attempt at staying dry. Rose watches him pull the heavy car seat out of the car and bring it inside. Just like that, the show is over and everyone is out of view.

It isn't until a few weeks later when William comes knocking on Rose's door that she gets the full story.

———

She senses him coming long before she hears his heavy footing on her front steps. She wasn't expecting a visit but knows that it's William at the door, his shadow in the frosted glass announcing his presence before he's even knocked. It wasn't his usually friendly *rat-a-tat-tat* knock, but a dull knock-knock-knock instead. His knock alone tells her the tone and purpose of his visit will be on a more serious note than his previous ones.

Opening the door, she plasters her best sympathetic smile on her face as William slowly looks up from his shoes to meet her eyes. He looks worn—exhausted. Rose imagines he hasn't had a restful night since they returned from the hospital. She steps aside and welcomes him in.

Rose fiddles with the kettle while William sinks into a chair, the weight of the world on his shoulders. Rose has barely placed the milk and sugar on her plastic-covered tablecloth when William begins explaining what has happened.

"Quinn has severe postpartum depression and has been inconsistent with her medication."

He brings the scorching mug of tea to his lips and winces at the burning liquid, placing the mug back down almost instantly, spilling a little of its contents in the process. He goes on to explain in a quivering voice that his wife has recently been feeling immense guilt over an oversight with Cole. William doesn't elaborate but it's clear to him that this incident tipped her over the edge.

"You poor dear! What a terribly sad experience for all of you," Rose offers kindly, placing a frail hand over William's, patting it lightly.

Hesitating and against her better judgement, she adds, "My late-husband, Max, killed himself a few years ago." She releases a breath, playing the part of the grieving widow perfectly.

William looks up suddenly with tears in his eyes. He's surprised by what she's shared. She appreciates the pity in his gaze as she does indeed miss Max terribly and doesn't enjoy talking about him very much.

She waves it off, silently trying to change the subject. She doesn't know why she felt compelled to bring it up. Max's death still evokes a lot of pain and mixed feelings for her.

When she looks up, she sees William staring straight down at the table, seemingly lost in thought and rhythmically tapping his index finger on the edge. When he looks up, Rose recognizes hope in his eyes, and it makes her squirm in her seat. She watches as he sits up a little straighter in his chair, looking directly at her as he speaks.

"Mrs. Westover, I was hoping I could ask you a favour," he starts.

Rose bites the inside of her cheek, chiding herself. Why had she mentioned Max's death? Now she's put herself in a situation she has no interest being in. Betraying her emotions, she forces a smile, nodding in encouragement for William to continue.

"Since you have experience with this—" he coughs, clearing his throat, "—sort of thing, I'm wondering if you would mind checking in on Quinn and Cole over the next few weeks, just to make sure they're okay."

There are deep purple bags under his eyes from stress and sleep deprivation.

"You see, there's an urgent situation in British Columbia. Some forest fires that are out of control."

He casually drags a finger in the spilled tea, making drawings on the plastic tablecloth.

"I haven't graduated yet, but my instructor asked me to head over there to help put out the fires."

His expression quickly switches to pride.

"They usually don't allow people with so few flight hours to go but my instructor says I'm ready." He smiles sleepily as he looks at Rose. "They need all hands on deck to fight the fires before they completely destroy the forest."

Rose smiles. She can see how pleased William is. To have been chosen to help save a large forest from a fire as a rookie pilot is a prestigious honour. She understands how special it feels to be offered this kind of recognition, to be noticed, and to feel important.

She has built a life on gaining the trust of her neighbours, of her church congregation, trying to make everyone feel comfortable around her, convincing them to tell her their secrets.

That had been their mistake—their weakness.

Lying is a funny thing. No one ever likes admitting that they lie. Yet everyone does it. Dirty little secrets kept close to the chest. The stain on the pillow that you turn over in the hopes that no one will ever find out. People like to cover up their lies, hide them from everyone, often by using more lies.

The cycle can get pretty confusing. Lie over lie—layers of them—it can be difficult to find your way back to the truth, or to make your way out of the lie.

She's watched good people do bad things her entire life. Liars always get what they deserve in the end, even if she doesn't have anything to do with it. Call it karma, or coincidence, whichever you like, it always works out that way... Liars never find true happiness. They live in agony from keeping all that evil inside themselves for years. The lies eventually destroy them from the inside out.

Every single one of them are liars. White lies, perhaps, but liars all the same. Rose has worked hard to remain unnoticed, hiding in plain sight, quietly cleansing the streets of evil just as her father had taught her all those years ago.

24

ROSE

When Bruce learned about his daughter's interest in the family hobby, he was thrilled. Rose had never seen him shine so visibly with pride. She immediately became his pet project. He taught her everything he knew.

"Over time, you'll find your own thing," he'd explained one night as he'd methodically washed his hands clean at the kitchen sink. The rust coloured stain coming off his palms had intrigued her rather than spooked her.

That evening, Rose had spent some time alone in her room contemplating what her contribution to society would be. That was when her quest for tracking liars began.

Driven by her childhood hatred of Maddison Thomas, Rose had confronted liars throughout her entire life. She thought that if she punished enough of them, she would forget about Maddison and get the bad taste out of her mouth from the deception and betrayal she'd experienced all those years ago. She'd been wrong.

———

Adhering to her father's advice, Rose had started with strangers. Knives were her weapons of choice—silent.

That part had been easy for her. Simple to obtain, easy to hide and no permit required. The hard part had been finding her first victim. She's wandered through the empty streets of town, looking for dejected teens to befriend. Her nerves and inexperience had almost gotten her in trouble. She'd found it difficult to get the liars to follow her to the building behind the house.

Over time, she'd honed her skills. She'd perfected her non-verbal communication tactics making her seem more approachable, friendly, and trustworthy. She'd become apt at luring her victims to the buildings beyond the shadows with the pretense of needing help with her gardens only to bring them to the most isolated spot on the property to finish the job.

Her father had acted quickly and impulsively, not doing much research before ending someone's life, resulting in a few too many close calls. Rose went about it differently. She was more careful—calculating. She didn't do it for sport like most of her family. She was doing the world a favour. Eliminating one liar at a time.

She'd hand-picked her victims and observed them for long periods at a time. She needed to weed out the liars from the honest folks. She studied them to make sure they made appropriate subjects.

Slowly, she would approach them, find something in common, and gain their trust over time so that later on they would willingly walk into her trap. She was careful to pick people from far away towns that her family had no connection to. It wasn't easy. It took time and effort and required every precaution necessary. She didn't want to lead the police to her door.

Her signature move was to cut off the pinky finger of every victim after killing them. No one ever saw her do it, of course. Even though many of her relatives used the house as their main spot, they were always careful to give each other lots of space. The family didn't watch each other work. It was her little thrill—knowing that even in the afterlife, her victims would never be able to pinky-swear to anything again. She kept the tiny digits protected and marinating in a sealed, glass Mason jar in the basement's cold storage.

This worked well until people started building new houses on the street. The economy had been bad and the farmer across the way had sold his land cheap, attracting a slew of new neighbours.

Houses were popping up all over the place. Their secluded lot was now surrounded by young families wanting to raise their children in the fresh air of the countryside, letting them run wild in the fields of wheat with the vast forest expanding behind the houses.

Rose's family had been forced to put their activities on hold for several years until they could adapt and adjust. It had been a nightmare; they'd struggled not to give into their urges. Old habits die hard. But Rose knew her time would come. Patience was the key to remaining safe and undetected.

This was about the time that Rose began her daycare business. Having had no children of her own, she wanted to care for other people's babies. She thought it would be the perfect cover-up— the caring and nurturing babysitter who's also a serial killer.

Rose had wanted to impact the little ones from the very beginning, in their early years when they were so impressionable. After all, children learn their behaviours and develop their personalities by watching their parents. She had naively thought she could alter the course of their lives, in spite of their predisposed genetic make-up and steer them in the right direction.

She soon realized that it couldn't be done.

She hadn't planned on killing a baby, but when the child's parents had been so terribly devious, she'd given in to her calling. She had reasoned with herself that if the parents had the lying gene, then by extension, so did their offspring. Therefore, they all had to go.

That had been a really bad move on her part.

An investigation into her daycare business had taken place. Police officers and lawyers had sniffed around, made her sweat, and lose sleep at night. She'd often wished her father was still around. He'd been a smooth-talker, able to get out of almost anything, an expert at disguise and distraction. When the "accident" happened at her daycare, people had started doubting her and asking questions.

They'd talked to neighbours to see if Rose had harmed any of her old clients' children. Thankfully, she had not—yet. She had also never had the chance to cut the pinky finger off the deceased child because another toddler had come stumbling through the secret library door, stopping her hand in mid-air, knife reflecting the light from the single lightbulb swinging on the ceiling.

The traumatized little girl had screamed, but being only two years old, Rose had been able to bribe her with ice cream. Once she'd woken up from her afternoon nap and Rose had cleaned up all the evidence, the little girl had seemingly forgotten all about it, passing it off as a nightmare.

Rose had called the parents to tell them the sad news of their son's passing—he'd died in his sleep, she'd claimed. Under a year old, there was always the risk of a baby dying of Sudden Infant Death Syndrome.

It had been fairly easy to leave him on his belly, his little head too heavy to lift for breath. It hadn't taken long before he'd become completely still. An autopsy revealed that the cause of death had indeed been from lack of oxygen. The investigation had been dropped when the grieving parents claimed they wanted to be left in peace.

Rose learned they moved a few months later, the memories too hard to bear. Rose felt cheated. She never got to finish the job she'd started. She never got to take care of the parents. She'd decided to seal off the secret room after that. She spent the last few years burying the old bones from the buildings in the yard claiming it was a large landscaping project just in case anyone came sniffing around again. Better safe than sorry.

———

When Rose's father died, he left the house and all of the land to her and her husband, Max. Losing her father was hard on her. He was her last connection to this part of her life no one else knew about. Her sister, Joyce, had lost her battle with breast cancer three years before. Their deaths had left a gaping hole in Rose's life.

Rose had endured a dark period when she didn't feel up to doing anything. Finding mundane things excruciating, Rose had struggled to get out of bed, eat properly and leave the house. Max had been worried about her.

He'd suggested many times that cleaning out the buildings on the property might help—something to keep her mind busy, he'd said.

Grieving, but alert, Rose had quickly made the excuse that the buildings held her father's things and she couldn't bring herself to go through any of it just yet. She had promised Max she'd deal with it on her on as soon as she felt better, and to her relief, he'd dropped it.

She loved Max very much and feared his reaction if he were to ever stumble into any of the buildings. He was sure to have questions. He might even spill her secret. If it came to that, Rose knew what she would have to do. She couldn't let Max destroy her family's reputation. She couldn't risk it. If he ever found out, she would have to get rid of him, which, in the end, is what she did.

———

After using her key in the building lock, Max had allowed his eyes to adjust for only a moment before his calm exterior broke. Rose had swiftly and unnoticeably caught up to him. She watched the horror play on Max's face and instead of shame all she could feel was anger.

Max had never before posed a threat to Rose's lifestyle or her family history. He'd never questioned, never pried. Yet, here he was, disgusted, judging her.

Rose panicked.

She wasn't ready to be a widow. She loved Max. She'd hoped for so long that someone like her could stand a chance at true love, but she'd been wrong. Max clearly didn't understand why she did what she did and no amount of explaining was going to change his mind or his opinion about her. She knew what needed to be done even if she was reluctant to do it.

When Max finally noticed Rose standing behind him in the building's entrance, blocking his way, the realization hit him just as it hit her. Rose was going to kill him. He instinctively backed away from her, two spouses suddenly strangers. Max slammed into the far wall, the small dark space not allowing much room for a successful escape.

She had him trapped—he knew it and she knew it.

Rose saw that Max understood, or at least she convinced herself that he did. He'd loved her blindly. Rose had counted on that, always careful whenever she'd shared personal details about her past. Being vague about old family traditions and childhood hobbies.

Rose gestured at him to move toward the door and walked behind him, leading him into the backyard, the gun pointed at his back. She stepped in front of him, kissed his shaking lips, and felt him jerk his head back as he tried to avoid her touch.

Stepping back from him enough to look directly into his eyes, she could feel hot tears escaping her eyes. She didn't trust herself to speak.

"Rose, please don't do this," he'd pleaded. Hands up, surrendering. Unblinking, he'd added, "I won't tell anyone." He'd lied.

She shook her head, disappointed.

She exhaled a heavy breath. Standing close to him, Rose grabbed her husband's hand and meticulously wrapped his fingers around the gun. She had to get this just right. She didn't want Max to suffer. She slowly lifted his hand until the barrel of the gun rested against his temple.

"I'll always love you," she uttered between sobs, and then she'd pressed her finger overtop her husband's, remaining quiet as his life had exploded out of him.

Shaking, she'd hurried to the house to change and wash her hands. There would be time to grieve later, but she'd had to play the hysterical widow left all alone by her husband's suicide.

She hadn't had to work too hard to fake the tears or the emptiness caused by the pain of losing Max. Her feelings had been genuine. She'd received sympathies from friends, dozens of casseroles, flowers, visitors. But not one person ever looked behind her closed garage door where the car was sitting, hidden from view under a green tarp.

Rose had gotten a new car easily and no one asked too many questions for fear of upsetting her. When people assume they know the reasons behind your actions, it can work in your favour.

She missed Max dearly but what choice had she had? He would have jeopardized everything her family had ever worked for. She was the last one left, but she wasn't done yet.

PART
THREE

25

DYLAN
JULY 1999

Dylan had taken the day off work at his computer programming job, to practice the bike ride ahead of time. One of the members of their group was typically assigned the responsibility of leader, of mapping out the route and being in charge of checking for potential blind spots and other problem areas. Gravel roads were their nemesis. The leader usually tried to find clean roads with clearly indicated, wide bike lanes to complete the long endurance cycling trips.

For years they'd planned long-distance rides with the same small group of friends they'd met at a spinning class during the long winter months. The group had always trained separately but met up for one long ride each year in July. Usually, the group aimed to travel 150 km to 200 km. They alternated routes every year, to keep it interesting. This year, Dylan was in charge of choosing the route.

They would be biking from North Bay to Verner, where they had a scheduled stop at The Village Café for lunch, before biking northbound towards Marten River and back to North Bay, closing the triangle with a 170 km ride, approximately nine hours of riding in total.

Since Dylan was leading this year's ride, he'd also been named honorary route inspector for the group. It would be his responsibility to warn the group about upcoming potholes, narrow bike lanes, and stop signs along the route. But no matter how prepared he was, even a fierce leader like Dylan had no idea that disaster lay ahead.

———

Dylan has been enduring a grueling work week of too many burnt coffees, hours bent over his keyboard, crunching formulas into a new system expected to roll out next month. The year is 1999 and they are getting ready for a new millennium in the IT world.

Even though Dylan has been working overtime almost every night, he still manages to get out a couple of evenings a week to train for the long ride. He's had to change his training schedule this year, to a more intense routine due to his grueling deadlines at work and a lack of time.

His wife, Maddison, had brought up a new technique a few months ago called interval training, where you bike harder, instead of longer. This, combined with weight lifting helps to get the muscles ready for endurance cycling after a long and dormant winter. It had sounded a little extreme, but he'd been willing to try it.

He only had to focus on sprint intervals of fifteen to thirty seconds each during which he gave it his all six to eight times with a few minutes of break in between to slow down his heart rate, before the next set. The total ride only lasted twenty minutes an evening. The goal was to bring yourself to the point of exhaustion, which would eventually train your body to become stronger and quicker.

So far, the theory was proving to be true. He was able to catch up and perform just as well as the rest of the group which had been doing longer endurance rides more frequently.

Maddison, a social worker, has been able to train with other cyclists as her hours are more flexible. On nights when Dylan works late, Maddison meets up with others from cycling class and cycles shorter routes.

The couple have two teenage sons, old enough that they don't need to worry about finding babysitters to watch over them while they go biking. Regardless, with Dylan working longer hours, the couple hasn't been able to spend much time together lately.

––––––

Dylan has a lot on his mind today. A good mental capacity is crucial to completing this long ride successfully. His mindset is just as important as his physical state. However, Dylan's state of mind seems off this morning and he's weary while gearing up. He's not sure if his new leader role is stressing him out more than he realized or if it's something to do with his upcoming deadline at work.

He'd taken a day off last week to do the practice run of the same ride they're embarking on this morning. He'd had nearly five hours of solitude—just him, the pavement and his thoughts. Maybe it was the fact that he'd had so much time with his thoughts that was causing him to be so moody today.

Dylan's eyebrows inch closer together as he is deep in thought. He shuts his eyes, willing whatever bad energy away. *Today will be good*, he convinces himself. To anyone passing by it might look like he's deep in concentration, but he knows he can't hide his nerves from Maddison.

Even though Dylan hadn't seen much of his wife over the last few months because of work and training, they've been able to remain a team in planning this ride together.

He's mentioned to her in passing that his boss hasn't been very receptive to some of the ideas he's suggested recently, and by default, Dylan has to redo an entire section of the program he'd been working on. It's been extremely frustrating and a huge waste of time, but it wasn't uncommon in the IT world. There's always new software or new technologies that can achieve faster and better results. IT is constantly dynamic. Always moving and improving. At least, that's what he has to tell himself to stay motivated.

Dylan remembers when he first met Maddison through a mutual friend. On their first date, Maddison had asked him about his work and he remembers how proud he'd been to have been a part of creating software from start to finish. He remembers feeling elated that he was heard and appreciated by his boss at the time.

Later, around the time of their tenth wedding anniversary, Dylan had been promoted to Team Leader. He remembers because it had been the first time he'd been home late, their dinner reservations having long since been cancelled. Maddison had been waiting up for him, her second large glass of red wine forgotten on the coffee table, almost empty. Dylan had felt a wave of emotion as he remembered the disappointment on her face. He'd felt so guilty for abandoning her but also a certain pride at having an important job to do.

He'd always been trying to climb the corporate ladder and he'd finally moved up. He'd worked hard for this. Still, seeing his wife's hurt expression as she watched him cross the room to the couch where she'd spent her evening had tugged at his heart.

She'd tried so hard to mask it and be supportive, quick to say it was fine. He'd reassured her it was a one-off, but little did they know that this was the beginning of a new regular occurrence for him. Dylan had assured her at the time that he would make it up to her for missing out on their date and dinner reservations, and he'd been set on keeping his word. To his dismay, he wasn't able to follow through.

On the make-up date, things had looked promising. The night had started well only to be interrupted by a system crash one hour into the evening. He'd had to leave before dinner and head straight to the office. Dylan and his team had worked through the night to correct the issue before things had a chance to escalate and customers began to take notice of the glitch in the system.

The IT world is so fickle. One wrong move and an entire system can come crashing down impacting thousands of users around the world at once.

Life can be like that at times. A small ripple over time can become a large wave. One mistake can lead to a lost friendship. One lie can lead to broken trust. One affair can break up a marriage. One moment of distraction can kill you.

26

DYLAN
JULY 1999

The Thomases take safety very seriously on their rides. They have new, reliable bikes, they always wear their helmets, they stop at every stop sign, they make sure to use the proper cycling signals, and they check the routes ahead of time.

They come prepared, ensuring one of them is always carrying a tire pump as well as an emergency tool kit to make small repairs along the way as is often required on long endurance rides. After a few years of doing this, they know what to expect and plan for it.

Today, they've packed protein bars and a couple of bottles of water each in their bike packs. Dylan makes sure to bring his cell phone along for the ride. Maddison, being an overprotective mother, can never distance herself too far away from her kids without being reachable. It gives her peace of mind that Dylan brings his phone, especially when they're leaving the boys home alone for such a long time. He's lucky to have gotten one from work so that he can bring it with him during their bike trips.

He tucks the phone in the bright, acid green fanny pack he always wears during his rides to hold his wallet and keys.

The boys never seem to mind when their parents leave them alone for these long days. As they have gotten older, the family's modest home sometimes feels stuffy and cramped with all four of them tiptoeing around each other. None of them do well staying indoors for days on end. Winter months are very trying for the Thomases.

While Maddison can keep up with her work-out routine by attending yoga classes and hitting the local gym in the evenings, Dylan typically works late most nights. He knows Maddison thinks he stays late at work just for the peace and quiet. And she's right. He doesn't do well with all the noise and busyness of home life with their growing sons. The boys almost always have friends over after school as they'd rather not be left alone with their parents. It's a sure way to avoid all the prying questions their parents might pepper them with the minute they walk through the door.

Dylan knows the boys cringe at the idea of family dinners at the kitchen table. The setting is all too formal for their liking. They really dislike being put on the spot and know they'll be left alone if they bring a friend. It was Maddison's idea to always eat dinner together as a family—a chance for them to catch up with each other and an opportunity for her to assess her family's state of mind.

She's the only one who enjoys those dinners though. Still, she insists on the multiple benefits they bring and continues to force them to do it even when she's confronted with disgruntled responses.

———

It was a quiet morning. Dylan woke up early and in a sour mood which he associated with being hungry. He's cooked himself and Maddison a large portion of steaming, hot oatmeal with a dash of cinnamon, sprinkled chopped pecans, and sliced bananas.

A healthy meal plan is necessary for the training leading up to the long ride as well as for the ride itself. The couple has been increasing their protein and grain intake, consciously cutting dairy and sugar whenever possible.

As Dylan locks the house and walks his bike down the driveway, he thinks of his eldest, Samuel, who, at thirteen years old, had been caught by his father in a precarious situation in his room this week.

A popular hip-hop song had been playing a little too loudly on the boy's laptop in the corner of his room. When Dylan opened the bedroom door without first announcing his presence, he'd surprised Samuel without his T-shirt on, passionately kissing a girl on his bed.

The blond girl had caught sight of Dylan standing at Samuel's door. Her blue eyes had widened like saucers as her face had turned tomato red. Without uttering a word, the girl had jumped up and off the bed and rushed by Dylan, squeezing past him through the door, avoiding eye contact at all costs. She'd been so mortified at being caught by her boyfriend's father that she'd run out of the house, shoes in hand.

Dylan decided to have a long talk with both boys after that about practicing safe sex. He'd thought his sons had understood "the talk" the first time when Dylan spoke with them when they were younger, but it had been obvious that day that the subject needed revisiting.

Dylan had always been nervous about having boys. Everyone knew that if you had a girl, you had to worry about her becoming pregnant. What people often forgot though, is that the boys who get the girls pregnant need just as much watching.

Dylan wasn't ignorant to the fact that his boys were interested in sex. He'd found pornographic images under their beds with no idea how they'd obtained them. Hormones and accessibility were a bad mix.

When Dylan was growing up, it had been generally accepted that, typically, boys' houses weren't monitored as strictly as girls' houses. For some reason, boys were left alone at a younger age than girls seemed to be. There was a certain mentality that girls needed more protection whereas boys could take care of themselves. It was certainly how Dylan had been brought up, and he'd done the same with his boys.

He was a very involved parent but honestly, he had many other things to worry about. His boys were growing up and needed to learn who they were. Part of learning meant they'd need to make some mistakes.

27

DYLAN
JULY 1999

"**Y**ou ready to go?" he asks Maddison, excited for the ride ahead.

"Yes," she replies enthusiastically.

They leave the house at seven sharp. Keeping a strict schedule is important to attaining their goals but also to ensuring they won't arrive late to meet the rest of the group. The gathering spot is only a few kilometres away slightly outside the city's bustling action.

The Thomases live in North Bay, conveniently near public bus routes for the boys and minutes away from Dylan's office, while the rest of the group is scattered across the countryside.

The sun is warm and bright. A slight glare reflects off the road. During their preparations this morning, Dylan had checked the weather and noted the high for the day was 25 degrees Celsius, but that isn't supposed to hit until around noon today. There are several clouds scattered across the sky offering temporary relief from the sun's warm rays. The light breeze is refreshing and welcomed as they begin pedaling. A perfect day for a long bike ride with great friends.

On these rides, Dylan usually spends his time looking around at the beautiful scenery and soaking it all up. There's just nothing like being outdoors. He spends so many hours bent over a desk that whenever he gets to go biking, especially first thing in the morning, he's very appreciative.

Taking a deep breath, he slowly fills his lungs with fresh morning air. There's nothing quite like it. His gaze sweeps the scenery, taking it all in—the vast green hayfields, the wind softly rustling the knee-high corn stalks.

His mouth waters at the thought of late summer barbeques where they often enjoy roasted corn and savory, almost charred roasted chicken breast, coated in his special homemade barbeque sauce. His secret ingredient—a pinch of cumin.

Every August, the Thomases head up to a friend's cottage in Cache Bay and spend the entire day basking in the warm sun, swimming in the cold lake, exploring the waters in their canoe, and hiking in the woods. There is always an assortment of fresh seasonal vegetables and cured meats at the cottage. Dylan looks forward to seeing the checkered picnic table full of colourful food ready to eat. His mind drifts to the atmosphere. The outdoor speakers at the cottage continuously blaring old songs, plenty of outdoor games for the boys and their friends, the joyful sounds of the kids running through the yard, throwing a Frisbee or splashing in the water.

Dylan and Maddison have been taking the boys to the cottage for over a decade and even as they approach the teenage years, they always look forward to going back and visiting their friends, Tom and Sue.

The Thomases don't own a cottage, but always consider the cottage weekend as their very own little getaway trip. Living in town, with two pre-teen boys to feed, Dylan and Maddison don't have much left in their budget to afford family vacations out in the country.

The cottage get-togethers in Cache Bay have always been a welcome break from the everyday grind. Dylan has fond memories of the cottage, of stepping out of the car and onto the soft green grass, shoes optional. Bathing suits instead of regular clothes, grilled meat, the unmistakable sound of ice clinking in a glass and no rules, made for some good times. The lack of curfews and late-night bonfires crackling accompanying a symphony of crickets added to the charm of the vacation.

When the boys were younger, the Thomases would put up their tent and spend the night, the drive home slightly too long to make back in the dark of the night. Nowadays, the boys are eager to return home to their city friends the following day, so the family very rarely stays up past midnight. The cottage weekend is quickly approaching and Dylan salivates at the thought of the food they will eat.

He sneaks a peek at his wife, riding along happily behind him. Her blue tank top clings to her tanned shoulders as she leans over the handlebars of the bike, stretching out her muscles, getting ready for the long haul.

It's going to be a hot one, Dylan thinks. He can feel it already.

Dylan is enjoying the silence surrounding them in the early hours of the morning. He really couldn't ask for a better way to spend a Saturday morning in the summer months. He's looking forward to the day ahead. Going exploring while exercising and spending time with their cycling friends.

What could be better?

And, this year, they have the bonus of riding their brand-new bikes. They'd bought them at the end of the season last year and saved a bunch of money. They'd both fallen in love with the slightly upright and comfortable new frames and all-terrain tires. The bikes make almost no sound at all as they cruise down the country roads.

Dylan feels like he is gliding on the pavement.

He holds his back straight, always one to keep his form while biking. He happily welcomes the strain of the ride on his aching muscles. Dylan also appreciates the silence of the ride. This is just what he needs to help clear his mind.

Since installing a new program at work, he's battled with anxiety and has been having trouble sleeping. After doing some research, he'd determined that there was nothing better to help deflect the effects than physical exercise. Good for the body, and even better for the mind.

Approximately two hours into the ride, they approach the town of Sturgeon Falls and Dylan hears a faint hum behind him. Turning around at the last minute, careful not to lose his balance, he spots a flash of red in his peripheral view before feeling a sharp pain in his left leg.

A painful cry escapes from his throat. He smashes to the ground, hitting the hard, rough surface of the pavement. There's a loud cracking sound—bones breaking. Stunned, he painfully turns his head over. In disbelief, he spots Maddison lying on the road a few feet behind him. A car speeds away down the long road, never once stopping to see what it hit.

Struggling to remain conscious, he fights the desire to shut his eyes for as long as he possibly can. He doesn't know Maddison's condition yet, and he's not sure if he'll be able to get cell service on his phone to call for help. They are lying on the shoulder of the road with their brand-new bikes shattered in pieces around them. Dylan glimpses debris from their bike bags, loose tires and his cracked helmet scattered across the pavement. It had happened so fast, he hadn't heard the car coming.

He has no way of knowing if his wife is alright.

As Dylan's heavy eyelids keep sliding shut, he sees brake lights, and notices the silhouette of a small figure peering over him. He strains to see any details but the person is standing in front of the glaring sun, completely obscuring any features.

The fight in him is quickly running out. The pain in his leg and back is too much to tolerate. Thick, red liquid drips down his forehead and into the ditch, and then the world goes black.

28

DYLAN

When Dylan regains consciousness a few hours later, he's lying on a stiff hospital bed with a green curtain surrounding his bed. He's completely disoriented.

He's stiff and strapped down to the bed—unable to move a muscle. He has a neck brace on, but when he strains his eyes, he sees crusty blood and dirt all over his uncovered arms and legs.

A shiver courses through him. He has to blink hard to keep his eye open, the other swollen shut. On his lips, he recognizes a metallic taste surely left there by a bloody nose. Running his dry tongue over his teeth, he notices that a few are missing, surprised to find gaping holes in their place.

When a nearby nurse clumsily drops her metal medical tray onto the ceramic floor in the hallway next to his room, Dylan yells in terror, hundreds of nerves on fire.

The images come so fast, he feels like he would have fallen off the hospital bed had he not been strapped down. The vivid images come quick—his memories fresh.

The red car. The red brake lights in the distance, the silhouette—the last things he remembers seeing. He shuts his eyes, but all he can see is the red blood everywhere. His wife sprawled on the side of the road, her head split open.

His monitor beeps and alerts his nurse who rushes over to check his vitals. She grabs his patient file at the foot of the bed and flips through the chart smiling kindly under her medical mask, her eyes creasing at the corners.

"How are you doing Mr. Thomas?" she asks, her eyes shiny and clean with no trace of makeup.

Dylan's mouth is sore and parched. He finds that his voice is hoarse and he can see black spots floating about, bouncing off the white walls. He'd hit his head pretty hard on the road, knocking him out almost immediately. He knows enough from having two young boys that he's most likely suffering from a concussion. He will probably need to remain here overnight to be observed before being released. And who knows what's wrong with his neck.

He slowly feels the panic set in as he attempts to move his arms and legs, which are tightly tied down. One of his legs is lifted in a sling and covered in a thick, white cast. He has no memory of breaking it, but the thought of it makes his stomach turn.

Dylan makes his best attempt at a grunt to reply to the kind nurse but only manages a low gurgle followed by a dry cough from somewhere deep in his chest.

Without missing a beat, the nurse gets the hint and seems to magically appear on his right side, holding up a plastic cup of water with a bendy straw that she holds up to his lips for him to drink. He gratefully takes a long sip of the tepid liquid mixed with the metallic taste of blood in his mouth before he forces it down his throat.

"There, that's better now," she remarks, placing the cup on a nearby table. "How's the pain today?" she asks him.

Today? How long had he been here? Hadn't he just gotten here a few hours ago? Where are the boys? Who's taking care of them? Where's his wife? Is she still lying on the side of the road, drowning in her own blood?

The memory of his wife's mangled body makes his body jerk, nausea overwhelming him. He doesn't even know if his wife is alive.

29

DYLAN
AUGUST 13TH, 2014

Dylan's head feels foggy when he wakes up. He's been dealing with chronic migraines for years—a result of the concussion he suffered during the accident.

Lying in bed for hours just waiting for time to tick by, he's watched the numbers change one by one on his digital alarm clock all night long. His eyes are red and irritated from squinting in the dark trying to make sense of the lurking shadows in the corners of the room.

He blinks a few times, trying to rid himself of the slimy film stretched over his eyes. He'd finally gotten a few hours of sleep around 1 a.m., but now he's wide awake. Something has woken him.

A loud crashing sound resonates through the house followed by heavy steps.

Someone's in his house.

Dylan jumps out of bed wearing only boxer shorts. His overweight belly sloshes, making it impossible to ignore the excess of beer he drank a few hours before. His head is pounding from the migraine and the adrenaline rushing through his veins.

The sound of the breaking glass makes him close his eyes instinctively.

The old, familiar fear is overtaking him again, and there's nothing he can do about it. No amount of therapy can remove the imprint left on his brain from the trauma of the accident.

Over the years, he's learned methods of dealing with his post-traumatic-stress-disorder—how to breathe and calm down his heart rate—but he can't stop the images from popping up in his mind.

His therapist has explained at length how all kinds of events, people, sounds, and even smells can trigger a memory. Dylan had already been well aware of that as the memories had been keeping him awake and unable to resume life as normal. No matter how many years had passed, Dylan couldn't forget—not even if he wanted to.

His obsession with finding his wife's hit-and-run killer has taken up every ounce of space in his mind since that dreadful day. Dylan's memories of the accident have remained at the forefront of his mind—all-consuming. His friends have tried to pull him out of this pit on various occasions, encouraging him to move away and start over. But it was no use.

He'd lost his passion for biking. He hadn't had the heart or the energy for it. He'd been in the habit of always making excuses until almost all of his friends had moved on, leaving him to wallow in his pain.

Nothing has been the same since the accident. He'd found it impossible to watch the world go on as usual, oblivious to the fact that he'd lost the love of his life. No, nothing would ever be the same again. After all, it was his route they had been taking. It was his fault his wife and unborn baby were dead.

In the dark of the early morning, it takes Dylan a moment for his eyes to adjust. The memory of his accident has shaken him, brought him back to that stretch of road and the red car.

He quickly and clumsily brushes his hand along the night table, only to knock his phone to the floor with a loud thump.

"Shit!" he mutters under his breath.

Someone has broken in and Dylan isn't doing a great job of being sneaky enough to surprise whoever has the balls to enter his home. Dylan can hear the intruder's loud steps, seemingly not at all concerned with the loud fall of his phone.

He sidesteps around the night table as quietly as he can, trying to make up for his earlier clumsiness and feels around the surface to locate his glasses. His eyesight was also damaged in the accident requiring him to wear ridiculously thick glasses to see anything of importance. Without them, the world resembles a Monet painting—blurry images made of quick brush strokes.

His bad leg has never been the same since that day either. The accident left him with a permanent limp on his left side.

Knowing every square inch of this house, he carefully moves towards the bedroom window to peek through the grimy, closed blinds, checking the front yard for any clue as to who might be roaming around downstairs.

His sons are away for the weekend as they often are nowadays. Since the accident, he and his boys have had trouble getting along on the best of days.

Anticipating every creaky floorboard, every whining strip, he makes his way from the window to the bedroom door just as his toe grazes the foot of the four-post bed. The king-size duvet is loosely draped over the queen-size mattress creating a pool of excess fabric on the floor.

Dylan exhales in relief at his close call. But his small reprieve is short-lived as he overcorrects his step and his thigh connects directly with the edge of the lower dresser. The impact makes the attached oval mirror sway slightly reflecting the faint streetlight coming into the room.

Dylan has to bite his bottom lip hard to stop himself from cursing. Ever since the accident, he bruises like a peach. As he lifts his head to continue on his quest, he catches sight of himself in the mirror just as a passerby's car headlights shine into the room. Suddenly not feeling so strong, he begins to wonder if it would be best to hide away, lock himself in his ensuite bathroom and call the police from there. Let them deal with it.

No. He won't do that.

He can't stand by again and do nothing. Dylan finds an old resolve and pushes on towards the door. He couldn't protect Maddison when the car hit them from behind, but this he can do.

He firmly grips the door's brass handle, squeezing it as he turns. He spots a light downstairs, a faint blue hue coming from a cellphone moving in one direction and then another. Dylan feels his heart tighten as he looks down from his safe place in the shadows of the upstairs landing. The intruder doesn't seem aware of his presence yet.

"OK, ok, what do I do now?" he mumbles to himself, encouraged, as he attempts to think quickly.

His mind is still a little bit jumbled. Ever since the accident, he has had a hard time concentrating and still struggles making connections, his thoughts just not as quick as they used to be.

It had taken him more months than he'd liked to admit before he'd been able to memorize more than five digits in a row. This had been particularly hard on him due to the nature of his career in computer programming. He'd been placed on modified duties for the better part of the following year until he'd been deemed capable of returning to his regular job.

Yet, his performance has never been quite the same. Whether it was attributed to lost motivation, grief, or the concussion, it didn't really matter. He'd been on his way towards a promotion to management back then. That was all forgotten now, never mentioned again. Not that it bothered him much. Work had become a necessity, a means to an end, not something he is passionate about anymore.

Rubbing the sleep out of his eyes, Dylan focuses all of his attention on the present moment as he attempts to figure out his next steps. He remembers there's an abandoned baseball bat behind his bedroom door. He retraces his steps and snatches it as quietly as he can muster. Putting all of his weight onto the front of his feet, he carefully makes his way out through the door avoiding many tripping hazards along the way. He wraps his fingers around the handle of the bat, getting ready.

The confidence that was lacking earlier seems to course through him. He's fired up with a vengeful energy he hadn't realized he had in him.

Dylan abruptly lifts the bat over his shoulder, wincing in pain as his back protests the sharp movement. He begins making his way down the dark hallway, doing his best not to breathe too loudly to give away his position.

He's so focused on his steps down the narrow stairs, trying his best not to slip on the hardwood floor in his stockinged feet, that he almost misses the blue light turning towards him. Caught off guard, he barely has the time to shift his bat. He does his best to maintain his balance on the stairs and takes a swing.

The intruder's light must have given him a warning of what Dylan was up to because the perp had time to react and duck out of the way at the last second. The bat collides loudly with the wall next to them creating a crater in the plaster.

"Dad! What the fuck are you doing?" the perp yells accusingly.

The voice, full of fear and anger sounds quite frightening and almost foreign to Dylan. Once his heart begins to slow a little, he realizes who he'd almost hit with his baseball bat.

Samuel, his oldest son, had come home in the middle of the night, scaring the living crap out of his dad. Dylan, horrified, watches as Samuel climbs the remaining few steps up the stairway and turns on the hall lights. Both men stare at each other, both out of breath and shaking from the near miss encounter.

Dylan feels the blood drain from his face and he collapses heavily on a step, allowing the bat to slide down the staircase and rattle loudly on the main floor below. He'd almost brutally attacked his own son with a bat. Or worse. He'd almost killed him.

The realization of how close Dylan had been to injuring his son crashes into him along with a deep guilt, one he hasn't felt for a very long time. Dylan's fear and left-over anger from his helplessness at the time of the accident had almost cost him dearly.

What had he been thinking about, going after an intruder in the dark? What if he'd connected with his son's head? How would he ever have been able to forgive himself?

Unable to explain the horror of this realization, ashamed by his actions, Dylan drops his head into his hands and weeps. He can feel the hot rage radiating from his son. The nervous energy between them is thick.

"What the hell were you thinking, Dad?" Sam demands. His son's fists are squeezed so tight, the knuckles have turned white. He angrily stares at the top of his father's balding head, looking for answers.

In the lit-up staircase, the idea of a dangerous intruder seems impossible even to Dylan. He's embarrassed, feeling pathetic and weak that he'd jumped to this conclusion as though the entire world was bad because something bad had happened to him in the past.

"I'm so sorry, Sam," Dylan tries, lifting his eyes to meet Samuel's. "I thought you were a thief," he explains, hesitant, confusion blurring his memory. "Why are you here? Aren't you supposed to be out with friends or something?" Dylan's brain is muddled as he watches Samuel shake his head, obviously exasperated with him.

"No, Dad. I was over at Julia's place, remember? That party I told you about?" Dylan seems to recall some mention of this but he must have remembered the dates wrong.

"By the way, my bag knocked over a picture frame on my way in. I cleaned up what I could, but I was worried about waking you." Samuel snorts. "Guess I didn't need to worry about that!" He waves a hand in dismissal.

When Dylan remembers what time it is he begins to puff up his chest, figuring he should probably discipline his son for staying out past curfew, but Dylan just doesn't have it in him. He feels the air leak out of his lungs.

He doesn't want to fight with his son—not tonight, not ever. His sons are all he has left and he can't stomach the idea of ever pushing them away by being too controlling.

Some of the other parents in their circle disagreed with his parenting style, called him a pushover, or negligent even. But Dylan had done the best he could. Raising his boys as a single dad had not been easy.

There was no other adult in the home he could lean on, discuss issues with, or get support from. He was left all alone to pick up the pieces his wife's death had left behind.

Maddison had been much more adept at parenting and discipline than he'd ever been. It was as though she'd had this sixth sense when it came to raising their kids. She always seemed to know what to do or say. Her background in social work helped her understand the boys' mindsets better, spotting trouble signs from a mile away.

Dylan had always adopted a more passive approach to discipline. His method hadn't changed much since Maddison's death.

The only difference now was that it was extremely apparent just how much of a backbone Maddison had been to their family and how much he missed the structure and order her presence had conjured.

She'd been the glue holding them together, the oil making their engine run. Without her, they were falling apart, drifting away from each other.

———

When the boys had first learned about their parents' accident, they'd panicked. Some family friends had brought the boys over to the hospital to see them, but of course Maddison was already long gone by then. Dylan had been in surgery for his leg, so the boys had learned about their injuries from the doctor.

After the initial shock, the boys had begun showing all the usual signs of grief. The healing had taken them all some time. It had taken a while to understand the depth of their loss. They had lost their mother. It was a lot for teenage boys to take in. They'd dealt with it in different ways, Samuel by partying, and Robert by isolating himself and playing countless hours of video games.

The loss of the baby had come as a shock to all of them. Dylan hadn't even known Maddison was pregnant. His loss had been two-fold and almost unbearable.

Busy recuperating from his injuries and dealing with his own grief, Dylan couldn't call himself *Parent of the Year*. He'd done his best to keep the boys healthy and happy. That was about all he'd had the capacity for. At the time, Dylan had convinced himself that he'd done enough, that he'd done his best.

But looking at Samuel now, a young man, Dylan saw the holes in his son's character and felt like he'd failed in his own responsibilities as his father. Dylan had been too soft in his discipline.

Kids need structure.

They might fight it at first, but if done right, it could help them thrive. Hoping it wasn't too late, Dylan refused to let his son go on like this, going out night after night with no job prospects in sights and no chores to keep him accountable. His boys needed him to step up his parenting game and help them become successful adults. Dylan could see that now.

He would talk with Sam in the morning when they'd both had some sleep.

After awkwardly hugging his son goodnight, Dylan retreats to the master bedroom to lie down for the remaining hours of the night until it's a reasonable hour to go cut the grass.

He knows he won't fall back asleep now, especially after the adrenaline rush he's just experienced. He isn't sure if he's more worked-up by the thought that only minutes ago, he'd been sure that someone had been breaking into his home, or if he's more terrified of being left alone with his own thoughts with nowhere to hide, and no escape in sight.

30

DYLAN

The warm rays of sunshine softly reach in through the bedroom blinds. Dylan groans as he rolls onto his back and scratches his thigh. His boxer briefs rode up during his sleep and he pulls them down to avoid squishing any important organs.

He's managed to get a few hours of sleep after all. Feeling groggy and exhausted, he knows that if he doesn't wake up now, his neck will begin protesting. The uncomfortable position he'd slept in and the flattened pillow he's had for longer than he cares to admit add to the strain and pounding in his head.

It's Saturday. He has nowhere to be.

He sighs. Begrudgingly, he takes his time getting up, slowly rising to a seated position, blinking several times against the bright light hitting his eyes. His right eye slightly better focused, he shuts his left eye as he struggles to stand. His muscles ache from all the excitement of last night, a muscle memory of sort.

Staggering over to the door, he grabs his old musty-smelling bath towel and recoils. He should probably wash the towels today. Glancing back at the messy, un-made bed, he resolves that he should probably give his sheets a wash, too.

The thought of house chores completely overwhelms him. He'd been quite content to leave those tasks to Maddison, while he'd been in charge of mowing the grass and taking out the garbage. He'd been surprised when they'd naturally landed on such stereotypical roles in their marriage, but they had both felt it worked. Sharing the load had created a peaceful harmony in their relationship. They were both contributing within their strengths and benefiting from their shared responsibilities.

Without Maddison here to help, the house now looked more like a frat house.

With three males in the home and no one to remind them of the ever-growing mountain of dirty dishes or the piles of laundry, there's usually a funky odor lingering in the halls at all times. Fluffy dust bunnies populate the floors and hold on for dear life on ceiling vents. The baseboard caulking is now a dull gray colour and, if the sun hits the room just right, you can see dust particles floating around with the pulse of the ceiling fans.

His feet feel heavy as he walks over to the only bathroom in the house. Happy to have woken up before Samuel, Dylan locks himself in the small room and starts his morning routine. He reads the latest news stories on his phone while sitting on the john and, once finished, he stands to trim his overgrown beard.

Turning the trimmer off, Dylan considers his grooming job as he decides what to do next. Since there is no work today, Dylan contemplates doing what he normally does to pass the time on Saturdays—drive around, looking for the red car that destroyed his life.

The steam rolls in, filling the small space by making a cloud of thick fog. The air hot, he steps over the tub's edge and under the scorching water. The jet is set to the highest setting, hitting his back like a thousand needles. It's something he used to find soothing, but that now makes him grit his teeth. Yet, he stands there, counting the minutes until it's over, refusing to change the setting.

This short-lived suffering is nothing compared to the aching he feels inside. If only he could do something to rid himself of the agony. Yell loud enough, cry an ocean of tears, or hit something until it's obliterated. He would do anything not to feel this kind of pain. He'd rather feel nothing at all than this excruciating torture of the memory of all he's lost.

Survivor's guilt is what experts call it. Dylan thinks it should be renamed *survivor's curse* as his beating heart haunts him every day. A steady and persistent reminder that he's still here, sucking air while his wife and unborn child are gone instead of him. His curse is living with that brutal reality everyday never understanding why they had to die and he has to live.

———

Stepping out of the shower, his skin red hot, he pats himself dry with the smelly towel from earlier, wrapping it around his middle before making his way back to his bedroom to find clean clothes. Leaning over the growing pile of dirty underwear and socks, he finds his glasses perched on the night table and puts them on.

Immediately, the out-of-focus room appears transformed before him and the sight of it discourages him. He can feel his shoulders sagging just by looking at all the work that needs to be done.

The room is humid and grimy. His sweaty feet leave imprints on the hardwood floor as he walks to the closet. The hot shower might have been a terrible idea. He feels greasier than he did when he got in the shower.

He picks out a golf shirt and khakis with a brown belt. He doesn't even play golf. Dylan hasn't felt like doing much to stay active lately, yet he's still in the habit of wearing the same clothes he used to wear before the accident.

As he bends down to tie his worn running shoes, he feels his nose tingle as though a small thread is coming loose on the inside. It's a tell-tale sign that it's nearly ready to start bleeding—another side-effect from that dreadful day. He barely has time to reach the tissues on the dresser before the dark red liquid begins dripping out rapidly, reminding him of an open tap of water.

"Great," he mutters to himself as he plops down on the unmade bed, his tissue box nestled next to him.

He'll remain in this spot for anywhere from ten minutes to an hour. With the intensity of this nosebleed, he can already tell it's going to be a long one.

He would plug the bridge of his nose and tilt his head like he knows he's supposed to do if it weren't for the inevitable blood clot that would eventually form and find its way up his nasal canal. The clot would then slide down and land in his mouth, making him choke before he could make his way to the bathroom sink to spit it out in time to take a normal breath.

Then, after all this, comes the impending migraine.

It's a strange time of year for a nosebleed but then again, the heat and stress can cause all kinds of unwanted and bizarre side effects. He hates the metallic taste of blood on his tongue and would love to chug water right now if it wouldn't make the blood drip quicker.

Although the nosebleed is painless, he feels dizzy with nausea as he watches the white tissue turn crimson under his fingers, the blood seeping underneath his fingernails.

Since he finds himself bound to his bed for an unforeseen length of time, Dylan decides to locate his fallen cellphone. Bending over to reach under his bed, Dylan's nose protests by running even more violently, making him grasp at several tissues to staunch the blood eager to drain out. In a desperate attempt to slow down the bleeding, he twists a wad of tissue and shoves it into his right nostril.

Feeling secure enough with his makeshift blockage, Dylan glances at the alarm clock stating it's now 7 a.m. He debates if it's too early to call someone, but decides to tap away on his phone, searching for George Feldman.

Detective Feldman has been on the case of the accident since day one and Dylan likes to check in from time to time to see if there's been any developments on his wife's case. He's always hopeful there will be news but, after all this time, he knows it's foolish to expect any.

Dylan's called the man so often that he's memorized the detective's number. Still, he prefers using the contact page on his phone, not wanting to risk embarrassment—given his past experience with memory loss and forgetting digits.

Fumbling with the phone now, he dials the number. He's about to tap the speaker button when a gruff voice answers.

"Detective Feldman speaking."

Although their relationship is strictly professional, Dylan has always wanted to be friends with George Feldman. He was the only one who had expressed interest in Dylan's account of the day's events. He'd been particularly interested in the strangeness of the accident and the car's brake lights that Dylan had noticed before losing consciousness.

Detective Feldman had been curious enough to press further, to ask different questions. He'd tried to make sense of it from every possible angle. Had the driver stopped to check on them? Who had called for an ambulance?

The call had come from an anonymous caller using a phone that was no longer in service. There were still questions that hadn't been answered regarding this case. The biggest one was, of course, who was responsible.

"Hi, George. It's Dylan Thomas," he replies sheepishly, doing his best to keep his voice normal, despite the tissue plugging up his nose. "Just checking in again."

He feels bad. He hates who he's become. A lonely man, a desperate man. He can't shake the need for justice that brews deep within him. He won't rest until he finds out who's responsible for his wife's and unborn baby's deaths. Every instinct in his body tells him it was a deliberate act. But who would ever want to harm his sweet and beautiful Maddison? Everyone loved her.

She'd been so popular in high school. Athletic, funny, and intelligent. And she'd been well-liked amongst the other parents at their sons' school—such a dedicated friend and wife.

He can't imagine someone wanting to hurt her.

Yet there has been a nagging doubt creeping its way to the surface. It's nothing much really. Just a tiny doubt that his wife's past wasn't completely innocent. It's small, like a splinter of wood in a finger—but hard to ignore.

He had been shocked by some of the comments he'd seen on social media from her high school peers after the accident, calling her a bully, saying she got what she had coming. But did anyone deserve to die? No one was perfect after all. What gave them the right to judge others when they weren't innocent themselves? Everyone had a past. Everyone has something they're not proud of, but surely no one deserves to die?

The detective sighs loudly in the phone as he automatically uses the same line Dylan's heard often. "Nothing yet, but we'll keep looking."

Dylan knew that it meant there was no more hope, and he was on his own.

31

DYLAN

Dylan hangs up the phone, disappointed. As his nosebleed seems to be remaining at bay for the time being, he decides to go for a drive to clear his head, but also to grab a much-needed dose of caffeine. He will try to get ahead of his migraine today and if he's really lucky, he'll be able to avoid it altogether.

He writes a text to Sam taking longer than he cares to admit typing out the simple message. He lets him know that he's going for a drive and will be back later. Not that Sam cares about his father's activities, but Dylan likes to tell the boys when he'll be away just in case they start worrying or they need something.

Knowing how late Sam came home last night, he expects he will make it back before his son wakes up.

Dylan runs a hand through his greying hair as he grabs his prescription shades off the entrance mirror. Even though he knows no one notices him much these days, he still likes to feel protected behind the shades, his sorrow and tiredness hidden.

Dealing with funeral arrangements, insurance claims, and obtaining a death certificate while working through his own recovery, grieving and trying to hold it together for the boys, took a toll on his health. His skin is rough and he constantly looks dehydrated—probably because he is. He mainly survives on strong black coffee and rye. His diet lately has consisted almost exclusively of burgers and donuts.

He doesn't even recognize himself.

No wonder his sons treat him differently nowadays. Dylan doesn't even respect himself—why would they?

He staggers down the front steps and locks the house behind him before double-clicking the key fob to unlock the car doors. Even though he's the sole passenger today, decades of unlocking all the doors for a family of four is a habit he hasn't yet quit. He settles into the warm car, thankful to be early before the heat of the day weighs down on him.

He starts the car, his Chevy Cruze LS humming to life. Rolling the windows down, Dylan risks breathing in with his fragile nose, not caring the least bit if it starts to bleed again. He's usually got two boxes of tissues floating around the backseat of the car. The air in the car is stale from the heat, the pine air freshener long since dried up.

He can feel the sting of the hot windowsill on his arm. The sun beats on the grey hood of the car. It will be sweltering in a matter of minutes. Dylan cranks the cool air. Even though his windows are down, he sets the air conditioner knob to the max. Indulgent. That's how he feels today. Readjusting himself in his seat, his thin shirt does a poor job of masking his pudgy waist. He can barely stand to look at his growing stomach, therefore he doesn't. He just lives with it, ignoring its existence.

He's tired of feeling sorry for himself.

Last night had been a wake-up call. It hadn't occurred to him just how paranoid and anxious he'd become, how much he'd lost control of his life until he had almost hit his own son.

That couldn't happen again. Not ever.

Dylan grips the steering wheel tightly as he curves it to the right and onto the dry pavement. He'd lost the love of his life on a day similar to this, years ago. The sun had been warm and bright, glaring on the dry pavement.

Dylan remembers how focused he'd been at the time, how stuck in his own head he could be back when he had everything, when his life revolved around his job or his status. Since losing Maddison, his job hadn't seemed all that important. It paid the bills. What was the point of getting up the ladder and being successful when you had no one to enjoy it with?

With his shades snug on the bridge of his nose, Dylan sniffles softly, careful not to aggravate his fragile nose once more. The dry heat makes it worse. The cool air isn't working quickly enough, and Dylan can feel a ring of sweat building under one of his stomach rolls. He winces at the thought. How disgusting he is.

He absentmindedly plays with the gold ring on his wedding finger. He's never removed it. Even after the funeral, it hadn't felt right. The ring was all he had left. This and the boys, of course.

He feels so ashamed by how distant he'd been in his marriage in the years before the accident. He regrets all the times he chose work over her.

He'd been such a prick.

So prideful and arrogant, thinking his work made him who he was. Hindsight's 20/20, or something like that. It had all been devastatingly clear after Maddison's death that Dylan had been wrong in his priorities. Where had work been the last few years, those esteemed colleagues who couldn't live without him? He could count on one hand how many of them had made an appearance at Maddison's funeral. Even fewer had called in the weeks following, and only one had brought over a casserole dish for Dylan and the boys.

He'd since vowed never to allow a workplace to take anything more away from his life. It was a place to earn a living, not a place to make a life. He'd give anything for just one more day with Maddison.

He misses her dearly. He often thinks of her curly, blond hair skimming across her face that day, how he'd longed to reach out and touch it, tuck a strand behind her ear. He'd been too focused on the bike ride, too busy to show his wife what she'd meant to him.

He'd never liked being affectionate in public back then. If Maddison were here today, he wouldn't hesitate to grab her and plant a kiss on her lips in the middle of the road. He grieved all those wasted opportunities he hadn't realized he'd never get again. He'd taken her for granted and hated himself for that now.

Once Dylan had gotten the okay from his doctor to drive again, he'd started going for drives on the weekend to clear his head, to get fresh air. Mostly, he'd been looking for his revenge. As he went driving today, like during all those previous weekends, he kept looking for that red car.

32

Quinn has been finding it difficult since William left to join the fight against the massive fires in British Columbia. When William had first told her he'd been asked to go to fight fires far away, Quinn's chest had tightened so much, she half expected it to implode. She hadn't felt confident in her abilities as she'd been battling with her mental health these last few months.

She hadn't been sure she had it in her. The idea of doing both the morning and evening routine with Cole had stressed her out. She hadn't slept for days before William left. She hadn't been sure how she'd be able to pull it off.

William had been so excited about the opportunity. He'd talked her ear off about what an amazing chance this would be for him. *An experience of a lifetime,* he'd said. That and a little bit of extra money to help them pay some of the school bills that had been piling up. A few months in exchange for a year of financial security.

Quinn had dreaded the idea of William leaving the moment he'd first brought it up. She'd only imagined the long, sleepless nights when she'd be alone cradling her screaming child, bouncing him from room to room. Without William around to offer support, or to take over when she'd had just about enough, she expected she would just crack.

Quinn didn't have very many people to lean on or to talk to as it was. With William gone, she has kept mostly to herself, except for a few outings a week, but even then, she rarely interacts with others. She's never been the kind of person to go out of her way to make friends.

She blames this on her lack of confidence, a flaw she never used to mind much, until now when she needs a friend to talk to. Other than Lena and Rose, Quinn has barely talked to anyone else since moving here. Her friends back home are too busy with their families—they wouldn't have time for her.

Quinn reminds herself of why they'd moved here. She really wants to support William, but with him away, she's finding it harder to keep up the facade. The truth is that being here scares the crap out of her.

It's not the first time Quinn's been here.

She'd never told William, didn't dare to mention it. She's so embarrassed by her past, so tortured by her behaviour that she can't risk telling William the truth about what she's done. About who she is.

This is one of those secrets she will take with her to the grave. William must never know or else he'd never look at her the same way again. Quinn shudders at a memory she'd long ago learned to push to the back of her mind. It's the only way she can move on with her life although she finds it difficult to carry on, pretending all is well with the world when she remembers so clearly what she did. The memory of that day still haunts her.

She understands evil better than most. She's seen it. She's done it. If it's in her, then Quinn believes that it's in everyone. A split second, a chance, a choice. To choose what's easy or what's difficult. To tell or to stay quiet. To come clean, or to keep hiding, while working so hard to forget.

No one in this world is completely pure. Everyone's screwed up in their own way. Quinn knows this. That's what she tells herself over and over. Yet, it doesn't change how she feels about herself. It doesn't stop her conscience from nagging at her. Since meeting William, she hasn't thought about that time as much. And as he doesn't know about that part of her past, Quinn can't talk to him about it. She wouldn't dare bring it up.

Quinn has somehow managed to block away most of the memory, effectively enough for it to seem like a long-ago forgotten nightmare. Yet she still has to deal with the flashbacks and the disturbing images that come to her regularly, changing her mood abruptly, souring even her happiest days.

A screeching tire in the distance or the resonating sound of a hammer hitting a nail can set her off. She has an aversion to red nail polish, is terrified of spilling some on the table, the sticky mess reminding her of something she's worked so hard to forget.

Some reminders were unavoidable. She was constantly on edge and paranoid. She isn't sure how she manages to live with herself, but here she is. How come she gets to have a child and a husband when she doesn't deserve any of it?

The accident with Cole in the winter months had spun her carefully woven life completely out of control.

She's tried her hardest to hold her secrets close to her chest, like a delicate vase. She's been so worried about what truths might come to light that she has squeezed tighter and tighter. She risks hurting herself, the glass beginning to crack under her grip. She fears her secrets being exposed and doesn't know how to stop.

All the fight had left her when she'd seen Cole in the hospital. She hadn't had the strength to fight off the memories anymore. They were still there like a shoebox of pictures just waiting to be opened. Cole's overdose had done just that—had brought it all back to her.

Quinn lives with the shame of her actions from that day long ago when she'd been so young and so afraid.

She'd been at the wrong place at the wrong time, some might say. Still, Quinn had had a part in it. She should have been more responsible. She could blame her age at the time to explain her actions, but she'd known full well that what she'd done was wrong. Anyone would know that. And yet, she'd done it anyway. She'd given in to the impulse, taken the easy way out of a sticky situation. And because of it, two people were dead.

33

QUINN
AUGUST 13TH, 2014

She struggles to place Cole in the car's bucket seat, his writhing body kicking and wiggling under her touch. He's never been fond of the seat, and in this heat, Quinn can't blame him, although she is quickly losing patience. She shuts the rear door of their car, carefully watching that Cole's flailing feet aren't extended and might somehow get pinched in the door. She runs on empty most days, but today she somehow feels even worse. She's never done well with heat.

Today is her grocery day. Even though Quinn is on maternity leave and could easily take advantage of going to the grocery store any day of the week, she still chooses to go on Saturdays. It might be out of habit, but mainly she enjoys feeling like a normal person, surrounded by other shoppers busy with their thoughts.

She loves to people-watch and imagine other shoppers' lives as they buy their food for the week. She enjoys guessing what people will buy. It's a game she plays with herself. Will the man with the prim goatee standing at the meat counter order a fillet of the fresh salmon or a slab of the finest AAA rib eye steak? She doesn't win anything when she gets it right. Nothing other than the small satisfaction that she's right about people. That she can know something about someone just by taking one look at them.

The other shoppers don't need to know she's been planning her grocery trip for days now, making one list after another, categorizing items by grocery, produce, dairy, etc. She's crossed and crumbled many lists before ending up with this final one she holds in her hand. For all they know, she's been just as busy as they have and wrote it that same morning. They don't need to know that she's cooking for two instead of three most days, or that she's lost all interest in food. That what she craves the most these days is caffeine.

With Cole eating mainly solid food these days, Quinn's constantly surprised by how excited she is at the prospect of having a decent cup of coffee. Without having to worry as much about her daily caffeine intake, she's finding happiness in this simple pleasure. A step forward, a glimmer of hope that one day, she'll be back to her old self.

Today she's making that small step. It doesn't matter that it's blisteringly hot outside, she's determined to get that long-awaited cup of coffee. She deserves this.

She climbs into the car and sits on the sizzling seat, wiping a bead of sweat from her brow. Frowning, she taps at the control panel. The AC doesn't seem to be working properly these days. She makes a mental note to book the car into a repair shop soon but dreads the thought of a steep bill. With William's school costs and her being on employment insurance, they don't have extra money for unplanned expenses like this.

She hopes William's work in B.C. will bring in some much-needed cash flow. They are both working extra hard and she hopes it will be worth their while.

Cole's face is red from the heat and Quinn lowers the windows to let the faint breeze cool them. She places the diaper bag on the passenger seat and backs down the driveway.

She can't help it if she feels deep in her soul that this place is judging her, too. She's pushed the uneasiness far from her mind, but the symptoms have come crawling back to the surface. Her demons don't take pity on her. They thrive on making her uncomfortable, keeping her up at night, torturing her with worry. They are eager to make themselves known, yet Quinn is determined to keep them hidden.

Whether it was the heat or just the accumulating exhaustion, Quinn has been feeling herself losing control these days. She's under the strong impression that everyone can see right through her. That they know she's falling apart. She doesn't hide her emotions well and she's had a hell of a time lately getting a grip on them. She's let her anxiety turn into aggression, especially when it comes to Cole.

The growing guilt over how she's so quick to snap at Cole is emphasized by the dreadful passing of time that results in no new evidence, making her both grateful and edgy.

She's walking on eggshells, trying to blend in and not draw any attention to herself, but she's not sure she's pulling it off. She might be paranoid, but she can't help the creeping feeling that someone is watching her. She feels eyes boring into the back of her head. She feels it in the way the stray hairs on her neck stand up at random.

She's not sure how long she'll be able to keep this up.

She's already on antidepression medication and knows all the anxiety regulation techniques, yet she's aware that the only way to rid herself of the weight of her secret is by spilling the truth, as ugly and as wrong as it is. She needs to own up to her mistakes and suffer the consequences so that the guilt will finally vanish and turn to forgiveness. She wants to be free from it. She doesn't want it hanging over her head anymore.

She feels wrong, all wrong. It's as though the entire world knows what she's done, conspiring against her, pushing her over the edge, trying to force it out of her. She's started checking behind her more often, walking around the house at night locking the doors repeatedly, just making sure. The beating in her chest resonates loudly in her ears.

In the mornings when she wakes at the crack of dawn, she feels as though even the crows are laughing darkly at her pathetic attempt at living a normal life. She realizes that coming clean would be terrible, life-altering, and most definitely relationship-damaging, and she can't imagine ever disappointing William. She wouldn't be able to bear the look of shock on his face. How he would undeniably look at her differently if she ever told him.

No. She can't do that.

She would rather suffer the consequences of her guilt in silence, rather than be freed by speaking the horrible truth out loud.

She convinces herself that she's lying for Cole. She doesn't want to lose him and she doesn't want him to grow up knowing his mother's past. Not the real one anyway. Only the rather carefully dissected version of it she chooses to share with him. She wants him to respect and love her, to grow to appreciate all the sacrifices she's made, all the doting she's done.

Quinn wants to be remembered for the good she's done for Cole, not the bad. What kind of mother does what she did?

Sure, she'd been younger then, but hadn't she had any moral compass at all? Nothing guiding her in the right direction? She supposed there had been one all along. Maybe she'd just chosen to ignore it. Her choice—the wrong one.

Her guilt has been eating her alive, terrorizing her nights, suffocating her days. The loss of control over every aspect of her life since moving here and staying home with Cole has increased her anxiety levels and makes it difficult to keep moving forward. It's been hard to envision a future—to imagine doing this, day-in, day-out.

The mind-numbing routine makes her grit her teeth and makes her want to pull her hair out. There's no easy road to take. Come clean and be free, yet lose everything and everyone she loves, or keep the secret close, remaining unhappy and tormented, but safe.

She knows she has to stay strong for Cole, but on the other hand, she wants to give up, turn herself in. She wishes for it to be over, for the truth to come out. Looking up at the imposing white house, she can't help but shudder. The fear of being caged mixed with the relief of everything being exposed and out in the open is overwhelming and complicated.

But she knows she has to come clean. It will be better coming from her than being found out, she rationalizes. She still has the opportunity to right a wrong.

She checks the rearview mirror, taking a long look at her son and makes a decision.

No more secrets.

34

QUINN

With her car windows rolled down, Quinn can't help but notice there's a faint odor of dog poop lingering somewhere nearby. This, mixed with the nauseating and strong smell of the pesky maggots filling her green bin in the garage, makes her almost get sick.

Quinn wrinkles her nose as the disgusting aroma fills her nostrils. She peers at Cole staring out of his open window with a certain air of curiosity, his nose barely reaching the bottom. He's apparently unaffected by the smell. She's amazed at how quickly he's growing these days.

Since he was born, her son has ranked on the higher end of the scale for weight and above average percentile for height. Some mornings, she's had to do a double-take because there's a noticeable difference in his height and the circumference of his head. She's been surprised more than once while struggling to fit a onesie over Cole's head, only to realize he's outgrown it overnight. She makes a mental note to look online later to buy some more clothes. She has a moment of panic when she imagines the talk she'll have to have with William later about the unexpected expense.

Money has been so tight lately.

Quinn sighs as she settles into her seat, making the car sway slightly. The car coasts smoothly down the driveway as she recites her grocery list out loud.

"Alright, Cole, can you help Mommy remember that we need bread, butter, eggs, milk, and cereal?" She glances in the rearview mirror, looking at his bright eyes, pretending he understands.

Maybe he does because, right at that moment, he smiles, his chubby cheeks like red apples.

"Do you want more avocados?" she inquires, knowing full well that he would very much like more avocados.

He had taken no time devouring the five she'd purchased last week. She needs to talk to fill the silence.

"How about some more bananas?" she adds, taking her eyes off the road once more to glance at her baby boy, enjoying their conversation.

Cole happily gabs away as the car's front right tire suddenly sinks into a large pothole and the entire car jerks. Quinn's backside lifts a few inches off her seat before slamming back down.

"Ouch!" she yelps. "What the heck was that?" Flustered, she fights with the steering wheel, the navigation almost impossible as she attempts to move over to the shoulder. Parking on the side of the road, she turns in her seat to find Cole unmoved, his eyes blinking in the sunrise. She can't believe he's not crying but is glad for it.

Quinn feels her blood pressure return to normal only to spike up again. What was that? Did she hit something? What happened?

She glances through the windshield for a hint but comes up empty. She turns the car off, leaving the windows down, and carefully looks out her window to see if there are any cars coming down the road before grabbing the keys and getting out of the car to inspect the vehicle.

It doesn't take Quinn long to discover what's happened. Her right front wheel is pointing in the wrong direction. The pothole must have caused it. She knows the car is useless and fumbles through the passenger window to grab her phone out of her purse to call William so that together they can discuss how to handle this.

Car repairs make Quinn extremely uncomfortable. The terminology, the mechanics of it, they go right over her head. William will know what to do. He'll be able to help her calm down.

Standing by her car, she feels the hot fumes radiating off of it, and she fans herself pointlessly. She's mortified by her look of a damsel in distress. Quinn sniffles back the runny nose threatening to come with the impending tears she's barely managing to hold back. She does her best to look confident and in control as she dials.

Who am I trying to impress anyway? she wonders.

After the third ring, the familiar sound of William's voicemail comes through the speaker. She relays the situation as calmly as she can possibly muster, and urges him to call her back soon.

Quinn stands by the car, cell phone in hand, as though William will call back right way, somehow sensing she needs him and check his phone at that exact moment. *What now?* She wonders.

Flustered, she doesn't notice her next-door neighbour standing a few feet away next to her flower garden, looking in her direction. Their gazes meet and the kind woman offers Quinn a sad smile. Her neighbour brushes her dirty gardening gloves on her beige pants and waddles over, her knee pads slowing her down.

"Are you ok, my dear?" she inquires. Mrs. Westover's sympathetic eyes seem to look through Quinn as they assess her.

Rattled by the heat and the embarrassment of her situation, Quinn replies, "I'm not sure. I think I hit that pothole back there. I must have been distracted or something. I usually go around it, but I hit it pretty hard. My right front wheel is completely crooked. I think it has to do with the axle?" Her tone is inquisitive, but she's sure Mrs. Westover doesn't know any more than she does about what's wrong with the car.

Mrs. Westover peers at the car behind Quinn, her head tilted slightly to look over her glasses, her sun hat blocking her eyes from Quinn slightly.

"Oh yes, that does look rather bad. I don't think a spare tire will be able to fix that mess." She laughs to herself.

Quinn doesn't think any of this is very funny, but perhaps she's being too sensitive because of their financial situation. She's already thinking of the large bill this new repair will bring, not to mention the towing fee to get it to a garage in the first place. Just one more thing to worry about. Will their insurance cover this kind of damage? Or a rental vehicle while theirs is being looked at? Not to mention the loss of freedom leaving the car at the garage will mean. All these questions and the intense heat are getting to her. Her head is beginning to swim, her brain foggy. Sweat is pouring down her forehead.

She needs to get Cole out of the sweltering car. She's not sure what she's going to do for groceries just yet, but she excuses herself to move over to his side of the car to get him out of his car seat.

Cole, content to be out and able to move his limbs, smiles happily up at her. When Quinn returns to the other side of the car, Mrs. Westover is swiftly removing her gardening gloves and gesturing at her to pass Cole over.

"Let me hold this sweet boy for you to give you a moment to think," the kind lady says, tutting lovingly at Cole.

Her son is enchanted by their neighbour's wide smile and eye contact, never steering from it. Watching them now, it's as though Quinn doesn't exist at all and they are the only two people in the world.

On one hand, Quinn is completely amazed. But on the other hand, something about their bond disturbs her. The ease this woman, a practical stranger, has with her son nags at her. It's like they have a connection that Quinn can't understand. A strong longing to share a closeness with her son overtakes her.

She feels her jaw clench as she watches them, Cole swaying gently in the woman's arms. A song on her neighbour's lips, entertains Cole for a few verses. Sometimes Quinn feels like Cole puts his best self forward for Mrs. Westover and that irritates and saddens her.

Her mood sour, she swallows her pride, attributing her son's interest in Mrs. Westover to her eye-contact and exaggerated facial expressions which animate her features like a cartoon character.

"You're too kind, Mrs. Westover. I don't even know where to start." Quinn hesitates as her gaze drifts back her broken car, looking pitiful on the side of the road.

The heat is getting worse and she still hasn't heard back from William.

"On top of everything, today is grocery day. We have nothing left in the house. And now I'm at a total loss of what to do." Exasperated and on the verge of tears, Quinn takes a deep breath, doing her best to regain her composure. She's never been one to outwardly express her concerns.

"Well, I'd be happy to give you a lift to town if you'd like," Mrs. Westover kindly offers, but just then, she lowers her head. "Oh dear, I've completely forgotten that I have the women's bible study this morning. I got so caught up in my gardening that the time just slipped right on by. My babies need so much time and care." She gestures to her beloved garden with her spare hand, the other holding on firmly to Cole.

Quinn always thinks it's odd of her to call her vegetables her babies, but the woman had never had children of her own, so this was how she coped with that. Mrs. Westover looks back at Quinn's car and a slow smile crosses her lips.

"You know what? I've got a spare car in the garage! I haven't taken it out for years, but you're welcome to it if you'd like. It might need some gas, but otherwise, it should do the trick." She winks at Quinn.

"Really?" Quinn can't believe her luck. "Are you sure you don't mind? It would be so helpful, at least until I can figure out what to do about this mess," she says pointing behind her to her Golf on the side of the road.

She knows she doesn't have the energy to deal with a towing company, a repair shop, and the insurance on an empty stomach. Getting the groceries done and food in the house will be the first step to helping her feel like she's getting a handle on the situation. Take care of her family first. Then deal with the car.

"Not at all! It's my pleasure!" her neighbour grins, happy to help out.

"Well, I don't know what to say. Thank you!" Quinn manages. "You're a lifesaver."

"More, right place, right time, I would say." Mrs. Westover shouts over her shoulder as she leads Quinn towards her garage, still holding onto Cole.

Quinn hears the woman singing a lullaby, but she can't make out the words. She feels herself shiver unexpectedly. She can't imagine what makes her do that, especially in this heat. She glances over at the garden Mrs. Westover was tending and tries to make sense of it. The flowers are all mixed together in one plot, spaced somewhat sporadically.

Quinn spies some black-eyed Susans, day lilies, pink peonies, blue sea holly, and purple bell flowers. She's struck by how beautiful the various colours look together, how the miss-match somehow makes sense, as though Mrs. Westover had known all along what the final result would be. Maybe she'd planned it to look like this all along.

Quinn is just beginning to think about asking Mrs. Westover for advice on her own sad, little excuse for a garden when she hears the faint groan of the garage door opening in the distance and turns her attention towards the house.

35

QUINN

Standing in front of her neighbour's garage, Quinn shifts uncomfortably. She can feel rings of sweat under her breasts. They are full and heavy—ready to burst at any moment. She needs to feed Cole soon.

She's surprised he hasn't started fussing yet. It's usually so easy to predict when the next feed is by Cole's cries that Quinn doesn't bother checking the time these days. Cole helps her stay on track. He is the ruler of their time, the dictator of when they eat, sleep, and even when she relieves herself. She lives her days on his schedule.

She only showers when Cole is having a good day or when he's asleep, and she only eats after Cole has finished his plate.

On any other day, a disturbance like this one would have set Cole off into full-on hangry mode. He normally would have been unsettled to the point that his breathing might have turned raspy from all his crying.

Quinn is relieved that today doesn't seem to be one of those days. The good days are few and far between, yet she's beginning to see a few more the older her son gets. This good streak won't last long though because Cole is teething right now and hasn't been getting the same quality of sleep.

It's just a matter of time before he realizes they're late for snack time. The baby crackers she's packed in the diaper bag will have to do for now.

Once inside the garage, Mrs. Westover balances Cole on her left hip, stretching to find the hanging cord for the light above her head. She pulls and turns it on.

"Here it is," she announces proudly.

She directs Quinn towards the vehicle covered by a green tarp.

"As I mentioned, it's been sitting in here for quite some time," she admits with a grim look on her face. "But you're welcome to it."

She motions for Quinn to remove the tarp to expose the car, Quinn feels slightly uncomfortable—it's covered in dust. Doing her best to avoid loose dirt landing on any of them, she lifts the material in one swift movement. Despite her earlier anxiety regarding driving someone else's vehicle, Quinn suddenly feels slightly exhilarated.

This is so far from her normal activities that she barely recognizes herself. She can't help but grin as the plastic tarp falls to the concrete floor in the garage revealing a shiny red sedan. The Corolla is in excellent condition and Quinn quickly relaxes. She can feel the inside of her palms drying and her heart rate settling back down.

Biting her lower lip, she can barely contain her excitement. She can't wait to hop in and take it for a drive. She can't believe the old woman's generosity.

"This is so great!" she finally exclaims. "I'll try it out today, and I'll let you know the minute I can get a rental or when I find out what's happening with the Golf. Thank you so much for this!" she adds with the best smile she can muster.

"There's no rush, dear," the woman waves a casual hand her way, still gazing admirably at Cole. "As you can see, it's not getting much use just sitting around here. It's yours for as long as you need it." She smiles warmly, and Quinn can't help but feel like all her troubles are melting away.

"Thank you so much, Mrs. Westover. I really owe you one," she promises.

"Let's see if it works first, shall we?" the woman laughs.

Quinn walks over to the driver's seat and notices the keys are sitting on the dash. She doesn't waste any time inserting the key and waits a moment before turning it all the way. She wonders if it will take a while to get the car running, or that if perhaps the battery is dead, however the car hums to life without a glitch.

There is almost a full tank of fuel in the car, and it appears to have been cleaned out before being tucked away all those years ago. Quinn is excited to try it out.

Mrs. Westover carefully steps away from the car to give Quinn enough room to reverse out of the garage.

When she's safely backed out of the tight door, Quinn rolls down the driver's window to let some air flow inside the car. The air conditioner is working hard to cool the interior, the outside heat only getting worse by the minute.

Quinn, almost skips back to the broken-down Golf, now abandoned on the shoulder, to grab Cole's car seat.

It's swelteringly hot to the touch and she yelps in pain as her fingertips touch the blistering metal. She puts her fingers to her mouth and sucks on them to help ease the pain, but it seems like the heat keeps burning through her skin even though she's removed her fingers.

She hurries to get the seat out, awkwardly walking back to the Corolla. The bucket seat is heavier than she remembers. She must be getting weaker.

She really needs to eat better.

Cole seems to read her mind and begins to wiggle in Mrs. Westover's arms. Before they can be delayed any longer, Quinn straps the seat safely into the backseat and relieves Mrs. Westover by taking Cole into her arms and strapping him into the car as best she can.

She's careful not to hit her head on the car door as she gets in since it's slightly lower than what she's used to. Cole starts fussing more profusely and Quinn feels impatience building inside of her.

"In a few minutes, Cole. I just need a few more minutes," she says in the calmest voice she can muster.

She turns around just in time to see Mrs. Westover's troubled expression but forces a smile so the woman doesn't worry. Quinn pretends to have it all under control, as though this is no big deal. She adjusts the rearview mirror and her seat.

"Thanks again!" She waves at the woman as she shuts the window and puts the car in reverse.

Using the rearview mirror and side mirrors to guide her, she has a hard time focusing with Cole's screams taking so much space in the car.

They drive past her broken car and the anxiety quickly returns. How will she fix this? She has no idea where to start. She risks a quick look at her phone siting in the car's cup holder, but William still hasn't called her back. She sighs. She will just have to figure this one out on her own.

36

QUINN

The grocery store is less than ten minutes away. The glare of the warm sun is bouncing off the freshly paved road and hitting Quinn right in the eyes. She forgot her sunglasses in the Golf so she needs to make the best of it for now until she can get back to it.

She's surprised at how comfortable she already feels in this borrowed car. Normally the thought of driving someone else's car would make her feel so anxious, but when Quinn rolls the window down and feels the air flow through the car and her hair, she casts her worries away. She feels good—so good that she decides to let her hair loose, out of its top bun prison.

Driving the car gives her an independence she didn't know she'd been craving. It makes her feel unstoppable, free. She wants to close her eyes under the sun's rays and rest for a while even though she can't.

She would love nothing more than to lie on her back and allow the warm sun to glow over her skin until it shines like thousands of tiny diamonds. But unfortunately, Quinn's skin is so pale that she easily burns any time she stays in the sun for too long.

Since she spends most of her time indoors, instead of the tanned version of herself she often dreams of, she looks more like a horror movie character with her long, dangly, overgrown, black hair and her white, porcelain skin.

She pulls herself out of her daydream and snaps down the sun visor to help her see the road ahead. She's quite proud of herself for becoming so familiar with this town in such a short time. Without William chauffeuring her around and driving all the time, she's been forced to push past her comfort zone and familiarize herself with the new roads.

"Here we are," she exclaims as she rolls up the window and carefully finds a large enough parking spot, somewhere between the cart parking and the grocery store entrance. She has a habit of sitting in her car for several minutes rifling through papers, packing snacks in the diaper bag, and counting her money, but she skips that today. It's too warm to sit in the car as the heat takes over quickly.

"Do you remember what we need to buy today, little guy?" she asks her son as she pulls him carefully from the car. Leaving the car seat behind, she carries him in her arms through the automatic doors where a rush of cold air conditioning barrages them at the entrance.

He's grown so much lately that Quinn is able to sit him straight into the grocery cart seat. He's quite happy to sit there and lean over the handrail to chew the plastic handle as best as he can. Quinn used to find it disgusting, but after the fifth time or so of him doing it, she'd given up. She draws the line at dropping his soother on the dirty floor. That she will always clean, but there are other things she's more lenient with nowadays.

She reads the list out loud to Cole as she pushes the awkward cart along the produce bins.

"Bananas, apples, sweet potatoes, and avocados. We don't want to forget those, right?" She smiles as she kisses the top of his head.

She lives for moments like this.

Cole is content, sitting happily in the cart, keeping quiet, and Quinn is in charge and in control. She's elated that she can get her groceries done after all. It makes her feel like she can conquer anything. She's quite pleased with how she's handled this latest crisis and how she's still getting her chores done on time. All without William's help.

Thirty minutes later, Quinn is standing at the check-out, desperately looking for a snack for Cole, who must have sensed the fun cart ride nearing an end since he's suddenly decided to throw a fit. He grabs at her loose hair insistently, and his cries pierce the silence around them.

Frustrated and feeling everyone's judgmental stares on her, she grabs the hair tie on her wrist and twists her mane back in a top bun before gathering her money. She's ashamed and disappointed that she hasn't been able to have just one outing without an outburst from Cole.

"Just one minute, Cole," she hisses, impatience on her tongue.

She feels rushed, the intensity elevated by having to bag her groceries while simultaneously trying to pacify Cole. She haphazardly places the items into the plastic bags.

The bags are so thin, she's not convinced they will last the short walk from the car to the house. She's flustered by the looks of the other customers urging her to do something about her crying child, all the while praying she gets out of the store quickly.

She's trying to make everyone happy but nobody seems to be, least of all her.

"That will be $234.40" repeats the cashier, hand extended, expectant.

The cashier, Barb, is arrogantly looking down at Quinn as though she's the scum of the earth. Seeing Quinn struggling, her bra strap falling down her bicep limiting her movements, Barb smirks at the bad packing job, offering no help. Although Quinn smiles politely, her insides are fuming. She wants to tell this lady to mind her own business, but she doesn't.

She can't bear the idea of yelling or even being rude to a worker in front of her son. Not so much for what it might do to Cole, but more so for what other customers would think of her as a mother. She wants to look like other mothers who seem to find motherhood a natural, peaceful change in their already perfect lives.

It seems every other new mom in the store has everything under control. Their babies are as happy as can be. They giggle and smile at strangers, they don't seem fussy or hungry at every possible moment, and they are always well-dressed.

Lately, Quinn has been skipping laundry day a little too frequently, leaving her and Cole wearing the same outfits for days on end. She doesn't see the point in always trying to dress him up in cute clothes when he's bound to throw up on them or have a diaper blowout at any moment. That, and they almost never leave the house. Still, she finds she's envious of the moms with well-dressed children, a vanity she doesn't seem able to shake.

Feeling the stares of strangers boring into the back of her head, she pays for her groceries and books it out of the store without looking back. It takes her a moment to remember what the borrowed car looks like, but then she spots it. Someone has wedged their vehicle so close to hers, she can't imagine ever being able to open the rear door wide enough to buckle Cole inside.

"Crap," she mumbles under her breath.

She'll have to scoot through the other side to strap him in his bucket seat through the other door.

She struggles to get the grocery cart near enough to the trunk to place the groceries inside. Quinn is careful not to touch the red paint, the colour and the heat reminding her too much of a big bonfire.

Suddenly, she finds herself craving s'mores. Maybe the next time William comes home, they could have a nice campfire in the backyard and roast some marshmallows. The idea of seeing William soon makes her relax and slowly forget about the stressful incident in the store.

Quinn leans over to start the car and gets the cool air flowing through the vehicle. She pops the trunk and begins loading the thin plastic bags in the back. As she loads, she realizes she's packed her eggs on top of her bread, squishing the entire loaf. She closes her eyes, annoyed at her carelessness, yet pride makes her continue loading the car as though nothing is wrong.

She's sweating and irritated beyond measure, embarrassed and disappointed that even in a small town such as this, people don't seem to have much respect for new mothers. Surely some of the judgemental women in the store had once been new mothers themselves? They could have given her understanding looks, nods of approval, some sort of help, but no. She'd been left to fend for herself.

She shuts the trunk with a little more force than she intends, startling Cole, making him cry out at the loud noise. She can feel her chin trembling slightly.

Keep it together, she wills herself.

Driving back to the house, she wishes she had a friend to visit right now. Someone to call on when things got tough. William isn't much help these days. His phone reception has been too spotty to talk. Quinn is desperate for someone, anyone, to talk to. She feels so alone these days. Even with Cole strapped to her hip most hours of the day, she's never felt lonelier in her entire life.

When she drives up the driveway, she lets out a long breath. She needs to muster enough energy to do this next part—the unpacking. Something she used to enjoy with all the organizing and time-consuming tasks to make the day fly by faster now just seems like a chore. All she really wants to do is to take a nap on the couch and disappear.

37

QUINN

Quinn has indents on her fingers from holding on to the heavy grocery bags. She tries to do the fewest trips possible when bringing in groceries, even if her hands protest in the process. She's always been that way, never one to waste time, even though all she has is time to waste.

Feeling the sweat under her armpits, she settles Cole down in front of her on the kitchen floor with some toys to keep him entertained. Turning her attention back to the bags, she places the dairy and meat inside the refrigerator and forces herself to stretch out the chore as much as she can, trying in vain to burn the day away. But she's too efficient for her own good.

Seeing as she hasn't yet heard from William, she decides to call Lena while she finishes placing the canned goods in the cupboard. Cradling her cell phone on her shoulder, she waits two rings before hearing Lena's cheerful voice on the other end.

"Hi Quinn! How are you?" Lena sings.

"Doing great, and yourself?" inquires Quinn, always polite.

Lena and Quinn have been spending more time together since their yoga class excursion. They've found other activities they both enjoy. From time to time Lena invites Quinn and Cole over for tea and then a walk in the neighbourhood so that the women can talk while Cole falls asleep in the stroller. They usually stop at a bench in a nearby park and sit down for a few minutes before returning to the house and parting ways.

Today, however, Quinn doesn't really feel like heading out again after her morning misadventures. Instead, she's just looking to talk to someone and not feel so alone for a moment.

Lena rambles on about her new love of using essential oils at home, some blend called 'Energize Me', telling Quinn she needs to look into it for herself, saying it's a life-changer. She speaks very clearly when she says this, and Quinn thinks she's trying to emphasize the change needed in Quinn's life.

"So what's going on, girl? I'm sure you didn't call to hear me talk about oils!" Lena laughs.

"No, you're right." She sighs, turning to glance at Cole. "I'm just having a rough day. The car broke down and today was grocery day. We had nothing to eat in the house, so I really needed to go out to get some. Mrs. Westover was kind enough to lend me a spare car she happened to have in the garage."

She tries to sound positive and encouraged, but Lena, ever so observant, presses her. She can tell by Quinn's tone that there's something else she wants to say.

"And, what else?" Lena questions.

"Well, I just wish William were here to help me deal with some of this. I swear, sometimes I feel like I'm a single mom!" she feels her voice quiver. "I know that sounds terrible. I'm so grateful for how hard William is working for us and for the fact that I'm able to stay home. I know so many women would love to have the opportunity to do this." She pauses before adding, "I just wish Jake had waited a bit longer before sending William on that assignment. At least until Cole was one or something, you know? Sorry, I know this is awkward—me complaining to you about your husband."

Quinn can hear water running in the background. She imagines Lena pouring water from the tap into her fruit infuser bottle, wearing tight leggings and a tank top, her hair in a high ponytail.

"Well, I understand that. You are doing almost everything while William's away. That's hard! It's a lot to ask of a person," she sighs. "But I think you have it wrong," she adds carefully. "William practically begged Jake for that out-of-town assignment."

She pauses for a moment before continuing.

"I remember that night. Jake had come home stunned by William's eagerness to take that assignment. He wasn't nearly qualified enough, but he seemed eager to learn. Jake questioned him many times to make sure he was certain you and Cole would be okay during his absence, and William assured him that you were on board," Lena continues hesitantly, suddenly nervous.

Quinn feels like a bucket of ice has been dumped down her back. William wanted to leave? He asked to leave them? But why? It doesn't make any sense.

"I don't understand," she finally utters, unable to think of anything else to say.

"I don't know what to tell you. I'm sorry! I didn't mean to stir up anything. I thought you knew." Lena speaks quickly now, clearly uncomfortable having unveiled this lie to her friend. Quinn hears Lena biting her nails through the phone.

"No, it's ok, it's not your fault. I must have heard him wrong back then or something. You know, mom brain!" Quinn quickly makes light of it and tries to justify the lie and cover for her husband.

Inside she's crumbling, tearing at the seams.

She quickly chitchats her way to the end of the conversation with Lena, pretending that it's time to feed Cole and hangs up. She grips the counter, steadying herself, her phone face down on the counter, as she tries to wrap her mind around this news.

It must have been a simple misunderstanding. Surely her husband wouldn't have left her alone by choice? So soon after her suicide attempt?

No, that can't be right, she decides.

She resigns herself to asking William about it when they speak next. He will explain everything, clear things up and all will be good again.

38

DYLAN
AUGUST 13TH, 2014

Time stands still. He's holding his breath despite the violent pounding in his heart begging for release. Dylan waits patiently in his car down the street, careful not to be seen. His clenched palms are sweaty and he's perspiring profusely from his forehead and underarms. His golf shirt has a circle of sweat on the back, but he doesn't care.

He's found it. He's found her.

Somehow all these years, Dylan had always assumed a man had caused the accident. But he's acutely aware now that he's not at all surprised to find out it's a woman who drives this car. Maddison had told him about how some girls from her past had been jealous of her popularity. He feels warm tears escaping from his eyes as he looks on at the woman in the parking lot.

———

Just like every Saturday since his release from the hospital, Dylan stops at the coffee shop across the street from his house, before heading down the rest of HWY 17. He has a large printout of a map posted on the wall of his bedroom showing everywhere he's searched. Every Saturday the route he's taken over the years is marked with a red Sharpie pen line.

He knows this map by heart. It rests on the wall opposite the bed so that he sees it every night before going to sleep. He looks at it every day—that and a picture of Maddison in an expensive silver, engraved frame he had made after her funeral.

Her smiling face stares back at him from the nightstand. He's placed it on her side of the bed, as though she's still there.

It's sad really, but everyone copes differently with grief. He's been in the anger phase for quite some time, unsure if he'll ever move on from there. This map has helped him deal with the blinding rage inside of him. It keeps him focused and grounded. It gives him purpose. Without this motivation staring at him every morning, he wouldn't have the strength to get on with his days. He's already lost so much.

————

He'd been close to turning around and heading on home, when the sunshine gleamed down on the red car. It looked brand new, as though it had just been through the car wash—like it was under a spotlight just for him. *Here I am*, it seemed to call out to him, begging to be seen.

At first, he hadn't believed it. Yet, after all this time, he'd finally found it.

He's found *her*.

Part of him is convinced his memory is wrong. That the car must have been a different colour, his memories distorted with time and as a result of the concussion. He's trailed dozens of red cars since the accident, but none of them had any identifying marks of a collision.

A car isn't that hard to hide when you need to keep it away from prying eyes. He'd been close to giving up the search, assuming the car had been fixed up at a body shop, but now he was glad he'd persisted.

He understands now that enough time has passed since the accident to make this woman feel safe enough to take it out again. She probably didn't think anyone was still looking for it.

But here he is.

He's been waiting for his wife's killer to make a mistake, sitting in his car with his hot coffee grasped tightly in his hand burning the pads of his fingers, his eyes squinting at the glaring sun bouncing off the smooth black pavement. His shades give him a casual look, while inside he's brewing. The AC in his car blares, cooling his skin, making it easier to drain the hot liquid in his cup.

His stomach is in knots. Hope has returned, and with it, a fresh new wave of anger. He's felt it many times over the years, always different, always associated with painful memories. But not today. Today, the sadness is quickly replaced with a need for vengeance.

Dylan watches the woman across the street, holding her little baby boy in her arms. Her movements are rough and almost robotic. Her mind seems to be elsewhere. From his point of view, the woman looks almost frustrated with the baby. This makes his skin tingle.

How dare she?

She took away his wife and unborn child. She's made a life for herself, avoiding any repercussions and has had a baby of her own only to resent it.

When the woman gets into her vehicle and starts for the road, he doesn't hesitate. He follows her.

He hasn't come this far, after so many years, only to spot the car and the person he's been searching for, and to let her get away. Not when he's so close.

He tails her for a few minutes through the town until she turns right onto a country road. They drive over train tracks and she keeps going. Either she knows she's being followed and is leading him astray or she lives here. Dylan doesn't remember ever coming down this way before.

He hadn't thought anyone actually lived down here, therefore he usually skips over it on his map. The road is surrounded by acres of forest. If he weren't following his wife's killer, he would actually slow down to enjoy the scenery. He can appreciate how peaceful it would be to live out here.

Furious, it takes everything in him to keep his pace steady so as not to give away his position. Resentment swells within him as he watches the red car slow down significantly, and finally take a sharp left down a cul-de-sac.

Dylan allows more space between them. They are the only two cars on the street and he would be seen fairly easily if she were paying attention. He decides to pull over to the side of the road in front of another driveway several houses down.

He hasn't thought about his next move or what he will do when the woman gets to her house. He wants to observe her without being seen. He's never thought to practice what to do if he found that car.

For a long time, he's come up empty-handed—years of searches yielding no results. His frustration has festered as his hope dwindled with each passing day.

Until now.

Dylan's skin tingles and his leg bounces nervously on the floor of the car as he puts the vehicle in park. He grabs aimlessly at an abandoned fast food coupon flyer. Something to stare at so that if the woman catches sight of him, she won't suspect anything.

Dylan hasn't felt this energized or this nervous since his wedding day. He's agitated and biting ferociously at a cuticle on his index finger, pulling hard, making it bleed. He sucks the blood off his finger and looks over the flyer hesitantly when there is a sudden, hard knock on his car window.

He jumps up in his seat, his shades falling down at his feet, startled by the sound and the small face staring at him through the window. It takes him a moment for his heart beat to settle before he can locate the automatic window button to roll it down.

"Hello?" he croaks, his throat dry from the scare.

"*Bonjour*," the woman says as she eyes the inside of his car suspiciously. "Can I help you?" she offers, but not in a friendly manner. She's got a no-bullshit look to her that makes Dylan uncomfortable, feeling caught and exposed. He's been so concerned that the owner of the Corolla would notice him that he'd neglected to pay attention to her neighbours. Evidently, he hadn't stayed under the radar as he'd hoped.

He's relieved that this is not the same woman he's been following, but rather, a slightly older woman with auburn hair. She's sporting a baseball hat and a tight-fitting neon yellow tank top.

Just by looking at her, Dylan can tell that this woman is spunky and thrives on gossip. Apparently she also believes in keeping tabs on the comings and goings around here, greeting every new passerby. She must be one of those Neighbourhood Watch people. He despises her already.

Fumbling for an answer, he finally manages a warm smile as he holds up the now creased fast food flyer. "I was looking for this restaurant and I seem to have lost my way. I'm not from around here, so I think I must have made a wrong turn somewhere." He tilts his head sheepishly, turning on his charm, doing his best to appear lost and confused.

Unfortunately, his act is rusty and the woman's not buying it.

She's onto him. Her eyes instantly narrow, her lips purse. Dylan isn't sure if she will press him for the truth or call him out on his lie.

The woman glances down the street, trying to spot whatever it was that Dylan had been looking at, but she says nothing. She gives him a dirty look before answering him.

"All restaurants are found within the town lines. Make your way back to HWY 17 and keep driving west a few minutes. You can't miss them," she adds in a tone of indignation, her accent thick as she looks down her nose at him like he's the biggest idiot on the planet.

"Oh! Well, alright then. Thank you!" he replies with a fake salute.

What a self-righteous bitch, he thinks to himself.

Whoever said small-town people were friendly had never met her.

Reaching around his feet, he locates his shades only to notice a crack on the right lens.

"Shit," he mutters. "Great, just great."

Knowing he can't dwell on it now, not with the nosy woman glaring at him, Dylan reaches inside the glovebox to retrieve a spare set of regular glasses, a prescription off, that will have to do until he gets home.

Dylan makes a big show of turning the car around and drives back in the direction he came from. He's driving slowly looking in his rearview mirror trying to spot the red car. As luck would have it, he sees it parked in front of a tall, two-story, white siding house.

Perfect.

He will leave now so the Neighbourhood Watch patrol doesn't call in reinforcements, but he will come back later for a stake-out. He grabs the coupons on the seat once more and decides that he is, in fact, hungry for a juicy burger and salty fries.

What the hell, why not?

He'll need to eat if he's going to be watching the red car all day. He doesn't have a plan yet, but he's hoping one will form sooner rather than later.

Glancing at his cell phone in the cup holder next to his empty cup of coffee, he wonders if he should let Detective Feldman know he's finally found the car and the person responsible for his wife's death. Knowing he should leave it to the police, he can't bring himself to place the call. Part of him doesn't want to let go yet. He wants to see it through—to be certain.

Dylan decides to wait until he's had a closer look at the vehicle. He needs to be a hundred percent sure it's the same car.

39

SYLVIE

Sylvie walks briskly home. Her encounter with the stranger has left her blood pumping. Her ears are ringing as she walks inside and makes her way to the refrigerator to grab a bottle of carbonated water. Today's heat has her neck perspiring onto her thin gold chain. Even her ears are sweating. She can taste salt on her upper lip as she chugs the water.

She can't shake the feeling that the man was acting suspiciously. He'd been so startled by her presence. She's almost certain that he wasn't lost as he'd claimed, but had been on her road for a very specific purpose. But why?

Sylvie is sure she's never seen him before.

She keeps a pretty good log of the comings and goings of everyone on this street. Having lived here for many years, she makes it a point to meet every new neighbour and to be welcoming. And yet, her guard had gone up today.

There'd been something sinister about that man. Something was bothering her about his sudden appearance on her road. She didn't like the way she had caught him staring at the rental house down the street. The new family, the Millers, has a little boy just under a year old.

Sylvie feels her inner mama bear instincts kicking in as she taps her perfectly manicured fingernails on her granite countertop. The sight of her white kitchen cabinets helps her think more clearly. She does most of her thinking and plotting in this room. She knows every bit of gossip there is in this town, knows almost everyone who lives here.

She's mad at herself for not asking the man his name. She did make a note of the colour and make of the car, for future reference, but she's having trouble remembering the license plate number.

She'd taken a pretty decent look at the man and easily puts him in his sixties. She also speculates that he's enjoyed his fair share of burgers in his life. And he wasn't a good liar, that part was obvious.

She'd managed to startle the crap out of him by knocking on his car window. She felt pretty proud of that. There had been a strangeness about him, a look she'd recognized so well. He'd had a cloak of sadness and desperation filtering over his aging skin. She wondered what that was about. She'd seen that same look in herself before.

She crosses the kitchen, enters her office through the two adjoining French-doors, and settles down in her chair at her black espresso desk. She places her half-drained bottle of Perrier on a coaster decorated with an inspirational quote and begins rummaging through the drawers.

When she opens the top right one, her heart skips a beat. She pulls up a water-damaged photograph that's yellowed and curling at the corners. Her breath catches as she traces her fingers over the young boy in the picture. Her son, Martin, had only been five years old when this picture was taken. It captured the very first moment he'd held a fiddle, after receiving it as a birthday present from his parents.

Her eyelids flutter shut as she remembers. It had been a few weeks after that, when the accident had happened. She tries not to think too much about that horrific day when their lives were changed forever.

There was so much confusion, so many questions unanswered. Still, all these years later, Sylvie has a difficult time trusting others. She's never been able to prove her theory, but she was convinced that what happened had been no accident—that it had been pre-meditated.

Sylvie gets up from her chair slowly and leans on the window to look outside. The trees, now abundant with large green leaves, were doing their best to shade the thirsty grass. Seeing the look in that stranger's eyes today brought it all back to her. That need to know. The look of fear mixed with anger. The sudden knowledge that life isn't as perfect as it once might have been.

40

SYLVIE

All the benefits of her long, five-kilometre walk, have been completely erased by her encounter with the strange man. Sylvie peers out her office window and exhales, glad to see the stranger's car is gone.

The very fact that his face had reddened slightly and that he'd been ashamed, even momentarily, at being caught, told her he had some core values that aligned with her own. This man was going rogue. He was acting out of character, going on instinct. Sometimes that was just as dangerous as someone who took pleasure in breaking rules.

Sylvie lost her faith in humanity long ago. She's lost too much over the years.

Her divorce had been a nasty business. Her husband Paul had sprung it on her, shocked her by revealing the truth—his long-standing lies. Until that moment, she'd held him in high regard, but everything had come tumbling down when Paul had come clean about what he'd done.

The memory of it still stings. She picks away a loose piece of lint from her shirt. Since finding out the truth, Sylvie finds it hard to take things for what they appear to be.

Ever since Paul opened up to her, she's seen every hair, every speck of dust, every crumb and scratch on the floor. She can't just glide through life ignoring all these imperfections. Now nothing ever feels clean to her. All she ever sees is dirt, doubt, and guilt.

After Paul had told her about his affair, she'd developed some silly rituals in the shower to get clean, trying to rub away the other woman's memory from her mind. It didn't work, of course; all it accomplished was to make her skin raw and dry from all the scrubbing. As a last resort, she'd taken up walking.

Even though years have passed, she's kept up with her exercise. She really enjoys walking. It helps clear her head. The first half-hour is almost always about *her*—the woman her husband of twenty years had left her for—but then Sylvie's thoughts usually switch to more peaceful, enjoyable things. She tries to walk every day, if possible; it helps keep her sane and balanced. It keeps her focused on the present and emotionally available for her kids.

Without it, she'd be completely lost.

She gains most of her energy from her walks. You'd never know it to look at her, but she struggles to get out of bed every morning. She feels pathetic and calls herself terrible things: loser, failure, ugly, and *stupid*. She's not sure when she started thinking of herself in those terms, but it was probably around the time of the divorce.

———

She'd loved Paul with all her heart. They had been high school sweethearts. It had been a dream come true. Well, at least it had been for her. She'd felt like such an idiot when he'd blurted it out one night before bed. Of course, neither of them had gotten any sleep that night.

He'd claimed he hadn't meant to hurt her feelings, that he had needs. All the clichéd bullshit she'd seen in countless movies. She thought he was joking at first, couldn't believe this was happening to her. Then he'd grabbed a gym bag and started filling it with clothes, talking about going to sleep at a hotel until they sorted things out.

Sylvie had watched in disbelief as her husband of two decades had walked out of their bedroom, a bag over his shoulder, never looking back once. She'd felt as though he'd slapped her. She'd sunk into the bed, her mind spinning.

This can't be happening, she remembers thinking.

She'd felt as though she was going to be sick. Instead, she had gone to bed and tried to maintain a normal routine finding that sticking to one was important during moments of panic. It had helped her to keep moving forward, to deal with what she couldn't otherwise control. She couldn't stop her husband from walking out, but she could put herself to bed, even though she knew she wouldn't be falling asleep anytime soon.

The next morning, she'd woken up with a fresh resolve to forgive him. What was one little hiccup after twenty years of marriage? It was actually remarkable that this was all there had been. Only, when she'd called his cell phone to tell him the good news, he'd rudely interrupted her to say he had no interest in rekindling their love, but that he, in fact, wanted a divorce.

She had been so shocked that she'd abruptly hung up. This man had been by her side since high school. He'd been her best friend—how could he turn his back on her, on his family?

She'd started walking to cope with her emotions since she hadn't wanted her kids to see her cry. Maybe that had been wrong of her, but she'd always seen herself as a strong person, and she'd been raised to believe that if you cried, it made you weak.

She knows differently now, but her father's voice still echoes in her mind each time she lets a tear slip through her stone exterior. Instead of letting things get to her, she becomes chatty or makes jokes. So far it seems to be working.

It was only years after the divorce and many miles down the same stretch of road that she had started to realize how wrong her perception of her marriage had been. Where it had been perfect for her, it had been a living hell for Paul.

Part of her felt bad for him that he'd kept things inside for so long, never giving them a chance to work on whatever was troubling him. But then she realized that he'd had twenty-years to tell her how he felt, two decades to work together on what was wrong. But instead, he had gone looking for something new.

Looking back at the picture on her desk, she allows the tears to fall. She's alone in the house with no witnesses. She can truly let her emotions run through her. She hopes the tears will begin the healing process, but after so many years, she's not convinced letting them out helps much.

41

SYLVIE

If she thinks back, she can pinpoint the exact moment when things with her husband started going down the wrong path. It was a few weeks after Martin's accident when they hadn't agreed on how to handle the situation.

It had been the first time they hadn't seen eye to eye on something so crucial. It inevitably created a wedge between them that they'd tried hard to bridge with dinners out, expensive renovations, and splurging on their kids.

However, the damage had been done and no amount of money could fix it. It was a difference of opinion strong enough to break them apart. Their relationship was never the same after that, acting more like roommates and less like partners.

They'd still shared some laughs over the years, but the enjoyment had been forced. Everything had been executed to keep up appearances, to keep the peace. It had been all for nothing. They couldn't change what had happened. The hurt that was wedged between them had followed them into their bedroom. They hadn't been intimate for years.

Sylvie hadn't cared much about this, content to have a life partner with whom she could share her days. Unfortunately, her husband had thought differently.

———

The accident had happened after Martin's fifth birthday. Sylvie was busy at home, taking care of Frank, her two year-old toddler, and Martin. She'd been feeling overwhelmed and drained of all energy, so her friend Kim had recommended she find a daycare program for Martin for a couple of days a week to give her a break. That would allow her to focus solely on Frank, or to run errands while only having to worry about one child at a time.

They were making good money back then, so Sylvie hadn't hesitated—too desperate to get some help. She trusted Kim and phoned the number she'd given her.

When she had found out the woman lived on her road, she felt the stars had aligned. She had visited the daycare provider's home that very afternoon and signed a check for the first two months on the spot for three days a week.

Sylvie still remembers how hopeful she'd felt on her walk home. She'd taken charge. It had been a big step and she could finally breathe a full breath. She was finally going to get some help. Even if she had to pay for it, it was worth her sanity.

Raising two kids under five years old had been a struggle for her. She had been glad she'd reached out and done something for herself. She was already walking taller, growing more confident with each step. She'd been looking forward to this next phase. She hadn't known what a grave mistake she'd just made.

For years after the accident, she had blamed herself for the oversight. She must have been so caught up in her own things to completely miss what was right in front of her.

Of course, no one believed her at the time.

She'd missed so many signs. *Overlooked* was a better word for it. Choosing not to see things that seemed off for the sake of convenience.

How she regretted that after.

A chill makes its way from her shoulders up to her neck, like a cool breeze blowing the stray hairs softly on the nape of her neck. She shivers though she is not cold.

The memory of that day haunts her still. She could never put her finger on it, but she remembers feeling that something was different that morning. As she'd been doing for weeks, she'd dropped Martin off at Mrs. Westover's place. Martin seemed to really like her. There were two other children his age there and one nine-month-old baby.

When Sylvie had visited Mrs. Westover's daycare that first day, she'd been excited and relieved to find a safe-looking place so close to home. She'd been swept away by Mrs. Westover's charm, her kind eyes, and her love of children. She'd failed to notice the undertones, the judgment.

Sylvie, along with Frank who was strapped to her chest in a toddler carrier, had walked through the daycare space, mesmerized by the bright colours on the walls, the tiny tables and chairs, the many books, and the educational posters lining the walls. The foam floors, quiet stations, and crafts table had made her elated at the thought of Martin playing here, making friends, while she focused solely on Frank for at least a few hours a week.

She'd started noticing a problem after a couple of weeks. Martin had appeared to have lost his excitement for going to play there. He almost seemed resentful, taking forever to get dressed in the mornings, refusing to eat his snacks. He had even begun to be aggressive at home with his brother.

Sylvie hadn't been able to make sense of it, other than assuming he was having a difficult time adjusting to not being the centre of attention anymore since there were other children around. But his behaviour had puzzled her. She had wondered if Martin was upset with her for spending so much quality time with Frank like she used to do with him. She'd felt so guilty about it and had even considered pulling him out of the daycare altogether.

In the end, she'd resisted the idea. Her emotional well-being had improved so much during those first few weeks. Caring for only one child at a time had been way more manageable for her. She'd just been starting to get into a groove and worried about having to change things again.

Against her better judgement, she'd fought her instincts and kept bringing Martin to the daycare. She'd downplayed her worries writing it all off as normal separation anxiety due to being apart from each other.

The day of the accident, Martin had been particularly difficult to dress. He'd rejected every outfit Sylvie had offered him. He'd also refused to eat his breakfast, ran around the house when it was time to leave, and ignored her pleas to put his shoes on.

Something was definitely off; unfortunately, Sylvie had missed the cues entirely. She'd associated his change in behaviour to his father working longer hours. Martin had always been a sensitive child. He'd sensed something was wrong but hadn't had the words to express it to her. How she wishes she would have slowed down and tried harder to understand him.

Sylvie had dropped him off at their usual time that morning. Around lunchtime, she'd seen the ambulance rush by and head straight to Mrs. Westover's house. Sylvie had been enjoying a quiet morning, cleaning around the house, having just put Frank down for his nap when she'd seen the lights whizz by the kitchen window. Her heart sized, a lump of steel heavy in her chest.

Somehow she'd just known it was Martin.

Mother's instinct, or whatever you might call it, she'd known. She'd rushed around the house gathering things. Picking up a groggy Frank from his crib, she'd grabbed her phone and seen a missed call from Mrs. Westover. Her breath had caught—she remembers it vividly. She hadn't bothered listening to the voicemail but had urgently called back.

"There's been an accident." Mrs. Westover had said without any greeting. "Martin's pinky finger got cut off," she said after a beat too long.

"Oh, dear God!" Sylvie uttered, unable to say anything else, the realization of his injury too traumatic to bear.

"The ambulance is here now and they're taking him to the hospital to see if they can save his finger," the woman added, sounding strange.

At the time, Sylvie had attributed the tone to guilt or worry, but later, her gut had told her it had sounded more like disappointment. As though Mrs. Westover hadn't wanted his finger to be saved.

Of course, everyone had rejoiced when his finger had been reattached successfully a few hours later with the promise of regaining full function, except for some loss of sensation in the extremities at times. Martin still had a nasty scar where his pinky had been reattached and struggled to keep it warm at times when the blood didn't quite circulate properly.

Sylvie had been so grateful that her son hadn't lost his finger that she hadn't pressed charges. It had been an accident after all. Paul hadn't understood how she could be so quick to forgive. He'd been outraged and had threatened to close down the daycare and sue Mrs. Westover for negligence.

Sylvie had never gotten the full story of how Martin came to lose his finger in the first place. She'd tried on many occasions, but Martin had always acted detached whenever she'd brought it up. After all, how much could she expect from a five-year-old? After a while, she'd let it drop and counted them lucky to have this ordeal behind them. Still, something bothered her about the whole event.

In the end, she'd pulled Martin out of the daycare with little convincing from Paul. She knew it was the right thing to do, although she was nervous about how to handle her days and keep her sanity. Still, having her children in her own care had to be better than whatever had happened at Mrs. Westover's.

Sylvie had kept Martin home for the remainder of that year until he was old enough to go to school. Nevertheless, she and Paul seemed to irritate each other more often after the accident. They'd been short with each other, spending less time together and speaking less. The gap between them had been expanding, but they'd pretended like everything was fine.

Martin's finger had been saved. Nothing had changed, except everything had.

42

QUINN

Cole is playing quietly with his coloured wooden blocks on the living room rug while Quinn busies herself unloading the groceries. The majority of the bread can be saved and she's relieved. She will make herself an avocado toast for lunch today and prepare homemade barbeque sauce to marinate some chicken breasts for dinnertime.

Putting things neatly away into their designated spots gives Quinn some much needed relief. Her tiredness is caused by not doing enough for herself. She likes order and organization—something that's been lacking these days. It helps to clear her mind. She's always thought she would enjoy a job with repetitive tasks, and although she does enjoy the routine of things, her days are just a little too predictable for her liking.

She's beginning to see motherhood not just as a new identity, but as a job. Only this is the most demanding job she's ever had. There are no breaks. She's on-call every night and barely gets to eat. She can never have a sick day and always needs to put Cole's needs before her own. She feels like she's being pulled by an invisible anchor to the bottom of the sea. Drowning in responsibilities.

The volume in the house is always high as Cole has recently been discovering his voice and loves to experiment with how loudly he can scream. The constant noise and the shrill sound of his cries almost tip her over the edge. Quinn has her jaw tightly clenched. She's barely started to feel her shoulders relax when Cole abruptly knocks the blocks over onto the hardwood, making a loud clanging noise, startling her.

"Cole, seriously? Can you play more quietly, please?" she begs, slowing her heart rate with every breath.

It's not as though her infant can control his movements with precision. She's aware she's asking too much from him, but she can't help it. She's cracking. As her son stares back at her, both mischievous and intrigued, she finds her irritation growing. She knows how silly it is for her to assume her baby understands what he's doing. She knows this is a normal phase and that he's learning, but it's driving her nuts.

Since they started him on solids, Cole has been enjoying spilling his food all over the floor for Quinn to pick up. Too often to count, Quinn has felt some mushed up produce splat on the top of her head as she knelt to scrub away the food that had landed underneath the high chair.

"What am I going to do with you?" she sighs, exasperated, feeling the sting of tears in her eyes. Closing her eyes, she takes deep breaths trying to steady herself.

It's not a big deal, she reminds herself.

She feels like a monster. This isn't how she imagined she would be as a mother. She hates this version of herself—so high strung, never taking time for herself, always tense. She barely recognizes herself.

She remembers catching sight of her face in the hall mirror a few weeks ago. She'd just reprimanded Cole for something silly, but her face had looked like he'd just committed a terrible sin. The degree to which she had scolded him made her even angrier. She was ashamed of her behaviour. She wanted to be a better parent.

Every day, she wishes for patience and understanding. She wants a good relationship with her son. There is a lot of pressure on her to be a natural at being a good mother because she was doing it all hours of the day.

A lot of her friends back home hadn't taken their full maternity leaves. They'd had exciting jobs waiting for them to go back to after they'd given birth, but Quinn didn't. She'd worked contract to contract. So when she'd gotten pregnant, the plan had been to stay home with Cole until he turned one before returning to work.

Even though her work had been meaningless and boring, the idea of spending a year with a baby hardly speaking to other adults for 365 days had seemed impossible to Quinn. She missed her friends back home. Hell, she even missed her shitty contract work.

Anything had to be better than this.

Quinn knows that how she's feeling isn't good. She's been feeling like this for a while, and it hasn't gotten better. She decides to send a text to William to tell him she's having a rough day. He knows what this means by now. She's not doing it to add to his guilt about being so far away, but she also hasn't heard from him since the car incident this morning. She just wants to hear his voice, to feel his presence. She hopes he will call her soon as he usually does after she sends a text like that.

Since Cole is in one of his moods where nothing seems to be pleasing him, Quinn decides to take him out for a walk to clear her head. She's been getting used to the solitude of her street. There's peace and a sense of security that comes from being the only two people on the road. Exercise and a change of scenery will do them both a great deal of good. At least, that's what she's counting on.

43

QUINN

Quinn pushes the stroller down the long, gravel road, her head pounding with every step. She scolds herself for being dehydrated—again. She's had a terrible time remembering to drink enough water during these harsh, August heat waves.

As a child, she used to get heatstroke often. Her parents never remembered to bring enough water for all of them and, being the middle child, Quinn was often forgotten. Most of the water went to her younger brother who ran around the most and whose skin got the reddest.

The first indication of dehydration for her is a slight headache followed by nausea. By then, it's too late. She'll be bedridden for the rest of the day, nursing an agonizing migraine, bargaining with God to spare her from the pain just this once—or to kill her quickly. Either way, it didn't matter. She had just wanted immediate relief. She hopes they can manage to get to the end of the road and back before it all really hits her.

She had known it was supposed to hit a high of thirty-five degrees Celsius with the humidity by two in the afternoon, but she hasn't prepared. She was so intent on getting out of the house that she forgot most of the things they'd need for their walk. What a disaster! The fluctuation in weather had made her brain foggy again, her impending migraine making her crave her bed.

At seven months old, Cole still isn't sleeping well. This morning, he had woken up at three A.M. and had refused to go back to bed. Quinn doesn't find it too difficult to wake up early, but then almost always crashes around two in the afternoon. That's when she has the most trouble staying patient. The lack of sleep mixed with the reflux of fussiness left Quinn running on empty most days.

Quinn had settled in her usual spot at the corner seat of the large, leather couch in the dark cover of night as she'd tried to nurse Cole back to sleep. Her butt print had made a deep U-shaped dent in the spot where she spent most of her days fighting with her bad thoughts.

It was usually in those early mornings, when exhaustion and desperation teamed up, that Quinn found herself scouring the Internet trying to find a solution to her situation.

For hours, she'd read blog posts and forums describing how precious these moments were supposed to be, reminding her to cherish every single second. She'd fantasized about these very moments during her pregnancy, but this morning all she'd wanted to do was crawl back into bed and get Cole off of her. She found it hard to understand how she could both feel incredibly lonely, but also have a desperate desire to be left alone.

———

As the stroller hits a shallow pothole, Quinn returns her attention to her walk. She's surprised to have made it as far as the train tracks at the end of the road before Cole starts to protest being in his stroller. She has him strapped in the seat, and he doesn't enjoy being tied down too tightly.

It must be hot in that seat without air circulating around the black fabric and foam. Quinn lifts the sunshade and takes a peek at his chubby face, his cheeks as round and as red as apples.

"I guess it's time to turn back. A short walk today," she sighs, more to herself than to him.

Might as well, she thinks. She can feel the migraine quickly approaching. As she turns the stroller around and moves to the opposite side of the road, Cole's blue fleece blanket falls out as his tiny feet kick at it. She doesn't even remember bringing it.

Mom brain, she derides herself.

Why would Cole even need a blanket in this heat? Her brain isn't working right these days. She shakes her head, trying to rid herself of the fog on her mind. She thinks back to earlier this morning when she'd almost placed a box of cereal in the refrigerator.

At home, she keeps a pile of baby things by the door to take with her every time she goes somewhere. Instead of constantly looking for things, Quinn has them readily accessible. It helps her not forget important things like diapers or wipes. But sometimes, she ends up carrying way too much with her. Like now, for instance. A warm fleece blanket on what she can only assume is one of this summer's hottest days.

She should be embarrassed. But when Quinn gets into this dark place, she rarely cares about what other people think of her. She's got so much more to worry about.

44

QUINN

As Quinn walks back towards her house, she moves off the road and onto the shoulder to allow a few cars to drive by. Even out here in the country, there's quite a bit of traffic. She never used to notice things like traffic before, but then again, she never used to walk on the road this much when she lived in Kingston. If she and William ever went for a walk before having Cole, they would go on the sidewalk. Here she has to share the road with the traffic and is often forced to move out of the way as the cars tended to drive faster on these country roads.

Today is one of her favourite days—garbage day. She secretly enjoys getting a little glimpse into someone's life just by looking at what they throw away. She now knows that the owner of the bungalow at the end of the road, the one with the blue shutters, has most likely gone through a divorce and enjoys a screw-driver as her drink of choice based on the empty orange juice containers and vodka bottles.

She'd noticed only one car in the driveway for months now and there always seemed to be empty bottles on garbage day. As she passes by, she sees that, yet again, the recycling bin is filled with empty vodka bottles.

Just by paying attention, she can easily see who on her road is a pop or a beer drinker, who has just purchased a new flat screen TV, or who has kids simply based on the assortment of toys littering their front lawns. She can also spot who's away on vacation by the long grass and the overflowing mailbox. She wonders what people can tell about her family when they look at their house.

Ever since realizing how revealing certain details are to strangers, Quinn has done her best to be discreet. Without being rude, she's managed to keep to herself. But during the agonizingly long days of feeling stuck inside the house, she'd finally decided to go out, needing a change of scenery.

Mrs. Westover mostly keeps to herself as well. Quinn has seen her only a handful of times since William left to fight fires. Once earlier in the spring, Rose's knees had been deep in the fresh dirt, working the ground with a small shovel. From their earlier conversations, Quinn is aware of her neighbour's love of her garden.

Thinking about Rose reminds Quinn of how helpful she'd been this morning, and she wonders if Mrs. Westover had a chance to attend her bible study as planned after helping Quinn with her car malfunction.

Last week as Quinn had walked by, her neighbour had offered her a few cucumbers from her vegetable garden. She'd asked about Cole and guessed correctly at his age.

Quinn had apologetically asked if his screaming had disturbed her, but the woman had assured her that it had been no bother. Rose had even offered to come over to help out again, and Quinn had been touched by the offer.

———

After the cars pass by, Quinn resumes her walk and continues to sweat. There are no clouds in the sky and the wind is warm. The slight effort it takes to push the stroller exhausts her completely. Her headache getting stronger and more persistent, making her grit her teeth. She rubs her temples, hoping for some relief but finding none. She curses under her breath.

Of course. Today, of all days, Cole is fussing in the stroller, eager to get out. He's feeling the heat, too. Unfortunately, while he might be hoping for some tummy time, Quinn's already planning on putting him straight to bed for his nap so that she can have a quick shower to wash off the grime from the road.

Pushing the stroller up the hill, Quinn spots a middle-aged man walking on the opposite side. He looks over and offers a polite smile and nod, continuing on his way down the hill she's just climbed. He looks vaguely familiar—something about his eyes—yet Quinn is sure she's never seen him around before. There aren't a lot of houses down this way and few people are home during the day.

Not many people walk along the road here.

Cole lifts an agitated fist and screams once more, urging her to get home as quickly as possible. Spotting the mailbox straight ahead, Quinn picks up her pace. She makes the final push up the driveway and locks the stroller.

The thought of a nice, refreshing shower is calling to her as she gets Cole out of his stroller, propping him on her hip, carrying the rest of the load in the crook of her arm. She unlocks the door and walks through, placing everything, including Cole, on the kitchen table, where he sits happily, mesmerized by the various items scattered around him.

A cool wave of air conditioning hits Quinn right away and she immediately feels better. However, Cole's cries have gotten to her and her head is pounding even more strongly. She hurries to pick him up, clumsily grabs the blue fleece blanket, and stomps upstairs where freedom is so close she can taste it.

In the dark corner of his room, she rocks Cole while he nurses urgently at her breast, his form of punishment for making him wait too long between feeds. The heat radiating off his tiny body is making Quinn slightly nauseous and claustrophobic. She can feel herself quickly reaching her breaking point.

She needs some time to herself.

Her head is now pulsing. She feels as unstable and unpredictable as a floating ember slowly making its way towards a dry hayfield.

After Cole has finished feeding, Quinn plants a kiss on both cheeks and places him in the crib. She carefully tucks his blanket around him snuggly so that the AC won't chill him too much. Tiptoeing out of the room, she exhales a long breath, praying he won't cry out and summon her back to his room. She desperately needs a shower to cool off and to calm her pounding head.

Beads of sweat roll down her back and between her breasts as she hurries to the ensuite bathroom to turn on the shower. There is a ring of sweat at her hairline and her hair is a mixture of salty crispness and smelly, wet frizz.

She feels the grimy road dirt coating her hair and her skin, sticking to her with the heat. Quinn can see a film of brown dust over her exposed legs and arms, and feels dirt on the back of her neck where the stray hairs are sticking to it. The wind must have blown some dirt up during the walk, covering her with a coat of dust, muting her colour ever so slightly.

Quinn checks the baby monitor to see if Cole has fallen asleep already. The video monitor has been so helpful in checking on him from anywhere in the house, saving her steps, but the technology isn't perfect. The grainy image, made even less clear with the lights off, makes it difficult to determine where Cole is lying in the large crib. After a few moments of zooming and scanning the screen, Quinn spots him in the corner and sees that his chest is slowly moving up and down. He's sleeping soundly. Thank God.

She sighs in relief as she steps into the large shower.

As the cool spray from the shower head washes over her, Quinn wonders if she, too, should nap after her shower. Sleep usually helps with even the worst of her migraines, though she's doubtful a nap will do it. She's been so exhausted lately. It might do her some good to rest for a little while. The old advice from her friends comes to her mind—*sleep when baby sleeps*. Now she understands.

She'd had more energy when Cole was a newborn. She couldn't turn her mind off during his naps, always busying herself with folding laundry, washing dishes, or catching up on emails. But recently, sleep is at the forefront of her thoughts. She can't function without it, even daydreams about it.

She knows her patience with Cole is thinning and that it isn't good for either of them. As she lathers shampoo into her hair, she hears a strange noise. A squeak and then a soft click.

What the hell? she thinks. *Is William home?*

Her heart beats quickly, excited to see her husband after all this time apart. But the absence of William's booming voice announcing his return concerns Quinn, suddenly making her feel vulnerable. Had she heard something else? Was someone else in the house?

Alert now, Quinn quickly rinses off most of the soap. Not bothering to get it all, she carefully shuts off the water, her movements automatic. A beat goes by as she stands there, quiet and listening.

She steps out of the shower warily, trying not to make a sound. Still wet and covered with soap suds, she strains her ears trying to make out the sound she's just heard. As she makes her way towards the baby monitor, her eye catches movement out of her bathroom window, down below in the yard. For a moment, Quinn isn't sure what she's seeing. She feels like she must be dreaming.

A man—not her husband, but one who reminds her of the man she saw walking on the road earlier—is running through the backyard heading for the woods, holding something. It takes Quinn a few minutes to realize that he's holding her son's blue fleece blanket.

The stranger has kidnaped Cole.

45

QUINN

Quinn can't digest what she's just seen. The man has taken Cole, and he's running away with him towards the woods.

Hastily, she grabs William's green bathrobe hanging on the back hook of the bathroom door and yanks it free when the hood gets stuck.

"Come on!" she mutters through gritted teeth, her heart pounding.

It takes everything for her not to collapse onto the cold tiled floor and whimper like a child—giving up. She only keeps the rising nausea at bay with the thought that it's not over yet. She still has a chance to get Cole back.

Quickly pushing down the dreadful feelings overtaking her, she takes another quick glance at the baby monitor just to be sure her eyes aren't playing tricks on her. Out of habit, she grabs it and clicks on the camera view, and as she'd dreaded, Cole isn't in his crib. She feels a scream rising in her throat, panic freezing her in place, her brain not working properly.

What's going on? Why is this happening? She panics.

She slaps her left cheek as hard as she can to bring herself back to attention and drops the monitor on the floor, unstartled by the noise. Focus returning to her, she rushes down the stairs two at a time, almost falling on the last step, the long bathrobe trailing behind her.

Quinn is barely covered and dripping with water and soap suds. There was a time in her life when she would have probably died of humiliation, been completely mortified at the very idea of doing this, but right now, she doesn't give a damn.

She has only one thing on her mind.

Getting Cole.

She bolts through the house and catches sight of the man still running with Cole in his arms. The man has just reached the edge of the woods. For a split second, she appreciates the ridiculously large property. She's glad she can still see them but is disgruntled at the seclusion. Calling for help out here would be useless.

She flings open the back patio door and dashes out after the man, not bothering to close the door behind her. Quinn's robe is flying behind her like a cape. She yells out to the man between sobs.

"Please, stop!" she cries, weaker than she'd like. "Give me my son back!"

As Quinn runs, her wet hair sticks to her face and she violently whips it away, getting angrier. Mama bear is coming out.

"You stop right there, you son of a bitch!" she yells loudly, surprising herself.

The man just keeps running ahead, never once looking back.

He's not very quick, but he's much farther ahead and Quinn isn't sure she'll be able to catch up before losing him inside the thick woods. She runs as fast as she can through the dry grass. Since it hasn't rained in over two weeks, the sun has burnt the lawn to a crisp forcing the city to impose a fire ban until the next significant rainfall.

She spots a deer trail where some of the foliage and branches have been slightly parted at the entrance to the woods and instinctively decides that following it will be her best chance at catching up to him.

Running through the woods, her bare feet scream in pain as she steps on sharp rocks and sticks. She can't stop now; she can see the man right up ahead. He's got Cole so tightly in his arms, he might even be strangling him in his run. He's gathering speed and distance, dressed in appropriate gear for the woods.

"Stop, you're hurting him!" Quinn pleads, her throat catching as she imagines her son turning as blue as his blanket.

Why isn't Cole crying?

Has the man already hurt him? Does Cole hear her voice? Does her son know she's running after him?

The woods are quiet and dark beneath the summer leaves. Their hurried steps, the crunch of the leaves, and the snap of breaking branches are the only noises she can hear.

The man is running fast, jumping expertly over rocks and mounds in the ground. He looks athletic and very comfortable in the forest like he knows his way around these parts of the woods. In all the time Quinn has lived here, she hasn't once ventured into the woods behind the house.

How she regrets that now.

Desperate, the man just out of sight, Quinn wills herself to run even faster, her breath ragged. For a split second, Quinn's mind flashes an image, almost blinding her. That man, his eyes. She's seen him before. Her pace slows as the memory surfaces. Her foot catches on a thick root sticking out from the ground, and she begins to fall but catches herself on a nearby tree. A few seconds. That's all it takes for her to lose a visual on her target.

Panting, she looks up but she can't see the man anymore.

"Cole?" She yells, bewildered. "No, no, no! This can't be happening!"

She holds back the tears as she frantically scans the woods. Every leaf blowing in the wind makes her heart skip a beat as she convinces herself it's them. Her shoulders slump. Despair starts to take over with the realization that she really can't see them anymore.

Quinn tries to quiet the pounding in her ears to listen more intently, but she can't hear anything. She feels like she's going to pass out or have a heart attack. Her vision is spotty, the exertion catching up with her. Her migraine returns full-force the first chance it gets.

She pushes off of the tree she was hugging for support, and resumes her aimless walk. Stumbling now, she does her best to see through the black spots in her vision, wincing with every step as the soles of her feet burn angrily.

She limps slowly, the race over. She's lost.

The man has stolen Cole right from under her.

Quinn has failed at the most basic motherhood task of keeping her baby safe from harm. She's let her son down. She'll never see Cole again.

Her eyes are heavy from exhaustion. Her pounding head makes her stumble and stagger over the forest floor. After another ten minutes of wandering in the vast forest, she knows she doesn't stand a chance of finding them on her own.

She shivers despite the lingering heat hanging above the ferns, a sign that her body is going into shock. She can feel herself giving up. The hope is floating away like dandelion fluff in the wind.

Her eyes close momentarily as she tries to steady her swaying body. She hears a rustling of leaves to her left. Opening her eyes, she jerks her head in the sound's direction and stops in her tracks. She crouches slowly, willing her body not to make a sound so as not to betray her position. She waits patiently, expecting to glimpse the man holding Cole. Instead, she sees a small black squirrel jump across the forest floor and find his way to a fallen tree to eat an acorn.

At the sight of the squirrel unbothered by her despair, Quinn begins to sob loudly. Snot drips and bubbles out of her nose. A string of spit spans her top and bottom lips, making her very own spider web.

When she'd gotten married, Quinn had been afraid of becoming a young widow. Losing William had seemed like the worst possible thing that could ever happen to her. Ever since she's become a mother, Cole has taken up a lot of her attention and a lot of her time, pushing William to the sidelines. Her days were entirely focused on keeping Cole alive, happy, and healthy.

Dread overcomes her. What will the man do to her son? Why wasn't Cole crying?

Since giving birth, Quinn has never allowed herself to consider the possibility of her son dying someday. She's forced herself to believe it would never happen. But mothers lose their children every day in this country. If a wife loses a husband, she becomes a widow. But what do you call a mother when her child dies? There's no name for it.

Stop it, she scolds herself.

"Cole is fine," she states out loud, trying to convince herself. "I'll find him unharmed and things will go right back to normal."

Right? He had to be okay.

Her whole body trembles as fear takes over. Fear is the gateway to an even worse emotion—doubt. *What if it's not all going to be okay?*

Images of finding her son's body lying on the forest floor terrify her. Her imagination is her worst enemy. Without meaning to, grief sneaks into Quinn's heart. Her eyesight compromised by the tears running down her face, she steps onto a sharp, broken stick poking out from under a pile of leaves, and it pierces the bottom of her foot.

She lets out a high-pitched scream as she falls forward. Her hands stretch out in front of her useless to stop her fall and her head collides with a large boulder. Before everything goes dark, the last thing that flashes through her mind isn't Cole's face, but the man's deep, green eyes.

46

QUINN

Quinn pushes off the forest floor and runs a tentative finger along her temple. She feels a warm sticky residue which she can only assume is blood. She'd hit her head pretty hard in her fall. The daylight is long gone. She's missed the sunset altogether, along with the last several hours. There is barely any moonlight coming through the leaves above.

The night is cold, despite it being the middle of August. A storm is brewing overhead, sending a brisk chill through the air. The wind is picking up and making her shiver. She's barely dressed, covered only by her husband's green bathrobe which fits loosely over her, her feet swollen from cuts and bruises. The dropping temperature has turned them blue hours ago. She's frozen to the bone. She pulls herself stiffly to her feet and staggers forward—one step at a time.

A raindrop falls on her cheek—a cold contrast to the steady stream of hot tears that haven't stopped since she woke up. Quinn has no idea where she is. She's scared, alone, and lost in the forest. The wind picks up as the rain begins to fall heavily. Her teeth begin to chatter. She wraps the damp fabric around her, but it's useless.

She remembers complaining about the thick humidity in the air only hours ago. She'd been annoyed that her clothes were clinging to her skin and disgusted by the ring of salt on her hairline.

How hot she'd been when she'd last held Cole!

Shaking her head, she reprimands herself. *Not going there.*

She can't get distracted. She needs to keep her mind focused and she needs to keep moving. There is no one who can help her now, no one who knows where she is.

Hell, she doesn't even know.

The forest is a dark place to be when the sun goes down. With no markers or clear paths, she'd been disoriented within minutes of waking up. Convinced she hadn't gone in that far, she tries to retrace her steps, but there's no daylight left to guide her.

She's been going ahead strictly by feel, extending her arms out in front of her as though she's been blindfolded. She might as well be. Letting her scraped hands brush against the bark and moss on the trees, she uses all of her senses to guide her.

She should have paid attention when she'd come running into the forest. Her body had propelled her forward, adrenaline coursing through her veins. She had been driven by a fierce determination to catch up to the man as quickly as possible. She hadn't noticed the trees or remembered her way. And now Cole was gone, and she was lost in the woods, unable to get out and useless to save her son.

"Cole!" she screams as loudly as she can in case there are houses nearby. "Can anyone hear me?"

She's met by nothing but terrifying silence. Nature all around her only adds to her fear rather than calming her down. What if there are wolves out here just waiting to chew on her limbs? What if the man dropped Cole in the woods and the beasts get to her son first?

Quinn muffles a cry, forcing it down her throat as quickly as she can, willing herself to remain calm.

255

She needs to keep her anxiety at bay. She can't let it win, or she will lose everything. She's come this far and she will see it through even if it kills her. She needs to keep moving forward, to focus on the hope she's clinging to so tightly.

It's all she has left.

Her body's shivering, the wet cotton doing little to keep the harsh winds and cold rain from going right through her, soaking her to the bone. Her throat is still sore from screaming at the man. She brings her hands up to her mouth to blow on them, only to find her breath isn't warm enough to make any difference. Her long black hair clings to her face in cold streaks and she brushes it away quickly, determined to find a way out—her motivation.

Every step on the cold forest floor sends a spike of pain resonating through her body. Her back cries in protest. Her injured foot is screaming in agony with every step. Quinn's breasts are painfully full of unused milk, making her feel feverish. She can feel her eyelids growing heavy—from a mixture of the harsh elements and the long journey. Her energy is running out quickly.

She's running out of time.

She has no water and no food to give her body the boost she desperately needs to keep moving forward. She slowly makes her way through the woods, even though she has no clear sense of where she's heading.

Her eyes are barely open, useless against the dark forest. The moon and stars are hidden by the heavy rain clouds, making it impossible to see anything in front of her. Quinn can't even see her own hand in front of her face.

She wonders if she should give up hope, stop walking around in circles in the dark, and lie down for a few hours until the sun comes back.

Would she even survive the night if she stopped walking?

On the other hand, waiting for daylight would give her a fighting chance at finding a way out of this immense forest.

She feels for an open area on the forest floor where the rocks aren't prominent before carefully lowering herself. Her head is pounding and begging for sleep. Sitting on the borrowed bathrobe, grateful for her husband's taller height, she tries to convince herself she can stay awake until it's light enough to see her way out of the woods.

The harsh rain falls in pellets, attacking her sensitive skin. The tiny shards force her eyes closed. She wraps herself in the bathrobe tightly, doing her best to cover every inch of her body. She will spend the night here and try again tomorrow. She needs to stay alive—if not for herself, then for Cole.

She wills herself to keep breathing until she loses consciousness.

PART FOUR

47

ROSE

She's been working in the backyard when she hears the young woman next door scream like a feral cat. At first, it shakes her, makes her hair stand on end, not because she's frightened, but because she's excited. She hasn't heard a desperate scream like that in ages. She's forgotten just how much she misses it.

———

She'd been attending to her babies—her flower garden. The sun had been particularly hot these past few days and she'd been worried the dirt would dry and shrink down to nothing.

Rose had been watering her garden twice a day in order to keep her flowers happy and growing. She knew to avoid watering the leaves while the sun was out so the rays wouldn't burn them.

Over the years, she'd found peace working out there for hours on end, often getting lost in the tasks of plucking the weeds, digging holes in the dirt for new bulbs or seeds, and watering the large plot.

She spent most afternoons back there. She liked looking out into the woods as she worked. The bugs were mostly done for the season and it had been enjoyable to spend some time in her gardens.

Shortly after she had heard the scream, Rose had seen a man running out of the Millers' home, holding a blue fleece blanket tight to his chest, and disappearing into the woods. She'd spotted Quinn following close behind, barely dressed, and looking out of sorts.

A smile had played on Rose's lips as she'd taken in the scene.

"My, oh my," she laughed to herself.

It hadn't taken long for Rose to recognize the man. He'd gained weight over the years, but there was no doubt in her mind that the man she'd seen running from the Miller's home was Dylan Thomas.

She was impressed—surprised. She hadn't thought Dylan had it in him to act on his need for vengeance. She'd spent many years studying his face, searching for him online, saving his picture on her computer to keep her fire fueled.

She felt giddy at how perfectly her plan had worked out. She'd taken a big chance, and it had paid off.

By lending Quinn her old car to take into town, she'd practically offered the girl up on a plate as bait. All Rose has to do now is to sit back and wait for the car to pop up on a police vehicle alert and have her dear neighbour arrested. Rose is pleased with herself. Her quick thinking has saved her once again. Things are working out according to plan. She'll be able to move on and keep her secrets.

She'd known Dylan Thomas had been sniffing around, that he had been for years, but she'd never thought in a million years that he would be in town on the same day Quinn took the car out for the first time, or that he would have seen her.

She wondered how often he'd come to town, searching street after street for the red car with damage to the right passenger side-her car. How many scared drivers had he tailed and terrified by coming too close to inspect every dent and bump, only to speed away, disappointed by the endless search?

Rose had strained her ears to hear as best she could as Quinn ran deeper into the dense woods. She could hear the woman scream something, but her voice had been drowned out beneath the loud crunch of leaves.

Quinn's voice had resonated at first, bouncing off the trees like an echo of sorts, but her voice had been muffled the further in she'd gone, blending in with the songs of birds and the screams of children playing down the street.

The old woman had wished she could've been a bird in a tree watching the scene develop before her eyes. She'd been disappointed at missing the moment Quinn's life had fallen apart but consoled herself that it didn't matter if it had been at her own hand or someone else's. It would be much more convenient legally if her neighbour's death was someone else's problem. No one would be sniffing around her.

———

When Mrs. Westover could no longer hear any noises coming from the woods, she'd waited several more minutes, and eventually she'd heard the rustling of leaves. Not sure what to expect, she'd hidden behind one of her buildings to observe without being seen.

She'd watched as Dylan came out of the woods looking terribly shaken up and sweaty.

He'd been limping along, looking awful and scared. He was no longer holding the blanket in his arms. Mrs. Westover had wondered what had happened to baby Cole. She liked Cole but with liars for parents, the poor boy had no chance. Dylan had taken care of it for her and didn't even know it.

Once Mrs. Westover had been certain that Dylan was out of sight back on the street, she'd ventured out into the woods herself to check things out. She'd struggled for a while to find the exact spot where Dylan had been and wasn't surprised to discover Quinn passed out on the forest floor with a bloody forehead.

"Good riddance," she'd muttered in disgust as a farewell.

As she'd made to leave, Mrs. Westover had noticed a splash of bright, blue fabric tangled in a nearby bush. Without thinking, she'd walked towards it, grabbed it, and hastily made her way home.

She'd wondered where Cole was as he wasn't in the woods and Dylan's hands had been empty. She'd spent a few moments looking around in an attempt to find the boy but had given up. She'd been careful where she'd walked, trying hard not to cover any of Dylan and Quinn's tracks. Maybe the police would assume it had been an affair gone wrong.

With Quinn's husband working in British Colombia for some time now, it wasn't an impossible theory. Quinn didn't have very many friends in town from what Mrs. Westover had gathered. Perhaps it would take a few days before she was reported missing or discovered.

As Rose made her way back towards her house, she'd heard a screeching noise.

She recognized it all too well.

It was Cole's shrill cry coming from inside her neighbour's house. Quinn must have left the back patio door open when she'd run out. Mrs. Westover pondered what to do. She could have just ignored it and let things play out however they might, but then again, she could finish what she'd started.

Dylan must have only wanted to lure Quinn out of the house by making her believe that he'd taken Cole in his fleece blanket and run away into the woods with him. Rose wondered what Quinn must have been thinking for his reason behind it. She'd probably thought he'd been some kind of pedophile. Rose had laughed to herself at the irony of the situation.

If only Quinn knew—Dylan was the good guy.

48

ROSE

Mrs. Westover slowly enters the house through the open patio door. She creeps up the circular staircase to where Cole is screaming at the top of his lungs.

He's hungry, she figures.

Unsure of what to do, Mrs. Westover decides to keep climbing the stairs until she's standing at the boy's bedroom door. She's surprised to notice that she's nervous. She's done this many times before, but it's been a while.

"Knock, knock!" she taps at the door playfully.

Cole's bright, wet eyes look up at her, and his red cheeks bunch up into big balls as he smiles at her. One of the benefits of having been Cole's babysitter in the past is that he trusts her.

"Hi there, little man. You're okay, you're okay," she mutters as she lifts his solid frame to rest comfortably on her hip.

He doesn't make a fuss when she picks him up from his crib. His attention immediately goes to the blanket she's holding in her hand. She wraps it loosely around him. Despite the heat outside, she is grateful to have something with which to shield his body from prying eyes when she takes him home with her. She looks around the room for a moment, grabbing a few diapers and wipes before heading down to the kitchen.

Once there, she inspects the fridge and is glad to find two bottles of pumped breastmilk prepared ahead of time and ready to be used.

"Now, here we go! Just what you need," she reassures Cole, balancing him in her arms.

She softly strokes Cole's hair and walks out of the house through the open patio door making sure not to touch anything else. Yet she doesn't need to worry if her prints are in the house as she's been there multiple times to babysit. If she's questioned later on, she can easily explain that.

She wanders over to her garden with Cole resting on her hip. The boy happily plays with her necklace as she softly hums a nursery rhyme. She strolls around her backyard gently rocking Cole in her arms, enjoying the sensation. The excitement of what she's about to do makes her feel so elated—she feels high. She tries to make the moment last as long as she can. She knows she will need to act quickly.

Cole seems to sense the shift. His smile is quickly replaced by a confused expression.

"Don't worry my boy. It will only hurt for a little while," she reassures him. *Kids are so intuitive*, she thinks.

She has to refrain from skipping over to the house, the excitement building up with each passing second. Closing the door behind her, she shuts the blinds and settles Cole down on the entry floor.

Old enough to sit on his own, Cole remains in his spot while Mrs. Westover moves to the kitchen. Exhilarated, she fingers the knives one by one. Swiftly choosing one, she feels her top lip twitch. It's almost time, but first she must get all the preparations in order.

First, she will need to sharpen the knife she's picked. She doesn't want the little guy to suffer. She will be quick about it, and make it as painless as possible. She doesn't lie.

49

LENA

Lena busily cleans the house, trying to shake off the awkward conversation she's just had with Quinn. Listening to the radio, she dusts the lamps and ceiling fans, vacuums behind the couch and chairs, and sweeps meticulously under the kitchen table and under the kitchen sink where crumbs always seem to collect.

Tiny rocks from Jake's boots litter the landing. Dirty piles of laundry are scattered throughout the house, some in their room, some by the front hall closet, and some on top of the washing machine just waiting for her to clean them. The sight of all the chaos is overwhelming.

She's grateful for her air conditioning for without it she would get nothing done. The heat has been intense these last few days, and she hasn't wanted to go out for walks. She's glad for the distraction that cleaning the house offers.

Lena moves around her home touching practically everything. She works quickly but messily. There is a strategy behind her cleaning methods, but to the unknowing eye, it might look like she can't keep her attention on a single thing at a time. Whereas most people prefer to clean one room at a time, Lena's tactic is to attack the entire house all at once leaving wreckage behind her like a tornado in the centre of a city.

She works well in the mess of cleaning supplies, overflowing mountains of clothes, heaps of dirty dishes in the sink, stacks of papers on every table, brooms leaning against doorways, and dust piles collecting in every corner with the music blaring.

This is the way she prefers it.

Get the house in enough disarray that she has no choice but to keep working at it until it's all done.

She empties every drawer and closet, cleans every nook, reaches high to get the cobwebs and wrestles her way around the toilets to clean the base that most people would rather pretend doesn't exist.

Lena might be meticulous at home, but Jake is a perfectionist at work. Her husband sometimes works late into the night preparing a course or agonizing over lesson plans, so worried about appearing professional.

She doesn't mind. She admires him for caring so much.

She understands his desire to be respected by others. Jake struggled in school as a teenager and he's making up for that by putting his best self forward every day.

He often worries that he won't be able to sustain a position of this status if people ever find out that he'd struggled academically in the past. But he's so passionate about aviation and anything to do with helicopters that he's always seemed extremely knowledgeable to his peers.

When it comes to things he's interested about, he gives it all he's got. He's worked hard to get where he is which keeps him humble. He's a kind and generous man who often helps struggling students by offering to pay for their lunches if they're short on cash. Jake had even recently helped the Millers find accommodations when William admitted that their finances might not permit them to make the move to North Bay.

Her husband often takes on everyone else's problems which sometimes drains him. Lena worries that Jake's good intentions will one day cripple him. However, helping others seems to only motivate him to do more good.

Jake and Lena live modestly but give generously. They like to support their community. They've both been lucky to have done so well in life, and they're always looking for ways to give back in any way they can.

As Lena wipes the countertops, she spots dog hair on her pants. The dog hair that accumulates in one day astonishes her. With two dogs, even though they are quite small, she finds she still needs to vacuum daily or she will have tumbleweeds of hair floating around her floors. She loves her black clothing but cringes at the amount of hair that shows up on it. It's a continuous battle to keep everything clean.

She does her best to clear her mind as she moves around the house, but she feels so bad. It's obvious to her that Quinn hadn't known about William's decision to push for the assignment out of town. Lena hates that she's the one who'd told her.

She had thought Quinn knew.

She hadn't wanted to hurt her, but she was genuinely confused when Quinn suggested that Jake had made him go.

She wants to talk to Jake about it, but it will need to wait. She doesn't like to bother him when he's at work. He teaches long classes for most of the day, but he should have a break coming up around 12:30.

She leans the broom against a nearby wall to pick up her phone to give Quinn a call. She's tried to call her several times since their conversation, but her calls keep going to voicemail.

She sighs and looks around her house for a moment. She feels stir crazy. She's been in the house since yesterday. She looks at her outfit. She's wearing work-out clothes, her usual go-to for cleaning, and decides she will get out of her funk by shaking it up a little bit.

She will go grab two iced-coffees and bring them over to Quinn's place to see how she's faring. She had been so excited about making a new friend and she's worried about the damage their conversation may have done. She doesn't want to risk losing Quinn over this.

Lena has never been good at making friends. She'd had no trouble finding boyfriends in her youth, but girls have always intimidated her. They always seem to want to compete. She finds herself constantly self-conscious, worrying if she looks right, if she has interesting things to say, and if she's funny enough. Despite acting confident around other people, she's the complete opposite. She usually ends up saying inappropriate things and making a fool of herself.

She knows what she looks like, and she worries it makes women uncomfortable especially if she's talking to their husbands. Lena sighs. She's more than her looks; she has a big heart. She just hasn't had many chances to prove it before being judged. She wants nothing more than to make friends and not be so lonely.

Quinn. She'd felt hope rise within her. Here was a woman who was new to the area, who needed a friend. She'd instantly felt relieved.

Quinn had been dressed fairly casually, her hair unwashed, her face free of make-up.

Lena had immediately felt relaxed.

Now, this was a woman she could see herself hanging out with. Someone with whom she could let her guard down and be herself.

But after her conversation with Quinn this morning, Lena's worried that she's thrown it all away by blabbing about the wrong thing. She bites her bottom lip, upset with herself.

Before she can talk herself out of it, she leaves the mess behind, grabs her purse, and steps out into the heat of the day. At her car she hesitates, unsure if this is the right move as it might make matters worse, but she decides she needs to at least check in since she can't get a hold of her friend.

Maybe Quinn is out for a walk or possibly asleep. Still, something keeps gnawing at her.

Lena's always had strong gut feelings. She believes in a sixth sense. She feels drawn to go to Quinn's house. She drives by the coffee shop and chooses two large iced lattes, topped with whipped cream and heads out of town to the Millers' house. She blasts the music as she drives with the windows down gaining confidence that she's doing the right thing. The warm air sweeps her hair gently around her face, and she feels free.

She's not sure what she will say to Quinn, but figures she'll know when she sees her. What's important is that she shows up. She knows that much. The words will come later.

50

LENA

Lena pulls into the driveway slowly, biding her time. She still has no idea what she's going to say to Quinn. The iced lattes in the cup holders are sweating droplets despite her best efforts to keep the air cold in the car.

The ride wasn't long enough for Lena to formulate a speech or even to decide which direction she will take when she comes face to face with her friend. She just hopes there's still time to repair the wedge forming between them.

Noticing Quinn's broken-down car on the side of the road, Lena also sees the new car in the driveway, the one Quinn borrowed from Rose. Annoyed since she assumes this means Quinn has been screening her calls, she sits in the car for a moment deciding what to do. Lena checks the time on her phone and eyes the coffees.

Finally, she decides to quickly check on Quinn and drop off her iced latte. There was no sense in wasting a good coffee! Lena is sure her peace offering will be welcomed. Quinn loves her caffeine.

Staring at the house, mustering all of her courage, she's struck by how dominant the house looks from here. Flipping the rundown house had been Jake's idea. *A couple's marriage-building exercise*, he'd said. Somehow, she'd allowed him to convince her that a renovation would be good for their relationship, them working together, making something new.

Jake had sold her on the idea by arguing that it would be a good investment—plus he'd let her design the new look. Limited by their tiny budget in their early years as a young married couple, she'd had to get creative with the limited resources available in town.

She'd been so proud then of her handy work, had felt that swell of pride building in her, but the house had been nothing but a money pit since day one. There was always something in need of repair—a leak in the ceiling, a broken appliance. They'd also had back luck securing reliable tenants leaving them with bills for repairs rather than cash flow. The whole ordeal had been hard on their relationship. It had done the very opposite of what it was intended for.

It had pushed them apart rather than bringing them closer.

Jake had dealt with it by throwing himself into his teaching, and Lena had used yoga and meditation into order to cope with the disappointments and emotional gap.

The house stands in front of her, its shadow looming over her. She doesn't like coming here. This house is a constant reminder of what could have been. Every time she comes here, she feels emptier than she does in her own, lonely home. She needs Quinn's friendship more than she'd realized.

Resolving to try her best to mend things, Lena decides that she will apologize to Quinn even though she's done nothing wrong. She's unsure what the next steps should be as she's never been in this situation before. Turning the car off, she opens the door and stretches out a leg to keep it from closing on her as she grabs the drinks, using her elbow to shut the car door.

She's suddenly feeling very nervous and slightly underdressed for the conversation she's about to have, but quickly rationalizes that Quinn is probably the only person she knows who wouldn't care about her appearance. This makes her relax a little.

Walking up the steps to the house, she notices that the stroller has been left outside by the garage. Ringing the doorbell, she instantly scolds herself for doing so, afraid to have woken Cole with the loud, resonating chime.

"Crap, crap, crap!" she mutters under her breath while hopping nervously on one leg, almost spilling the lattes. "I'm such an idiot!" she reprimands herself as she leans over to the vertical panel window of the door.

Peeking inside, she sees no one coming to the door. No angry Quinn barreling down the stairs with a red-faced Cole. No meal preparations left on the counter from lunchtime. Come to think of it, Lena can't make out any noise. In fact, there is no movement whatsoever.

No visitors then. She exhales.

No one has witnessed her freaking out.

Seeing a tipped-over diaper bag at the entrance as she turns to leave, something else catches her eye. Squinting through the harsh glare of the window, she finds it almost impossible to identify what she's seen. Focusing on it, she realizes that the patio door is wide open.

She shivers. The iced lattes are making her cold.

A drop drips onto the concrete steps as she ponders what she should do. She places the drinks down on the front porch before making her way to the backyard.

She's grateful to be wearing her running shoes as it makes the walk through the long grass much easier to manage. She makes a point to let Jake know that some landscaping will be required in the near future.

She convinces herself that Quinn and Cole must be playing outside, which explains why they didn't hear her at the door. Gathering up her courage with every step, she stops abruptly when she rounds the corner of the house.

The yard is empty. There is no sign of Quinn or Cole.

"What? Where are they?" Lena mutters to herself as she wanders deeper into the yard and quickly turns towards the open door.

"Hello?" she calls out in the empty space.

There's definitely no one else here. She can feel the house's emptiness. It's an echo that only comes out when the house is vacant. Feeling the hair rising on the back of her neck, she begins to worry. Quinn and Cole aren't anywhere to be found. They seem to have vanished into thin air. There is also the strangeness of the open patio door. Curiosity overcomes her.

She needs to find out what's going on.

Lena cautiously walks through the doors careful not to touch anything. Wandering around the house she feels like an intruder even though she and Jake technically own this place. Her eyes skim over every single detail and item the Millers have lying around. Continuing her search through the house, the adrenaline that has propelled her forward starts to fade as she begins her climb to the second floor.

If the first floor shows nothing out of the norm, the second floor is entirely another story.

Lena can tell that something terrible has happened here. The floor is wet and dripping with soap suds. The shower curtain has been ripped from the shower rod and pulled halfway down to the floor. Lena also discovers Quinn's discarded clothes lying abandoned on the tiled floor of the master bathroom.

"What the hell?" Panicking now, Lena begins to frantically search each room. "Quinn? Cole? Anybody?" she yells out.

Where the hell are they? she worries.

She rushes to the hall and practically runs down the stairs and out the front door. She fumbles with her key fob to unlock her car door, trying to locate her phone resting in the center console. She's about to call the police when she spots the next-door neighbour, Mrs. Westover, looking through her living room window at her.

The old woman stands still, seemingly trying to blend in with the curtains, wishing to hide behind them. With a determined air, Lena gets out of her car, abandoning her cell phone and her previous resolve to call the police.

With surging confidence, Lena walks up Mrs. Westover's driveway.

She hears a strange noise coming from inside the house, but barely has time to identify it before Mrs. Westover opens the door tensely and backs up so Lena can enter. Lena just stands there, frozen in place, taking in the sight.

Usually tidy in appearance, Mrs. Westover looks slightly frazzled, as though she'd just run a marathon. Lena thinks that maybe the woman doesn't have an air conditioner in her home, with it being so old, but as fast as the thought hits her, so does a rush of cool air.

Not that then.

Something bothers her, but she can't figure out why her hair is standing up on the back of her neck.

Perhaps she's been gardening? Lena knows how much Mrs. Westover enjoys gardening. She pushes these feelings aside waving her hand in front of her face, seemingly erasing the uneasiness from her mind. She needs to get to the point.

"Rose, have you seen Quinn? We had a tense conversation this morning, and now she won't return my calls. I'm worried about her and Cole. The patio door is open and there's no one there!" Lena speaks quickly as Mrs. Westover keeps her face void of any emotion, completely oblivious to her appearance.

Watching her intently, Lena tries to read Rose's expression. She sees wispy, white hairs out of place frizzing around her head, creating a halo of sorts, yet at this precise moment Mrs. Westover looks nothing like an angel.

Lena also notices that the woman's shirt is untucked which is unusual for her. Frowning, taking this all in, Lena's eyes land on a light, blotchy, red stain on Mrs. Westover's apron. It appears the woman has recently scrubbed it as Lena can still see the water circle around the stain. As her eyes scan the room, Lena takes in the scene. There is a strong smell of bleach in the air, a brilliantly clean, white, porcelain farmhouse sink reflecting the sunshine, and a beautiful quilt on the dining room table where a mismatch of colourful fabric is being sewn together.

Lena's gaze returns to the kitchen, her heart beating quickly. Something doesn't feel right. Rose isn't herself. Her demeanour and her appearance are all off.

The house is eerily quiet. What was that sound she'd heard before?

Straining her neck to see past the elderly woman, Lena spots what is undeniably a bloodstain on the linoleum flooring and her breath catches.

Mrs. Westover remains quiet and still, watching her guest assess the scene, letting her come to her own conclusions. Lena is suddenly terrified. Whatever is going on here, she wants nothing to do with. Her heart pounds faster and she feels like she might pass out. A tingling feeling takes over her, and Lena thinks that this must be what a heart attack feels like. Gasping for air, glued in place, she watches as Mrs. Westover acts quickly.

The old woman lunges to the block of kitchen knives and grabs a large, sharp blade, striding back, bridging the space between them in mere seconds. Lena barely registers what's happening when Rose plunges the knife straight into Lena's abdomen.

As she feels the blade penetrate through her clothes, skin, muscles and organs, Lena finally understands what had seemed off. Mrs. Westover hadn't limped. There was nothing wrong with her leg. The old woman had been faking it all these years. What else had she been hiding?

51

ROSE

Lena is in shock—Rose can tell. She's seen it time and time again.

The girl's adrenaline is pumping through her veins. It always takes a moment for the brain to catch up to what's just happened.

She watches as Lena crashes to her knees, both of her hands holding on to the knife, hesitating, trying to decide if she ought to leave the blade in or remove it. She leaves it alone, only for the blade to sink further inside of her body as she falls.

Although Mrs. Westover would have preferred to skip this inconvenience, she's also rather thrilled. She cannot remember the last time she's had two victims in one day. She'd taken care of Cole fairly quickly.

She'd wanted the least amount of screaming possible and also the least amount of blood to wipe up. All she'd had to do was hold a pillow over the boy's face until he'd stopped breathing. She'd cut off one of his pinky fingers seconds later, opening the sealed pickle jar from the pantry in the basement, and tossing it in next to Maddison's and a few others whose names have escaped her.

She felt rather proud of her achievement. She'd taken a page out of her father's book, acted quickly, and it had paid off.

She's calm as she watches Lena convulse on the floor, allowing the blood to seep where it may, knowing just how to clean up the mess.

Rose isn't worried about being found out—she has a plan.

Lena's unplanned visit had worried Rose at first, but then the woman had offered a perfect solution to get Rose off the hook. By telling Rose about the tense conversation she had had with Quinn earlier, the girl wriggling on her floor has given Rose a way out.

Quinn has a history of depression and had recently attempted suicide. Rose starts toying with the idea of how to spin the story. Just how far would Quinn go? How unstable is she?

Finally, repulsed by Lena's twitching, Rose quickly checks the window to the front yard. She steps into her garage to grab the old tarp that had protected the Corolla. Knowing she needs to act quickly, she returns to Lena's side and uses all the strength she has to drag Lena's body onto the tarp.

Keeping her eyes and ears open for anyone curious enough to peek in, she makes sure that the coast is clear before dragging her victim through the kitchen and towards the basement door. Rose pulls the tarp forcefully down the stairs, Lena's body making a dragging, slumping noise with every step down.

THUMP, THUMP, THUMP.

Rose brings Lena right into the cold space. She stares down at Lena's motionless body, enjoying the sight of the dark blood seeping out of her. Before leaving the girl behind, Rose makes sure to swiftly remove the knife, offering a kind smile to Lena.

"Sorry, dear. You're just a fly who got caught in the wrong web. It won't be long now," she explains calmly before heading back upstairs leaving the woman to die alone in the basement where so many others have taken their last breaths.

52

WILLIAM

William wipes the sweat off his brow. He throws his head back, enjoying a cold one with the boys from his Emergency Service helicopter team. They'd worked relentlessly for sixteen hours straight, only stopping a few times to fly down and get more fuel.

They've been paired up two per aircraft. One person is in charge of the maps, wind direction, and reporting back to the base, while the other can solely focus on flying. William has been flying the entire day. His eyes are burning. He rubs them with the palm of his hand seeing stars behind his eyelids.

It feels like a vacuum has sucked all the moisture from his eyeballs and they're getting increasingly irritated. He knows he probably looks like shit with his eyes bloodshot like in his younger days after parties when he used to smoke something other than cigarettes.

His hair sticks out in various directions from being pulled at during the more stressful moments of the flight, his shirt is soiled from wiping his sweaty forehead on it throughout the day, and there's also a hint of a five o'clock shadow trying its best to make a fierce comeback.

William is doing his best to pay attention to the 'shop talk' as the boys recount the day's events.

"That was a grueling day out there, man," William's partner remarks. "I don't know about you, but I'm feeling that last one. I'm beat," he adds before he slams his drink down on the coaster in front of him and gets up to use the men's room.

They've managed to put out only about a quarter of the fire but, after only a few weeks of fighting the raging flames in this dry climate, they consider that a success. William is eager to get back out there, but he knows it wouldn't be safe.

He desperately needs sleep.

He's barely able to stand on his own two feet, swaying from side to side as though he's reenacting his prom night dance. Feeling pathetic, William carefully rises from his bar stool.

"Alright boys, I'm calling it a night," he bows towards them in a geeky goodbye.

"See you, man," somebody mumbles back, waving an uninterested hand in the air.

He slaps a heavy hand on several shoulders on the way out of the bar, unsure if he knows the men he's waving goodbye to or if they're other pilots on his team. He's had quite a bit to drink tonight. Alcohol has been his remedy for dealing with the long, stressful days fighting fires and the lonely nights away from his family.

Remarkably, William successfully crosses the poorly lit parking lot and finds his way to his prepaid motel room. It's no secret that the school didn't splurge on the rooms.

William tries to push away the memory of the dirty toilet that had welcomed him several weeks ago. He'd be surprised if the staff cleaned the rooms regularly. Crumbs and dust had stuck to the bottoms of his feet when he'd dared to remove his socks. He'd only made that mistake once.

Rather than picturing himself at a regular motel, like he's accustomed to, William likes to pretend he's living with roommates who are out for the night. Thinking about it this way helps him feel better if he randomly discovers more unsanitary housekeeping.

After living with Quinn for several years, William has gotten used to her need for everything to be tidy. His wife's constant demands regarding laundry, cleaning, and organization used to make his head spin but he misses that now. He misses her.

Shutting the cheap plastic blinds which propels more dust into the air, William exhales. He's finally alone. Being with someone else for sixteen hours straight is exhausting, even when you don't talk constantly.

You're always on guard. Always keeping yourself in check, never letting your hair down, so to speak.

Christ, William had needed to fart all day and had been holding it in. It feels good to have a few hours of solitude. He doesn't feel like seeing or talking to anyone until he's showered and gotten some sleep.

Staggering to the tiny bathroom, he nearly trips over the duvet lying on the floor. The cleaners haven't been here today, then. He isn't surprised by anything anymore. William absentmindedly grabs his phone on his way back from the bathroom and scrolls through social media, liking and commenting on various posts.

He feels a little homesick. He misses his friends from Kingston, but he doesn't want to admit this to Quinn. He's well aware that she's not entirely pleased with the move and worries that any hesitation on his part might just give her the push she needs to change his mind.

Ever since Cole was born, William has been struggling to connect with Quinn. She'd first claimed they couldn't be intimate—doctor's orders, she'd said. That was months ago. He'd done his best to wait for her to be ready.

He rubs a hand over his face feeling guilty for his impatience. His wife needed his support, but William's patience was growing lean. He craved that physical connection with her. He wasn't going to be connecting with her that way anytime soon.

And they'd talked about what might happen when she'd gotten pregnant. They had known it was a strong possibility that Quinn would relapse into depression after Cole's birth. They just hadn't imagined how hard it would be.

Quinn's attempted suicide had burst his optimistic bubble forcing him to face the fact that his wife was indeed very ill. That devastating event compounded with the stress he'd been facing in his studies had sent him spiraling into old habits he'd been trying to avoid for years.

He knows exhaustion is a major trigger, starting the snowball effect, yet how can he possibly avoid where his mind goes automatically?

His work requires him to work long hours, expecting the same from all pilots. He'd practically begged for this assignment, and now he has to prove he's been worthy of getting the chance. Jake had graciously pulled many strings to make this opportunity available to him, and William refuses to let his boss down. He needs to push through even though his muscles ache and he feels lonely.

Unfortunately, since being here, the lack of sleep was being medicated by golden liquid from glass bottles. Feeling the familiar buzz from the alcohol radiating through his body, William's innocent social media browsing quickly escalates to visiting pornography sites.

Although he hasn't visited these sites in years, he has no trouble remembering the web links by heart. It was a nightly habit he'd had for over a decade, one often triggered by an excess of alcohol. One just simply doesn't forget something like that, no matter how much self-restraint one might have.

After clicking through several videos, feeling satisfied, William checks the time in the top right corner of his phone. Noticing the low battery symbol, he plugs the device into its charger for the night. He won't be getting much sleep again tonight, but he's determined to take advantage of every second of solitude.

He does a cursory check of any missed calls and notices several from Quinn. He doesn't bother checking the voicemail, deciding that it would be too late to call her back now anyway. Besides, his head is starting to spin and he feels a desperate desire to close his eyes. He resolves that he'll call her first thing the morning. Whatever it is, she can wait a few hours.

53

DYLAN

Dylan is terrified. *What was he thinking?* He climbs up the stairs to his house as quickly as he can and shuts the door behind him turning the lock. He rushes around the house shutting all the blinds. His hands are shaking. *How could he have been so stupid?* He should have called Detective Feldman when he'd first seen the car.

All sense had escaped him once he'd seen it and that young woman holding her baby in her arms. He'd been struck with such intense grief and jealousy that he'd acted purely from instinct and pain. He hadn't been thinking clearly. He shouldn't have followed her home. He shouldn't have gone inside.

He'd been so careless, acting impulsively. He'd touched the scratches on the car, practically caressing the indent with his fingers, reminded of the last time he'd ever seen his wife alive. His prints would be easily detectable.

His heart is pounding hard as he thinks of the baby boy. What has he done? He's destroyed that family. He's done that—no one else. He's completely to blame for the decisions he made today.

He can try to justify it, but he knows deep in his soul that it had been nothing more than a vengeance. He's wanted his wife's killer to pay—only now he's the one with blood on his hands.

He can't shake the image of the woman—a woman whose name he doesn't yet know—lying on the cooling forest floor, looking almost angelic. Only he'd known better. There'd been nothing pure about her. Knowing what she'd done to his family, Dylan is surprised he'd resisted bashing her head in himself out of pure rage.

The woman hadn't been moving when he'd stood over her. He'd risked a glance before he'd cowardly run away. How wrong it had all gone in a mere matter of minutes!

He's sore and gulping for air from his earlier stunt in the woods. Who was he kidding? He wasn't the young, fit man he'd once been. The sprint through the thick foliage had taken every ounce of energy he'd had. The earlier adrenaline he'd felt was quickly seeping out of him and he feels weak in the knees. Collapsing on his bed, he lies on his back with his arms thrown in abandon above his head.

"What am I going to do now?" he moans to himself. Turning his head to look at his wife's picture on the nightstand, he feels judgement radiating towards him from beyond the grave. This isn't him. He doesn't do things like this. Why has he taken such a great risk? Why has he been so stupid?

As scared as he feels, there's a small part of him that's relieved. *It's over*, he says to himself. At least, that's what he thinks. He's taken justice into his own hands and righted a wrong. He can finally put all the questions regarding his wife's killer behind him. As he lies on the bed, his anger finds him like a warm blanket—a welcome, old friend.

Dylan doesn't care who the woman was. He doesn't care that she was a mother and a wife. To him, she'd been a killer and she'd gotten what she deserved.

54

HENRY
AUGUST 14TH, 2014

His belly full of fried eggs, beans, and toast, Henry sets out early in the morning to get his bearings for the upcoming hunting season. He's dressed in full camo gear, the abstract pattern of brown, black, and green helping him to blend in with his surroundings. He carries a compass, a map, and a notebook in a small backpack. He's seeking the perfect hiding spot to track and shoot deer.

Henry has been hunting deer for over thirty years. He's known around the area for his scrumptious venison pepperettes. He has a waiting list of orders started already, and hunting season hasn't even begun yet.

His thick skin is weathered by the sun and the years. He has grown out his beard out over the last few months, despite the heat. He doesn't want to risk his shaving cream putting off a scent that would alert the deer giving away his position. He's so committed to deer hunting that he even recently quit smoking cigarettes to see if his chances improve this season. He discovered scent-free soap at the grocery store in town and it's proving to be worth the extra money.

He's careful not to say words like "kill", or "dead" when he talks about his hunts. Some of the townspeople look down on his hobby. He's not the only one around here that hunts, but since he's the most successful hunter, he gets the most heat for it.

Last night's heavy rainfall has finally let up. The sun is starting to peek through the tops of the trees as he walks out into the vastness of his property. He owns nearly a hundred acres between North Bay and Sturgeon Falls.

His father had previously owned a hobby farm on half of the acreage, but the rest has always remained wooded. Henry's heavy boots are like feathers on the ground as he expertly wanders the forest like it's his second home. He's mindful of every step he takes, careful not to disturb the land.

For years, he's trained himself to walk through the forest almost undetected by walking slowly and avoiding dry leaves. This won't be a problem today due to last night's rainfall. He wanders throughout the tall trunks, avoiding broken twigs. He pauses regularly to take in the sun's few rays penetrating through the thick foliage. Hunting can't be hurried. It takes patience and skill more than strength and haste.

A couple of black squirrels scurry past him. Unaware of his presence they playfully chase each other up a nearby tree trunk. He blends in with the wildlife. This is one of his favourite things to do. He feels so good in the woods, as though he's amongst friends. Some of these friends he will eat for dinner later.

The air deep in the forest is different under the cover of the trees. He can smell leaves rotting, fresh ferns growing, and new mushrooms sprouting from the rain last night. The scent of pine needles scattered throughout the forest is intoxicating. The colours are vivid and dark at the same time.

Henry tries not to step on the fragile moss even though it would make a good sound barrier. He respects the life growing in the forest. So many trees have been lost over the years to man or fire. The hunter does his best to keep the forest healthy. He maintains it as best as he can, cutting down dead trees to make space for others to reach the sunlight and rain they desperately crave. Even though he's not hunting right now, he tends to get right back into the groove of things the moment he enters the forest. *A creature of habit*, he's been called.

Although he's walking ahead, his eyes are constantly scanning the forest floor for any large roots or boulders to avoid. The uneven ground is a signature of the northern forests.

He spots movement to his right and before even seeing what it is, he already knows by the rapid rhythm of the sound that it's a chipmunk. The hurried rustling of leaves is more noise than one would expect such a little creature to make. A Blue Jay calls loudly above as a cloud of fog lifts through the air.

His eyes staring upwards, he sees a few silent crows, watching him watch them. They remain silent trying to decide if he's a friend or foe.

Henry learned long ago to never cross a crow.

Their memories last forever, and they share knowledge about their enemies with each other, remembering the faces of those who've wronged them, ganging up to attack. He'd rather stay on their good side. He has a lot of respect for them. They are smart creatures that often get a bad rap—kind of like him.

Henry sees no indication of wind this morning in the leaves as his gaze lifts to watch the birds fly above his head. He loves being in these woods. It's where he feels at his best. The fresh, pine smell, the cedar, the soundtrack of birds, and the natural light have always been favourites of his.

Having grown up on a hobby farm, he's always enjoyed the smell of fresh-cut hay and grass. Henry stops walking for a moment to close his eyes and appreciate the moment of solitude. His backpack is purely for show this morning. He knows his way around these woods and won't be needing it.

He wipes a bead of sweat from his brow as he removes his brown and green, camo ball cap. Without the wind, the air feels thick, like he could slice it with an axe.

He sports heavy, lined pants, a warm sweater, and thick socks. A bad call on his part. Saying he's warm is an understatement. His clothing is glued to him like a wet shower curtain sticks to a wall. He needs to find a spot to make camp before he completely melts away.

There is sweat on his upper lip that matches the dew on the grass, but Henry presses on further into the woods. The deeper in he gets, the cooler he starts to feel. The thick leaves provide good coverage from the sun rays. Henry's ball cap has been doing a poor job of keeping the harsh rays off his skin. He's grateful for nature's fix to his problem.

He thinks of these trees as family and comes to visit them often. With a gloved hand, he touches some of the tall giants as he passes by—greeting them, thanking them for the reprieve from the sun, liking the feel of the rough bark gripping the fabric of his glove. It's almost as though the trees don't want him to leave. He could spend all day out here away from people. He's always preferred solitude.

His four-legged companion, Kip, trails along behind him, sniffing widely at the ground eager to find something to sink his teeth into. He's a real teddy bear at home, but out here in the forest, the dog purely goes off of a deeper instinct.

Kip is a beautiful, chocolate brown Pointer of about six years old. He's been good company to Henry and enjoys running around the forest floors almost as much as Henry does. The pair get along great and understand each other.

Kip is happily wandering off the path, as he usually does, while Henry busies himself looking at tracks in the mud, scuffs on the bark, and visible pathways through the ferns and grass that deer might have taken recently. He's looking up high to try and find a solid tree on which to install his tree stand when he hears a distant whimper from Kip.

Usually, if Kip finds an animal carcass, he barks three times to get Henry's attention. This whimper is different—unusual. Henry doesn't know what to expect as he strains his eyes to see where Kip has gone off to.

Stepping off the path slightly, he sees his dog running towards him with what appears to be a piece of clothing in his mouth.

When Henry picks it up, he realizes there are splatters of blood covering the garment. His heart beats in his chest as he quickly understands what Kip must have found. Gripping the fabric in his gloved hand, he steps over several large, fallen tree trunks, and carefully hops over a small stream as Kip hurriedly shows him the way.

There is an urgency in his step although he's wary of what he'll find.

He discovers the body a few meters away from the path. As he carefully steps closer, he realizes he is looking at a woman. Her long, black hair covers most of her face, and he cannot make out any identifying features. She is lying on her side, wrapped in what appears to be an oversized, plaid bathrobe. The belt is missing, and he realizes that this is what Kip had brought him.

Kneeling to take a closer look, he observes the small rise and fall of her shoulders. She's alive! *Thank God!* It takes everything in him not to yelp for joy. Although he's a hunter and used to seeing death, he's never seen a dead human. He's quite uncomfortable at the sight of this barely dressed and unconscious woman but knows he will need to go and get help—fast.

She appears to be younger than him, approximately in her thirties. Her skin lacks colour. Through some parts in her dark mane, he notices a deep, bloody gash on her forehead that will surely require some stitches. Henry's more concerned about injuries he can't see.

He feels ridiculously overdressed as he's in close proximity to her. Hastily, he removes his coat and drapes it over her body, partly to cover her exposed parts, but also to keep her warm until he can get help.

Seeing no other alternative, he holds on to the belt from the robe, calling Kip to his side with a whistle between his teeth. Henry stands up and turns around heading back to the trail. Once back on familiar ground, he ties the blood-splattered belt onto a large tree to make it easier to find the spot when he returns with the authorities.

Without wasting another second, knowing he can't do more to help the woman by standing idle, he abruptly turns on his heel and heads back towards his truck. He needs to hurry. He needs his phone. He's worried about the woman in the woods. Her breathing had looked laboured and her colouring ghostly.

If humans die in similar fashion to animals, Henry knows the woman doesn't have much time left.

55

HENRY

He's wheezing by the time he reaches his pickup truck and reaches for his phone. He makes the call to emergency services and waits by his truck as instructed. While he waits, the operator keeps him on the phone and asks more details about what Henry noticed at the scene and of the woman's condition.

Two patrol cars arrive promptly only ten minutes after Henry placed the call. They drive towards his cabin, their lights flashing, and find him standing by his truck. Kip remains by his owner's side the entire time, sitting alert and anxiously wagging his tail back and forth on the ground. He's been quiet otherwise and Henry is grateful for his company. A man's best friend.

The driver's door of the first car opens and the police officer awkwardly steps out of his vehicle, grabbing the steering wheel to push himself up. Henry doesn't fail to notice that the vehicle isn't sitting as low to the ground anymore. He sees the man's partner, a younger female officer stepping out of the car, shutting the door with a soft click.

"Hello there, sir. Are you Henry Darch, the one who called in about a body in the woods?" The male officer introduces himself as Officer Jones. He gives Henry a solid handshake, pumping his hand hard several times before releasing it.

"That's right. Found her up the path some, a few meters off to the north." Henry gestures in the right direction before offering more.

"I tied the belt of her bathrobe to a tree to make it easy to find the spot." His face is serious as he speaks with the police. He feels his cheeks redden due to his earlier jog to the truck and the sudden realization of his mistake.

"I know I probably shouldn't have touched anything, but my dog here brought me the belt from the woman's robe, which is how I was able to find her," he adds sheepishly. "I also dropped my jacket over her to keep her warm," he mentions. "It didn't feel right leaving her out there like that." He shakes his head, the memory fresh.

Both officers nod in understanding and the woman makes a note in her notepad.

As they are speaking, Henry watches two more police officers exit the second car. He stiffens, suddenly feeling uncomfortable and outnumbered. He doesn't have any plans of getting on their bad side, not today anyway. But the sting of the past is still there. Henry knows they won't need his prints to eliminate him from the scene. They already have his in their system.

He's not unfamiliar with the police. He has his own history with them, although his days of drinking too much alcohol and getting kicked out of pubs in his college years are long behind him. Still, he can't escape his past in this small town. His record follows him wherever he goes. He's not the police's biggest fan, but in this circumstance, Henry hopes they can all work together to get this woman some help.

While the police officers write down more information, Henry spots the shining blue and red lights of an ambulance coming down the path towards them. He can't remember the last time there were so many vehicles at the cabin.

He watches as two paramedics hop out and begin working efficiently, opening the back doors and preparing a portable gurney to carry with them into the thicker parts of the woods. There isn't a moment to lose. The woman's condition can only worsen as her injured body remains exposed to the elements.

"Right. Well, you better lead the way," one of the male officer gestures ahead when they are all set.

There's a haziness to the air. It's the kind of day when you can literally see the heat waves hovering over the ground. Henry pushes through the path, focused on being silent. The hunter doesn't mind skipping the mindless chit-chat.

This isn't some leisurely nature walk. He's leading a team of emergency responders to a woman's body. Today, he's not a drunken low-life—he's a hero. He's enjoying the importance this new title gives him.

"It's not much further," he reassures them after walking for a good ten minutes through the thick foliage. He hasn't bothered being careful with his steps. He knows his efforts at protecting the forest floor won't be shared by the rest and would only slow them down. He hopes the forest will forgive him for it.

With a lump forming in his throat, he chances a glance behind him as he leads the group down the isolated path. He can tell some the officers aren't used to being this deep in the woods. Some of them are breathing heavily and are struggling to avoid the large boulders sticking up from the ground and the slippery mud. Kip remains silent beside him like he knows that this situation is serious.

As Henry had hoped, they easily locate the belt tied to the tree, and he leads them down the brush to where the woman is lying. Henry is relieved when he sees she's still breathing. Officer Jones informs Henry they will need to keep his coat for analysis to rule it out when they test for any fabric samples.

"Just a formality," the officer reassures him.

"That's no problem, sir. Like I mentioned, I just didn't want her to be cold, lying like that." Henry awkwardly gestures to the barely-dressed woman, who's still unconscious.

"That was good thinking on your part, Mr. Darch," one of the paramedics remarks as they move to inspect the woman's injuries, and presumably to decide how to move her.

Henry feels a tingle of pride at being addressed with such appreciation and respect, but it quickly evaporates when Officer Jones turns towards him and asks him to step back to give the team room to work.

Looking on from a few paces away, Henry feels weak. He's never had any children, but he imagines how he would feel if this were his daughter, lying half-naked in the middle of the woods, left for dead. A deep anger stirs up within him.

His father had been physically abusive, throwing punches whenever he'd felt like it. Henry had been on edge for most of his childhood, never knowing what mood his father would be in when he came home.

Over the years, Henry had built a life for himself and moved out on his own as soon as it had been possible. He hadn't needed much and had easily adapted to a life of solitude, low stress, and routine. He preferred when things were predictable, and he didn't like surprises.

Today's events made him uncomfortable. Seeing the young woman injured brought back memories he'd much rather push away. Sensing his discomfort, Kip lifts his head, butting his nose to Henry's hand for support, bringing him back to the present.

After examining her for several minutes, the paramedics carefully lift the woman's body onto the gurney. Henry hears them talking about a faint pulse. There is a sense of urgency as they place an oxygen mask over her nose and mouth and tie her down so as not to move her around too much just in case she's broken something they can't yet see.

From what Henry can tell, she doesn't seem to have any obviously broken bones, but then again, he knows nothing about internal bleeding. The cut on her forehead looks even more ghastly than before. Henry is used to seeing blood, but the sight before him disturbs him deeply.

He has to turn his eyes away so as not to be sick. He can feel the nausea climbing up his throat. He needs to sit down. Who was this woman and why was she out here looking like that? Henry feels tears prickling his eyes.

Who would do this to another human being? What kind of monster would do this?

When Henry hunted deer, it was for their meat. *But what purpose does killing or trying to kill another human serve?* he wondered.

Tears streak down his cheeks and he turns away from the scene, Kip nuzzling at his elbow. A person who could hurt another human was pure evil, he decided. Feeling the bitterness entering him, he leaned on a tree and sobbed.

56

WILLIAM

William and his flight partner, Chris, have been in the air for several hours when Chris gets a call in his noise-cancelling earphones. William keeps his eyes trained on the flight path, but notices the shift in the energy of the cabin. Whoever is on the other end of that phone call has just delivered his buddy some bad news.

The poor bastard, William thinks.

He busies himself with the flight once Chris ends the call. William doesn't want it to look like he's been eavesdropping. He triple checks the switches, clears his throat, and does his best to appear normal, but the air in the cabin is suddenly thick—tense.

William takes a quick glance in his partner's direction, his curiosity winning him over. Chris's face is pale, like he's going to be sick. William feels his heart drop.

Shit.

It had been bad news after all. Giving the man some time to process the news, William feels a lump forming in his throat. Chris had been beaming with joy just a few days ago after getting a call from his wife telling him she was pregnant. With Chris's face so serious, William takes a deep breath, unsure how to support his new friend. He imagines Chris's wife has lost the baby and feels devastated for them.

After a few moments of silence, Chris, with his face still blanched, turns to William and requests to return to the ground. William figures his partner needs a moment to collect himself and turns the helicopter around heading for base.

As soon as they land, he turns off the aircraft and looks over to Chris with the intention of offering him some words of comfort, anything to ease the pain his friend is experiencing. Only, when William turns to him, Chris is staring right at him, his eyes wide with fear.

Confused, William is about to ask Chris what's wrong when out of the crew cab window he notices two uniformed police officers standing against the wall, looking sullen.

William opens the door and both he and Chris step out onto the concrete floor and make their way over to the other men. They are accompanied by William's team leader, Fred, whose hair is standing on end and is wearing a creased shirt badly tucked in, looking as though he's just gotten out of bed despite it being mid-morning.

"Mr. William Miller?" one police officer asks, expertly flipping through his notepad.

"Yes, that me," William's voice cracks in response coughing a few times to clear it.

"May we step inside?" the other officer asks, pointing to the tiny room in the corner of the flight bay.

Without uttering a word, William nods and follows the police officers into the small space, almost holding his breath as the door shuts behind him.

William can see Chris through the large window which opens into the flight bay but looks away from his friend's terrified expression. Chris must assume William knows what this is all about, but he's wrong—William is just as lost as he is.

Having vacated the only chair in the room, the bay supervisor stands along the wall next to Chris, a stern expression on his face. No one dares to take the only available seat, and the men awkwardly remain standing in a circle facing each other waiting for someone to speak.

"Mr. Miller, I'm afraid we've come to share some bad news," the first police officer tells him, looking sympathetic.

William's throat goes dry. He's not certain he's heard him correctly. The officers are here for him? Bad news?

"What's happened?" he manages nervously.

"Your wife is in hospital after being found unconscious in the woods behind your house and your son, Cole..." He refers to his notes, flipping pages with his thumb before adding, "...has been reported missing." He frowns, as if on cue, doing as he's been told to do with his mouth when delivering bad news, but lacking any sort of understanding of the worry and pain that he also causes.

"What?" William croaks, fear and emotion taking over. He leans on a nearby wall to compose himself. Pressing a hand over his heart, he looks down at his boots, one of the laces undone and lying loosely on the floor.

"I don't understand," William finally adds. He goes through every possible scenario in his mind, coming up blank. "What's going on? What do you mean missing?"

William would be lying if he said that he was surprised to hear about his wife's state, but the news that Cole is missing bothers him.

Had Quinn taken Cole somewhere? Where was she heading?

With Quinn's history of mental health issues, William had been concerned about her state of mind when the opportunity presented itself to fight fires in British Columbia. She'd been looking grim the last time he saw her. He shouldn't have left her all alone in a new town, especially not so soon after her suicide attempt. He understands that now, but it's too late.

The truth was that William had needed a break from the responsibilities of home and the exhausting school work. He'd wanted to get his hands dirty, be a part of the action, and prove himself with the big guys in the hopes that one day he would be able to easily get a job there.

Northern Ontario certainly had some gorgeous outdoor spots with lush forests and wide bodies of water, but William's dream had always been to move to British Columbia. He's always wanted to escape from the busyness of city life and live in a small, off-grid, log house. To raise his family. Perhaps own a few goats, some chickens, and even a horse. He often imagines this scenario to help him sleep at night, keeping his ambitions at the top of his mind to help persuade him to try his best every day.

Hearing one of the police officers clear his throat, William's attention returns to the small room. Lifting his head, he quickly notices that all eyes are on him. Whether they are analyzing his reaction to the news or waiting for him to ask more questions, he can't be sure.

He's aware that in cases like this, the husband is typically the prime suspect. Is that why they've come here tonight? Surely they know that William's been working up here for weeks.

Maybe they have reason to believe Quinn and Cole were forced to leave. Just the very idea of someone hurting his family sends a strong wave of nausea rising up his throat, last night's binge drinking coming back in full force.

He feels his knees buckle, imagining the worst. Sensing his distress, the officer addresses him kindly.

"Mr. Miller, our colleagues are doing everything they can to locate your son. They have multiple search parties being organized as we speak," he states in reassurance before switching to a more interrogating tone. "Can you tell us the last time you had any contact with your wife?" he questions. His notepad is at the ready to record any information William is willing to share before requesting the presence of his lawyer—which William hesitates to do.

Shaking off the paranoia, William considers that the police officer's question is probably aimed at building a usable timeline to help pinpoint when Quinn and Cole were last seen.

He hesitates as he wills himself to remember. His memory is still fuzzy from alcohol and lack of sleep.

William finally answers, "I didn't talk to her today. I saw she called, yesterday but I haven't returned her call yet." He rubs a hand over his stiff neck, tears threatening to fall as the guilt builds up.

Maybe Quinn had needed his help and he hadn't been there for her. What could he have even done from so far away? Something—he could have done something.

"How did she seem the last time you talked to her?" the police officer presses.

"Fine. She seemed normal. I didn't notice anything off," William replies, feeling his stomach churning. Where was Quinn? What's happened?

Brushing him off, the police officer closest to him holds out a standard white paper with a printed, coloured photograph of an old 1994 red Corolla.

"Mr. Miller, can you please identify this vehicle?"

William shakes his head.

He doesn't recognize the car but it's clear that the car is parked in his driveway. He notices the rental house's white siding in the background.

William's pretty certain he's never seen this car before in his life, but something about the question and the sudden silence in the room tells him he must answer carefully. His answer might drastically impact the chance of the police finding his son. William looks at the photograph for a long time, trying to remember if he's ever seen this car before.

"No, I don't recognize it," he finally answers, weary of considering the consequences that may arise from his response.

The room remains silent for a beat before the officers exchange a glance and stand up in unison.

"Mr. Miller, we're going to have to ask you to come with us," the police officer indicates.

"What? Why? Am I under arrest? I need to go home to my wife and to look for my son!" William's patience is wearing thin. He wants to know what's going on, but no one is telling him anything. So far, they've only asked questions. He's tired and frustrated, and he feels utterly useless. He needs answers.

"We will fly you back home so that you can go see your wife but in the meantime, we have more questions for you," the one officer replies.

William can only nod. It's obvious that he's not the one in control of this situation, so he may as well go willingly and not get into more trouble than he already feels he's in. Without wasting any time, the group exits the tiny room and walks over to the waiting police car sitting outside the garage. William and his team lead exchange concerned glances on the way out.

Thunder roars in the sky threatening a heavy rainfall. William can't help but think of the meaning of the sudden change in weather. While it will be great to fight off the fires, it also looms with the threat that something terrible has happened.

57

QUINN

Quinn can hear the faint beeping sound of a nearby monitor. The beeps match the beats of her weak heartbeat. She's alive, but barely. How she's still living is a mystery to her. She was so sure she was going to die alone in that forest.

She aches all over, every muscle is sore and stiff. An oxygen mask is strapped to her face making her feel claustrophobic. Quinn keeps her eyes closed, shielding herself from reality for a brief moment. Focusing all her energy on inhaling and exhaling, filling her lungs, keeping her alive. It takes everything for her to remain calm.

"She's waking up," someone says to her right.

She hears the squeak of running shoes on the floor as the person gets closer, and she opens her eyes.

"Hi, sweetheart, my name is Jill, and I'm your nurse. You're at the Sturgeon Falls Hospital," she waits a beat to allow Quinn to process this.

Memories of how she ended up here come flooding in. Quinn's eyes fill with tears and she blinks them back, trying to focus on the woman standing over her. Seeing Jill's gentle face smiling down at her is reassuring. Quinn instantly begins to feel calmer.

Jill's eyes are kind and full of love.

Quinn is in good hands.

Just as she allows herself to relax, she remembers that she doesn't know what's happened to Cole. She jerks herself upright, the wires attached to her tightening against the pull. The beeping on the machine increases at an alarming rate.

"My son! Where's Cole?" she croaks out as loudly as she can.

Jill begins to move around her quickly. Quinn has trouble keeping her eyes on her. Her head is bandaged, some of the white gauze falling over her eyes making the edges of her vision blurry. Jill firmly shoves Quinn back down on the bed and pushes medicine through the IV. A sedative surely, Quinn thinks as the warm liquid courses through her, sending her into a sleepy state again.

She dreams of Cole and of his blue eyes. She imagines his chubby cheeks and his laugh. She can feel hot tears dripping down her cheeks and into her ears as she cries, but she doesn't want to wake up—not yet. She doesn't want to face reality yet.

She feels heavy. She can't move.

The fear and the sedative are working their way through her system, paralyzing her. Seeing Cole this happy in her mind pulls at her heartstrings. She cannot remember the last time she saw her boy look this happy. She doesn't know how long it's been since she's held him. She tries to calculate it, but the exercise hurts her brain so she releases it. She lets go and falls asleep.

———

Quinn feels someone holding her hand. The skin, which is rough and warm, comforts her. She smells a familiar scent and begins to tear up.

William. He's back. He's here with her.

Slowly, Quinn opens her eyes and looks into the eyes of the man she loves. They haven't talked in several days. William looks as terrible as Quinn feels. The pair look at each other for a long time without speaking. So much has happened since they last talked, neither of them knows where to begin.

Quinn recalls her conversation with Lena, about how William had lied to her about being chosen to go fight fires in B.C. She remembers how she had needed him when the car broke down, but couldn't get a hold of him.

How desperately she'd needed him when Cole was taken but she had been forced to deal with it on her own.

Her husband, the man who'd moved her away from all she knew, had abandoned her for months in an isolated town, alone, caring for their young child in a strange home.

Resentful, Quinn starts to pull her hand away, feeling bitter, sensing her heart growing cold with every memory of how William has let her down. Her mind turns dark as the negative thoughts begin spinning faster as she contemplates her husband's selfishness. She begins to wonder if he truly loves her or if she was simply an accessory to his piloting dream. Quinn begins to doubt her love for him, the vile taste in her mouth becoming more prevalent.

William's smile fades. Like candle wax getting hot, his skin seems to melt as his lips curve down. Quinn's unexpected rejection to his touch hurts him deeply, she can see the pain on his face.

Part of her feels sorry for him, but she's so furious with him that she cannot bear the thought of comforting him when she's the one needing comfort.

She feels miserable—her heart aches and her head throbs. She's unsure if she's broken any bones, but her spirit is definitely shattered into a million pieces. Every ounce of her wants to rip out the IV pinned to her hand and go search for Cole. She's completely shattered by her son's kidnapping and William's lie. Neither of them has been entirely truthful.

The idea she's had of her perfect marriage of love, respect, and honesty has been destroyed and now she cannot un-see it.

"I'm sorry," he finally says and she can tell that he means it. She's not sure what he's sorry for, but she'll take it.

Quinn knows she will need her husband by her side for whatever's next. They will need to work as a team if they are to survive this. She starts to cry, not knowing how to tell him that she's failed. She can't bear the thought of admitting that she's lost Cole.

Looking into his eyes and seeing the layers of pain in them, she can see that he already knows. She breaks down once more. William knows but he's still here, sticking by her.

Jill comes up next to Quinn and checks her oxygen levels. Happy with the results, she removes the mask over Quinn's mouth and smiles kindly at the couple. Before they can talk, two police officers enter her hospital room and address Quinn.

"Mrs. Miller, welcome back," the female police officer smiles at her, but the smile doesn't last as she gets right to business. "We'd like to ask you a few questions regarding what happened to you."

"OK," Quinn manages to mutter, before responding with a slow nod.

She isn't sure she'll be much help. She can't even remember what day it is or how she's ended up in this hospital in the first place. She must have hit her head pretty hard. A bandage is taped to her forehead and the skin feels tender when she frowns.

"How did you know I was here?" she turns to William.

The officer closest to her answers for him, "The triage nurse in Emergency saw you when you came in with the paramedics. She watched your stretcher being pushed through the doors and heard one of the paramedics refer to you as Jane Doe." He absentmindedly rubs his cheek before he continues. "She recognized you as the same patient who'd been admitted not too long ago for a suicide attempt." At this he lowers his voice and his gaze.

"You know, small town..." he offers as though that explained everything. "With the approximate date of your last visit, she was able to find your file, your name and your emergency contact—William." He indicates her husband as though she might have forgotten who he is.

"We sent some local B.C. police officers to get William and fly him back here to be with you before you woke up."

Impressed, Quinn remains mute, looking at her wrists, the scars still pink and healing.

Without further delay, the police officer goes on. "Mrs. Miller, could you please start at the beginning and explain how you ended up unconscious in the middle of the woods?" the officer inquires as he prepares her notebook.

Quinn hesitates. Scratching an itch on her arm to kill time.

Where should she start? With the man running away with Cole? Or the car breaking down? Or perhaps even with her conversation with Lena that sent her out for a walk, only to come home sweaty and longing for a shower.

She decides to start with the man. She needs them to focus on finding her son, not on her own mental state. She gives a detailed description of the man as best she can remember from her casual glance in his direction during her walk. She remembers him clutching Cole's blue blanket and herself grabbing William's plaid bathrobe.

The specific details are still hazy in her memory. She closes her eyes to remember better.

She remembers yelling, but had anyone heard her?

58

ROSE

A shadow hovers at the front door. Rose notices the light change in the window. She quickly gets to her feet as she hears the hard knock on the door.

When she opens it, she finds two uniformed officers standing there with hats on their heads, their eyes slightly obscured. She feigns surprise at their presence. While one of the police officers talks to her, the other peers over her shoulder, trying to see into the house. He's not being subtle about it, therefore Rose moves aside and invites them in.

She's been expecting this visit, yet she hadn't been sure how long it would take them to find Quinn's body in the woods. Proud of herself for having the foresight to drop Lena's car back in the Adkins' driveway and dispose of the iced lattes at the same time, she feels calm. Now there's no indication that Lena had been to visit Quinn at all.

"Please, have a seat, officers," she motions for them to sit in the kitchen, doing her best to keep her voice frail and her movements slow. A smile plays on her lips as she turns to face the sink patting down her apron.

She's well-practiced at dealing with police officers after watching her father interact with them. She keeps up the charm, as she'd learned a long time ago that being friendly can go a long way. Her willingness to help also makes her appear innocent.

When people have something to hide, they can get pretty defensive—evasive. Rose knows how to play her part perfectly. She knows how to appear appropriately concerned by police officers' presence but has perfected the appearance of fretting, letting the police officers know that she's a little unsettled by their presence as most would be if officers were paying them a visit at home.

She busies herself by filling the kettle with tap water and setting it on the stove to boil, turning back to the officers so they can discuss what they've come for.

"We're investigating the disappearance of a young infant by the name of Cole Miller, your neighbours' son," he nods his head in the direction of the Millers' house.

"Cole is missing?" Rose pretends to be shocked by the news and overcome with grief. She expertly places a worried hand over her heart as though distraught by the news. "Oh, dear, how terrible! I wonder what happened."

She knows that she's doing a good job of appearing concerned, but she can't help but wonder why they haven't mentioned that Quinn is missing as well. Rose doesn't offer any new information; she lets the police officers lead the way.

"There appears to have been a struggle at the house next door yesterday. Do you remember hearing or seeing anything unusual yesterday afternoon, August 13th?" the police officer queries, his attention on her every move, while his nosy partner, the silent observer, remains standing and looking around.

He begins to move over to the living room, making Rose nervous. Yet she holds her tongue, plays the part and smiles sadly, returning her attention to the police officer at the table.

She shakily pours hot water into a green pot with a few bags of black tea and lets it steep for several moments. She needs to appear bothered by the officers being in her house and not be too forthcoming with her answers and comments or they might suspect that she knows more than she's let on. She's enjoying this. She loves having the upper hand and knowing more than they do.

Pretending to think, Rose replies with laughter, "I'm sorry, but I'm having trouble even remembering what I ate for lunch today!" She chuckles at this truth. "I believe I may have been gardening," she finally answers.

"Did you see or hear anything?" Sitting straighter, alert, he presses.

"I heard a scream and then silence," she casually states.

The police officer in the living room slowly turns his gaze towards her and steps back into the kitchen. He's about to ask a follow-up question, when Rose sighs and smiles adding, "But then again, the lady next door, Quinn, well, she's always screaming at her son. To her, he never does anything right. I babysat Cole a few times for them. Mrs. Miller couldn't get rid of him fast enough," she shares.

She's managed to captivate the attention of both police officers. She carefully stands up from her chair to get some delicate teacups and saucers, milk and sugar. She sets everything down on the round table and waits for the next question.

"You didn't suspect anything else was going on?" the police officer asks.

"Not really. Like what?" she questions, wondering what they know, but the police officers remain expressionless—they won't give anything away. "When I'm gardening I kind of block everything out. I'm in the zone, you know? Taking care of my babies is my favourite thing," she smiles.

"Your babies?" the officer raises an eyebrow.

Shit, Rose thinks.

She should have used a different word.

"Yes, sorry, that's what I call my flowers."

She brings the steaming cup of tea to her lips, blows on it, and takes a sip. She's telling the truth, therefore she's got nothing to worry about. She has no trouble looking them in the eye. The police officer sitting across from her taps his pen in a repetitive manner against the surface of the table growing frustrated. She senses the switch as he starts on a new line of questioning.

"Other than gardening, what are your other 'hobbies', Mrs. Westover?" he asks, treading carefully.

Rose can almost see the air quotes around the word hobbies. Taking it literally, Rose plays along.

"Oh, I love reading books, quilting, canning, making jam and pickles, and drinking tea, of course!" Rose says enthusiastically.

The police officer smiles and nods politely, bored out of his mind. Thinking this is a dead-end—a waste of time, he tries to end the interview as fast as he can. The other officer is still snooping around and is nearing the basement door. Rose remains seated, taking a sharp breath through her nose.

Feeling exhilarated by the cat and mouse game and the adrenaline pulsing through her, at the thought of almost being caught, she feels edgy.

Without any reason or motive to search her property, the officers end the interview, their cups of tea still steaming remaining untouched on the table.

They wish Rose a good rest of her day and let her know that if she remembers anything else she should give them a call. Instead of agreeing, Rose takes the business card and tells them she will put it on her fridge which she does the minute they are gone. She's enjoying playing the part of the concerned neighbour.

Proud of herself and how she handled the questioning, Rose decides to drink the rest of her tea, and snaps a square of dark chocolate to go with it as a reward for the deception. She's surprised at how easily she deterred them. Had they been paying closer attention, they would have spotted what they were searching for right in front of them, laid out casually on her couch in the living room. In plain sight, as though she's got nothing to hide. She chuckles.

She hopes her comments about Quinn will force the police to take another look at the woman's parenting skills and how Quinn's fragile mental state may have been the cause of the entire incident. She bites into the bitter chocolate and licks the broken slivers from her lips. She's feeling quite content with herself.

The dark, bitter chocolate has never tasted so sweet.

59

QUINN

Once she finishes recalling the events, Quinn requests some water.

Her throat is dry and she feels like she may never quench her thirst. A nurse brings her a disposable cup three-quarters full, but Quinn has trouble bringing it to her lips. She feels weak with exhaustion. Remembering every detail of what's occurred has made her so tired, as though she's just finished running a marathon. Her head hurts and her eyes feel heavy.

"I think that's enough questions for today," William states protectively. "My wife needs to rest. She's been through a lot," he adds, holding back tears, his voice trembling.

Quinn notices his body shaking beside her, his eyes glassy.

"We understand, Mr. Miller." The officer directly in front of Quinn closes his notebook. His partner remains unmoved at his post by the small window as he addresses William. "But we need to find out as much as we can to locate your son." The importance of his statement is evident.

After a moment, Quinn seems to get a second wind and nods for the police officer to continue with the questioning.

"Thank you for your cooperation, Mrs. Miller. We're almost done here for today," he reassures her. "Can you tell us again what you remember of the man?" he asks, pen in hand.

Quinn feels an intense itch on her legs and gives it a sudden jerk, startling William and the officer.

"Sorry," she apologizes sheepishly. "My legs are incredibly itchy."

William lifts the covers slightly and he sees red, blistery bumps on Quinn's legs.

"That looks like poison ivy," William states in concern. His eyes move over her body landing on her arms. "Yup, definitely poison ivy. Look," he points to her forearms, "you've got some here too."

The very mention of poison ivy makes the itchiness worse.

"Don't scratch it," William warns. "It'll just make it itch more. I'll get the nurse," and with that he stands and leaves the room.

Closing her eyes, Quinn does her best to ignore the blisters on her skin and the strong desire to rip through them with her fingernails. The nurse walks in and checks her over.

"Oh dear, that can't be comfortable," she looks over at Quinn in sympathy. "Here, take this. It'll help with the itching," she explains as she hands her a tablet to swallow.

"Thanks," Quinn croaks as she takes the pill and props herself on her pillow, willing her body to quit attacking itself.

She needs all of her focus to be on finding Cole. They can't afford any distractions right now. She looks over to the patient police officer still poised with his notebook and pen. He nods, ready for her.

She again describes the man who kidnapped her son and feels William's body stiffen at the mention of him. He's uncomfortable, or perhaps he's angry—most likely it's a mix of both. They haven't seen each other in a few months and already Quinn has trouble identifying her husband's subtle body language cues.

She used to know every micro expression, the slight shift in the intonation of his voice. Over the years, she'd become apt at understanding the meaning behind every pause in his speech and pace of his breaths.

Looking at her husband now as he talks to the officers, she has trouble recognizing the man she used to know so well. The lie he's hidden from her covers his skin, like plastic wrap, making him unrecognizable to her.

His hands are rough and calloused, his hair seems to have more grey in it and is thinning, and there are new creases by his eyes that she's never noticed before. She can also spot a shift in his weight when she focuses on his gut. Perhaps his time away from her hasn't been as joyful as he had hoped. Most likely, William's been drinking a few too many beers.

Quinn does her best to describe the man who'd taken their son. She guesses at his age and mentions noticing he'd had a slight limp in the right leg. She closes her eyes and swallows hard. Attempting to remember any small detail, she feels frustrated when she comes up empty.

Yet something is bothering her.

"There is one more thing," Quinn mentions, immediately hating herself for not allowing her brain to catch up to her mouth, regretting the words as soon as she's said them.

Now with all eyes on her, expectant, eagerly waiting for her to elaborate, she has no choice but to go on.

This is the moment of truth. She has no idea what the repercussions of this admission will be, but she is willing to put everything on the line if it might help them find Cole.

Hesitating for a moment, Quinn shuts her eyes. She can't look at them as she admits this. She doesn't want to risk seeing the disappointment on William's face—the shock that is likely about to cast a shadow over everything else.

"The man—he looked vaguely familiar to me," she explains as the police officers do their best not to appear stunned by this news.

Quinn opens her eyes briefly, trying to commit to memory the way William is tenderly looking at her now, full of love and kindness. She takes a mental picture of how he's gazing at her, knowing full well that he probably won't look at her like this ever again.

"I'm not sure if it's relevant, or if I just hit my head too hard, but I just can't seem to get something out of my mind." She steadies herself trying to work up the nerve to say more.

"Sometimes it's the random details that help us solve cases," the officer prompts her, shifting in his seat.

Looking only at the police officer, Quinn continues. The words come out all at once, seemingly in one breath.

"When I was twelve years old, my parents and I were camping near North Bay with some of my aunts and uncles and their kids. I, along with the rest of my cousins had heard a rumour that the woods there were haunted. That someone was always watching your every move." With a shaking hand, she pauses to pick up her glass of water. She brings it to her lips and swallows a large gulp. Some of it goes down the wrong way almost choking her. Quinn's throat is tight with emotion with what she's about to reveal.

"We had this idea of going out at night, after our parents had fallen asleep, to spend the night in the woods. My cousins, Steve and Andrew, were older than me by five years. They were leading the rest of us. We had a secret call and everything," she smiles weakly at the memory.

"It was thrilling to leave our tents quietly in the middle of the night without anyone knowing. The campground was still—so quiet. I remember how strange it was. During the day the place had been loud, full of life with noisy families. We'd heard far away sounds of kids splashing water at the nearby lake, teenagers playing sports or biking down the narrow dirt paths, new families arriving and setting up camp for the weekend," she stops for a moment, collecting herself.

"Only, at night, the campground was an entirely different place. The curfew was eleven o'clock and everyone had to be in bed. There wasn't a light in sight. Everyone was obligated to pour water over the hot coals of their fires before going to bed, so we didn't even have those to guide us. We didn't want to risk using flashlights for fear of the campground workers finding us and reporting back to our parents. We were scared to get in trouble or get kicked out of the campground," she twists her hands together, anxious about telling the rest of the story.

The police officers play along, but she can tell they're wondering where she's going with this tale.

"Well, we had quietly found our way through the forest using only the moonlight to guide us. We'd walked for a while before finally stopping for a few hours to sleep. One of the girls had brought a blanket and we all tried to get curled up in it. The boys got us girls all scared with ghost stories. Spooky cracking noises in the dark forest kept us awake for most of the night. We were shivering slightly, our shorts and T-shirt PJs not quite cutting it. We were all huddled together, trying to stay warm when we eventually fell asleep." Quinn pauses here, steadying herself.

"The next morning, we woke up startled by the sound of a loud crash. I was the first one up and the only one who ran towards the sound while the others ran the other way." Quinn smiles weakly, embarrassed by her naïve pre-teen self. "By the sound of that crash, it was clear to me that something bad had happened and I was determined to get to it and see if I could help. I know it doesn't make sense for a young girl to run towards chaos, but I've always been the type of person to want to help others, never expecting anything in return." At least, that's how she used to be, she thinks to herself. "I believed in the good of others and that everyone deserves a second chance," she adds.

She bites her lip before continuing.

"The others ran away, too terrified to follow. As I got to the road, I saw something strange. There were two cyclists badly hurt lying on the road. A woman was bent over one of the cyclists. At first, I assumed she must be helping them, but then she just ran back towards her car, got in it, and sped off." Quinn closes her eyes, doing her best to remember the details she'd been pushing away for years.

"I couldn't understand why the woman had left them there. I went up to the man first as he was the closest to me. His eyes fluttered momentarily, just enough for me to notice their deep green colour." She pauses to swallow another gulp of water before adding, "The man who took Cole had the same eyes. I'd recognize them anywhere. I know it sounds crazy, but I think he's the one who took Cole, only I can't figure out why." She nervously glances between William and the two officers, afraid to lead them in the wrong direction.

"Thank you, Mrs. Miller, this information is very helpful to us. We will do a search of reported hit and run accidents involving cyclists in that area around the timeframe you mentioned and hopefully, we'll get our guy and then find Cole," the officer sounded optimistic, flipping his notebook shut and quickly rising from his seat.

"I never talked about it before because I worried I didn't remember it correctly. I'd been so young," she adds.

Reaching out a hand to him, Quinn stops the officer. "There's another thing I remember from that day." She hesitates. She waits for the officer to sit back down. He looks at her intently, slightly annoyed at being delayed in his search.

"When I reached the woman cyclist, she was missing a finger—her pinky finger." She shuddered before relaying, "It appeared to have been cut off." Wincing, she sticks out her tongue in disgust.

She relays the scene as she can best remember, but the nauseating feeling she'd felt back then and the exhaustion from the last day catch up with her and she needs to still herself to gather her thoughts.

"I remember being confused by that. How would her finger get cut off if she'd been hit by a car?" she asks, genuinely puzzled. "I did look around briefly, but I never saw her finger anywhere," she admits. "My cousins called for me at that point and I turned around and ran back, scared and shaking. I never told anyone what I'd seen." She looks down at the hospital bed unable to meet anyone's eyes. "I've been ashamed of keeping silent for years." She allows the tears to finally fall.

Her hand finds her husband's through the veil of tears and she squeezes it hard, willing him not to let go—he doesn't. She's surprised by his loyalty. She's basically just admitted to negligence in reporting a crime and here he stands by her side, unwavering. She doesn't dare meet his eyes, scared of what she'll find there. For now, she's content with the feel of his hand, the warmth and reassurance it brings her.

She notices one of the officers shifting in his seat, slightly inclining towards her. His interest is clear. "Thank you for sharing this with us, Mrs. Miller. Your account of past events will be very helpful to us," he adds. "Can you recall what the vehicle looked like?" he inquires.

"No, unfortunately, that's where my memory fails me. I think it's partly from the shock of seeing two people mangled," Quinn grimaces, bile rising in her throat at the thought. "I was so scared after seeing all that blood, the stark whiteness of bones poking out of twisted limbs, the missing finger..." she trails off as the tears fall once more, remembering. "I'm sorry. This is hard."

The police officers nod to each other and stand in unison.

"We understand. Thank you so much for all of your time. We best be on our way to relay this information to our commander."

Looking over at the nurse as she enters the room, a signal that it's time for the officers to leave, the officer adds, "We understand you will need to remain in the hospital until you're well enough to go home, but if you remember anything else, please give me a call." He hands Quinn his business card, and she notices he's hand-written a cell phone number.

That's how she knows he's serious about her calling.

"We will be in touch later on, or as soon as we have more information," the other officer chimes in. He'd been quietly watching the entire exchange, surely playing the role of the observer during the interview.

William nods solemnly as he walks them out of Quinn's room. At the door, he exchanges a few more words with the officers and shakes their hands, thanking them for all their hard work. When he returns to Quinn's bed, he stands at her feet, focusing on the blanket. She can tell that he's struggling to keep it together. He's trying to be strong, but there's been so much information floating around, she knows he's having a hard time piecing it all together.

As she watches her husband crumbling before her, Quinn can't help but lie there motionless, unable to move to him to comfort him—her rock. She finds it almost unbearable to watch him be so lost, so powerless. It hurts her to not be able to help him, just like she never did anything to help those people back then. Yet, part of her, maybe a bigger part of her than she'd like to admit, revels in seeing her husband suffer.

After all this time, she's held onto this secret, this part of her past that he didn't know. She wonders how he feels now, knowing that he isn't the only one capable of keeping secrets.

60

WILLIAM

William leans on the wall outside of Quinn's hospital room with his head pressed on the cold white wall. He's struggling to come to terms with all the new information he's just learned in the last few hours. He feels his mind spinning and starts getting queasy.

On one hand, he's enraged at his wife for keeping this secret from him, but on the other hand, he hasn't always been honest with her. He feels very stuck. He can't point a finger at her for keeping quiet about this when he's been holding back on her also. William drops his head, his eyes closing as a wave of exhaustion overtakes him. He is too tired to think this through properly.

His wife's confession explains so much. This incident would have tormented her for years. The guilt built up from keeping a secret this big would have made her defensive, angry, and drained her mind of energy.

Squeezing the paper cup of hot coffee in his hand, the feelings he's been working hard to keep inside bubble out. A drop of the scalding liquid burns his skin and he sucks on the tip of his finger to ease the sting.

As he does, he thinks of his little boy—Cole's smiling face and chubby little feet. He thinks of his son's little fingers, how Cole's entire hand would fit over his thumb, holding on tightly. How safe he'd been in his embrace. How trusting Cole had been and how his own father had let him down.

William weeps at the thoughts, feeling weak in the knees.

Where is Cole?

Sadness and anger mix together building into a surge of emotion resembling a whirlwind. He wants to hold on to the anger, to feel something other than the crippling feeling of sadness that settled in his chest.

Allowing the emotions to wash over him, he clenches his free hand into a tight fist. He breathes in and counts to five like Quinn taught him to do many years ago, allowing his heart to fill with anger but on the exhale, letting it all go. He knows he and Quinn won't get anywhere by being upset with each other.

William is doing his best not to get angry at Quinn. After all, it wasn't her fault their boy had been taken. But after hearing her admit that she recognized the man who took Cole, William finds it hard not to blame her.

What else is Quinn hiding?

William hadn't seen the man in question, but after hearing his wife describe him, William feels like he was also there and saw the stranger take their son into the woods. The rawness of the image he's built up in his mind makes it feel so real. He closes his eyes briefly when he feels a hand on his shoulder.

"Sir?" the doctor addresses him carefully. William startles and lifts his head to meet the doctor's eyes. "We're going to be keeping your wife overnight. We'll see how she's holding up in the morning. Why don't you go home and get some rest," he gently offers. With that he turns around to head back down the narrow hallway, his white coat floating behind him.

Without much hesitation, William takes up the offer. He needs to get out of here.

Peeking into Quinn's room, he sees the slow rise and fall of her chest. She's out like a light and won't even notice he's left. William is grateful to not have the added guilt of leaving her behind.

He walks into the elevator and presses the ground floor button. Distraught and confused, he knows he desperately needs some sleep and a hot shower. He rubs at his face, feeling the grime on his jaw, the grittiness of his unwashed hair.

Stepping out of the elevator, he's about to call a taxi when he spots Officer Rogers, one of the officers that had interviewed Quinn, near the nurse's station.

"Mr. Miller, is everything alright?" Officer Rogers inquires, a concerned look on his face.

"Yes, just fine. They are keeping Quinn overnight to monitor her." He rubs his hair absentmindedly, a habit he has when he's tired. "I think I'll call a cab and head home and try to sleep for a few hours," he explains.

The police officer straightens. "Why don't you follow me out? I'd be glad to drive you home, Mr. Miller," he suggests.

Grateful for the offer and the free ride, William nods his thanks and follows the man out to his car. Officer Rogers isn't very chatty during the ride maintaining a professional presence the entire time. William is extremely grateful that he doesn't have to make mindless chitchat where he could inadvertently divulge something that might unwittingly tie him to the case.

When they pull onto William's street, he sees police cars everywhere. Bright yellow lights shine into his eyes and a sea of onlookers block his driveway.

The officer mumbles something inaudible and pulls over to the side of the road to park. There appears to be multiple search parties organized, bundled in pairs. They watch in silence as a few groups leave in different directions.

William catches a glimpse of a pair of men making their way through the woods, quickly losing sight of their bright flashlights as they disappear into the dark cloak of the thick forest. He feels a surge of anxiety. That should be him out there looking for his son. The officer scratches his head before addressing William.

"I'm afraid we'll need to walk the rest of the way unless there's somewhere else you'd like to go?" he offers.

"Actually, I think I should go out there and join the search." William suggests, his adrenaline pumping, his hand already on the door handle, ready to spring into action.

With a stern hand held up in a full-stop and a warning tone, Officer Rogers replies shortly, "Sir, with all due respect, you need some rest. We need you and Mrs. Miller to be in top shape for questioning in the morning so we can get to the bottom of this," he explains. "Let's leave the volunteer search teams to work through the night. We can see about getting you on a search team tomorrow if they haven't found anything by then," he adds kindly.

William considers this and fights the urge to disagree. He worries there might be other reasons why the police officer doesn't want him walking around the woods contaminating any evidence. What else is Officer Rogers withholding from him?

Frustrated, he shuts his eyes. His son is out there somewhere. He should be out looking for him.

He feels useless just sitting here, but he can't deny his exhaustion. Maybe his distressed state would actually cause him to overlook something important. He needs good rest to be sharp so that he can join in the search tomorrow.

That is, unless they find something tonight. He shudders.

As though Cole could be reduced to a thing, no longer a living being.

William watched many crime shows in his twenties. He remembers the gory pictures of decaying corpses, buried bones, burnt flesh, and spilled blood. The images had been filed away in a distant and unreachable place in his memories, but they've suddenly rushed to the surface.

One by one, every horrible image he's ever seen or even imagined begins reappearing in his mind. Newspaper images, terrible accidents, wars in foreign countries, cancer patients, open caskets at funeral homes, a friend's broken leg in middle school—horrible pictures displayed in front of him one after the other like a silent horror show.

He forces his eyes to open, to erase the gruesome images. William is shocked by how many people have already heard the news and have come by so late in the evening. He feels both irritated at the loss of privacy and touched at the onslaught of people that are willing to help.

His Volkswagen Golf stares at him, broken, willing William to help it. Rubbing at his face, William is struck by how much there is to do, how useless he feels at the moment. He spots a red Corolla in the driveway, the one the police officer in B.C. had shown him. He still doesn't know how it got there or whose car it is. He makes a mental note to ask Quinn in the morning.

Another piece of the puzzle that doesn't add up.

He is overwhelmed by fatigue and emotion. As the officer looks on, waiting for his answer, William quickly realizes that he won't get much rest here. He considers checking into a nearby hotel, but doesn't have the energy to go through the routine of getting a room, a key, and a designated check-out time.

His leg jitters, a reflex reaction to the stress he's under, but he barely registers it. A thought has just popped into his mind and he turns to the officer.

"Would you mind giving me a ride to a house ten minutes away? My boss lives in town. I'm sure I could stay with him for tonight," he says, hopeful. "Then, I'll be able to come back here refreshed in the morning to help with the search," he convinces himself. Being around others, even if he doesn't feel like talking is better than being completely alone.

"Sure, that's not a problem," the officer nods in agreement, reversing the car swiftly before heading back towards town.

William watches the emergency lights fade away in the passenger side mirror. So many questions twirl around in his mind. The officer turns up the music gradually using his thumb to press the volume arrow on the steering wheel.

The music enters William's ears, but he doesn't pay much attention to it—he's physically here, but mentally so far away. He's convinced that a few hours of rest will help him think more clearly and help him to absorb some of the information that's been thrown his way. He badly wishes he could recall some of the conversations he's shared with Quinn in the past months.

Had she hinted at anything that would explain this? Had his wife been hiding anything else from him?

Had there been any background noise he should have paid closer attention to? What had he missed? William wasn't the most observant person. Quinn was always telling him that he often missed what was right in front of him as he got lost in his own head. As the car moves further and further from his house, William can't help but feel the dread creep in.

He hates how Quinn's one admission of holding back a secret makes him second-guess everything she's ever told him and everything he thought he knew about her.

61

WILLIAM

When they arrive at Jake and Lena's home, William sees a police car in the driveway. The officer next to him stiffens in his seat and abruptly shuts the music off, and the car becomes eerily quiet.

Without a word, they quickly step out of the car and make their way up the few steps of the high ranch to the front door. A light is on in the kitchen, giving the men a perfect view of the interior, as though it were a large, movie theater screen. Jake is sitting at the table, his elbows leaning on the surface, his hands holding his head, his gaze down.

Something's wrong, William thinks.

The men hesitate a moment at the door suddenly feeling like they are intruding on something personal, unsure if they should proceed or turn around. Thankfully, an officer on the inside is paying attention and sees them hovering at the door. He quickly comes to greet them, positioning himself so that he is effectively blocking the view of the inside of the house.

"Officer Rogers," he addresses the police officer with an undertone of confusion. "How can I help you?" he offers, his expression remaining professional. The Adkins' two dogs begin barking excitedly, but their yapping quickly turns to low whimpers. Even the dogs can sense the tension.

"Good evening, Officer Taylor, I've got Mr. Miller here. I believe Mr. Adkins is his boss," he gestures with an open hand towards Jake who still has his head buried in his hands.

With a hushed tone he adds, "Mr. Miller was wondering about the possibility of spending the night here as his home is being used to facilitate the search for Cole Miller, his son." William shifts his body from one foot to another, quickly losing confidence in the idea as he takes in the serious look of the other officer and of the other members of his team standing around the kitchen.

Hearing the low mumbles at the door, William watches Jake slowly raise his head to meet his eyes. William hasn't seen his boss since he'd left several weeks ago to fight fires in B.C.

Pain is etched over Jake's face and tears have stained his cheeks; Jake's hair is void of any styling gel and stands at odds in various directions. William has never seen his boss look so disheveled—it's startling.

If Jake's appearance is a mess, the house is in complete disarray. There's an assortment of kitchen tools and containers all over the counters. A mop and broom are lying on the floor, seemingly abandoned before doing their jobs. Piles of laundry litter the floor like tiny hills to maneuver around.

What happened here? William can't make sense of it.

"William," Jake croaks, his throat raw from emotion. "I'm sorry to hear about Quinn and Cole, man."

Pushing past the officers, William steps into the home and climbs the stairs two at a time without bothering to remove his shoes. He pulls a kitchen chair close to Jake and sits down, placing a hand on his back to offer support.

"What's going on, Jake?" William asks as gently as possible, pushing away his own pain to help his boss, his only friend in this town.

"Lena's missing," Jake whispers, all his strength escaping him, the force of saying the words nearly making him crumble. "I came home yesterday, but she wasn't here. Her car's here with her purse and cellphone in it. I just don't understand."

Turning to face William, Jake eyes him with urgency. "Where is she?" he growls, sounding borderline hysterical.

William is shaken by the news, but even more so, he's confused.

"Wait," he says, looking around the room. "So both Lena and Cole are missing?" he asks the officers. "Did they go missing the same day?" His question seems to hang in the air for a moment before Officer Taylor nods.

The modest home feels like it's suddenly begun to shrink with the five men in the kitchen. The tension is high. They all want answers.

"What the hell is going on?" William wants to know, exasperated, but his question is met with silence.

No one knows, he realizes.

With both elbows pressed on the table, Jake stares mindlessly at the salt and pepper shakers on the table in front of him. At first, it looks like he's just lost in memory, but then he grabs one of the pottery pieces and abruptly throws it across the room, through the living room until it collides with the decorative brick wall, smashing it into hundreds of tiny, sharp pieces.

William stands abruptly—startled. He's half-impressed at Jake's physical strength but also terrified by the sudden outburst.

"Mr. Adkins, please restrain yourself," Officer Taylor warns with a controlled growl, stepping closer, his voice authoritative. One hand rests on his gun holster, the other on his hip.

William has never heard anyone address Jake in this manner before. His boss is usually the one to speak like this. As the senior teacher at the flight school, Jake has his title and has earned his status. He commands respect from others by his presence alone. Jake hadn't had it easy and worked hard to get to where he was. The entire class looks up to him.

The tension in the room is so thick it's almost palpable. The clutter around him makes William's mind race. This is too much.

Alert, William begins pacing around the kitchen, moving between the sink and the fridge and back again. He focuses on his breath, trying to calm his rapid thoughts, and make some sense of this. Could there be a connection between Lena and Cole that could explain why they've both gone missing on the same day?

He watches Jake pitifully get up from his seat and wander over to the living room only to kneel down calmly. William sees his boss picking up the tiny pieces of pottery with one hand while collecting them carefully in his other hand ironically cushioning the shattered pieces protectively.

Alone on the other side of the house with the stairway between them, Jake begins to weep. The desperation resonates through his body, making his form shake. The sight is heart-wrenching. William watches, lips trembling as Jake's pain takes over his need to control what's going on around him.

The officer nearest to the living room seems to notice this as well and approaches Jake carefully to assist him in getting seated on the nearby love seat wrapping him with the grey throw cover resting on the back of the sofa. William stops pacing and watches, mesmerized and in awe of his boss's expression of pain. Jake has been a rock to him during the last few months, and seeing him like this is disheartening. William keeps it all inside, but his emotions are nearing the surface.

"Don't worry about the mess, sir. We'll have someone come in and clean this up for you," the young officer's tone is reassuring and kind as he addresses Jake. "Why don't you get some rest? Tomorrow is a big day for both of you," he adds, glancing between William and Jake.

William looks over to Officer Rogers whose been quietly taking everything in. Worry is etched on his face.

"Excuse me, Officer, but I think I'd like to go to a hotel for the night after all," he struggles to speak. "Jake has enough to worry about without me being here," he explains.

"Don't worry, William." Jake waves him off from across the room. "I could use a friend right now and so could you," he locks eyes with him. "You're staying," he states, making the decision for him.

His assertive boss is back, if only for a moment. William hadn't realized how much he needed things to go back to normal, even if just briefly.

"Sure," William replies gratefully.

He's glad to be able to be with a friend tonight. He really doesn't want to be alone. He doubts he'll get any sleep, but the idea of a hot shower sounds incredibly tempting.

After some questioning, the police officers exit the house to join the search. Feeling drained emotionally, Jake retreats to the master bedroom and William settles in the basement guest room. Finally alone, William allows his mind to drift to Quinn, who's all by herself but not really, lying in a hospital bed down the street. He thinks of Cole. Who knows where his son is, or if he's even alive? Covering his face with a pillow, he weeps heavily until no more tears come.

62

HENRY

Kip's tail wags happily as he prances around the yard. He's helping Henry and the other volunteers look around the Millers' place while evening sets in around them. Everyone is out looking for the couple's lost son, Cole. After finding the boy's mother in that terrible state, the hunter feels compelled to help with the search.

Henry is fueled by adrenaline, eager to find out where the boy could be, and nervous to find out what happened to him. His gut tells him something terrible has happened. He senses it crawling under his skin—feels it in his bones. He's always had a sixth sense about these things. It's as though the trees whisper the world's secrets to him.

Henry's dressed in a thick, flannel, button-up coat and black Dickies pants. After all the sun this week, yesterday's rainfall has cooled the air down significantly. The leaves are rustling and curling in on themselves. A dark cloud, heavy with rain, hangs over the volunteers; the threat of a downpour is imminent. The purple sky is layered with scars of white and yellow.

Henry is reminded of a scene in one of his favourite childhood movies, Bambi. Only it's not the mother the hunter is searching for but the baby.

———

Kip seems to be enjoying helping with the search and being a part of the action—it's so different from their usual quiet nights in the small cabin. The pointer sniffs the earth and the grass like he's never seen it before. He seems to have completely recovered from his earlier shock at finding the woman's body in the woods.

Henry feels uneasy as the crowd gathers around him. He's not used to being around so many people at one time. He recognizes a few volunteers as customers of his—deer pepperrette enthusiasts—but most of them are strangers. A tall, lean, clean-shaven police officer walks to the front of the crowd gathering on the Millers' front lawn.

Dusk won't be for a few hours. The energy is high amongst the volunteers. Everyone wants to be a hero—they are all hoping to be the one to find a clue to help find Cole. A few people have brought their dogs along with them. Most people seem to be between the ages of their late thirties to their early fifties.

Henry spots a group of older ladies he recognizes from the quilters' group at the local church. They are speaking in hushed tones and immediately stop chatting once the police officer starts to speak addressing the crowd.

"Good evening, everyone, and thank you for coming. I'm Officer Boileau and I'll be in charge of the search here tonight, so if you have any questions as the night progresses, please report them directly to me." He looks down at some papers, his hands still as he holds them with a firm grip before continuing.

"As most of you already know, we are searching for a little boy named Cole. He's nearly nine months old, weighing around nineteen pounds. He's got light brown hair and blue eyes. His picture has been printed on flyers which are over by the volunteer registration tent. Please make sure to grab a flyer as well as a map of the woods before venturing out to search. The woods here are dense and not maintained as they are mostly private property and haven't been used for years," he explains matter-of-factly.

"We've been told that Cole was wearing a green onesie the day he was taken on August 13th. A blue fleece blanket is also missing." He pauses. "We will be searching from five p.m. to midnight tonight. Depending on the results of this search, we will follow up regarding whether an additional day of searching will be necessary." He rubs a spot beside his eye, a headache coming on surely.

"We appreciate you being here and helping us search for this little boy in the hope of bringing him home. If you find anything, please be sure to tell me or Officer Peters." He gestures to his right at a bulky man sporting a thick, black moustache. "You never know what might help us find Cole, so keep your eyes open and let's get searching." His tone is tired but he's trying his best to motivate the crowd.

Still, the importance of the task is clear to all. A child's life hangs in the balance—the importance of finding him or any clues to his whereabouts is a high priority.

Once the speech is over, the crowd looks lost like a herd of confused sheep waiting for further directives. A bright spotlight is turned on blinding most of the volunteers as it illuminates the yard, preparing for the descending darkness.

The volunteer registration tent has been installed on the lawn in front of the large bay window of the Millers' house.

Henry has never met the Millers. Before finding Quinn in the woods this morning, he had never seen the family around town. He's not familiar with the house they're renting either. He's never had a customer on this road, so he's never had a reason to come.

He's a little surprised not to see Mr. Miller amongst the volunteers. The couple's picture had been splayed on the news along with Cole's ever since the paramedics dropped Mrs. Miller off at the hospital. Mr. Miller must still be getting questioned by the police, or perhaps he's with Quinn at the hospital.

Henry begins making his way towards the volunteer tent when Kip abruptly pulls him to the side, his leash going tight with tension in Henry's grasp.

"Kip, you old boy, just what do you think you're doing?" Henry mutters. "Come back here, you silly boy," he pleads in confusion and annoyance as he struggles with the leash.

They need to be looking for the child, not sniffing out other dogs' favourite pee spots. Kip forcibly pulls Henry across the lawn and towards the backyard. There are no volunteers back here yet, which makes Henry feel uneasy. Irritated, Henry pulls hard at the leash.

"Come on Kip, that's enough."

To his surprise, Kip begins to whine and pulls back even harder. Kip presses on, continuing with his initial mission, ignoring his master's commands.

Seeing the dog's determination, Henry's curiosity wins over his earlier frustration, and he gives in. He allows himself to be led to the neighbour's yard. Henry is unbelievably uncomfortable.

Every second he's back here feels wrong to him. He lowers his voice to a whisper, as though someone might see them trespassing and make a fuss.

"OK, now that's enough, Kip. We can't be here."

A slight pull at the leash sends Kip growling at him. Henry blanches. Kip's never acted like this towards him before. "What the hell? What's gotten into you, boy?" Henry hisses angrily, exasperated and insulted by his dog's lack of respect for his owner.

Kip appears not to hear the anger in his voice, or if he does, he chooses to ignore it. The dog's nose leads him further into the backyard, where he begins to sniff at the ground intensely. Kip stops sniffing when he reaches the garden.

Here, Kip sits and waits patiently as Henry has taught him to do when his dog is retrieving prey. When Henry doesn't move, Kip begins to frantically paw at the dirt, all the while emitting loud, whining sounds.

"Can I help you?" someone asks. An older woman wrapped in a long purple coat wearing a knitted hat makes her way barefooted through the tall grass towards Henry.

It takes the hunter a moment to steady himself. He'd been so focused on Kip that all his other senses had failed him. He couldn't remember the last time something had moved in his peripheral view and he'd missed it.

The woman's tone isn't quite accusatory but it's also not friendly. Henry feels his cheeks flush with embarrassment.

He's about to speak when Kip suddenly stops digging and turns towards the woman with bared teeth. He starts to growl taking an aggressive stance. The woman backs up instinctively. Her trembling right hand covers her mouth in fear.

"Kip, stop that right now!" Henry insists through his clenched teeth, astonished at his dog's behaviour.

"I'm so sorry, ma'am, he's not usually like this. I don't know what's gotten into him." He pulls hard on the leash. "He must have seen a squirrel or something," he says as an explanation. "He's a hunting dog, so he doesn't let off easily when he finds what he's been searching for." Apologetic, he adds, "We better be getting back to the tent. I'm sorry for disturbing you."

"Well, there are no squirrels buried in my garden if that's what he's after," the old woman replies with her nose in the air.

Her arrogant tone matches her dignified expression, but as Henry turns toward his dog, he's sure he sees a sly smile play on the woman's lips sending chills down his spine.

A creeping feeling climbs up his arms followed by an urgent need to get back to the other volunteers. He forcefully tugs on the leash, causing Kip to let out a sharp yelp at the brusqueness of the pull. Once back at the Millers', Kip calms down. Henry crouches next to him and pets him fiercely doing his best to slow down his own heartbeat. Kip has never reacted this aggressively before. The dog's behaviour troubles him, but it also arouses his suspicions.

What had he found?

Kip has never led Henry down a false trail in the past. He's been the best hunting partner Henry has ever had and has proven himself to be extremely reliable.

In the seven years, they've hunted together, Kip has never led Henry astray and definitely never growled at someone before.

Henry trusts him more than he does most humans which is why he doesn't hesitate to reward him with a few dog treats that he keeps in his pocket.

"I trust you, boy," he whispers reassuringly to the dog. "Good boy, Kip." He pets him gently on the head a few times and stands up.

Kip has landed on something—something big.

Henry knows it. The woman next door is hiding something and he's determined to find out what it is.

63

SYLVIE

While washing the dishes, Sylvie picks at the stubborn food left hardening on the dinner plate with her fingernail. From her vantage point at the kitchen sink window, she notices a police vehicle making its way down the street.

She's by herself tonight, Martin and Frank are staying with their father. There's still plenty of light left in the day, but the heavy clouds warn of a downpour quickly approaching. Sylvie has heard from some of the neighbours that there will be a search occurring soon for young Cole Miller.

Her chest tightens when she remembers how little the boy had been the last time she'd seen him. Cole had been sitting in his stroller happily gazing up at the sky and pointing to a bird. His eyes had been full of wonder as though nothing bad ever happened in the world. She remembers watching him and thinks that Martin had been the same at that age. How long ago that was!

She rinses the soap off the remainder of the dishes and places them on the drying rack for the evening. She'd been planning on painting her nails and watching a *Friends* rerun tonight, but what the hell. She could do that any night of the year.

This was more important.

She has an opportunity to make a real difference here—to help a neighbour and assist in finding a missing child. How scared must little Cole be, alone in those woods!

Sylvie feels a wave of nausea as she considers the possibility that Cole might no longer be alive. How could a baby survive that long alone in the woods? Steadying herself on the counter with both hands, she waits for the moment to pass, watching the sink until the last of the soap bubbles pop and her fear dissolves.

"Right, OK," she coaxes herself, trying to shake it off.

She's been talking to herself more and more since her husband left. At first, it had helped battle some of the loneliness she'd experienced. Talking to herself had made the days more interesting and less eerily quiet. But spending too much time by herself wasn't good for her.

She finds a thin jacket hanging on the entrance hook and slides it on, hoping it will be enough to keep the impending evening chill off of her. Checking herself in the mirror, she grabs a ball cap and snuggly fits it over her hair. She's not expecting much for bugs this late into the summer but she's about to enter the forest at night, so she wants to be prepared.

She makes sure to grab her phone in case the boys needs to reach her while she's out. She's not sure how her cell reception will be in the woods, but she figures someone will have a walkie-talkie of some sort for communication in case of an emergency.

She shuts off the interior lights, leaving only the light above the kitchen sink on. Turning on the sole outdoor light for her return, she locks up the house and zips her house key safely away in her jacket pocket.

Her running shoes make a crunching sound on the dry gravel driveway, her footsteps echoing back to her from the vastness of the woods. She can hear the booming sound of someone with authority addressing the crowd of volunteers down the road.

Making her way down to the Millers' house, she notices a large number of people are gathered around a simple, white tent. As she reaches the mass, she needs to strain her neck to see over some of the taller volunteers. She's glad to see that so many people have offered to look for Cole. She feels proud of herself for coming to help out as well.

Her eyes dart from left to right, trying to see if she recognizes anyone. Spotting a few familiar faces from down the street, a couple with preschool-aged children, she offers a tentative wave. It's hard to know how people will react to news like this. Some hide away in their homes, some spring into action, while others hug their children close and become paranoid of any stranger they see—this is where Sylvie fits in.

She wonders if she should tell someone about the suspicious man that she'd caught idling on their street earlier yesterday. She'd almost put him out of her mind, but hadn't he been watching the Millers' house?

Looking at the couples grouping together, worried looks on their faces, she wonders who's watching her neighbour's kids tonight while they are out searching. Remembering a post on social media about a teenager offering to watch the little ones while their parents helped with the search, Sylvie marvels at how the community has come together when tragedy strikes.

Scanning the crowd, she notices a few of the town's Monday coffee gang, some middle-aged men dressed for a long trek in the woods. She's smiling at the thoughtfulness and care of her neighbours—her town—happy to be a part of the action.

The line for volunteer registration is moving slowly. Two officers are seated behind a grey, plastic, foldable table taking down names and pairing volunteers to specific locations to search. It appears as though they are forming several search parties to cover as much ground as possible.

There is a poster-sized map of the area, laminated and taped to a stick, planted firmly in the ground next to the registration tent. The flimsy poster is reinforced by a plywood cut-out. Colourful flyers showcasing Cole's picture are being handed out to everyone by a woman sporting a blue, nylon windbreaker. Sylvie has never seen her before.

Approaching the table, Sylvie is next in line when she notices a man and his dog crouched on the ground, off to the side of the house between the Millers' and Mrs. Westover's place. Something about the man's stance and the way he's reassuring his dog makes Sylvie look on a minute longer. She watches the man briskly walk back towards the road, anger showing on his face. His dog is alert and excited as he keeps looking back, barking at something or someone in the shadows of the backyard.

Is there someone standing there or is Sylvie imagining things?

She tries to shake the thoughts from her mind but they won't leave. When she gets something stuck in her head, it's hard for her to let it go. She's been working on focusing more on the present lately, but this time she just can't set her thoughts aside. Perhaps it's a gut feeling or her previous history with the woman next door that makes her undeniably intrigued.

A part of her has always wanted to sneak into Mrs. Westover's backyard and look around. For what, she's not sure, but she feels like there must be something there. The old woman keeps to herself and gives Sylvie the heebbie-jeebbies.

Sylvie absentmindedly leaves the registration line and wanders casually over towards Mrs. Westover's backyard, curiosity winning out. She's only slightly aware that she's placing a significant distance between herself and the rest of the volunteers—not the smartest thing she's ever done.

She keeps moving as though pulled by an unknown magnetic force, determined to figure out what's just transpired, if it was anything at all. The strange scene she's just witnessed between the man and his dog, and possibly a person standing in the shadows. She needs to look—if only to calm her racing heart. The backyard seems much darker than the front of the house. The house casts large shadows leaking into the edges of the woods.

There is no one back here, she discovers.

Only her.

Her heart is beating fast as the built-up adrenaline begins to settle. She makes her way back to the tent scolding herself for being so silly. Always the inquisitive one.

She started having trouble trusting others around the time her husband left. Sylvie now understands that people can pretend to be one thing while being someone completely different all at the same time—how they can lie and fool everyone around them. She's promised herself that if ever a seed of doubt enters her mind she will pursue it. She isn't ready to let that gut feeling go anytime soon. She owes it to herself to not be taken for a fool again.

With her mind in a haze, busy analyzing what she's seen from a distance, she considers reasons for it all. She watches a shadow move inside Mrs. Westover's home. Strangely, it paces quickly, frantically. If Sylvie had to describe it, she'd say the person looked to be panicking.

She draws in a breath and watches from the corner of her eyes trying her best not to be too obvious. She knows all too well that if ever you're watching someone in secret, someone else could very well be watching you, and you wouldn't even know it.

64

The night had been long and miserable. The hospital is not a place to get a good night's sleep. The loud sounds, bright lights, screaming patients, and beeping machines had kept Quinn awake all night long. Her blistery skin and pounding headache along with the sound of rushing feet scurrying down the halls as nurses hurried from room to room, and the gut-wrenching cry of children makes it almost impossible to rest.

If the never-ending noises weren't enough, there was also the very distinct smell that adds to an unsettling stay. Clinical and sterile, the sickening odor lingers permanently in the air as though it's been painted on the walls. The smell alone is motivation enough to will your body back to health just to get out of there.

Similar to her rental house, the hospital is a canvas of various shades of white everywhere; eggshell-white, snow-white, and cotton-white. There's so much white that it feels like there are no definitions between the walls and the floors. It's like a large tarp or a blanket has been draped over the surfaces in a weak attempt to cover the horrid smell, or perhaps to hide the many lives lost within these walls.

Quinn has tossed and turned throughout the night, unable to rid herself of the images of the man taking her son away just hours before.

She'd tried running after him, her feet glued to the ground, her screams muffled. The images moved in quick succession as though they were on a merry-go-round stuck on their individual horses, going around in circles, never reaching each other. She'd woken up screaming, her throat sore, with Jill by her side holding her hand.

The hospital bed sheets were twisted around her legs and her pillow had fallen on the floor. Then she'd cried, despair overwhelming her.

She feels like the worst mother in the entire world.

The world will be judging her. She knows it. They will call her names, thinking her unworthy to be a mother. Yet no matter what stones they throw at her, Quinn has already thought it. She's judged herself the hardest.

Depression has settled in taking its rightful place in her body, starting with her mind. Black ink splatters over every last good thought ensuring any hope she has left gets swallowed up, and destroyed.

Her own mind is her worst enemy.

The effects continue throughout her body, making her muscles ache and scream in pain. Her bones feel weak with fear, she's unable to move or get out of bed, and her head spins easily back into the dark place she knows all too well. It doesn't matter how hard she tries to fight it. The darkness always wins.

Quinn thinks back to when she'd first spotted the man rushing through the backyard—how hard he'd been clutching Cole in his blue blanket, and how tightly he'd held him in his arms. She can't figure out what could have possessed him to do it.

Why had he taken her son away?

357

Had the man seen her that day, years ago, when she'd witnessed the accident? Had he been searching for her all this time?

She couldn't imagine someone doing that—holding a grudge for that long. Yet, a part of her was beginning to understand it. The pain could easily turn towards anger propelling her to spring into action and seek revenge.

The man had lost his wife and unborn child, she remembers reading an article about the accident a few days later. Could that be his motivation? Could he have taken her child as punishment for the child he'd lost?

Surely no sane person would ever dream of taking someone else's child. But this man, with all these years of torturing pain, is probably far from being sane.

She shifts uncomfortably in the hospital bed, the scratchy sheets complaining under her weight. Her skin feels irritated and she represses the urge to scratch.

The pill must be wearing off, she concludes.

The thin, white mattress is doing the bare minimum to support her lower back. The doctor had visited her earlier this morning to tell her that she would be discharged soon. She should have felt grateful, but she'd only felt heavy dread instead.

———

Swinging her feet to the tiled floor, Quinn steadies herself on the edge of the bed before standing up. Her head still feels a little dizzy. She's unsure how to handle the next steps—with Cole and with William.

Mostly she feels tired. Too tired to deal with any of it.

She knows she ought to be jumping out of bed and rushing home, grateful for the early release allowing her to join the search party but her gut tells her it will be useless, that it's too late.

How she knows this, she's not sure—a mother's instincts perhaps.

As the tears sting her eyes, she shakes them away. Nothing has been said to her, either way. Yet, she feels the hope draining with each passing hour. She has no way of knowing if her son is okay. As she feels the panic rising, she starts doing her breathing exercises to steady her heartbeat.

One, two, three, inhale. One, two, three, exhale.

Sitting on the edge of the stiff bed for a few minutes, she focuses on inhaling deeply to allow her breathing to return to normal. She needs to focus—she needs her medication.

"Hey, babe, you okay?" William's voice seems far away, as though she's underwater.

Her body feels tingly and oxygen-deprived. It takes him asking again for Quinn to resurface from her meditative state. She watches him as he hesitantly wanders into the room and stands beside her, carefully placing his hand on her back. He means it as a reassuring gesture, but Quinn doesn't feel the kindness of the act, only the weight of it—the lies between them.

"Hey," she says, finally responding. "Yeah, I'll be okay," she replies as close to the truth that she can muster for the time being.

I think.

Giving him the silent treatment now would be juvenile and extremely unhelpful to their search efforts. If they are going to find Cole, they need to work together. There will be time later to work on healing the trust that's been broken.

359

William is pulling something out of a bag.

"I swung by the house earlier this morning and grabbed you some clothes to wear," he explains, pulling out some of her loungewear from a plastic grocery bag.

She feels tears in her eyes, incredibly touched by the gesture. She's grateful to spot her shoes, pants, undergarments and a comfy shirt.

"Was it awful?" she asks about his stop at the house and the reporters crowding their lawn—vultures waiting for a scoop.

"Actually, there weren't too many, and I just ignored the ones that were there. I wasn't long. I only grabbed your clothes from the laundry room and left to come here," he smiles gently. "Here, let me help you."

Closing the privacy curtain, he helps her to get dressed. She's surprised not to find herself mortified by the experience, having more awful things to worry about. William assists her to a standing position and takes her arm to help with her balance. Her feet are swollen and badly damaged from her night in the woods.

"Ouch!" she moans. In a matter of seconds, her nurse, Jill, rushes over to her and helps her sit in a wheelchair.

"Here you go, darling. This will help you get out the door and to your vehicle." Jill smiles kindly.

She glances at Quinn's bare feet briefly, making a decision. Without any mention of it, she carefully places Quinn's shoes into her bag to bring home with the rest of her personal items. Normally, patients need to wear shoes on the way out, but Quinn is touched by the nurse's willingness to overlook this little detail.

"Thank you." Quinn exhales, wincing in pain, but incredibly grateful for the gesture.

She is glad to have the comfort of the leather seat, even if it's only for a few minutes. William and Quinn wave goodbye to the staff as they roll away. William is pushing Quinn towards the elevators by the nurses' station when a television screen above switches to a news report about Cole. Quinn starts to shake as she watches, mesmerized.

Emotions overwhelm her when a picture of her little boy fills the screen. His chubby grin sets her off and she starts to cry. The police have used the picture she has on her nightstand for the report. Seeing it there on the screen makes it all too real.

She feels like she's going to be sick.

Her skin feels prickly and a rush of heat hits her. She tears her eyes away from the screen, doing her best to zone out the news anchor's voice. Gripping the handles of the wheelchair, she keeps her eyes tightly shut. Gritting her teeth against the pain coursing through her, bee-lining for her heart, she feels a panic attack about to erupt any moment.

Someone must have recognized them as being Cole's parents, because just then, the sound goes mute. Carefully, opening one eye at a time, she looks up and sees the same television now showing only a black screen.

It's so oddly sudden that she wonders if she had imagined Cole's face on it in the first place, as though missing him had conjured his image. She thinks that perhaps she is losing her mind. She really needs to take her medication. She's been behind on it.

She feels unbalanced—unpredictable.

65

WILLIAM

Leaving the hospital, William notices that the rain has stayed away for at least another day. Good news for them as they are eager to head home and join the search. His jaw is tense as he grinds his teeth. He hasn't been sleeping well, but there's no surprise there. His stomach is in knots and his muscles are exhausted.

He maneuvers the rental car through the herd of people on the street and at their house. Parking the car in the driveway, the couple takes a deep breath as though preparing for battle. They can't go unnoticed with all these people blocking their front door.

William struggles to usher his wife towards the house through the sea of reporters on his front lawn. Microphones and cameras are thrust in their faces, making it difficult to get to the door without breaking into tears. The couple does their best to keep their faces blank, focusing all their energy on getting into their home.

"Mrs. Miller, do you know where Cole is? Is he alive?" a reporter asks her, shoving a microphone at her mouth almost knocking Quinn's teeth out.

The question is lacking emotion. Quinn shivers beside him, her steps slowing and uncertain. Her face contorts in pain with every step. The bandage on her forehead, the torturous steps, and the obvious grief plastered across her face makes her the perfect target for the reporters.

Unable to watch his wife struggle, being taken advantage of by their unwanted guests, William grabs Quinn's hand—it's strictly business-like, a means to an end—and pulls her towards the front door.

"Mrs. Miller, how are you sleeping while your baby is still out there?" another reporter questions, making Quinn cringe at the insensitive question.

It stabs at his heart that they're treating his wife like this. It takes everything he's got not to spin around and give the reporter a piece of his mind.

Large posters of Cole's face are stuck to sticks and planted in the yard. Volunteers walk around holding smaller versions of the same poster, and hand out copies to others. There is a hushed murmur as the couple get closer to the door. When it's clear the Millers aren't going to be answering any questions, most of the volunteers make a path to help them get to their front door.

Touched by their gesture, William feels himself well up with heavy emotions, as he looks at their worried faces. It seems the entire world is silent as they climb the front steps, the jingle of William's keys echoing against the forest, bouncing back towards them.

As they step inside, the soft click of the door behind them seems to snap everyone out of their hypnotized state, and the voices get loud again, only slightly muffled by the windows.

The couple watches in silence for a few moments. William is in awe of all the help they've received, grateful to see they won't have to do this alone, but also feeling overwhelmed at the sudden loss of privacy. He quickly rushes around the first floor shutting all the curtains, plunging them into darkness.

What a change from, when Quinn had been alone in this house for weeks on end with Cole.

Turning on the lights, William sees the shock in his wife's eyes, her body trembling. He sits her down on a chair in the living room and fills the kettle to make some tea. He rummages through the pantry to find something herbal in the hopes of helping her relax.

He hasn't been in this kitchen for almost two months. Quinn has rearranged the pantry once again making it difficult to find what he's looking for, but he refuses to ask for help.

His wife sits motionless on the chair, seemingly staring at a dirty spot on a faraway baseboard. Finding the tea box, he takes out a bag and plops it into Quinn's favourite mug. While he waits for the water to boil, he looks over at his wife. She's lost some weight since William left. Her body seems fragile, older somehow.

"Are you cold?" he ventures.

"No," she says faintly.

"Are you hungry?" he asks but she shakes her head. "Do you want to go sleep?" he wonders, but again she shakes her head.

Her upper lip quivers and her eyes shut.

Shit, William thinks as Quinn begins to sob into her hands.

With the faint sound of the water starting to boil on the stove, William rushes to his wife's side and kneels beside her on the floor. He doesn't know what to say, so he just holds her in his arms, hoping to provide, at the very least, a physical comfort.

His own grief and worry join hers, and together they cry silently.

The kettle's cry jolts them back to the moment, forcing William to stand. He wipes his tears and continues on to his mundane task of preparing the tea. He pours the scalding water into the mug, the scent of chamomile wafting through the air.

With a shaking hand, he brings the hot drink over to Quinn's side along with a spoon and saucer and places it on the nearby coffee table. He's quite sure she won't touch it, but it helps him to do something, anything, rather than just sit around and wait.

He's jittery. He hates feeling useless. He would be much more helpful out there with the others, searching. But he knows Quinn needs him right now, seeing as they've got no close family nearby.

There's also the upsetting news that Lena is missing.

Where has she gone? William still hasn't dared to let Quinn know her friend has disappeared. He's holding off on telling her, hoping she was sheltered from the news at the hospital. He has no idea how she will react to learning that her friend has gone missing. That upsetting news along with Cole's kidnapping is sure to push her over the edge. Watching his wife now, William wonders if it's already too late.

He doesn't want to risk upsetting Quinn further, at least not until he has all the facts. Telling her now would just make her worry even more. Or worse. Come to the same conclusions that he had— that Lena had something to do with Cole's disappearance. That somehow, she had worked out a deal with the stranger to steal Cole.

He knows it's farfetched, but it's all he has. It's the only plausible theory he's been able to come up with that explains the sudden disappearance of both his son and their friend. It's the only connection he can imagine.

William remembers when Quinn had mentioned the strange salt and pepper shakers that had looked so out of place at Jake and Lena's house that first evening they'd had dinner there. Quinn had speculated that maybe they had some secret history, a child unmentioned. Now, Jake had smashed one to pieces in anger as though it had meant something significant.

William shakes his head. Surely Jake would have told him if they'd lost a child? The two of them had grown quite close over his time here. Jake wasn't the type of guy to keep any secrets. He was a straight shooter and a genuinely good person. Yet, there's a difference between being honest and avoiding the truth.

If only William could figure out if Lena and the man were connected. Had Lena been at the house when Cole was taken? Quinn had been in the shower, but he knows from the report the police officer had shared with him earlier today that Lena had been on her way to their house around that same time. If so, had she seen something?

Shaking his head, he pushes the thought away. He's getting distracted. He needs to focus on finding Cole and discovering the identity of his kidnapper.

Feeling his heartbeat getting faster, an idea begins to form in William's mind. His thoughts keep returning to the man, this stranger that Quinn thinks she recognizes. He might be the one responsible for Cole and Lena's disappearance.

He shakes his head defiantly. He needs to sleep.

Trying to find reasons for this situation is maddening, bordering on impossible. The possibilities are endless. William looks over at his wife as though she might hold all the answers, but he comes up blank. She hasn't so much as blinked since he set the tea beside her, the steam growing fainter by the minute.

"Babe, why don't you go and have a nap upstairs?" he suggests gently, knowing she probably got little to no sleep at the hospital. He'll wait to tell her about Lena later.

"No, I need to stay here in case Cole comes back," she says urgently, as though the very idea of her falling asleep would mean that Cole is never coming back.

William looks at his wife, feeling terrible for her.

Quinn has always been superstitious about much of what happens in her life. For example, if she forgot to change the bed sheets, then that meant that Cole would be fussy that day. If she put too much cereal in her bowl, then it would rain.

It's utter nonsense to William, but Quinn strongly believes this. As though her forgetfulness or clumsiness could attract bad karma. Everything matters. Every oversight, every wrong move—a butterfly effect.

His wife used to do her absolute best not to stray away from routine. Before having Cole, she'd been predictable in her daily activities to a fault. She'd always walk at the same time, on the same route, eat the same thing for breakfast every morning, drink the same tea at night, and style her hair the same way she'd done since he'd met her.

William wonders if the stranger had taken note of his wife's routine as well and used it against her.

Quinn had been so overwhelmed with Cole lately, so sleep-deprived and focused on getting everything done, that she'd forgotten one crucial little step along the way—locking the front door. Something so automatic, yet, something they rarely did whenever they were home. Quinn had learned to sleep when their son slept, therefore locking the front door had been the sensible thing to do. However, with all the stress caused by the breakdown of the car and the intense heat, Quinn had forgotten this simple step. The police had told William that the front door had been unlocked and this detail was engraved in his mind.

Who knows if this would still have happened had she remembered to lock the door before going upstairs for her shower? William knows he shouldn't blame her. Turning against each other would be counterproductive and useless at this point. They needed to stay focused and work as a team if they were to have any chance of finding Cole.

"Quinn, come with me. I'll tuck you in. You need some sleep." He helps her off the chair and guides her up the stairs to their bedroom.

Her sore feet slow them down. William holds her arm pushing her to the top, resisting the urge to pick her up in his arms and carry her the rest of the way.

He tucks her into their bed, laying the fluffy white comforter over her. Swiftly, he shuts the blinds and curtains, instantly removing any remaining light from the space.

Quinn sighs at the softness of the bed and sinks right into it, disappearing under the covers. Stepping quietly towards the door, William looks at the shape of his wife's body buried under a mountain of cotton.

"I'll come back to check on you in a little bit," he whispers softly before pulling the door shut and making his way quietly down the stairs.

Back in the kitchen, he doesn't waste any time. He picks up his phone and dials a number he's now learned by heart.

"Hi Jake, it's me. Listen, I need your car." He pauses, then explains, "I'm going to find this guy. I'm sure he took my son and I think he might have Lena, too." For a moment, he considers his actions, worried about Quinn waking up to an empty house. But he reassures himself that he'll be back before she wakes.

After a beat, Jake replies, "I'll pick you up in five minutes," and the line goes dead.

66

WILLIAM

With clenched fists and a tight jaw, William paces angrily in his living room as he waits impatiently for Jake to arrive.

Trying to keep his mind focused on the goal, fighting the instinct to talk himself out of it. William searches on his phone to find the details of the hit-and-run accident Quinn had mentioned to the officers. All he has is an approximate location, the year the accident happened, and the fact that two people were hit.

Several hits-and-runs were reported that year, but only one article mentioned a deceased wife. William easily finds a name for the male victim, Dylan Thomas. He copies it with his phone, switching the browser to the national People Search website. He pastes the name into the search bar, and easily finds who he's looking for.

A professional networking site with some details on Dylan Thomas appears on his screen along with an unflattering picture of the man and his current place of work. After searching for Dylan's workplace website, he finds a short biography of him.

His bottom lip curls at the mention of Dylan being high up in the IT industry with a dozen raving reviews from colleagues over the years. William has always been jealous of IT guys. Ever since he was a kid, he'd always preferred working with his hands taking pleasure in seeing progress.

It's why he's always chosen blue-collar jobs through the years. Others had teased him about his intelligence, but William knows a degree doesn't make them any smarter than him.

Years after graduation, those same guys had been unrelenting about how smart they were and how much money they were making. For William, it wasn't about the money, yet those guys had gotten under his skin and left a bad taste in his mouth. Every time he learned of someone working in IT, his reaction was visceral.

Feeling smug, William looks down at the man's address on his phone. He'd found Thomas's home number in an article about his work. All it had taken was a copy-paste of the number into the 411 Reverse Look-up on the Yellow Pages website. The man's address was linked to his home number. Apparently, he's one of the last few people who still has a house phone number listed in the phone book.

A part of him hopes Dylan Thomas isn't home today, because William isn't sure what he'll do to the man once he finds him.

———

When Jake's car finally pulls into the driveway, William can feel sweat dripping down his forehead.

This is nuts, he chides himself.

He can't believe he's considering confronting an alleged child kidnapper. He's thankful that Jake has offered to drive because he isn't sure his nerves would allow him to concentrate on the road. He hastily opens a kitchen drawer and grabs a notepad to write Quinn a note to let her know he's gone out for a bit, and that he has his phone on him. He hopes his writing will be legible as his hand is shaking pretty badly.

Before he shuts the drawer, he notices something shiny reflecting the sun's rays through the kitchen. He grabs it and stuffs it into his pocket before rushing out the door, careful to lock it behind him.

Avoiding the crowd's judging eyes, he climbs into the vehicle. Doing his best to repress the unpleasant memories, William relays the directions to Dylan's house to Jake, feeling the bitter taste of revenge on his tongue. Sitting in Jake's car, the two men are silent as they begin driving.

———

The intensity in the car is heavy. It's almost as though it's slowing down the vehicle with its weight. The air is hot. William feels like he's suffocating. He presses the switch on the door and the passenger window rolls down. His own Golf still has a manual crank, but Jake and Lena's Lexus is in pristine condition, not one candy wrapper, Kleenex, or gum packet littering the floor of the car. In a sense, the car could belong to anyone.

The lack of personality is apparent and slightly staggering. It appears that Jake and Lena have no real attachment to the vehicle, but use it purely as a mode of transportation. William's own vehicle has been with him for so many years, it's almost a part of the family. So many memories are linked to it—most recently the one of bringing Cole home and moving into their rental.

The car hums quietly along the road, the minutes stretching as long as the highway when suddenly William spots their exit. His emotions on his sleeve, his tone is curt.

"Turn here," he indicates to Jake, pointing a finger towards the exit.

His anger is bubbling to the surface, but his mind is clear. He is extremely aware of his surroundings, seeing everything in great detail, but remaining focused on what's coming. He imagines breaking into Dylan's home and beating the crap out of him while Jake holds him down.

The men have an advantage. There are two of them and one of him.

Also, William is hoping they catch him by surprise before the police get there, although that seems unlikely given how easily William was able to find the man's information and address. Determined, he resigns himself to finding out what Dylan's done with his son if it's the last thing he does.

67

ROSE

Rose has been in a frazzled state ever since that damned dog snooped around her garden. How is it that animals can detect so much more than humans can? She grits her teeth barely containing her anger. That dog could ruin everything.

She saw the look in that man's eyes, that hunter. He could sense something was going on. He understands animals and how they behave—he trusts them. How close that dog had been to finding something that could unravel everything Rose has worked so hard to keep hidden.

Years of family history could have come crashing down around her.

Somehow she'd managed to keep her composure, acting only upset at the dog's presence on her property, but things had quickly unraveled after she'd stepped back inside her home.

She paces around her house, too worked up to slow down, no longer caring if anyone is peering through her windows. She feels itchy. A rash has starting to erupt on her skin. She's forgotten how sensitive she is to some of the plants in the woods. Mixed with the intense heat from the sun, she can't escape the allergic reaction. She feels like she's suffocating under her white blouse, the material irritating her skin.

She hastily undoes several buttons, her chest red from being flushed and the reaction to the poison ivy.

As a child she had always had severe reactions to the poison ivy that lined the edge of the property. She usually skipped over the plants or wore rubber boots to trek through the woods at this time of year, but Rose hadn't had any reason to venture into the forest for several years, content with her small garden plot to continue her activities. She'd forgotten how ruthless the tiny plants could be.

She scolds herself for being so careless and going into the woods. The rash was sure to give her away. If anything it would create a hole in her story, placing her in the woods around the time of Cole's disappearance.

How could she have been so stupid?

As it turns out, Quinn is alive. Rose could kick herself. She'd been standing right over the girl only a day ago.

Quinn had been mangled and unconscious—Rose could have easily killed her. She'd forgotten to check for Quinn's heartbeat, assuming she'd succumbed to her injuries. Rose had cut corners and now she was paying for it.

She'd been glued to the television ever since discovering Quinn in the woods. Her jaw had dropped in disbelief when the news anchor had announced that Quinn had been discovered and was alive. The only saving grace was that Quinn had been unconscious for a long while, and probably had no memories of Rose standing over her.

She takes a deep breath and rolls up her sleeves. The red bumps on her forearms are almost intolerable. She does her best to resist the urge to scratch them. Her skin still has remnants of old scars from her childhood encounters with the plants. The reaction is worse than it was last time, developing more quickly as it usually does after each exposure. Rather than building a tolerance to the plant, her body goes into full attack mode.

"I'm such an idiot!" Upset with herself, she feels her anger coming in like waves, her peaceful exterior cracking.

The pressure is high.

She doesn't want to be the one responsible for destroying decades of good family history, and the one to blame for exposing all of them. They'd all worked so hard keeping up appearances, sacrificing lifestyles to keep their good standing with the community. Now, Rose has jeopardized everything. She'd been out of practice, sure of herself, and she'd made mistakes.

Her heartbeat is running wild, making her head spin. Fear has come—she senses it. She hasn't been this scared in years. She hates how vulnerable she feels.

The inability to predict the outcome is terrifying. Her thoughts are erratic, just like her movements. She barely recognizes herself right now. Like a caged animal stuck in a corner, she feels trapped—desperate to rectify the mistake. She's in trouble.

She lights a cinnamon-scented candle to ground her mind, but the spicy smell does nothing to soothe her. With her eyes closed, Rose jumps at the sound of a car door closing next door. Her heart skips a beat as she practically glides to the window, her feet floating on the floor, doing her best not to make a sound.

Peering out of the bay window, she watches William and Quinn walk up to their front door and disappear into the house.

Her eyes narrow at seeing Quinn, alive and well, walking on her own two feet as though nothing's happened. Rose releases a shallow hiss at the frustration of having been so close to getting rid of her next door neighbour.

Her rash intensifies with her growing anger, as though her inner darkness is pushing its way out to the surface, refusing to hide any longer. Rose doesn't see it that way, however. In her mind, she's doing the world a favour. Rose doesn't count herself as one of those evil-blooded people. She's one of the only ones seeing sense and cleansing the world—purifying it.

Unable to fight the urge to scratch the blistering, red bumps any longer, Rose rapidly drags her nails over her forearms, scraping at the raw skin until she draws blood. Seeing the bright, red liquid oozing out of her arm helps her breathe easier, yet it doesn't take the itch away. She watches the red droplets fall onto her linoleum flooring and is mesmerized for a moment by the colour of her own blood.

She ponders a lifelong question. Young or old, honest or liar, does the blood appear the same to the naked eye? She knows it does and doesn't blame people for not seeing what she sees in others—how easily she can spot liars. Although they look like regular people walking on the street, Rose has always been adept at being able to tell if they have evil in their blood.

She wonders what others see when they look at her.

68

ROSE

She decides to wait an hour as she watches the house next door.

She imagines the Millers are desperate to find Cole and eager to join the search, assuming their son is lost somewhere nearby. She laughs bitterly at the irony that he's not at all far from home, but rather, in her basement. She toys with the idea of letting things settle down before moving the boy, but another thought occurs to her.

If she's quick and takes extreme precautions, she might actually be able to place Cole back in his crib at his parent's house without them noticing her. She's left the boy pretty well intact since killing him, minus the severed finger, of course.

As a woman who's lost many of her own children, she's struggling to accept her impulsive decision to kill Cole. Had it really been necessary? He was just a baby after all. Who knows how he would have ended growing up? Would he have grown up and lived a pure, honest life even though he'd been raised by deceitful parents?

Rose had made that mistake in the past. She'd doubted herself and had experienced similar remorse before, but time usually proved her first instincts had been right.

She hadn't really hesitated when she'd killed Cole, although the boy had grown on her over the few months since she'd been tasked to watch over him sporadically. She'd watched him grow, had gotten to know him. It had been harder for her to proceed with her decision. Yet, once Rose had made up her mind, there was no turning back—no chance of redemption. Evil was evil, and it couldn't be cleansed. There was no stopping her. She was doing everyone a favour.

She'd known full-well what she'd had to do. She hadn't had a choice. Cole had to die. His parents had placed that curse on his life the moment they'd become liars. There was no place on this earth for people like the Millers.

Looking out her window, Rose spots fewer volunteers out today. She recognizes a few familiar faces from the night before. It will be tricky for her to get around unnoticed. She will need to be quick on her feet and have some kind of explanation ready in case someone catches her.

Thinking about it for a moment, she comes up with the perfect explanation. She'll say she's just found the boy in the yard, someone must have left him there when no one was looking. She will send them on a wild goose chase through the woods to find this 'someone', while she leaves town for a few days.

As luck would have it, just as Rose starts getting ready to bring Cole back to the Millers', most of the volunteers begin to gather at the back of the house. She decides that this is her best chance.

With the reporters away for the time being and the searchers in the back, Rose knows it's time. As though God is smiling down on her, Rose watches Jake Adkins pull up in the Millers' driveway, and spots William running out of the house two steps at a time, quickly joining him in the vehicle.

The two men drive off quickly—on a mission.

Rose can't imagine where they are headed, but she heard about Lena's disappearance on the news earlier. The men are probably letting Quinn rest, while they go off to the police station or out looking for Lena and Cole. She doesn't actually care why they've left because it's given her the perfect window of opportunity to proceed with her plan.

69

QUINN

Quinn stirs in her sleep. She feels restless, her feet hurt and her mind is spinning. The house is quiet—too quiet. The drastic difference between her house and the hospital makes her feel on edge. Drifting in and out of consciousness, she feels like she'll forever be between these two stages, never in the present. Her body aches from being immobile for several hours, lying on her side the entire time since William tucked her in.

For the briefest of moments, Quinn lies there with her eyes closed, tuning into the familiar sounds of the house; the creaks of the rotating ceiling fan, the smell of the overflowing garbage in the kitchen downstairs, the feel of her soft pillow and comforter.

For just a few seconds, she pretends that everything is ok, that this terrible ordeal has been nothing but a nightmare. None of it is real. She imagines Cole's whimpers from down the hall, his cries for her. But, unfortunately, no matter how hard she strains her ears, she can't hear a thing.

She's brutally assaulted by the terrible reality that she will most likely never again see her sweet boy's face and never get to hold him in her arms again.

Her eyelids fly open, only to close once more as the tears come pouring out. She shrinks into the mattress as though she's glued to it, weighed down by her pain.

The comforter seems to weigh a hundred pounds, filled with heavy rocks rather than fluffy, down feathers. She feels nauseous at the thought of never seeing Cole again.

Where's her baby boy?

How could this have happened? Was all of this her fault? Could her secret from so many years ago have caused all of this? The butterfly effect, karma for staying quiet about what she'd seen. The gut-wrenching guilt takes over again and she whimpers.

The agony in her heart radiates throughout her entire body and lands in her stomach with a heavy thud. It feels as though the bed is moving on its own, but it's only her heart beating strongly, shaking her to the core.

It's been two days.

Two days since she saw the man running through the woods with her son wrapped in his blanket. Three days since she'd held Cole in her arms, held his tiny fingers and kissed his palms.

Quinn's body aches from head to toe. Her feet are in rough shape from running on the forest floor. Her breasts have already started to get smaller, her milk supply surprisingly almost completely dried up as though they've given up hope of ever being called on again. The gash to her head had been stitched up neatly, but she can't help feeling like Frankenstein.

She finally has an exterior that matches how she's been feeling on the inside since becoming a mother.

A monster.

Some people were maternal, graceful mothers, while other women like herself should never become parents. Cole deserved better from her. No matter what the outcome of all of this was, Quinn had let her son down way before he'd been kidnapped.

Her job was to love him and keep him safe and she'd failed at both. She'd failed him. For someone who thrived on routine and stability for her own life, Quinn had been unstable emotionally for Cole. She feels a sinking feeling in her belly at the realization that Cole would have been better off with anyone else but her. Quinn exhales slowly, steadying herself.

She can't lie in bed forever. She slowly sits and rubs her eyes. Slowly moving her tangled hair away from her face, she grabs a forgotten hair elastic from the nightstand, and makes a messy bun on the top of her head.

Swinging her feet over the side of the bed, she places them heavily on the ground beneath her. The soft plush carpet feels nice against her bare feet. Again, she's acutely aware of how strange the house feels being so empty, so quiet.

Even though it's painful, she slips some shoes on as recommended by her doctor, to avoid damaging her feet any more than they already are, and she stumbles to the bathroom door wincing slightly with every step.

She's still sporting the loungewear she wore home from the hospital. Her grey sweatpants and plain white t-shirt feel loose on her. She peels the gauze back to reveal the healing gash, stitched up expertly. Her head is throbbing. Looking at her arms she's glad to see that the rash on her body from the poison ivy has reduced slightly.

She wants a shower, but she can't help but feel guilty about it. How can she possibly go on with life and continue with these mundane tasks when her little boy is missing, out there somewhere?

Thoughts of the last moments she saw Cole come rushing to her, making her lose her balance and lean against the wall. The cold surface helps her come back to the present and focus on the bathroom. Her eyes burn from all the tears.

When was the last time she ate something? She can't remember.

The hospital food had been dry and unappetizing. She'd left most of it on her tray as the thought of eating anything had seemed impossible in her current state.

Wiping angrily at her cheeks, she scrapes her fingers against the raw surface of her skin, wrecked by her salty tears. She feels more alone than ever. A small part of her even misses the steady, numbing buzz from the hospital.

She misses Cole's presence and his smile. She misses feeling needed. She craves William's embrace and wants to hear his soothing voice reassuring her that it will all be okay.

Where is William?

Pushing herself from the wall, Quinn suddenly stiffens. Something feels off. She searches her mind trying to assess what has sent her entire body into high alert mode.

There's a smell she doesn't recognize. It's unpleasant, even nauseating. Quinn hesitantly moves to the bedroom door and tries to find the source of the stench. Her nose leads her down the hall towards Cole's room. The smell is very strong here, and she covers her mouth and nose with her hand. Her eyes sting and her heart rate increases.

She doesn't want to go in there but she knows she has to. She needs to find out what's behind that door.

A million thoughts run through her mind.

Did an animal climb in an open window and die in there? When was the last time she'd emptied the Diaper Genie? Can human feces cause this horrible smell? Did the police leave some chemicals behind?

None of it makes any sense to her.

Feeling weak in the knees, Quinn falters. She draws in a quick breath and holds it as she twists the doorknob.

In the dark room, she immediately sees that the bedroom window is closed shut, curtains drawn. She's terrified and almost dizzy from the disgusting smell all around her. The room feels hot and heavy. There's been no air circulation in here for days.

Everything is telling her to get out and run. But instead, she steps further inside the room pinching her nose. She's shaking uncontrollably as she turns on the light, waiting for her eyes to adjust. As they do, Quinn spots a familiar shape in the crib.

"Cole! Oh my God, Cole!" she screams in terror, running towards the crib.

The lifeless body of her little boy laying before her makes her scream once again—a sound of pure anguish she didn't know she could even make.

"No!" she cries. "You can't be gone! No!" She barely hesitates before picking him up, hugging his tiny frame in her arms. "My sweet boy!" she wails a gut-wrenching cry.

Feeling the room spinning around her, the mixture of smells, the stiffness of her dead son, and the weight of her grief hits her like a train. Quinn keels over and vomits. Still holding Cole, she falls to her knees, crying.

Her little boy is dead. How could this happen?

Quinn sobs hysterically. Stricken by grief, she stares at her boy lying still in her arms. His skin is an unnatural grey colour. Life has long ago drained from his cheeks. His tiny eyes are glued shut forever. His body feels heavy in her arms.

Dead weight.

She releases another scream as she realizes she will never again see his smile. She won't see his first steps, hear his first words.

Heavy sobs make it harder and harder for her to breathe. She runs frantic fingers through his hair, swallowing down the bile threatening to come up in her throat. This is her boy. She made him. Quinn feels guilty for being uncomfortable to look at him like this.

Crumpled on the floor of the nursery, surrounded by mountains of baby clothes, toys, and diapers, Quinn suddenly feels overwhelmed and exhausted. She hugs Cole's body close to her, refusing to let him go, even though she knows she must do exactly that, eventually.

She knows she needs to call the police. Oh, William! How is she ever going to tell him?

"William!" she cries out. After a beat, she calls out to him again, yielding no response. Her husband must have stepped out to assist with the search.

She pushes the thought away.

This moment is all she has. This is the last time it will ever be just her and her boy alone. She feels a lump in her throat and leans over to kiss her son's corpse.

His face is perfectly preserved, for the time being, making him resemble a porcelain doll. Quinn traces the outline of his face with a shaky finger.

"You are my sunshine, my only sunshine..." the words choke out as she's unable to continue singing the lullaby.

She feels his chubby cheeks one last time, praying she will never forget even the smallest details; his thick eyelashes, his tiny nose, and his partially opened lips. She kisses his fingers one by one feeling ridiculous for her complaints over the last few months about his razor-sharp fingernails.

As she moves down his pudgy hand, kissing each of his fingers, she notices something strange. Cole's pinky finger is missing. Confusion mixed with anger hits her at an alarming speed.

What had this man done to her son? He had stolen him from under her, then tortured and killed him. The very thought of Cole suffering makes her stomach twist again. She moves her head to the side expecting to be sick again, only this time, it's only dry heaves.

Her stomach is empty. She desperately needs to drink water.

Quinn hesitates at the door, still holding Cole's body in her arms, unsure what to do next. She hates the thought of leaving Cole here, but rationally, she realizes he doesn't need her anymore. Even when he did need her, she'd done a pretty poor job of being there for him. The worst possible thing has already happened. Her son is dead.

Between heavy sobs, Quinn reluctantly lays Cole's body back into the crib, kissing him one last time before backing out of the room and shutting the door, leaving her son behind.

70

LENA

Her movements are slow and calculated. With a shaky arm, she grabs at her side and winces at the touch. She feels weaker with each passing hour. Her wound is serious and she has no idea how long she's got.

There are no windows in the damp basement. Only the furnace and hot water tank, a small cold storage room and one ceiling light that barely illuminates the room.

Lena can hear a buzzing murmur just outside the walls. She feels the thumping of people walking on the ground, their steps vibrating around her, but she has no way to reach them.

Why are there so many people out there? Are they looking for her? For Quinn? Is her friend still alive?

Mrs. Westover is obviously deranged. Has she also hurt Quinn? Is that why Quinn's patio door was left open and why Lena couldn't find her? So many unanswered questions with new ones forming every minute.

With all the noise outside, no one has been able to hear her hammering the hard walls with her fists. She's pounded on the walls for hours, until her hands are purple with bruises.

She rubs her sore hands gently and decides to change tactics. No one can hear her but maybe after a while, they'll notice that she's missing and start looking for her. Frustrated at being so close to being saved, yet finding no way to get noticed, she grits her teeth.

She begins to frantically search the cramped space but there isn't much down there. The glow of the light casts strange shadows on the walls, making the room feel spookier than it already is. Lena is weak and terrified.

"No," she resolves. "I will not die like this," she says decisively.

She searches every corner of the space where she's confined. If this is going to be the last place she sees before she dies, she might as well know every inch of it.

She's grateful to be in decent shape, from all her yoga classes. She's been able to move in slow, consecutive movements, altering her poses to accommodate her wound. It helps her frame of mind and helps pass the time.

She wouldn't mind more clothes or even a blanket. She's wrapped her tank top around her wound to help slow down the bleeding, but the dampness of the concrete space and the absence of warmth make her shiver in only her sports bra. It's been a long time since she's eaten.

She starts towards the cold storage room, tucked away behind a heavy, grey, steel door. The door jams a little bit and she has to use all of her strength to pry it open.

Inside she finds dozens of shelves lined with glass jars filled with preserves. She spots different kinds of berry jams, jars of marmalade, apple butter, pickled beans, relish, and canned pickles. There is no water in the cold storage room but there's enough food to keep her strong for a few more days. At least, she hopes.

With sore hands, Lena chooses a jar of strawberry jam first.

"A bit of sugar might help me stay awake longer," she says to herself and she dips a finger in the jam.

The sweet, delectable, gritty jam tastes heavenly against her tongue. She hadn't realized just how hungry she is. She never did have that iced coffee with Quinn and she feels a pull at the sudden realization that she's in caffeine withdrawal. It would explain the throbbing headache she'd had all day. The food is a welcome source of energy.

She continues searching the small room's food supply and finds a jar of pickles. She struggles to twist the lid, her side throbbing in protest until she hears a soft pop as the jar opens. A full-bodied odor of vinegar, garlic, and dill enters her nostrils and makes her salivate.

Pickles have always been a favourite night-time snack for her and Jake. The tangy taste with the salty-garlicky bite always seems fitting for any occasion. The perfect healthy snack to satisfy a junk-food craving.

She reaches a shaky hand into the cold glass jar and pulls out a pickle. The colour of it catches her off guard. The pickle is dark brown, with a pink hue, not a vivid green like she's used to. She turns the jar around to check the label. On a white label is a handwritten note: *Liars*.

Lena's eyebrows stitch together as she considers the meaning. Her stomach growls and she shrugs off the confusion brought on by the label.

Food is food, she rationalizes.

She's about to take a bite into the pickle when she spots a strange bump she can't identify on the tip of it.

Stepping outside the cold storage room, still clutching the open jar under her arm, she brings the pickle closer to the basement light to see exactly what it was that struck her as odd.

As the light shines directly onto it, Lena lets out a piercing cry and drops the jar and the pickle onto the concrete floor. The glass shatters and all of its contents spread out onto the floor beneath her.

"Oh God, oh God!" Lena falls to the ground, her voice brittle and barely audible.

She backs away as quickly as she can, ignoring the pain in her side, pushing with her legs and arms until her back hits the far wall on the opposite end of the basement. The storage room door remains open, a room of secrets. Lies captured there for who knows how long.

Lena feels weakness taking over and retches in the corner, still too shaken up to stand. She blinks repeatedly, trying to erase the image sprawled out before her. Tears stain her cheeks. She's incapable of keeping them in as she rubs her hand on her pants trying to rub off the wet brine left on her skin.

She must have hit the overhead light when she dropped the jar for the light swings back and forth on its wire adding to the ominous feeling. Although the light is weak, Lena has no doubts about what she's seen.

What she'd found in that jar were not pickles. They weren't even food.

The bump had been a fingernail still attached to a severed finger.

The jar had been full of them and now dozens were laid across the floor, surrounding her, blocking her way to survival. Shattered glass covered the ground reflecting tiny slivers of light, exposing the truth.

71

ROSE

The noise coming from the basement seems to have quieted down.

Lena must finally be dead. Rose sighs as she moves the needle steadily through the colourful material. The girl had simply been in the wrong place at the wrong time.

She hadn't known Lena well, but Rose hadn't ever felt that the woman was deceitful or a liar. She knew Lena was married to the helicopter pilot. They had no kids but they did have two annoying dogs.

It pained Rose to have to let her die alone in the cold basement while she was warm upstairs in the comfort of her living room, just one floor higher. She's been keeping busy putting the finishing touches on the quilt she is working on while casually sipping herbal tea.

She's finally allowing herself to relax after the last few chaotic days. Cole is back home and will soon be found, she imagines. Her plan to move him, although highly risky, had been a way out for her, keeping her name off the radar for now. Sitting in the silence, Rose's mind works as her fingers bind two pieces of fabric together.

She still hasn't figured out how to deal with Lena's body once it begins decomposing. She may just toss it in the back garden along with all the others.

The volunteers have slowed down and the search parties have been put on hold, now that a suspect has been identified—Dylan Thomas. Rose had once been so jealous of Maddison having found someone to love her regardless of all of her flaws. Now all Mrs. Westover feels is pity for him. The man has more in common with Rose than she's ever imagined.

Revenge had flowed through his veins and hadn't allowed him to rest for years.

Rose chuckles morbidly at the strangeness that she and Dylan both owed their need for revenge to Maddison—in different ways of course.

72

QUINN

She can't face this alone. Now that she knows the truth and has said her goodbyes to Cole on her own terms, she's ready to call the authorities to come and take over. She wants justice for her boy.

This man will pay.

She may have been a bad mother, but this man is the real monster. He's killed her little boy. He's still out there, freely roaming the streets. Who knows who he's watching now?

Gripping the banister, Quinn slowly and methodically walks down the stairs. Her knees buckle at the last step, almost making her trip. Walking towards the kitchen, she finds William's note.

In a trance-like state, she picks up her phone, calls the police, and recounts her discovery of Cole's body, empty of any emotion, her tears all spent. She hears the far away voice of the operator urging her to stay on the line before she ends the call and the room is plunged into silence.

She can't.

She feels unbalanced, reckless. What's the point of following the rules, doing the right things, trying your best when none of it is in your control? Bad things still happened, and there's nothing anyone can do about it.

Quinn feels overwhelmed. The cold air and closed windows feel suffocating. The white walls are closing in around her. She shuts her eyes to try and find her centre, but her mind is spinning.

Questions. So many unanswered questions.

Her breathing is laboured and she knows that she's going to be sick again. Fighting the urge to let it all go on the kitchen floor, Quinn barely makes it out through the patio doors and retches in the flower bed.

Hunched over, hands on her knees, she takes deep breaths. After a moment, she slowly rises, wipes her mouth with the back of her hand, and rubs her eyes. Goosebumps form on her bare arms and she hugs herself, trying to settle the unease in her stomach and in her heart. Thick tears fall down her cheeks, and she brushes them away angrily.

A strange sound catches her attention and she quickly snaps her head towards it. Could it be an animal in the woods? The muffled noise sounds vaguely familiar, yet she can't make it out.

She walks through the overgrown grass until she's in the middle of her backyard, ears strained, doing her best to locate the source of the sound. Her blood pulsing from her highly alert state makes it difficult to hear the noise properly, but the closer she gets, the better she can decipher it—a faint pounding followed by a faraway cry. Her nostrils flare as she does her best to quiet her pounding heart.

What is that? More importantly, who is that?

Curiosity gets the best of her as she inches closer and closer to the noise. Before she knows it, she finds herself in Mrs. Westover's backyard. The noise is definitely louder here. Quinn leans towards the ground placing her palms on the grass for support. It seems like the noise is coming from the basement.

Is Mrs. Westover hurt? Does she need help?

Quinn hurries to the front door, knocking several times before the door opens to a weary Mrs. Westover.

"Mrs. Westover, is everything alright?" Quinn inquires with her brows furrowed together in worry as she scans her neighbour from head to toe for any obvious signs of distress.

She notices Mrs. Westover's arms and cheeks are covered in tiny, red, blistery hives much like her own. Frowning, she sees that some of the scabs have been picked raw, dry blood coagulated in splotches.

"Why, of course, dear. Why do you ask?" the woman replies, the calmness of her voice not matching her appearance.

Confused by her neighbour's appearance and overwhelmed by the unsettling noise, Quinn feels terrified. Finding Cole dead had set her mind spinning, and now nothing was making sense. She runs her fingers over her bare arms, scratching away at her own rash, suddenly itching with a vengeance. She needs comfort, even if something about Mrs. Westover's appearance unnerves her. Moving closer to her neighbour, she wails, "Cole is dead!" and throws herself into the woman's arms. "Then, I went out in the yard and heard a strange pounding noise..." She doesn't finish because just then the sound resumes, louder this time.

It's coming from inside Mrs. Westover's house.

Quinn eyes Rose's unnaturally still posture suspiciously and instinctively, carefully backs away. The women exchange a slow, knowing glance.

"Mrs. Westover, is someone down there?" Quinn asks rising terror filling every cell in her body. The constant banging almost makes her come completely unglued.

Inching further away, Quinn slowly stands straighter, wary of the woman she's called a friend. "What's going on?" she asks bluntly. "Who's down there?" she demands, pointing to the door.

As Quinn looks beyond Mrs. Westover's shoulder, the woman slowly reaches into her back pocket and pulls out a long, sharp knife. With Quinn's remaining strength and instincts, she spots the blade and swiftly jumps away just in time to avoid the hard blow coming straight for her neck.

Surprised by the sudden attack, Quinn dashes through the kitchen, tossing a chair behind her as she rushes towards the basement door. She grabs the doorknob and twists but the door won't budge. She hears a creak coming up behind her and spins around to face Mrs. Westover, arm raised, knife gleaming in the overhead light.

At the last second, Quinn ducks.

A whoosh of air moves the stray hairs on the top of her head. With Mrs. Westover slightly off-balance from her thrust, Quinn lunges at her and punches her in the stomach. Rose stumbles backward and collides with the hallway wall.

Picture frames crash down around her.

Quinn quickly returns her attention to the basement door. The noise has stopped during the scuffle.

Glancing behind her, she tries the knob once more, but when it doesn't budge, she doesn't linger. She backs up a few feet, aims to the left of the knob, where the locking mechanism should be, and kicks the door with all her strength, sending a jolt of pain through her injured foot.

Quinn watches as the door swings open abruptly against the force of her kick. Gritting her teeth, she smiles grimly, satisfied with this small triumph. She looks behind her to see Mrs. Westover slowly getting up on her feet.

Without a moment to lose, Quinn races down the stairs. Ignoring her throbbing feet, she descends through the darkness seeking the source of the noise.

73

WILLIAM

William spots flashing blue and red lights as they turn down Dylan Thomas's street. *That's not good*, thinks William. The police must have beat them here.

"Jake, what do you think happened here?" William turns to him, both men stunned at the scene before them. An ambulance idles nearby with its back hatch open. An unmarked van sits near the house, the windows tinted so dark the glass looks like it's been painted on. There are dozens of officers, a few K-9 German Shepherds snipping the lawn and concerned neighbours gathered behind yellow crime scene tape, blocking access to the street.

"I think we're about to find out." He lifts his chin slightly, his eyes on a police officer coming toward them. He pauses in his stride to take a long, hard look at their license plate.

The officer signals to Jake to roll his window down, "Hi there. Sorry, but no traffic is allowed on this road right now." He indicates behind him, the caution tape making his statement redundant.

"You guys from around here?" he asks.

Hesitating, Jake speaks first, "I teach at the helicopter school here in town, and this here is one of my students," he adds pointing to William.

Leaning in, the officer takes a good look inside the vehicle, pretending to be casual. "I'm afraid you'll need to go back the way you came and follow the detour route. This road will be closed for a while."

His tone seems apologetic but his body stiffens at the sight of William.

"Hey, have I seen you before?" he asks, causing William's forehead to perspire slightly.

He's got a feeling the officer already knows who he is.

"Nope, don't think so, sir," William replies as sweat begins to pool at the base of his back. He rubs his clammy hands over his jeans as subtly as he can manage.

Squinting at them, the officer is quiet for a moment, assessing them before advising them once more to return to the main road and go back the way they came. Jake and William's quick, shallow breaths finally return to normal once they're back on the main road.

"That was close, man." William exhales, relieved. "I felt like he could read my mind for a minute." He chuckles apprehensively before adding, "That was kind of stupid, coming all the way out here. I mean, what were we going to do if we found the douche-bag? Beat him up? Kill him?" He laughs nervously, mindlessly fingering the Swiss army knife he'd grabbed from the kitchen on his way out to meet Jake. "I think that officer just saved our asses back there." He feels embarrassed and strangely thankful for the interruption.

"Yeah, I guess you're right," Jake finally responds, never taking his eyes off the road. After a beat, he adds, "Look, I know this is probably the last thing you want to do, but I'm too worked up to drive back home just yet."

As he takes a side glance at William, Jake's eyes are covered with a sheen. William clenches his fists. He's feeling the tension too and can relate to Jake's pain.

"Yeah, man. It's all good, no problem at all." Slapping a flat palm on Jake's shoulder, he suggests they try and grab a bite to eat—not that either of them are hungry. It's merely as a way to pass time and calm down.

———

They arrive at their usual bar, and William's stomach rolls. Both men have been here many times during lunch breaks between lessons, but the bar doesn't offer its usual jovial atmosphere. Instead, William finds himself noticing the lack of light, the old, ripped seat cushions and sickening smell of stale beer and greasy fries.

They need to shake off the adrenaline from almost getting caught by the police officer near Dylan Thomas's house. William is still shaking at the idea that the officer might have recognized him. What would have happened if he had? Was William allowed to be so close to the house of the man who might have abducted his child? William guesses it would have looked pretty suspicious had he been caught.

Jake hastily grabs a nearby menu, abandoned on the table. He scans it hungrily while clutching his glass of water

"Man, I'm starving," William finally realizes.

Food is another one of William's impulses. It helps him deal with his emotions. William takes a quick glance at the menu before him, trying his best to touch only the corners, the rest smeared with a sticky residue. As he looks up he catches sight of an overhead television news broadcast.

The sound is off, but the captions can be read at the bottom of the screen. A slender female news anchor is standing outside a modest, two-story home, clutching her microphone. The wind is whipping through her long blond hair as she speaks, looking sternly at the camera.

The screen reads, "Hello, I'm Jennifer Douglas, and this broadcast is brought to you by North Bay News." The station's logo appears for a brief moment before the camera pans out to the house situated behind the news reporter.

"Behind me is the residence of Dylan Thomas, a man who was recently a suspect in the kidnapping of Cole Miller, a nine-month-old boy taken from his home on August 13th in Sturgeon Falls." she pauses briefly. "We've just learned from the lead investigator on this case that Mr. Thomas was found dead earlier this morning. The investigation into Mr. Thomas's death continues, although the police do not suspect foul play."

The camera moves slightly to show an officer in his mid-fifties with a balding head and a serious, clean-shaven face.

"Officer Liam Purdy of North Bay Police, can you tell us a little bit about what's going on here and the cause of Mr. Thomas's death?"

"Thank you, Jennifer. I can confirm the deceased man has been identified as Dylan Thomas, the prime suspect in the Cole Miller case. However, we can't release any details on how Mr. Thomas died at this time. Further investigation will be required. His family has been notified of his passing, and they've asked for time to grieve."

"What about Cole Miller? Was he also found in the home of Dylan Thomas?"

"After a thorough search, we can confirm that the child was not in the home. The search for Cole Miller is still ongoing." He nods curtly, finishing his sentence.

William's jaw is tight as his eyes glaze over. So, the bastard died. He should be relieved, but he isn't. They aren't going to get their answers now. The unknown is driving him mad. He feels so powerless.

"Are you seeing this?" Jake pipes in, staring at the screen above them. William hadn't noticed how many screens this bar had until pictures of Dylan, followed by Cole's sweet face, flash on every screen in the place. It makes him dizzy.

"Yeah. I'm guessing that's why there was caution tape and police everywhere," William gathers.

"I wonder how he died..." Jake muses. Bringing his hands together under his chin he scoffs, "I hope he suffered."

William looks on at his friend, his boss. He's surprised to find that he doesn't wish Dylan Thomas had suffered. He just wants to find Cole.

74

QUINN

The stairway is dark, and the room is musty. Quinn fights the growing dread inside of her. She has no idea what's waiting for her at the bottom of the steps.

Someone's down there, but who will she find?

The steps creak sharply under her weight, making her wince in fear. As she moves closer to the bottom, she holds her breath, trying to protect herself in this small, insignificant way. She knows it could be a trap, that Mrs. Westover could lock her down here along with whoever had been making the noise.

She doesn't dwell on the newly discovered persona of her next-door neighbour—she just knows that she needs to keep moving.

She needs to know.

The guilt of not having been able to save Cole propels her forward. She'll do what she can. It's the right thing to do. The room is damp and cold. She feels goosebumps on her skin. Stretching her arm to steady herself as she steps down, her hand touches a spider web and she shakes it off.

The walls are bare cement and some unfinished framework is laid across them. The structure lacks proper insulation save for the low-hanging ceiling. Wires, plumbing, and furnace ducts run along over her head, the aluminum pieces reflecting the small amount of light seeping in from the hallways on the main floor.

Quinn hears a muffled sound to her right and squints her eyes to see. Spotting a dark lump on the cold, concrete floor, she hesitantly moves closer. Taking in sharp breaths, she forces her legs to move.

Something touches her hair. She screams.

Her heart beats a million miles an hour, she is frozen in place. Her breathing is slow and raspy. With a shaky hand, she reaches above her to feel what's rubbed against her hair. She grasp a thin, metal chain, and exhales, realizing she's walked under the ceiling light chain.

With the low light from the ceiling light, Quinn spots bare feet in the corner of the basement. They appear to be covered in scratches and bruises, visible under the beam of light from the bulb swinging above Quinn's head. The rest of the body remains hidden from view hovering in the shadows.

A crack on the concrete floor seems to lead her to the person sprawled on the ground. Her breath catches as she gets closer and realizes who it is.

"Lena!" she shrieks. "What are you doing here?" Confused, she rushes over to her friend's limp body, forgetting for a split second all about Mrs. Westover. When she reaches Lena, she crouches to check for injuries before helping her sit upright.

Her friend is in terrible shape. Quinn notices that she looks dehydrated. Her colouring is pale and her lips are dry. There is blood all over the floor, indicating a serious injury. Quinn feels tears running down her cheeks as she imagines the pain of Lena's wound.

Lena's movements are slow and almost unnoticeable in their subtlety. Her eyes gloss over as she tries to mumble something incomprehensible. Quinn sees that the trail of blood extends to the wall behind where Lena is now slumped.

"What happened to you?" Quinn insists.

Lena is getting weaker by the second. Quinn watches her head bob down as she begins to lose consciousness. Again, her friend mumbles something inaudible.

"Lena! Stay with me!" Quinn panics. "You need help! She needs help!" she yells turning around, addressing no one in particular.

Her mind is whirling, first from finding Cole dead, followed by her terrifying encounter with Mrs. Westover, and now from watching her friend's life seeping out from her.

A creak on the step above brings Quinn's attention back to the moment. She twists her body around instinctively protecting Lena, shielding her with her back. As Mrs. Westover slowly descends the steps, Quinn realizes that her neighbour is in no rush. There is literally nowhere to escape to.

They are trapped down here.

Quinn swallows. Her throat is parched. Lena's bloody hand reaches out to hold Quinn's, catching her off guard, startling her with its coldness. Quinn doesn't take her eyes off Mrs. Westover for a second. She doesn't trust her one bit. Her motherly instincts finally kick in a little too late.

She shields the woman who's become like family to her in this strange town. She's no doctor, but she knows Lena's condition is serious. Quinn knows that, without a doubt, Lena is dying.

Panicking, Quinn's adrenaline kicks in.

She frantically scans the room for anything she can use as a weapon. Letting go of Lena's rust-coloured hand for just a moment, she hears a faint gurgle behind her in protest, but she doesn't look back.

There's no other way.

She doesn't have time to change her mind. To save them both, she needs to let her friend go or they will both die at the hand of this deranged woman. Mrs. Westover is clearly evil. There isn't time to waste.

The old woman is slowly making her way down the steps. She's almost reached the last one.

Quinn's chest heaves heavily, but she manages to hold herself together. Their lives depend on her next move. She was too late to save Cole. But protecting Lena—this she can do.

An animal-like growl escapes her lips as her throat closes from the stress. She barely recognizes herself. She is crouched low but on high alert, her posture almost primitive. She's ready to fight. She's ready to do what it takes to defend her friend. Quinn can barely comprehend the situation she's in, but at the moment, she's simply focused on saving Lena.

Spotting the cold room door ajar, she sprints across the basement floor, her shoes providing traction and protection to her injured feet. Hurriedly, Quinn scans the small space, dampness chilling her bones, her thin t-shirt providing no warmth. The overwhelming fear of finding herself confined in the small space quickens her gaze.

Her eyes dart from wall to wall. There isn't much here, she realizes. The sound of glass cracking brings her back to focus. She must hurry.

She spots a weak, narrow, water-damaged piece of wood at the bottom of the cold room. Quinn acts quickly. Without hesitating, she begins kicking at it hard, breaking the ends into splintered edges. In painful heaves, she finally lifts the two-by-four a few inches off the ground and manages to pull it away from the wall. Along the bottom of the slab of wood, Quinn spots a rusty nail sticking out. It's bent out of shape but is still sharp and very capable of inflicting pain.

The sound of another noticeable step and more breaking glass bring her attention back to the room where Lena is now sprawled on the cool floor unmoving. Flinging her makeshift weapon over her shoulder, Quinn heads back towards the main basement room, worried about what she'll find on the other side of the door.

75

QUINN

Mrs. Westover is standing over Lena. Her friend's body is limp—still, except for the small rise and fall of her chest to show her fight for life.

"It won't be long now," whispers Mrs. Westover.

"What happened to her?" Quinn asks, taken off guard by her neighbour's non-defensive stance.

"I stabbed her," she answers, nonchalantly.

Quinn takes a quick breath at Mrs. Westover's indifferent statement, as though it's no big deal. A picture begins to form in Quinn's mind. She must be in shock. No normal person would be so passive about stabbing someone, about watching life drain from their body. But Mrs. Westover seems unaffected by the pain she has inflicted.

"Why?" Quinn wearily asks.

There's a long drawn out pause as Mrs. Westover ponders the best way to respond.

"She was going to share my secret." The old woman's eyes hold Quinn's, and a chill runs down Quinn's spine.

She swallows, but her throat is parched. She needs water desperately. Her nose flares as the tears threaten once more. Seeing the state of her friend, her life expiring before her, Quinn's grief takes hold. She has no more energy, no more patience for games. She doesn't have the stamina to ask the questions she needs answers to.

Mrs. Westover stands between her and Lena. In a split second, her stance changes from that of a passive, remorseless bystander to a fearless attacker. Quinn barely has time to register movement when the old lady charges and slams directly into her.

Stunned, Quinn falls to the floor, hitting her head on the concrete, and dropping the timber beside her. Her head throbs and her vision goes spotty. As she tries to regain her balance, Quinn hears a weak voice calling her name.

Lena, on the other side of the room, is talking to her. The colour of her face lets Quinn know that it won't be long now before her friend dies. Mrs. Westover stands in the shadow, watching Quinn struggle to stand.

"...Cole..." Lena mumbles through half-closed lips, her tear-stained cheeks pressed to the cement floor.

"What? What about Cole?" Quinn begs to know while feeling around for the piece of wood with the nail in it as she struggles to stand.

"...killed him..." a weakening Lena adds, her eyelids closing.

"Please, Lena, what are you saying? Who killed him?" Quinn is hysterical.

With all of her remaining strength, Lena manages to briefly lift her arm and with a shaky finger, she points to the shadowed figure in the corner of the room.

Mrs. Westover steps out of the shadows, finally in full view. Unashamed, a sly smile plays on her lips. Rose's skin is covered in angry blisters and fresh scabs raw from where she's scratched them. Her face holds a snide expression, no effort or desire to deny the allegations.

Rather, the woman looks proud and confident. Such a contrast to the frail, old woman who used to limp around talking about her beloved church and her daycare business. How wrong Quinn had been. How blindly she'd trusted her. Rose wasn't the old lady she pretended to be.

Quinn and William hadn't even asked for references from previous clients before asking Rose to watch Cole. They'd been too desperate for a night out, rashly trusting a stranger out of convenience and the assumption that neighbours could be trusted. Yet, they truly hadn't known Mrs. Westover at all.

Confused, Quinn takes her eyes off Mrs. Westover for a brief moment to chance a glance at Lena. Her friend's eyes are open, a terrified look frozen on her white face. Quinn whimpers at the sight of her friend's lifeless body, moaning loudly as sadness overwhelms her. She's lost two people in the span of less than an hour. Losing her balance, Quinn crouches back down, nausea overtakes her. The room spins around her forcing her to place her hands on the ground to steady herself.

When she opens her eyes, she recoils at the sight of dozens of discoloured, severed fingers scattered all over the floor. How had she missed them before?

Getting to Lena had been her priority and she'd ignored the mess on the floor at her feet.

The broken glass and fingers make her want to shut her eyes, click her heels three time, and escape this reality.

In her squatted position, a small, yet very distinct detail on one of the fingers catches her attention. Feeling the bile rise up in her throat, Quinn forces herself to look at it more attentively. Possessed by an external strength, she picks up the tiny finger and drops it in her palm to inspect it closely.

The tiny fingernail is sharp and in need of cutting, and there next to it, just as she fears, she spots a small, brown freckle to the right of the nail. Dropping the finger to the floor, she wails louder than she thought possible. She stands abruptly, rage building up inside of her. Her veins feel like they are supercharged with anger, her skin hot to the touch.

She is boiling with fury.

Noticing a sudden movement to her left, she bends down quickly and grabs the two-by-four. With all her force, she swings the large timber as though it were a baseball bat until she feels it collide with something, or rather, someone. The bat smashes Rose's arm, snapping it like a twig, making her scream in agony.

Quinn's eyes are enraged, she's not finished yet. She bit her lip when she swung the wood and wipes blood onto her sleeve as she wipes her mouth. A twinge of fear flashes in Rose's eyes as Quinn rushes towards her, her arms raised above her head. Her pain pushing her forward, Quinn uses all her force to slam the wood directly into Mrs. Westover's skull. A loud yell is immediately followed by a sharp cracking noise.

The frenzy inside Quinn releases. She watches numbly as blood begins pooling around her. Mrs. Westover's body lies in a limp pile next to the basement steps. Her white hair is now crimson red, and a pool of blood seeps out from underneath her head as her fractured skull releases the pressure from the impact. Her skull is bashed in, the rusty nail imbedded so deeply inside her head that Quinn can't even see it anymore.

Quinn's breaths are shallow, and she feels herself coming in and out of consciousness. She stumbles backward feeling the coolness of the wall meet her bare hands, and allows herself to slide down to the floor, reaching to pick up the cut finger.

Dropping her head into her hands, she sobs uncontrollably, one hand in a fist, curled around the severed finger of her dead son.

76

WILLIAM

William and Jake drive back to William's house, surprised to find the road blocked off with yellow tape just as Dylan's street had been.

Quinn. William panics.

He had left her alone at home during the most painful event of her life. How could he have been so stupid? His heart beats quickly and he runs a hand roughly through his messy hair making him look ragged.

"Hurry up, man!" William voice's shakes. "Why did I leave Quinn alone?" he ponders weakly. "I shouldn't have left her alone." He begins to shudder as sweat lines his armpits despite the blast coming from the air conditioner.

Unable to offer any reassurance, Jake focuses on parking the car up the road, and the two men waste no time leaping out of the vehicle. They jog down the road towards the Millers' house where the activity seems to be concentrated.

William gets there first and begins to frantically pant as his eyes search to connect with someone, anyone, who can tell him what's happening. The blood drains from his face. There are three ambulances parked between his house and Mrs. Westover's.

The navy blue uniforms everywhere make it seems like he's in the middle of the ocean about to drown amongst the waves. There are people everywhere, coming in and out of his house as well as Mrs. Westover's. Crowds of people are on the lawn and walking around the backyard. No one seems to be in a hurry. William spots a few paramedics pulling out a stretcher and his heart sinks.

If no one is hurrying, it's probably because Quinn is beyond saving.

She's already dead, he thinks to himself.

William doubles over, clutching his stomach as he tries not to be sick.

"Mr. Miller?" A police officer William hadn't noticed before is suddenly standing before him, a grave expression on his face.

William wishes he didn't have to hear what the officer has to tell him. He'd give anything to turn back time to before any of this had ever happened. He wants to start over and never move to this cursed place. Cole would be in his arms and Quinn would be beside him as she'd been for years. He couldn't imagine his life without her or Cole in it.

"Mr. Miller, I'm Officer Sanders." He introduces himself and shakes William's hand. "I've been working on your son's case," he informs him. William nods, waiting for the blow. "There's been a development."

His grave expression weakens William's knees. Doing his best to help him stand, the officer glances over William's shoulder and his expression turns to one of shock.

"Mr. Adkins, I'm surprised to find you here. We've sent an officer to your house, but I'll let him know you're here."

And with that, the officer quickly retreats, leaving them standing there confused and lost. *A development*, thinks William. *What the hell does that even mean?*

Both men look like scolded toddlers, waiting for their punishment. They won't even look at each other as fear and pain is written on their faces. Once the officer returns, he addresses them both.

"May we sit down inside?" Officer Sanders motions towards the house.

William nods reluctantly. He looks back slightly at Jake whose downcast gaze is made more pronounced by dark hollow circles under his eyes. *None of this is good*, William shudders.

He's led to his living room where he plops himself down on the couch with a sense of defeat. The now-familiar house still doesn't feel quite like his. William has always felt like a stranger in this place. He'd been unattached to the furnishings, unmoved by the light coming through the kitchen window, untethered to the place, with the intent to move shortly after graduating from helicopter school. The move here had been purely practical.

Jake sits next to him on the couch in a similar fashion, yet it doesn't even stir William sitting on the cushion next to him. The level of self-restraint his boss is showing is remarkable. The two friends are emotionally exhausted and can't imagine hearing any more bad news.

"I'm afraid I've got some bad news." The officer looks from William to Jake, as though reading their minds. The look of confusion is etched on both men's faces, as they look to each other, struggling to understand why they are being addressed at the same time.

"We received a distress call from Mrs. Miller approximately an hour ago and sent officers to the house immediately, but I'm afraid we were too late."

William's eyes fill with tears at the sound of his wife's name. He imagines her waking up and searching for him through the house, distraught. He shouldn't have left her alone.

The officer stares at William, unblinking, trying to see if William had any notion of this information beforehand. When he's assured that this is new information, the officer continues, despite the white faces of both men.

William knows what the officer must tell him next. He's already two steps ahead. On all the police shows, the police officers have to be very clear when they deliver bad news so that nothing can be left to interpretation. He's also aware that once the man speaks the words, there is no going back. William will never be able to un-hear them.

"I'm sorry to inform you, Mr. Miller, but Cole is dead." He pauses. "Your wife found him earlier, already deceased, lying in his crib." He stops for a moment, before adding, "We're unsure as of now how exactly Cole's body ended up back in his room, as my team had done an extensive search when Cole was reported missing. But I assure you, we are working on it," he says before sadly adding, "I'm sorry for your loss." The last words echo deep into William's head as emotions swirl about.

Having a hard time swallowing, William finally finds his words.

"Where's Quinn? Is she..." His eyes scan the room unable to find his wife.

"Your wife is talking to one of our officers in the house next door." He indicates Mrs. Westover's house with his head. "I'm afraid there is more I need to tell you. Both of you." He now turns his attention to Jake, who's been surprisingly silent so far.

"Mr. Adkins, I'm so very sorry to let you know that we've located your wife, but she was badly injured when we got to her. Unfortunately, she succumbed to her injuries before our emergency workers could assist her. We estimate she died within the last hour."

"My wife is dead?" Tears run down Jakes cheeks as he shakes his head, refusing to accept the information. "I don't understand. What happened?" he demands angrily.

"I understand this is upsetting." The officer looks between the two men. William notices that he looks like he hasn't slept in days. William imagines he must have a similar appearance. At that moment, another officer comes over to stand behind Officer Sanders.

Looking up at the other officer, Officer Sanders nods and stands up. "I'll need both of you to follow me for a moment, please, when you're ready." He excuses himself and waits for the men to gather themselves off the sunken couch and join him by the backyard patio doors.

On shaky legs, the men move forward, their legs taking on a life of their own, guiding them where they need to go as their minds float away somewhere else to process the information they've just been given.

They are led out of the house and into the backyard.

Turning to William first, Officer Sanders asks him, "What do you know about Mrs. Westover?"

Surprised, William instinctively looks up at his neighbour's house remembering that Quinn is somewhere inside being questioned. He should be with her. She found Cole dead in his crib all by herself, and now he's only a few feet away but still letting her down by not being by her side.

Jake solemnly walks behind, struggling to keep up. Overwhelmed with grief, he kneels on the grass. Two nearby officers approach him and crouch by him, offering water. Their voices are low and kind. William and Officer Sanders watch and they slow their pace. Shaking off the terrible scene, William is filled with a longing to hold Quinn in his arms.

"I'm sorry Officer Sanders, but I really need to see my wife." He pushes past the man and circles the house.

He walks into Mrs. Westover's house without knocking and is welcomed by half a dozen uniformed officers in white masks and gloves moving around the house inspecting every inch.

He finds Quinn sitting at the kitchen table, her legs up on the seat of the chair gathered up in her arms in a makeshift hug. Her eyes are red making it clear that she's been crying. William's lips quiver at the sight of her, emitting an audible sound. Quinn hears it and lifts her head to meet his eyes.

"William..." she utters faintly, almost in a whisper.

William takes two quick steps and he wraps his arms around her. Quinn sobs loudly on his shoulder, and he lets his tears fall over her matted hair. Pulling apart for a brief moment, their eyes speak volumes. Their son is dead.

"She killed him," Quinn tells him.

"Who? What do you mean?" William doesn't understand.

"Mr. Miller, please take a seat," the officer across the table from them motions to the seat beside Quinn, and William gratefully takes it, never leaving Quinn's eyes. He takes a hold of her cold hand, her icy fingers, interlacing with his. He tries his best to warm them up to no avail.

"Mr. Miller, my name is Officer James. I was just in the process of asking your wife some questions regarding the events from earlier this afternoon."

Addressing Quinn, Officer James asks her to continue relating what happened.

William listens in awe as he hears his wife recall finding their son's lifeless body and placing a call to the emergency service. She goes on to explain how she ended up in their backyard after a strong wave of nausea, and how she heard a muffled noise from next door.

With her eyes glued to William's, she tells them about walking into Mrs. Westover's, how the old lady had charged her. How Quinn had kicked open the locked basement door to find Lena injured and dying. She tells them through heavy sobs about finding Cole's finger and about Lena's last words.

Quinn sniffles loudly.

William watches her and admires her strength. She's doing her best to remember these moments that might take years, if not the rest of her life, to blackout from her memory forever.

When she tells them how she hit Mrs. Westover over the head with the plank, Quinn looks down, seemingly worried of what William will think of her. He wants to pull her close and tell her he doesn't care, that he doesn't judge her the least bit. He wants to tell her how brave she was, how proud he is of her, but he can't.

At least, not here—not yet.

77

QUINN

The statements take several hours. Quinn shivers in the room and wants nothing more than to leave this house and this town for good. She doesn't belong here. There's nothing left for them here.

This town is now forever stained with her son's blood and she wants nothing to do with it anymore. She wants to get as far away as she can from this place. By the way William is holding her hand in his, she knows that he's on the same page.

They're a team again. The horrible events have remarkably brought them back together—closer than ever. Strange how that can happen. Some couples break under pressure, while others lean on each other and grow stronger together.

The officers lead them back home, the backyard search still underway. Reporters litter the lawns of both homes as the Millers numbly tread through the grass not caring who sees their tear-stained faces and what they trample on in their path. The news will come out soon exposing their loss to their town. The entire province will cry with them.

When they reach their front door, Quinn can't bring herself to enter. The last time she was inside the house, she'd found her son's dead body. Where was Cole now? Had they moved him?

Looking up to William and back to the officer, the unspoken question seems to hang in the air between them. The officer reluctantly offers the information.

"The coroner has taken Cole's body to the morgue for autopsy to find out the cause of death." Quinn can sense there is more he wants to say, but he seems to be deliberating wheter he should.

"What is it?" Quinn pleads with him. "Please tell us what you've found." She turns to face him as William wraps a protective arm around her waist, she assumes for comfort but also to hold her up depending on the findings.

"Perhaps we should step inside for this." The officer opens the door allowing them to step inside and closes it behind them.

None of them move from the entryway, all standing looking at each other.

"The coroner did confirm that Cole's little finger was severed from his right hand." He looks down, trying his best to remain professional in his delivery. "We will run some tests, but we strongly believe that the finger you found in Mrs. Westover's basement will match Cole's DNA," he says, meeting Quinn's eyes.

The officer says something else, but Quinn doesn't hear. She's so focused on the information she's just heard about her son. Mrs. Westover had killed him and cut off his pinky finger. Although it's disturbing, Quinn can only wonder why.

Why had Rose taken her son's finger? What had her son done to deserve this? A single tear escapes her eye and runs down her cheek, seemingly gluing her eyes shut for some time.

"What about the man? What's his part in all this?" she asks suddenly.

"Officers in North Bay found Dylan Thomas dead in his home earlier this morning." He scratches his head.

"Dylan Thomas." Quinn repeats, trying out the name on her tongue. "He's dead?" Quinn's eyes widen. "How?"

"It appears that he took his own life," he says sadly. "When they inspected the scene, they found a large map with red Sharpie lines and marks of where Mr. Thomas had been. Phone records showed that Mr. Thomas had recently been in touch with Inspector George Feldman. Upon looking into it, we discovered that Mr. Thomas had been obsessed with locating a red Corolla, the same one responsible for the hit-and-run that took the life of his wife, Maddison, and their unborn child." He pauses, allowing the information to sink in. The officer looks exhausted.

"Mrs. Westover let me use her red Corolla the other morning for my grocery run after our Golf broke down." Quinn's face is a mix of understanding and anger. "She's the one that killed that man's wife, isn't she?" Her eyes scan the officer's face.

"We believe so. We ran the plates and the car belonged to a Max Westover, Mrs. Westover's late husband. We believe Mr. Thomas had been looking for a red Corolla with a dent in the bumper and found you at the wheel. We think he mistook you for the one who killed his wife and child." He waits a beat. "Inspection revealed Mr. Thomas's fingerprints all over the bumper of the Corolla which was how he became our primary suspect in the first place. That and a concerned neighbour had tipped us off about a strange man having been parked on your street earlier on the morning of August 13th. Autopsy reports also identified a minor reaction to poison ivy."

"I wonder if he remembered me from that day long ago when I heard the crash and went over to see what had happened." Maybe he'd recognized her as she'd recognized his eyes.

"It's possible. What we suspect is Mr. Thomas recognized the car and entered your home with the intent to kidnap Cole. What he did with him, we're unsure of at this point. We still need to find out how Mrs. Westover came to find Cole. As you'd pointed out when we first came to you today, Mrs. Westover also had a significant poison ivy rash on her arms, similar to yours, indicating that she'd been in the woods at some point. Cole however did not have any reaction to poison ivy, so it's possible that Mr. Thomas never took him from the home."

"You think Mrs. Westover went looking for Cole in the woods but didn't find him. Then she grabbed him from his crib and brought him home to kill him?"

"Or it's possible that Cole had already died when Mrs. Westover found him and that she brought him home in a panic." The officer adds, "The coroner will have more information soon. The cut finger seems to indicate that Cole's death was premeditated." It's difficult for them to hear this information, hard to believe that they are discussing the death of their son.

Quinn remains still as William and the officer keep talking. Quinn's body is shaking, yet she begins to feel a strange calmness within her. Slowly, the questions are being answered. Now she knows in part what's happened to her son. There is a strange peace in finding out the fate of a loved one, even if only for selfish reasons.

There is comfort in knowing that she has Cole's body to place to rest which is more than some others have when they lose someone they love. She can arrange a funeral, install a beautifully marbled gravestone, and visit the site as much as she wants.

The anger that's been building starts escaping like a tire with a slow leak. It gives her lungs the space to expand to their full capacity once more. The grief is there but it isn't crushing her anymore. She's distraught, nauseous even, but in a way, she still has her son close to her. His body will be given back to them which she guesses is a small mercy from the old woman. A tiny gesture of grace between them even after death.

"Excuse me, sir?" says an officer coming through the patio doors, crossing through the living room to join them in the entrance where they've remained this entire time, unable to move further into the house.

All at once, the three of them turn in his direction. Quinn reluctantly opens her eyes, disappointed to still find herself in this house. The officer is holding a bundled-up quilt, the fabric made of equal-sized square pieces of various materials.

"I think you need to come and look at this." He motions to them to join him in the living room.

Making their way over, the officer swallows hard as he unfolds the quilt before them. Quinn gasps, painfully and loudly as she spots the familiar blue flannel blanket—Cole's blanket.

The blanket has been expertly stitched between two perfectly cut yellow and green squares.

Part of her wants to reach out and touch the fabric one more time, while another part of her wants to rip it from the quilt and take back what's theirs. Yet, her body remains still. Her legs are like concrete slabs keeping her from moving even an inch, unable to remove herself from this situation.

The officer gets confirmation from William that the blanket in question had belonged to Cole. He swiftly folds the quilt, unevenly, as though in a hurry to shield them from pain and hands it to an officer nearby to place in evidence—out of sight, out of mind. If only it worked that way.

William's warm hand covers Quinn's and she finds the blood rushing through her again, warming her from the inside out. Part of her might have died today, but William's hand over hers reminds her that she is very much alive and still has much to live for.

She looks over at her husband with newfound love, surprising herself. He's all she's got now. They are both experiencing this together.

The death of a child can build wedges between couples, cause them to fall apart and often leads to divorce. But they need each other.

William's hand squeezes hers and she feels reassured that they will make it through, one day at a time.

78

QUINN
NOVEMBER 2014

Quinn walks down the road hand in hand with William. It's been months since they buried Cole's body in a beautifully selected plot on a green landscape overlooking the Saint Lawrence River. Quinn hadn't known the best place to lay him to rest, but she was adamant that it wouldn't be near a forest.

The service had been a beautiful one, and thankfully no one had mentioned the old woman's name keeping the focus on Cole. His grave has been covered with dirt and hundreds of white flowers—daffodils and calla lilies. Many of their friends had attended and offered support. The autumn air had been chilly, and they had brought several blankets to huddle underneath.

There had been journalists present, but even they had honoured Cole's last moments by reserving the picture taking to appropriate moments during the ceremony, not willing to break the respectful silence.

It seemed the entire province had fallen in love with their son and many had offered their condolences by sending letters and flowers.

The ceremony had been short and intimate. A local violinist had serenaded them with an emotional and haunting rendition of "Angel" bringing everyone to tears.

Quinn had had Cole's picture printed and placed in a large black frame at the front next to his tiny casket. They had chosen a beautifully crafted, solid poplar, wood casket with a soft, white, velvet interior. The framed picture of Cole was now hanging on a wall in their new house in downtown Kingston where they could look at it every time they walked by.

Seeing as Mrs. Westover had been clearly responsible for at least two deaths, the investigation had expanded to the rest of her property, revealing make-shift burial sites for dozens of unidentified victims. Mrs. Westover had been living a secret life right under everyone's noses.

The old woman's house, as well as any remaining buildings, had been torn down. The yard was in the slow process of being carefully dug up to make sure they didn't leave any human remains behind. Cole's and Lena's deaths had exposed decades of killings and provided many families with the answers and closure they'd desperately needed.

The community had been supportive and helpful with the investigation. After hearing of Lena's death, Jake had taken a month off of work and begun the process of selling the rental house.

It was still unknown how Lena came to be in Mrs. Westover's basement, but the investigators had recovered the knife Rose had used to stab Lena.

Sylvie had organized a meal list and had been lending a hand in any way she could to make the process bearable.

William and Quinn had told Jake of their plans to move back to Kingston shortly after Cole's death. A fresh start, they'd said. They couldn't bear to live in the house where their son had been found dead in his crib. Jake had understood.

Quinn was still terrified of what evil monsters lurked in the forest behind the house. She wasn't too keen on the idea of having an isolated plot of land next to where her son was murdered either.

The decision to move wasn't easy. Even though they'd transferred Cole's body to Kingston, they had still debated the best thing to do to honour him. They had worried his spirit would stay behind somehow. In the end, they'd realized that they themselves carried their son's spirit in their hearts and that wherever they went, Cole would be with them.

———

The first few weeks following Cole's death had been a heavy blanket of emotions. It had been difficult to readjust to life with just the two of them.

There are no words to call parents who have lost a child. They find that they no longer fit in with their married, childless friends, nor do they fit in with their friends with families. They are just kind of floating around, trying to find their place with this new identity.

The psychologist that Quinn started seeing once they moved back to Kingston had given her a pamphlet with the details for a support group for parents who've lost a child. They have their first meeting tonight.

Quinn squeezes William's hand as the two of them take a walk down to the burial site to visit Cole. The idea of having more kids hasn't been discussed yet, but Quinn knows they will need some time before going down that road again.

She needs more time.

Quinn knows she needs to heal herself first. She still blames herself for not disclosing the information she had about the accident all those years ago. She also feels like she didn't give Cole the best of herself, and she's working on forgiving herself for that, knowing her state of mind wasn't at its best while she had been raising Cole.

Quinn now runs an online forum for other women with postpartum depression to share stories, and offer advice and support within a safe community, so that no one ever feels as overwhelmed and isolated as she had.

Arriving at Cole's gravesite, she closes her eyes, bringing to memory her son's beautiful face as she feels a tear run down her cheek. It's hard for her not to get angry. Cole's death could have been prevented. Swallowing the guilt, she knows she can't change the past. She needs to forgive herself and Mrs. Westover, even if she has no idea how to.

She can't shake the old woman's face from her mind, the pure evil in her eyes—what she'd failed to notice when she'd first met her. Going to Sturgeon Falls had terrified Quinn. She was used to noise, people, traffic. The silence that had greeted them in that town had been unnerving and unsettling to her. She'd been so scared of what wicked things or predatory animals were hiding in the woods behind their rental house when she should have been more afraid of what lived inside of herself and those around her.

Quinn now knows the terrifying truth. The worst kinds of monsters aren't animal—they're human.

———

ACKNOWLEDGMENTS

This story is close to my heart as many of the locations referred to in the book are special to my family, even though the story is completely fictional.

I wanted to write a story to raise awareness of the daily struggles of mental health and post-partum depression, which is how Quinn's character came to be. The rest of the story was based on a single, two-second vision that I imagined one day while looking out my bathroom window after stepping out of the shower while my daughter slept in her bed.

The relentless what-if questions and fears that this vision brought to me and the countless nights they kept me up meant that I just had to see where this story would take me. This wasn't an easy story for me to write, and if you read it, you will understand why. As a mom, this is my worst nightmare.

Thank you to all my readers for following along my writing journey and believing in me along the way as I stumble through it.

I owe many thanks to my incredible parents, André & Danielle Landry for inspiring the locations of this story and for their continuous encouragement in the writing process.

I'm forever grateful to my wonderful husband John for giving me time to work on this story during many evenings and weekends. I'm also grateful for the many glasses of wine, hot cups of tea, and all the hours you spent listening to my plot ideas. I'm so thankful for your support and encouragement to help me achieve my goals.

I'm also very blessed to have the support of my grand-parents Lucien & Hélène Landry, my sister Karine Landry, and the rest of my extended family and friends. You are the best cheerleaders.

An endless amount of gratitude goes to my Beta readers, Robert Gleitz, Krista Walsh, Karine Landry, Laura Porc, and Melanie MacKay for giving me feedback, identifying plot holes and helping me make this story even better.

I'm grateful to my editor and friend, Sherry Torchinsky, for going over this book with a fine-toothed comb, making it what it is today.

I can't forget to thank my author/writer friends, Karen Harrison, Lynn McCain, R.J. Jacobs, Robert Charles Gompers, Arti Manani, and many more for listening to my struggles with developing this story. A special thank you to my dear friend Natalie Banks who came to my rescue during the months of Covid-19 and mailed me a proof copy of my book so that I could stick to my publishing timeline.

Thank you for reading the story that's been haunting me for years. Now that you've read it, hopefully it will finally let me sleep.

ABOUT THE AUTHOR

Michelle Young is the author of the psychological thriller, *Your Move,* and two poetry books, *Salt & Light* and *Without Fear*. She holds an Honours BA with a major in psychology; and a minor in communications from the University of Ottawa. Young lives in Ottawa, Canada with her family.

If you enjoyed this book, please make sure to leave a review and follow Michelle Young on Facebook, Instagram and Goodreads.

Facebook.com/michelleyoungauthor

Instagram @michelleyoungauthor

www.michelleyoungauthor.com